TARNISHED LIES AND

NEITHER THIS, NOR THAT

Book #5

MariaLisa deMora

Editing by Hot Tree Editing

Proofing by Whiskey Jack Editing

Photography: 6:12 Photography by Eric McKinney

Model: Enrico Ravenna

First Published 2021

ISBN 13: 978-1-946738-66-0

DEDICATION

"You can't really love someone else
unless you really love yourself first"
~Fred Rogers

Shoutout to all of those still waiting on their
soulmates. Somewhere, someday. We
just gotta make sure we're ready, yeah?

Contents

ACKNOWLEDGMENTS

When I first penned the short story for Wildman as an entry into a holiday anthology, once I had a handle on him it flowed like butter in a hot pan. Smooth and easy, and so sinfully delightful I nearly left him in that short story purgatory.

This book is proof I couldn't do that to Wild, much less Justine. And if anyone ever deserved a happy ending, it's those two. But I'm getting ahead of myself, aren't I? So Wildman, the quack-quack master, the fuck-you shouter, the coulda-been-me advocate for lusting after something you didn't want, wasn't happy about just becoming a member of the IMC. He wasn't happy with his cameos in the other books. And he surely wasn't happy with his short story. The man wanted a longer tale, even if it took a while.

It took a while.

Big thank yous to my editing and proofreading teams, Hot Tree Editing and Whiskey Jack Editing. Through your nudges and outright shoves, the story came together in a way it wouldn't have otherwise. You folks rock, and I'm so pleased to have you in my corner. Thanks to to Megan and Kori, because your encouragement helped me keep the faith when I might have faltered.

So that brings me to here, and the story you're holding in your hands. I'm so proud of this one—okay, I'm proud of all of them, I admit—but once Wildman launched himself full-tilt and dragged me deep into his history I was hooked. I *needed* to know what happened next, hell, I needed to know what happened first!

As we made our way through the story, him telling his side of things and Justine chiming in about her path, I came to the conclusion that while this is at heart a love story—it's more truly a story about loving oneself first.

Hard lesson, yeah? We're conditioned from early on to be conscious of how we behave or look. Holding our outsides up against images we see in magazines, or online. What's harder for us to understand is that it's the inside that matters most. We have to love ourselves before we're anywhere near ready to love someone else.

I'm just glad Wildman and Justine learned that particular lesson early on, so by the time they met, they were ready. I hope you enjoy their story as much as I enjoyed discovering it with them.

Woofully yours,
~ML

Tarnished Lies and Dead Ends

Wildman learned a long time ago that trust in others wasn't healthy and might not lend itself to a long life. Blind trust gave a man false confidence and could get a man dead. His first experience in a club told him only a twist of fate would determine if that ending came quick—or slow. It took being brought into the Incoherent MC to overcome his beliefs, and he came to learn that his patch brothers of the IMC were his only allies. Then, in an instant, everything changed. A flash of lightning, shadows on a wall, blood on his fists—and a beautiful woman on her knees. His life would never be the same.

Justine LaPorte had been born MC royalty. Daughter of Justice Morgan, sister of Davis Mason, she thought she'd fought free long ago. Justine had focused on carving her own path, becoming the antithesis of everything any MC stood for—including her brother's beloved Rebel Wayfarers—carrying her federal badge with pride. Then a federal investigation puts her in harm's way, and she finds herself deeply embroiled in club politics when she's rescued by an officer from Incoherent. The IMC is a southern club at odds with all of the organizations in her past. Just her luck, that man who did the rescuing? He has the potential to fulfill all her desires, in and out of bed.

Chapter One

Chin dipped to his neck, Ogre stared into the mirror and let his fingertips trace a series of bumps along his hairline, indications of irritated flesh remaining from his freshly removed stitches. He caught the gaze of his reflection and studied himself, marking the age that had crept into his features over the past week.

"Hey, FourQ." He raised his voice with the call and waited until he heard a grunted response. "Remind me. What time's the ride supposed to start?"

Boots shuffled in the short hallway between the bathroom and kitchen, and Ogre glanced at the doorway, unsurprised to see the man wasn't alone.

He couldn't blame them for running in pairs around him. Not given the events of the previous days.

"Yeah. About that."

Ogre straightened and turned at the tone, abandoning the reflection of his pain and anger and directing the beam of his rage on a man he'd called brother so recently. Just from the expression on FourQ's face, Ogre already knew what he would say but wanted to force him to put words to it. FourQ and Puggs stood and stared at him, mouths closed, lips pressed into thin lines of fear.

Yeah, they should fucking fear me.

"What about what? You had a call, right? That's what you said. Had a call about the ride. So what fuckin' time is it supposed to start, man?" The man's phone had rung, pulling him from the living room to the kitchen so he could take it privately.

Private. Away from me.

Ogre snorted in disgust. Until last week he'd been the resolute arm of power for their club. Hell, less than a month ago, he'd been standing on FourQ's roof, pounding shingles into place to help keep his family dry and safe. And now this man was taking calls away from where he stood, to keep club business private.

"It's been recommended we postpone the ride."

Ogre, Lyle Woolsey to the government, kept his muscles loose and easy, limiting his respirations to a quiet and even cadence. He forced peace and calm throughout his body, controlling as much as he was able to, utilizing form, fit, and function beaten into him over the years, standing at his blood brother's side. Once he was locked down, he blinked, lids scratching across his dry eyes.

"Postpone." One long breath in. "The ride?"

"Brothers are sayin' it's not in the club's best interest." FourQ glanced to the man at his side but Puggs kept his mouth shut, not giving FourQ anything. No support, but also no condemnation, which damned the man in Ogre's book.

Teeth gritted, Ogre flexed the muscles in his jaw as he forced out, "Not in *their* best interest?" He knew the word drew a line between him and the rest of the club, but Ogre couldn't find it in himself to give one single fuck about the unstated difference right now.

"Yeah, brother—"

"Don't 'brother' me. Do not call me your *brother*." He thrust a finger out, shoving FourQ back two strides without touching him. "Do not presume. My old lady's dead. She's dead because of the club, buried in the woods, because it wasn't in the club's best interests to have her declared officially and have a fuckin' funeral. She's dead and buried, and this ride was the only thing you motherfuckers offered to speak to her memory."

"Ogre—"

"No." Scarred fingers tightening into aching fists, he planted them on his hips and glared at the two men. "Get the fuck outta my house, man." Lifting his chin, he stared down his nose, taking in the pallor left behind as blood leached out of their faces. "My old lady and my baby, still in her belly, are layin' in the woods next to fuckin' snitches and drug dealers. Not even a goddamned marker to tell the world part'a my soul was ripped from my body and laid to rest. All because it was in the best interest of the club for her death to be swept under the rug. What with the bullshit my brother pulled, and the attention he brought to our patch of ground, and all of that—I understood the reason. But now"—he leaned forwards, still keeping his voice under careful control—"there's no fucking goddamned reason to shove this shit in my face."

One week ago, Lyle Woolsey's life had come to an end.

A few people had read an unhealthy ambition into his efforts to fully support his club, and those few—two—had taken steps to sever the relationship.

His half-brother, Powell Durrell, had been vice president of the South Florida MC Keyz Krewz for three years. They weren't big, but weren't small, maintaining a club just the right size to make a difference in their community. Keeping the dealers off their turf was a full-time job, but one the members had been driven to continue. For more than two of those years, Lyle had stood at his brother's shoulder, cleaving strongly to his enforcer role and ensuring the safety of his blood family. Same daddy, different mothers, raised in different homes—but a solid relationship had grown between the two brothers.

Then a hurricane had swept in, wreaking destruction all across the southern tip of the state. The storm had taken the clubhouse roof, and as Lyle had taken the time to check in with the members across the region, each had varying stories of loss and ruin. Without having to think too hard about what was right, Lyle had turned his attention to helping their brothers, while men he'd stood shoulder to shoulder with to face down enemies pooled their resources and abilities at his requests. They worked through a long laundry list of damages, beginning with the president's, and then his brother's, house. After, they'd moved to repair the members' residences if possible, then circled back to fix up the clubhouse, because Lyle knew as long as the building was repaired, they could offer longer-term shelter to members whose homes weren't salvageable. Fundraisers had brought in money to buy materials individual members couldn't afford, and all along the way, Lyle's old lady was at his side doing her part.

That had been a factor in his downfall. Shelly was ambitious, more so than Lyle, and she saw the goodwill he was building with the rank-and-file members of the club. She saw it, recognized it, and wanted to use it to propel him higher in the club. Officers got a bigger percentage of the club's business earnings, and with a hurricane baby on the way, she'd pushed for the stability.

Powell didn't appreciate the idea, brought to his ears by his own woman, a club whore turned old lady who was jealous and whispering, telling pillow tales.

In retrospect, Lyle knew he should have seen it coming from a mile away. Should have expected and derailed it somehow.

He hadn't, and the sudden knowledge had struck deep and hard, piercing the bubble of belief and loyalty inside him.

Saturday night at the clubhouse should have been a loud, rowdy party, with the wilder old ladies mixed in with the sweetbottom girls who liked to play rough. The moment Ogre walked through the door and into the room spanning the width of the house, he'd clocked something was up by the mere fact every face that swung to stare at him was male. There'd been no greeting either, friendly or ill, which factored into a definite heads-up because he'd broken bread at every member's table over the past couple of months. Even those where he'd held no friendship previous to the storm, needs dictated he'd built a companionship and brotherhood warranting at least a passing hello.

It seemed as if the rumor he'd picked up in a backroom chat was true. The officers were gunning for him for no reason, that attack led by his own blood.

Ogre stopped next to the first member he came to. "Where's Powell?" He swung his gaze around the room again, still not seeing his brother's face. "FourQ, you know where he is?"

No words in response, just a tip of a chin to point to the office, door closed tight against the men in the main room.

"Obliged."

"Ogre, he's—"

"Lookin' to oust me, I know." He shook his head. "I heard but don't understand. I don't get it. I wanna get it from his own lips before I make a wrong turn somewhere in my response."

"It's more."

He stopped and swung around, staring at FourQ, a man who'd stood next to him on many a roof since the storm, swinging hammers in sync.

"He's lookin' for more."

"More than just strippin' the club off my back? Brother, ain't that enough?" Ogre turned on his heel and strode towards the door, scarcely noticing how the members cleared a path in front of him. Fist raised, he hesitated only a second before he brought his hand like a hammer against the surface. Three booming knocks, then he stepped backwards and waited.

Powell was the first one through the door, coming at him like a freight train, moving fast so his shove had extra momentum, throwing Ogre back three feet before he could dig in his heels. They stood like that, braced and straining, faces close enough Ogre could feel the heat, smell the sweat, and see the fear.

It was fear in his brother's eyes. Great, heaving amounts of the emotion, constricting his pupils, whites showing all around the edges.

Fear.

"What the fuck are you doing here?" Powell's first question didn't make sense.

"Where else would I be?" Ogre dropped his hands, letting his brother surge forwards a couple inches so they were chest to chest as he spread his arms wide. "I'm here, in the middle of my brothers, breathin' in the camaraderie, communin' in unity."

"You were meant to be at home." Powell disengaged abruptly, taking three long steps backwards. A wide circle of space built around Ogre. "With your old lady."

"My old lady." Ogre scanned the faces surrounding him. He decided to share his news. They'd learned a month ago, but Shelly had wanted to wait and be sure. "She's pregnant with my babe, and is probably sleeping, arms wrapped around her belly." Shocked murmurs filled the air, but not a man came forward with a congratulatory backslap. Oh, yeah, they're ready to do me ill. Powell's face drained of blood. "I don't got no cigars, but I'll buy a round for any man who wants it."

Nobody moved. There wasn't even the shuffle of boots against the floor.

"FourQ." Powell's shout broke the stasis, and Ogre felt the room's heavy pressure bearing in on him. This is it, *he thought.* This is my beatout. *"You're up."*

"No, brother." FourQ stepped out of the ring of men towards where Ogre stood. He was still yards away when he paused. Distanced himself from what Powell demanded, but he sure as shit hadn't come close enough to show support for a man gettin' unfairly railroaded. Can't ride middle of the road for long. *"I won't be your hands in this. You want it, I say you gotta do it. I don't agree, but I ain't an officer. Means I got no vote, but I won't do it."*

"You wanna be treated the same?"

"You do that to every man who argues with you, won't be no club left for you to try and rule over."

Ogre looked through the crowd, stunned not to find their president in the ranks around him. He zeroed in on the patch on Powell's chest, riding just underneath his nameplate. No longer the VP, the new officer plate proclaimed him their leader. The placement for the patch was off, wrong, because the club was meant to come first, with the individual subservient to the position. Powell's the prez. How the fuck did that happen? *His mind reeled with the knowledge of the behind-doors business conducted tonight.*

"Bassil." Powell called out his best friend's name, someone he'd run with since they were kids. The Keys were the playground for rich tourists—and a mecca for light-fingered kids. Powell Durrell and Curtis Bassil had worked as a pair, fleecing and stealing whenever and from whomever they pleased. Ogre remembered more than one night hearing the phone ring and his daddy getting up and going out, coming back, shaking his head about bailing his oldest son out again. If anyone was

going to step up and toe the mark Powell had drawn in the sand today, it'd be Bassil.

"No, brother." Stepping out from behind Powell, Bassil bored his gaze into Ogre. "It's got to be you. Makes more of a statement that way. You said you wanted everyone to know."

"Know what?" Ogre swung his gaze from Powell to Bassil. "What in the fuck are you talking about?"

He had an idea now. Between this scene and the few words spoken in his direction, he had an idea. One of the benefits of having more than thirty brothers believe in you was someone would spill early, asking for confirmation of what was happening. Powell wanted him gone, afraid he'd been angling for the seat Powell had clearly had his eyes on. Ogre just wanted to hear the betrayal from his brother's lips.

"Gotta be me, then might as well get to it." Powell came at him with a heavy, overhand swing, looking to take him down and out. "You're gonna go." Ogre swayed backwards, the strike hitting him a glancing blow across the temple and cheek as he took a step to the side to avoid the initial rush. "Gotta go. Gonna be out bad."

"What the fuck for?" Ogre danced sideways again, noting how the circle around them expanded, inserting various pieces of furniture into the mix. He grabbed a chair and lifted it in front of him, using it to fend off Powell's next attack. Powell grabbed the chair leg and yanked, shoving it against Ogre when he wouldn't let it go. The heavy wood struck his head with a whack. "The fuck you doin'? You gone mad?"

"Wasn't mad the night I heard you plotting behind my back." Powell attempted a leg sweep, but Ogre planted the chair in the way, a meaty thud telling him Powell would be sporting bruises from the hit. Powell snatched the chair away and tossed it at Ogre, lips pulled back from his teeth in a feral snarl. Ogre barely got his arm up to knock the chair behind him. "Plottin' and schemin' to take what's mine."

"I don't know what you're talking about." Without the chair to divert the attacks, it was only moments before they were grappling in the middle of the floor. Ogre took three hard hits to the kidneys, then one to the edge of his jaw, while churning out punishment of his own in two quick jabs against Powell's head, followed up with a knee to the gut before he broke free. "What's the real story?"

"Always in the way. Even as a kid. Daddy always favored you." Heaving in great panting breaths, Powell shook his head in a short, sharp burst, then lumbered towards Ogre in a laughable rush. He tripped when Ogre skipped to the side, tried to adjust his trajectory, and went down hard, his head smashing against the corner of the bar.

Stillness settled around them, all talk ending abruptly, Powell's sudden silence so heavy it nearly took Ogre to the ground.

"Brother?" Uncaring if it were a ruse, he fell to a sliding stop on his knees next to his brother's crumpled body. Blood covered Powell's face, flowing from a gash ripped in his scalp. "Powell, man. Talk to me."

More silence. No one spoke. He couldn't even hear his brother breathe.

"Call a bus." Ogre looked up, his gaze flitting from face to face, taking in their uniform looks of shock and fear. "Call a goddamned ambulance for him."

He cupped his brother's face in his hand, startled to see Powell's eyes were open. The pupils were uneven, one far larger than the other, and he bit back a scream of anger. Fumbling his phone out, he snapped at the man closest. "Bassil, meet the EMTs at the door. I'm callin' it in now."

"We should think about things."

Ogre lifted his chin, phone pressed against his ear, and shouted, "I don't give a fuck what you think. My brother deserves better."

The operator connected and gave her expected intro lines, and Ogre gave her the update as best he could, the address he knew by heart, then turned to pleading, "Please, God, get them here fast. He don't look good at all."

Powell never woke up. He died two days later.

Two days where Ogre didn't leave the hospital.

Two days of the police in his face every time he turned a corner.

Two days of the club coming to terms that they were leaderless. Something they didn't like for a myriad of reasons, Ogre finding out not the least of those reasons was due to the dominant club in the region pushing for stability. Outriders didn't like negative attention, and a headless club would wreck the area around them as it writhed and died.

At the end of day two, FourQ had come to him with the president patch in hand.

Standing beside his brother's deathbed, machines silenced and stillness in the room, Ogre turned him away without a word, shoulders hunched against the arguments and pleas.

He'd gone home, not having been able to connect with his old lady during that time, the cops having confiscated his phone as evidence of something.

There he'd found the rest of what his brother had planned.

Assassin in his kitchen, eating the leftovers of the meal Ogre's wife had cooked for him. The man had been taken off guard after waiting for so long without his target in sight. Ogre hadn't questioned him, hadn't taken the time, because taking up all the space in his head was a drumbeat of urgency shouting the question, "Where's Shelly?"

Once he'd dealt with the man sent to kill him, Ogre tore through the house, screaming her name.

He found Shelly dead in their bed. Covers defiled by her blood and more, the run-at-the-max air conditioner no competition for the natural course of things in the Keys, where hot and humid was every day. She was cold and pliable, deep purple along the backs of her legs and arms where the blood had pooled in place.

His baby dead in her womb.

Ogre's calls for help went unanswered. The club, his brothers, unified in their determination to ignore him if he wouldn't take up their yoke of authority. It was only when he'd shown at the clubhouse, gory and raging, that he got their attention.

Bassil had known the full story. He was the only one, though, which was small comfort for Ogre.

Powell had bought a paper on Ogre, had intended him to be beaten out of the club as a traitor, so the loyalty of the members would pass back to Powell upon Ogre's death. The paper hadn't included Shelly, but the hired killer hadn't been known for having a mercy streak.

It had taken four brothers to pull him off Bassil, leaving the man spittin' teeth on the floor, his nose a bloody mess.

That's when the club had shown its true colors. After everything he'd endured, everything that had gone on, when he picked up a phone to call the cops, the men had ripped it out of his hand. Talking about "for the good of the club" and "brother, you know this ain't the way." They'd talked and talked until he'd given in, making his own move to give over a secondhand marker, which ultimately led to a man he'd only heard tales about. President of the Bama Bastards and reportedly owner of an intelligence network second to none. The dom club had made the call, so at least Ogre was kept at arm's length from any fallout.

For a price, the man had organized a cleaner for Ogre's house, care and transport of Shelly to the stretch of woods the club used for disposal, and the materials to put her in the ground with. Ogre would have been willing to pay twice to see her handled with grace and compassion. The Bama Bastards president had come through in unexpected ways, the women he'd hired to wash and prepare her not turning away from the mottled monster she'd become. Ogre's last view of Shelly was with her hair clean and pulled to the side, lifelike face tinted with tasteful colors, and a serene upturn to the corners of her lips.

Now, here they were a week out from that day, and he'd wanted just one thing from the club. They might not have stood behind him, might not have helped with the cops, and might not have given him permission to deal with Shelly's death like he'd wanted—but they were damned sure going to do a memorial ride.

"If you won't give her respect, then I got nothin' for you." He advanced on FourQ, grabbed the man's vest lapels, and gave him a forceful shake. "Get the fuck"—he shoved hard, FourQ landing on his ass on the floor—"out of my house."

So it was a respectful parade of one who rolled past the woods, engine revving, pipes blatting out his pain. At the next intersection, Ogre rolled to a stop and looked left, then right, then left again. One way was north, and the rest of America. One way was south and the oblivion the ocean promised.

He glanced down and saw his nameplate. The vest already felt tons lighter, the club patch having been ripped off the back, tossed to the floor of the house without a second thought where FourQ had fallen.

He grabbed one corner of the nameplate and pulled until the first few threads snapped, then gave it another hard yank without dislodging the fabric. *Shelly did a good job with her sewing.* His throat closed up, clicking dryly as he tried to swallow. Wedging his finger into the space where the threads had broken, he strained, pulling hard, the wind seeping out of him as the patch slowly came free. He held it on one palm, staring at his name as the wind ruffled past it, lifting one corner. *Ogre no more.*

Another gust came after that one, and then another, and a moment later, the patch was airborne, sailing out into the road.

It had scarcely come to rest in the northbound lane of the highway when he rocked his throttle over, gunning the engine as his back wheel spun free, squealing as it found traction. Then Lyle was gone, headed north and away from the only place he'd ever called home.

Chapter Two

French Quarter, New Orleans, Twelve Years Later

Lyle shook his head in a slow arc, scratching across his chin with the tip of his thumbnail as he studied the man in front of him.

Jonah Warner was someone he trusted. Ruger, nicknamed for his preferred type of iron, stood as tall as Lyle but twice as broad. Not a man to be trifled with, he was known for being slow to anger but quick to respond when pushed. "Man, you know it ain't right."

Lyle shook his head again, flattening his palm on top of the table they shared. "Ruger, it might not be right, but it ain't wrong, either."

"There's only so much a man can stand." Ruger turned and leaned straight-armed and stiff against the railing in front of him. Lyle stepped up next to him and surveyed the scene below. They were on an external balcony on the second floor of a building in the French Quarter. The street in front of them was flooded by the typical weekend mass of tourists milling, drinks in hand. They'd been called to the place earlier in the afternoon by Torment, the president of the Common Enemy, a motorcycle club both had been hanging around, the reason for the call still unclear.

Sure the club was partying in the room behind them, but that was not much different from the open clubhouse parties they'd attended. If anything, the group had been less welcoming than normal, murmurs of surprise accompanying their arrival.

Then the girls had shown up. Bought-for-the-night whores from a known cathouse, experienced women for the most part. One girl was obviously new, claiming a barely legal eighteen as her age, but her blushes and shy stammering labeled her more innocent than not. The club president had latched onto that one, and from his persistence, would not be letting go. The girl had been schooled in how to comport herself, not resisting or complaining, even when the man's hands turned rough underneath her clothing. But her physical flinches of pain were visible, and Ruger wasn't on board with what was clearly going to happen tonight.

Shouts of laughter filtered through the closed glass doors behind them, and Lyle turned around in time to see Torment strip the girl's dress from her body, leaving her standing in a scrap of fabric for panties.

Ruger snapped upright at Lyle's groan and whirled around. He'd taken two steps before Lyle stopped him. "She signed up for this."

"You cannot tell me she knew what this party would bring." Ruger's neck twisted, and he glared at Lyle. "She's just a fuckin' kid."

"Give me ten minutes. All I ask. I'll have a distraction here, and you can whisk her away if you want." Lyle shoved past him and opened the door, looking over his shoulder to return Ruger's glare. "Ten minutes, brother."

Inside the room, he scooped up a jar of the potent moonshine the members had been drinking and lifted it to his nose, suppressing a shiver when the rancid scent hit him. "Torment." His call was calculated to distract, loud enough to reach the president, not sharp enough to warrant alarm. "Thought I could do a demonstration for y'all." He shrugged, lifted the jar to his mouth, and pretended to take a drink.

Rolling his head back, he shouted towards the ceiling. "Whoa, Jesus. That's the *good* shit." Lyle shook his head as if disoriented, then took another step towards Torment, reseated now with the naked girl on his lap. "Heard you were interested in my…interests, so to speak." He dug in his pocket and withdrew his phone, wagging it in his fingers. "One call, and you'll see it all." Lyle tipped his head to one side and pursed his lips. "Interested, or nah?"

"Oh yeah, brother." Torment slipped out from underneath the girl, letting her settle into his seat as he stepped towards Lyle. "I'd be very interested in a little demonstration." The hunger on the man's face was vicious and dark. "Been asking for this for a while. What do you need?"

Lyle made a show of looking up, marking the high ceiling. "Nothin' special. That's about twelve feet, wouldn't you say? Plenty of room for what I need." He tapped a number on his contact list and put the call on speaker as it rang the second time. The call connected, and he spoke gruffly, tone strict and hard. "Monique, this is Master Lyle." He rattled off the address, conveniently close to his sometime playmate's apartment. "I expect you prepared and here in five minutes. You and I will be providing the entertainment for the night."

Smooth as silk, she responded, "Yes, Sir."

Lyle disconnected and locked gazes with Torment. "I gotta get something from my bike."

"Of course." Waving his hand magnanimously, the president granted permission. Behind him, Ruger had maneuvered the girl out of the chair, retrieved her dress, and was already walking her through a door on the far side of the room. Torment had heard the door closing and whirled around, a slow rage beginning to roll off him as he realized what had happened. *Do I really want to be part of what this guy stands for?* He wasn't patched, not yet, but if he didn't change trajectories, Lyle knew he'd become part of the club in days, not months.

Lyle left the shouting man behind and made his way downstairs. He grabbed his small bag from where it was strapped on his bike, then waited in the doorway. Monique strode up soon after he'd taken up his position. He watched her from half a block away, her hips swaying as she stalked the sidewalk in her heels. A camel-colored coat was wrapped around her torso, tightly covered from throat to knees, regardless of the heat of the New Orleans evening. *That's promising.*

Monique stopped in front of him, chin to her chest as she threaded her fingers together behind her back. Her posture was impeccable: shoulders back, breasts lifted, the language of her stance spoke of a confident submissive. Open, ready, and patient. Waiting.

He reached for her and drifted the back of a single finger along one cheek, smiling as she subtly leaned into the touch. "Monique, you'll use the stoplight system tonight. But you know me well enough I hope you'll trust me to push you as far as I think you can go. These men who will be observing will not touch you. From the moment we walk through that door, until I say the scene is over, you're mine."

"Yes, Sir." Her breathing was shaky and shallow. From the flush in her cheeks, he read it as excitement, not fear. Her tongue darted out, slipping across her bottom lip. *Oh, yeah, she gonna be all the way into it.*

As long as he could remember, he'd enjoyed having total control over his sexual partners. *Since Florida.* That was a thought he couldn't afford tonight, and he cast it out. Shelly had fulfilled the emotional portion of what he'd seen as a perfect relationship. She might not have wanted his natural, untrained dominance, something he'd had to tone back for her, but he'd been deeply bonded to her. *Long ago and far away.*

Lyle had been in the scene since one of his more memorable attempts at forgetting had resulted in being introduced to the broad world of BDSM. It was at that moment Lyle had found his casual interest in that all-important control had bloomed into an exploration of pleasure and pain, paired with tenderness. Safe, sane, and consensual was the backbone of what he enjoyed and the tenet of various clubs he'd frequented. That was how he'd first encountered Monique, scening at an exclusive club in New Orleans.

Pleasure was a major factor for Lyle. He liked pleasure for himself, but even more, he liked turning on his partners, and as a chaser, also had a deep enjoyment of denying them when it suited his mood. All part of the lifestyle's control aspect he found so appealing. Part of what Monique enjoyed was impact play, which was what they'd be demonstrating tonight. Lyle had already intended to go to the club after the party, and the bag he'd retrieved held everything he needed to put on the scene Torment would be expecting.

As he continued to caress Monique's cheek, then trailed his touch down her throat to the collar of her coat, he tracked her emotional state. She settled, steadying underneath his hand, until she blew out a long, deep stream of air, releasing the last of her nervousness.

"I plan on fucking you." From the sound she made in her throat, he knew Monique was on board with the idea. "And beyond that, I have a couple of surprises for you, but my intent is to make you fly, sub. Do you want to fly tonight?"

"Ye—" Monique's mouth dropped open, forming a perfect "O" of arousal. "Yes, Sir."

"Remind me of our agreement." He knew her desires by heart, but giving her a direct order to voice them would empower her while also framing her expectations for the scene.

"Impact play with intimate contact, Sir. Restraints permitted if it pleases Sir."

"And the rest?" There was a longer list of desires, but she'd previously also communicated a group of hard limits. He wanted to know for certain there'd been no shifts in her boundaries. *No surprises for the Dom, darlin'.*

"No breath play, no fisting or double penetration, no humiliation, no incest role play, and no bodily fluid exchange." Underneath his thumb, her heartbeat still pounded away, even as her shoulders relaxed and lowered. "Sir." The simple statement of the rules affirmed not only that she was in control of her emotions but also that they were about to do a scene that would turn her on. Turn them both on, something he'd do his best to minimize on his side of the line so he could stay alert to potential threats in the room. *And the fact I gotta do this shit with a group of men I'm considering patchin' with says a lot about the quality of my friends. Ruger excluded.*

His palm grazed her shoulder, traveled down her fabric-covered arm until his thumb and fingers encircled her wrist. He gave a sharp tug, and she flowed with the physical demand, swaying as she took a step towards him.

Without a word, he turned and strode into the building, pulling her along behind him.

Time to pay the piper on his diversionary tactic. *I just hope Ruger knows what he's doing, pissing off Torment like this.*

Chapter Three

Common Enemy Clubhouse, Baton Rouge

Knees locked, Lyle stood in the center of what could be a makeshift fighting ring. He was lined up shoulder to shoulder with men he'd come to call brother, staring at a raggedy band of assholes who'd rolled in an hour ago. He knew the patch they so proudly wore, of course—there wasn't a biker along the Gulf Coast who didn't—but knowing it and then seeing it as a large contingent of the Incoherent MC lounged comfortably around his club's house wasn't a good thing.

"Wildman, what you make of this shit?"

The concerned confusion on Ruger's face matched the rolling of Lyle's gut. His new club name had settled on Wildman, coined following his and Monique's exhibition months ago. Since that day, he'd reconciled himself to doing the best he could for his brothers while under Torment's thumb.

"Either it's a parley request, and what the fuck we got that IMC could want is a mystery…" He grimaced. "Or we're about to be ex-members of the club formerly known as Common Enemy."

"You think it's a takeover?" Ruger caressed the butt of his favorite handgun, sitting low in an appendix holster strapped into the front of his pants. "Hostile, or amicable?"

"Fuck, brother, your guess is good as mine. This is IMC, though, so they wouldn't be in our house if it wasn't an invite. If it were hostile, we'd have met them in a field or on a road—not here in our own fuckin' house in Baton Rouge." Staying near Ruger, Wildman surveyed the IMC members, matching faces to the names he knew in passing. "Twisted is the big man, in case you didn't know. That's him standin' next to the bar cuttin' Torment to pieces with his stare. He's mean as a fuckin' snake, twice as lucky, and blood to the IMC founder. But don't let that fool you. Man earned his place in the club with blood, sweat, and tears."

"Yeah, way I heard it is the president patch still has the bullet hole in it that killed their previous president." Ruger shook his head. "Takes balls to wear somethin' like that, knowin' the tales that patch could tell."

"Then you boys both heard right."

Wildman whirled, shocked to see a big IMC member had squeezed into the space next to him. Face battered by what looked like a thousand fights, the man grinned, that expression so light and pleasant it was at odds with the hard glare turned Wildman's way. He flicked a glance at the man's chest, then back up as he nodded and greeted him. "Po'Boy." Wildman tugged off his fingerless glove, shoved it in his back pocket as he reached out a bare hand. "Good to meet you."

Their palms collided with a violent smack, the sound reverberating through the room and dragging several sets of eyes in their direction. That immediate scrutiny and attention included Torment and Twisted. Po'Boy's fingers wrapped around Wildman's thumb, and he returned the gesture, meeting every show of strength Po'Boy poured into their grip, ounce for ounce. Teeth gritted, Wildman lifted his chin, keeping his gaze fixed on Po'Boy, who was sending the same ruthless attitude back at him. They stood like that for several breaths, and neither man visibly allowed a flinch from the brutal show of force that had the bones in Wildman's hands grinding to dust. Then Po'Boy shocked him by grinning broadly just before he yanked Wildman forwards with their joined hands, pulled him to his chest, and pounded his back as if they were long-lost brothers reunited at last.

"Well met, Wildman. Well fuckin' met, brother."

Minutes passed like hours, and the clock over the front door tracked each elongated moment. The short hand had passed the apex of the circle four times before Wildman saw any real business underway. Once it began, however, it went fast, over in a flash. One moment Torment was standing in front of Twisted, left palm lifted to rest over his own heart as if he were making a vow. The next, Torment lay crumpled at the man's feet, and Wildman saw the tiniest puff of smoke from the old-school revolver Po'Boy held from across the room, residual effects from the shot that ended the man.

Fighting broke out all around them, Wildman and Ruger quickly standing back-to-back in a small cleared space. His pulse pounded, threat assessments happening in split seconds, separated by blinks of time. Grab, bring a face down to an uprushing knee, release. Catfish joined them, quickly followed by Mosser, and the four men shifted into a tight formation, vulnerable backs protected as chaos surrounded them. Few IMC members came within reach. Those were mostly staggering reactions to a shove or blow, but even as infrequently as that happened, the knocked-out bodies and groaning voices accumulated around the foursome's tiny square of safety.

A second gunshot tore through the air, and Wildman jerked his head to the side, staring up to where Po'Boy stood on top of a table. *Man needs a keeper. He's a fuckin' officer. Enough of a target already, shouldn't be makin' a spectacle out of himself if he ain't a foot soldier.* Twisted stood directly in front of Wildman, a dozen strides separating them, and Wildman's breath froze in his throat at the banked rage in the man's eyes. The leader of the IMC lifted his hand to his mouth, and a shrill whistle split the silence that had followed the report from the gun.

"Stand down. My guys, stand the fuck down. IMC stand *fucking* down." His repeated shouts were orders and had an immediate effect as the overwhelming numbers of IMC members disengaged and moved back from the outnumbered Common Enemy. "Stand down now."

Wildman stood, hands lifted in front of him, panting hard from the terror and exertion over the past minutes. Sweat rolled down his temple and he blinked as it got to his eye, stinging fiercely. He spat, not surprised to see the saliva tinged with red. For every man he'd laid out, he'd taken at least one blow.

"Common Enemy."

Wildman swung his gaze to Po'Boy when Twisted spoke, noting that, like Twisted, the man didn't seem to have so much as a hair out of place. As if the brawl started by the blindside assassination of the CEMC president hadn't touched either of them. Everyone talked about the two, how in sync they were, the shared driven sense of purpose making them unstoppable. It was awe-inspiring to see in person.

Twisted continued, "Listen to me. You're going to lay your vests down, and those who want, you'll possibly pick up a new set of cuts. Possibly. *Possibly.*" Wildman shook his head, and Po'Boy arrowed a scowl in his direction. "You don't want that? You decide—given the day's activities—this life, uncertain as it always is, is no longer a fit for you, then this right here's your chance to get out without even a beatout. Lay down your CEMC and walk out the door, won't a man in this room lift a hand to you. I get it, how a club isn't the right place for every man. How something which seemed to fit so well a few years ago rides uncomfortably on your shoulders now. This is your chance."

"Fuck you." Wildman lifted his chin as he shouted the words, an expected proclamation if Po'Boy's expression was anything to judge by. "Not handin' over my vest." His words were echoed, but only by a few. The men who stood at his shoulders and back, and about three others who'd dragged Torment's body to the wall and now stood watch over the lifeless form. "Not doin' it." Wildman shifted his focus away from Po'Boy and shook his head, ends of his sweat-sodden hair stinging as it lashed his cheeks. "Not takin' a beatout either. You came in here and did this. IMC askin' for war." He stretched his neck, looking down his nose into Twisted's face. "You got—"

He was on the floor, the unexpected collision with the immovable boards shocking as his lungs seized, refusing to take in or expel air.

"Now listen." The voice came from directly over his head, and Wildman rolled to his back to see Po'Boy standing above him, one boot on either side of his body. "My man here was about to write a check his ass couldn't cash, so I stifled him for a moment. You wanna see what started this, look in Torment's hand, motherfuckers. Fuckin' look at the asshole."

Wildman's stomach and chest hitched, searching for air as he stretched out, angling so he could see. Leather-clad feet scuffed the floor as they cleared the way, men stepping back and to the side, creating a lane of visibility meant for him. Torment lay against the base of the wall, legs tangled in on themselves, one arm stretched far over his head, the other palm-up at his side. That hand, his right hand, the dominant one, had a gun dangling from his index finger. Wildman recognized the pistol. It was one Torment kept in his jeans pocket. A just-in-case sneak-attack weapon he'd crowed about never needing, but kept anyway, brought out for show and threat.

"His check was countered, and my counter hit the bank and cleared, that deposit of lead one that won't be swayed by any argument. Saw the gun aimed at my president, and I acted accordingly." Po'Boy shuffled backwards until he was well out of reach and squatted, weight angled to one side as he rested a knee on the floor.

From this closer position, Wildman could see the lines of tension surrounding the man's eyes and mouth. This hadn't been a death he sought, and Wildman thought the man would own it for a long time. Ending Torment's life was going to weigh on Po'Boy.

Po'Boy asked, "Did he tell you we'd been invited?" As their gazes locked, Wildman shook his head in a side-to-side sweep. "Did he tell you we've been in talks for more'n half a year?"

"No fuckin' way."

"Yeah, fuckin' way." Po'Boy held still, staring into Wildman's face intently. "Half a year ago, he needed a helluva lot of money and IMC was in a position...well, I'll let my brother explain the business if he wants, but you need to know your dicktwat of a president sold you out. Every man in this room, sold out, regardless of time spent in the club, and freely pledged loyalty."

Po'Boy stretched out his hand, and Wildman hesitated for only a second before grabbing it like the lifeline he knew it was. From looking at those hands, it hadn't been Po'Boy who'd struck him down. That credit would likely fall to the prospect casually restrained nearby by Mosser, the straight armbar easily held against the struggling man flat out on the floor much like Wildman. Only Wildman was being offered a hand up by the IMC VP, while the prospect would be eating dirt for a long time.

"I hear good things about you, Wildman." Po'Boy stood and pulled, lifting Wildman to his feet. "You and me, we're gonna get along just fine."

Once on his feet, Wildman wagged his jaw side to side and winced. He caught Po'Boy staring at him with a smile and gruffly asked, "What?"

"You've got a remarkable amount of restraint."

Po'Boy thumbed over his shoulder to where Mosser still had the prospect on the floor. The man was lying still now, but his shoulder looked deformed. *Dislocated it.*

"Just bodes well for what comes next."

Wildman looked back at Po'Boy, who'd turned to give Wildman his profile, now facing Twisted. Following the secondary altercation, the IMC president had hopped on the bar, sitting with thighs apart, boots on the seat of a stool. He leaned on his knees with his forearms, looking weary.

"What comes next?" The curve of Po'Boy's cheek lifted at Wildman's question, corner of his mouth stretching into a smile. "What's that grin for?"

"Oh, it'll be a dance. You just watch and see. Twisted's gonna pick up where he left off before. Now, though, all of y'all know the truth of how things went down. We'll see how many change their tune and start steppin' to ours." He nodded, and Wildman glanced across to where Twisted was in time to see the man's head dip in response. "Watch and learn."

"Land this house sits on belongs to IMC. The house also belongs to IMC. While IMC—and make no mistake when I say IMC I mean *me*, because there is not a shred of difference between the two—wants to open new charters in strategic locations, Baton Rouge is already under my wing. I see no value in two charters competing for territory with all that would entail." Twisted ran a hand down his face, stroking his beard to the point. "My understanding is prospects live on site. How many prospects are we talkin' about?"

Wildman searched the room, seeing a dozen gazes turned his way. Seemed the silent consensus had deferred to him to speak. *Fuck.* Discounting the man still on the floor, he ran through names and numbers in his head and blinked. *Eight.* That couldn't be right. It was about half again as many as they'd ever held before. Not enough solid members and officers to mentor so many potential members. "Catfish, I come up with eight. That sound right to you?"

"Yeah, brother. Was nine until a couple minutes ago, but we got a cut right here for sure." Catfish rested his elbow on Wildman's shoulder, propping himself up.

Wildman dipped his chin as he spoke to Twisted, "Half live here, half in the trailer out by the road."

"Trailer in good condition?" Wildman's head wasn't the only one that shook. "No worries. I didn't relish movin' it anyway. If we held a vote right now, would any of the eight make it through? Be honest, men, if it's what they want, they can roll back to hangaround status, start comin' to IMC parties to see if we're a fit. Not like you're takin' the life from them." He rolled his shoulders as one hand came to rest on the gun strapped to his hip. "Unlike little mister no-name over there."

Wildman looked at Catfish, then Mosser and Ruger. He swept the gazes of the other CEMC members, seeing the same negative expressions. "None of them. There's been so many layered on, we haven't had a chance to get to know any of them enough to give a thumbs-up. There's promise in a couple I've interacted with, like Randy there." Wildman gestured to a prospect manning the door, not having moved during the brawl, holding his post with a dogged control. "And Mark." He nodded at the prospect to which Mosser had given over control of the traitor on the floor. "Steady Eddie kind of guys, both of them. They'd have earned my vote in a couple of months."

"Noted." Twisted's gaze swept him up and down. "Since you've been elected the de facto spokesperson, any members you wanna speak up about definitely keepin'? I ain't sure I wanna layer on—to use your words—too many new faces for IMC either. As you noted, it's hard enough to get to know a man under normal circumstances, but under what's looking a fuckton more like a hostile takeover than I wanted it to be, gettin' past the coating of suspicion's gonna be a bitch."

"You're talkin' like it's a done deal I'm gonna drop my patch and pick up yours. Like it's a done deal you'll even want me." Wildman shrugged, dislodging Catfish's elbow as his shoulders lifted and moved back, posture straightening. "If Torment hadn't pulled his particular brand of bullshit, what was the process you'd intended to run with us?"

"Patch the club entire as nonvoting probates. Give Torment a downward trajectory in the officer ranks, drop a minimum of four of my guys in here twenty-four seven. Determine in thirty days who would stay and who would go." Twisted rolled his shoulders, settling his vest on his back. "Timeline's changed. Process changed." He flashed a grin at Wildman. "Gotta be fluid as fuck, man. This is me goin' with the flow of circumstances."

"And now, where's that flow of change takin' you?"

"Men livin' in the house and trailer got thirty days to vacate. Every man I decide to keep will be assigned a new town. They'll enter the club as prospects without a minimum time before movin' up. Lets me break up the burden of evaluating potentials between my houses, eases the way for some needed one-on-one time to see if you all are really IMC material." Sweeping the inside of the house with his gaze, Twisted somehow made Wildman see every flaw through his eyes. Broken windows boarded over, broken floorboards covered in multiple layers of cardboard, and dirt and trash everywhere. "Thirty days, we have a bonfire."

"When will we know who you're takin' on?"

"Right the fuck now." Twisted hopped off the bar, heels landing with a thud that shook the floorboards. "I gotta know who wants it first. Then I'll separate the wannabes into winners and weepers." He lifted his head, sweeping his hair over his shoulder. "Give me a thumbs-up you want to petition for the patch." Arms relaxed at his sides, Twisted spun in a slow circle, pinning each man with a glare. "Fifteen seconds to decide which way you're gonna throw yourself. I'll tell you right now, if you want the life and don't pick my playground, I'll make fuckin' certain you don't patch in anywhere in southern Louisiana." He'd made it full circle, gaze latching on Wildman with a solid weight he could feel. "And before you ask yourself if I have so much pull and sway, remember who you're talkin' to." He grinned, white slash through his beard. "Or listenin' to, as it may be. Tick tock, boys. Time starts now."

Wildman didn't look away, keeping their gazes locked as he shrugged, the leather of his vest sitting uneasily on his shoulders. A second shrug told him what he wanted. CEMC was dead, and that light feeling was the sloughing of the unwanted drama and bullshit Torment always seemed to pull in around them. With a sigh, he shoved one hand deep in his jeans pocket and pulled out a pocketknife. Flicking the blade open, he held it fisted as he raised his arm shoulder height, aligning his thumb alongside the sharp edge. Only once he had declared himself did he glance around, finding his closest brothers had done the same, along with several other men he had been unsure of when Torment had patched them.

Ignoring the others, he gave Catfish, Ruger, and Mosser a nod, then swung his attention to Po'Boy, who was grinning widely as he counted down the remaining seconds. "Three, two, one-thousand fuckin' one. You got fuckin' nads, man. We'll let you take care of business quick, then do our thang." Po'Boy gestured to the prospect still held against the floor. "Regain that center, man, and pass it over." He held out a hand, patience seemingly unending. Flicking his fingers against his palm, Po'Boy waited silently.

"Anything?" Wildman gave Po'Boy his back, turning his attention to Catfish. "If not, I'm gonna cut him now."

"Go for it, brother." Catfish dropped a knee on the man's thigh, taking control of his arm from the prospect. "Got him, Mark. Go stand near Randy, man. Good job."

"Patch or vest." Wildman stepped closer, the tang of the knife pinched between thumb and finger. "Fuck it, vest." He snipped through the leather laces holding the sides of the vest together and wrapped a hand in the leather collar. Giving a yank, he ignored the yell of pain from the man who'd stepped far outside of his role today, retrieving the club's property. "Drag him out. He don't need to be in here for this." He gestured at two prospects still nearby, ones he hadn't gotten to know yet, not even their names. "Take out the trash, pros." Standing, he shook the vest once, then folded it carefully. It might not have a center on it, but it didn't matter. It represented the club. "Prospects, all head outside."

"My job, man. Give it over and let me tell them what's next, yeah?" Twisted stepped close and held out his hand. As he waited through Wildman's hesitation to hand over the vest, the man called out orders. "Prospects outside, far edge of the driveway. Do not let my men catch you tryin' to fuckin' overhear shit." As Po'Boy had, Twisted flicked his fingers against his palm, and Wildman set the folded black leather in his grip. "Any member who did not thumb-up, and I fuckin' marked you, trust me, leave your vest on the bar. Po'Boy, wanna count we have eleven after they're done?" Footsteps from behind Wildman told him Po'Boy was on the move. "After you drop off the vest, you are fuckin' dismissed. Free to leave." Twisted walked away from Wildman, confidence in his swagger. "And I recommend you get the fuck outta here fast-like."

Men throughout the room moved, walking towards where Po'Boy stood next to the bar. Twisted laid the vest he held on the surface and patted it once. Po'Boy slid it closer to himself and counted down, much as he had through the seconds the men had been allowed time to choose. "Twelve, because I keep good records. Eleven, ten, nine. No, fuckmonkey, you don't get to just leave the goddamned patches. Boss said vest, you leave the fuckin' vest. You ain't gonna patch in anywhere, don't need no raggedy cut-ass vest on your back ridin' around here. There now. Ain't that better? Eight, and I'm waitin'. Eight needs another to get to—there we go, good man, drop it and leave, you had your little bitty boy say. Seven, don't matter anyway, you're fuckin' out, and six." Wildman made his way to the edge of the room, putting his back to the wall as he watched the dismantling of the club. "Five, four, three and two, and here's the final one, don't let the door hit ya where the good Lord split ya, one. All in, Twisted."

"Movin' on." Twisted waited for the door to close behind the last ex-member, then whirled, arm extended as he pointed in rapid succession at Wildman and those nearest to where he stood. "You, you, you, both of you, guy with the head—"

"Twisted," Po'Boy interrupted, "they all got heads."

"*Bald* head," Twisted said with heavy emphasis. "Jesus, the shit I put up with." The mutter accompanied an eye roll. "And you." He waggled his fingers. "Go stand near Po'Boy." Wildman hoofed it quickly, not wanting to make the man say his instructions a second time. "Yea, man, put a hustle on it. I like to see that shit. Take fuckin' notes, Po'Boy. You're the one told his prospect to whack him over the head, and he's still gonna put his hat in the ring to join Incoherent. Well fuckin' done."

"Prez." Po'Boy coughed, then sniffed delicately as he grimaced. "Maybe we should take this outside."

"The fuck why?" Twisted shook his head. "Everyone not standin' by Po'Boy as of right now, you're out. Leave your vest, and if you don't want to do that, trust me, Po'Boy will be happy to deliver your beatout. Oh, I got an idea. We should let—" Twisted's head turned sharply. "What the hell?" He coughed. "The fuck is that?" He sniffed, less delicately than Po'Boy had. "Oh, Jesus. Outside, for fuck's sake, outside."

About then, the smell hit Wildman and he choked back a gag.

"Your ex-president shat himself. That seems incredibly appropriate, doncha think, Wild?" Po'Boy flung an arm around his neck and steered Wildman towards the door. "Leave him. Do not fuckin' move him" was called back over his shoulder. "My guys, and that means every one of you motherfuckers Twisted sent my way, follow me and my new friend here." He patted Wild's chest with his free hand, then shoved the door wide. "Fresh air, praise Jesus. That was incredibly rank. I'd venture a guess the man had digestive issues before he became all asshole, but this surely showed his true colors for ya. Shat all over himself and the club, the clubhouse, members, every fuckin' thing. Damn. What in *hell* have you been feedin' that man?"

Wildman straightened his shoulders, angling to the side and out from under Po'Boy's arm. He still held the open knife in his fist, taking care to keep the blade away from this man who seemed to have taken—a liking didn't seem the right word, an interest might be the better explanation—whatever it was, Po'Boy was sticking to him like a sandbur.

"What's next?" Wildman angled his head to indicate the pocketknife. "You takin' our vests, too?" The idea swelled inside him like a sickness. Some of the patches on his vest had been sewn into place by long-lost hands, and he wasn't ready to give any of that up yet. *Probably won't ever.* If they asked for the vest, he'd cut the colors of the dead club off and walk. *There's plenty more states than Louisiana. I've picked up and drifted before. I can do it again.*

Po'Boy studied his face, then gave a fluid shrug as he angled his chin towards where Twisted stood apart from them, talking to the group he hadn't singled out inside. "Up to the man. I'm just the muscle." Po'Boy flexed an arm, biceps pumped and ready, veins in his forearm bulging. "I learned a long time ago I'm better served by following than leading."

"Could say that about ninety-nine percent of us." Wildman studied the external façade of the clubhouse. "How'd we not see this comin'?" The clapboards were faded and checkered with peeling paint. Each broken or fractured windowpane was boarded from inside, giving the house a jack-o'-lantern look. "Roofline's saggin', means support is entirely gone. It ain't that it's not pretty on the outside, but if we were to dig into shit underneath, guarantee we find ants and termites boring through the pillars and posts." The roar of motorcycles made him look over his shoulder to watch as the rest of the men he'd fought for and tried to call brother threw a leg over their bikes and rode off with naked backs. Twisted's arms were loaded with vests grabbed from the top of the bar. He'd handled them respectfully, and it took Wildman a minute to realize the actions meant something to him, and how he reflected on this man who might become his president. "That shit's hard to see."

"I didn't have to do a single beatout either." Po'Boy stepped up beside Wildman and shrugged. "Bummer. I was all set to go two-one-two on a dude." He postured, miming swinging at an invisible foe, jabs and haymakers slicing harmlessly through the air. "Oh well, day's not over yet." He ducked his head and gave Wildman a knowing grin. "Might still get my chance."

"Common Enemy is dead." Wildman shrugged out of his vest and flipped it around in his hands until he could angle the blade against the threads holding the center patch in place. "Gonna get a head start on this shit."

"You do that, brother," Twisted called from the end of the line of men. He'd walked to where Catfish stood next to Ruger. "I want you, these two"—he tipped his head at the men, then clapped a hand on Mosser's shoulder—"and this one with us in Hammond." Lifting his chin, he called to a man who stood near their bikes. "Busk, you and Pony take the rest of them to our house here in Baton Rouge. Get them all settled in, yeah?"

"Patches, Prez?" Po'Boy stood shoulder to shoulder next to Wildman, appearing ready to do battle on his behalf.

"Yeah, yeah, get all the colors. We'll put them in a pyre with the vests we confiscated." Twisted looked around and seemed to find what he needed. "Prospects, you want to do hangaround time, you petition the Baton Rouge house. Trust me when I say you do not want to go anywhere else. Year and a day, same as our probate period. Year and a day and you can approach a different club." He thumbed over his shoulder at the clubhouse. "Anyone still gonna stay in there or y'all vacating? Trailer is still open, but I'm thinkin' we don't want to let Torment ripen much beyond today. Fuck thirty days, we'll torch the motherfucker tomorrow."

The prospects had shuffled together, their civilian clothes making them stand out even more than they had before. One by one, they angled away, heading to their cheap rice burner bikes or cages, and within only a couple of minutes, all that was left in the clearing were IMC members and the men busy removing patches from their vests.

"It's not all bad, Wild." Po'Boy's hand slapped directly between Wildman's shoulder blades, his thin shirt doing nothing to relieve the sting from the hit. He jerked his head around to scowl at Po'Boy, who had that damned infectious grin plastered across his face.

"Why isn't it all bad?" He finished the bottom rocker and closed the knife, slipping it back into his pocket. With the way his head throbbed, the oppressive heat was boiling him alive, and he just wanted to get out of the sun somewhere. "Tell me what's good about today."

"You got to meet me." Po'Boy accepted the patches, not giving them a second glance. "No, seriously, you found out you were gonna be fucked over by someone, had them dealt with so you didn't have to, and are in a prime position to join a well-respected club. We're the doms in the area, and no one ever dares forget that fact."

"Yeah, join as a nonvoting member." Wildman shrugged. "Guess it could be worse."

"Oh, my bad. Did you think you could join Mother without a probie period? Naw, man." Po'Boy shook his head, laughter glinting in his hard eyes. "You're my bitch for the foreseeable future, you feel me?"

He held out a hand, and Wildman accepted the fabric Po'Boy offered him. He smoothed it across his palm, stomach rolling as he realized what Po'Boy meant. A wide straight bar meant to go across a man's shoulders, giving no room to hide the fact he'd be in a far lesser position than the lowest member of any club.

"I'm a fucking prospect?" He glanced up, then around the clearing, seeing Catfish, Mosser, and Ruger held the same patches. Anger simmered through his veins at the joke these men had played on them. *And we thought we were the cream of the crop. Fuck.* He decided to push, see if there was any wiggle room out of this mess IMC had trapped them in. "We're bounced back to the lowest of the low? How is this not worse, Po'Boy?"

"Because you're *my* fuckin' prospect." Po'Boy threw his head back and crowed, flapping his elbows like chicken wings. "Gonna teach you all the right moves. Show me what you got. Hands like beaks." The man hummed loudly, the song unmusical but also unmistakable. "Flap your wings, and now shake your tail feathers." Wildman stood stock-still and stared at him. "Come on, probie. Dance with your goddamned sponsor."

"Fuck my life."

Chapter Four

Justine, Adken, Florida

"No, Mr. Yawas, that was not a rhetorical question." Justine LaPorte narrowed her eyes, pinning her subject to the chair. "It was an actual inquiry that deserves careful deliberation and a considered response. Something I find myself wondering if you'll be able to achieve given your current attitude." Head pounding, she refused to allow anything other than disdain to show in her expression. In negotiations like this, admitting discomfort or even any emotion could prove to be a death knell for a continued productive conversation. *Been doing this job a long damn time.* She denied herself a glance at the clock, trusting her gut, which told her they'd reached the four-hour mark a while ago. *Maybe too long.* "Which means—" She casually gathered up the papers and images in front of her, tucked them inside a yellow-edged folder, and straightened the corners until things lined up exactly. "You need some time to think."

She stood and thudded her fist against the solid metal door, ignoring Yawas' sputtering behind her. *They've got to know I won't back down.* He spit out a name, and she nearly paused, but when he didn't follow with anything else, she held firm and, once the door was opened, stalked through it, listening to the clunk as it set back into place.

Greg Anderson stared at her as she entered the observation room, his sharp gaze missing nothing. She hated him sometimes. Her counterpart on the anti-trafficking task force wielded the same authority as Justine, but his tactics couldn't have been more different. Where Justine evoked cautious respect from her colleagues, Greg Anderson left behind the stench of fear, perhaps especially when it was unnecessary.

"Yawas is a dead end." Anderson shoved a handful of folders into a box, careless with what amounted to hundreds of hours of labor to piece together the things they knew so far. Justine shook her head, carefully stacking the folders on her side of the table into color-coded columns she then tucked into one legal-sized box. "You knew it when you walked in there. Pretty sure you didn't have to make me wait out here half a day before you cut him loose."

"I didn't cut him loose." Justine gestured to the screens, showing Yawas still cuffed and chained to the table. "He's being detained another seventy-two hours on obstruction charges. I'll be back here day after tomorrow, giving him forty-eight before I peck away at his battle armor again." She shrugged. "He knows what I need. The only challenge will be if I can extract it before the window closes on when the information can be used." She fit the lid of the box into place and draped her jacket across it, hooking her computer bag and purse strap over her shoulder. "I'm going home for now. You can either show back up tomorrow for a rehearsal of the next talk with Yawas, or I'll know you aren't interested in this takedown."

Without waiting for Greg to finish spitting out whatever complaint he'd been storing up, she opened the door, held it with one heel as she lifted the box, and pivoted through the opening. She used the subterranean tunnel connecting the justice center with the jail and made her way to her office at the back of the building. The small window set in the outside wall was triple-paned detonation-proof glass, which distorted everything, but it afforded her a view of the nearby forest instead of concrete and glass.

Dumping the box along the wall, she toed open the bottom drawer of the desk and deposited the computer bag inside. That same toe tapped the drawer shut, and a slide of her finger locked the desk. She picked up the jacket, swished it through the air with a flourish, and slipped her arms through the fabric. A tug of the collar, and she grabbed her purse, ready to head out the door and to her home as advertised.

Where she'd go later was a different beast altogether.

***

Eyes safely closed behind the satin blindfold, Justine let her focus drift. The effortless way her body took in each breath was mesmerizing, how the muscles of her chest and back worked in seamless coordination. She listened to the rushing sounds within her own head, the quiet symphony of blood pounding and air cascading through her nostrils, drowning out any external distractions. Heat bloomed across her upper back, traveling side to side along her skin, then encircling her throat as it moved up to her face.

A tap against the side of her head was a well-known signal, one ingrained enough to pull her from the soothing quiet. Justine lifted her chin in response and clenched her lids closed tightly as the blindfold slipped free of her head, care taken so the ribbons didn't tangle in her hair.

"You are doing very well." The smooth praise reached her ears as fingers pinched her chin hard, yanking her forwards. She kept her balance with effort, remaining in the awkward position the hand had placed her—bent at the waist, chin lifted so the skin of her throat stretched taut. With her wrists and forearms bound together behind her back, Justine's muscles protested the new pose. "I'm proud of you."

She consciously smoothed her features, brows retreating to their normal neutral place, mouth closed as best she could, with the corners tipped up in a slightly positive expression. As blank and open as she could be. The hand reappeared at her chin, this time the grip gentle instead of brutal, and Justine had to fight to keep the dispassionate expression in place. Cold leather settled between her legs, and she rose a little, more an instinctive flexing of her thigh muscles than an intentional creating of space. The shoe-covered foot swept side to side, nudging her knees wider than before. She lost the sense of ease the steady focus on her breathing had provided, instead paying brief flurries of attention to all the places her body hurt. Knees, the outside of each thigh, her hips as they pivoted into a new position, shoulders from being held immobile for this length of time—*however long that was.* She stilled the instinct to shake the idea from her head, shoving it aside as she tried to find the place of gentle peace again.

Fingers danced the length of her arms, each miniscule easing of the bindings an unwelcome reminder that the serenity she'd found was ever fleeting. Tiny tugs at the end of each finger presaged the slow degloving that left her skin bare to the air, goose bumps chasing the worn leather. Her hands and wrists were chafed in turn, each arm carefully returned to a more natural position along her sides as the massaging touch moved to her shoulders. Weight landed on her upper back and neck, realigning her torso with the floor, easing the pressure on her hips. The harness holding the ball gag loosened, fingers teasing around her mouth to retrieve the device while a soft terrycloth towel was used to wipe her chin, cheeks, throat, and chest free from saliva that had spilled over.

A cushion whooshed out air nearby as someone sat, and Justine, so accustomed to the routine by now, anticipated the touch that would urge her slump to the side, resting her cheek against a fabric-clad thigh. A soft blanket settled over her shoulders, and as heat pooled against her skin, Justine slowly relaxed. A moment later, the hand grazed over the top of her head and gently removed the tie holding the tight braid, then stroked down the fall of hair. Some set of minutes later, Justine finally blinked her eyes open for the first time. The soothing cadence of fingers threading through her hair didn't change or falter, but she knew her partner was fully cognizant of her progress rising through the levels back to complete awareness.

She wrapped her fingers around his ankle, as clear an indication she was ready to move things along to the culmination as his signal earlier about the blindfold.

"Justine, you went really deep tonight."

She nodded, cheek rubbing against the expensive fabric of his suit pants.

"These cases are killing you a little inside."

She couldn't argue, not when the truth of his statement was something she witnessed in her mirror every day. Each of the latest rounds of trafficking busts was worse than the previous ones. The victims a little younger, a little more damaged, and way too often, a little too dead.

"It had been too long." *Damn.* Her admission came out hoarse, rusty as a gate no one bothered to maintain. "It was good." She took a deep breath and snuggled a little tighter against his leg. "Thank you, Sir."

"It's my honor as always, Justine." His fingers sank into her hair and gripped, turning her face up so their gazes clashed. "It would please me if you called more often."

She schooled her features as the gentle scold lashed like a whip. "My joy is to please, Sir." Not please him, specifically, although he'd been her first choice of a top when she'd realized where her car was aimed. Leaving the office, she'd turned the opposite way from the route that would take her home, only realizing it a few minutes into the drive. *Sometimes the subconscious response is right.* She'd sleep well for the few hours remaining tonight and be back in the office tomorrow with a vengeance. Justine gave her shoulders and arms a subtle stretch, arching her neck the slightest amount, the twinges from muscles and ligaments soothing, not painful. "You're very good at your job."

Greg Anderson smiled at her. "I'm good at all my jobs, Justine."

She smiled back and straightened, pulling away from his touch in preparation for rising from the floor. *Time to get the hell out of Dodge,* she thought, and inclined her head in acknowledgment of his words.

"We both are."

Chapter Five

Wildman, Two Years Later

"Trust is a thing of beauty." He stared at the woman lashed to the wall on the opposite side of the room. Not Wildman's sub; he wasn't playing tonight, just found himself at the club in an observing role. Something he'd been doing more and more. The woman's body jolted at the solid smack of a paddle applied to the bottom curve of her ass, the contact hard and stinging enough to send ripples throughout each of her limbs. The Dom pulled back to inspect his work, running a tender touch along the raised red strip of skin.

"Been a while, Master Lyle."

He turned to look at the man seated next to him. "Yes, it has, Master Jonah." Ruger grinned back at him.

In the years since joining the IMC, the two men had drifted apart and then back together again, following where the club led. Years of turmoil presaged by the aggressive takeover of their previous club, but both men had agreed it had all been worth it. Forging friendships with good men, then getting to watch as things turned on a dime for them, and then finding themselves in the middle of history-making events—all worth it.

Ruger's initiation to the scening world of BDSM had been that long-ago night in the Quarter when Monique had come to the party at Wildman's invitation. He'd watched avidly from the balcony as Wildman set things up, then—according to his retelling of the event—been mesmerized by the beauty of Monique's submission. Days and days of questioning had led to a casual invitation to the club, which had, in turn, led to an unexpected deepening of their friendship. Wildman couldn't have foreseen the benefits of having a close companion to bounce ideas off and talk through the nuance of a planned scene.

Monique had long since retired from casual play, finding the kind of committed partner she'd longed for, but Wildman still loved to watch her when the couple played publicly. Another loud smack of leather against skin brought his attention back to the bound woman across the room. Monique's head tipped backwards with a low moan as the heat from the strike flooded through her system.

"I received a personal invitation." Wildman shrugged, lifting a bottle of water for a drink before twisting the cap back into place. "Never been one to turn down a chance to be a voyeur."

"Why not find a sub and play? There's four or five I've seen who are just waiting for that crooked finger to call them over." Ruger leaned an elbow on the arm of his chair, angling closer. "I see a pair that enjoy doing twosomes, if you were interested."

Shaking his head slowly, Wildman let out a grunt. "Just not feelin' it tonight, man. Don't let me be the anchor on your boat, though. Feel free to bob off over the waves and catch yourself a keeper for the evening." Movement along the edges of his vision pulled his attention, and he stared at the man who'd just walked into the room, crossing the space with purpose in his stride. "Hol-ee shit on turd toast. Don't act like an idiot lookin' around, but glance towards the hallway leading to the back rooms. Is that Po'Boy?"

The response was slow but sure. "Nah, can't imagine him here. That guy's too tall or something. I didn't get a full look at the face, and he wasn't my sponsor or anything, but I'd recognize Po'Boy anywhere. That ain't him."

Wildman grunted, watched the man's back as he paused in front of a closed door and lifted a fist. Even such a minor gesture felt familiar, but he didn't draw Ruger's attention away from Monique again. She'd just taken another strike and looked to be near orgasm. Her partner opened his pants as he moved behind her, hands gripping the globes of her reddened ass as he pulled back and out, opening her for his cock. Either he'd already sheathed himself in a condom, or their agreement was vastly different than Wildman and Monique's had been, because the man plunged deep inside her with one thrust.

By the time he looked back at the hallway, Po'Boy's doppelgänger had disappeared, and Wildman lifted one shoulder, shrugging away the uncertainty. *Quack.* It'd been a hot minute since he'd been Po'Boy's prospect, but some jokes never died.

"I'm out, brother." The word slipped so naturally from his lips that it shouldn't have been jarring, but in this setting, it truly was. Here they were not MC members, but Doms and Masters. His usage of the different kind of title was telling, and Wildman grinned. "Gonna get me some wind therapy."

"Enjoy yourself, Master Lyle." Ruger's tone was wry, and as Wildman stood, he watched his friend crook the aforementioned finger, calling an unattached sub away from a quietly chattering group. "I have other cravings to tend to."

Wildman retrieved his belongings from the desk and quickly located an empty changing room. It was the work of moments to put away his club persona and don the one that fit just as comfortably. Phone in hand, he stared down at the screen, scrolling through the messages that had come through while the device had been locked away. Trouble brewing in Alabama, and Twisted wanted an all-member meeting later tonight. Wildman wavered a moment about retrieving Ruger, then decided the man had time to play. He'd bring his friend up to speed soon enough.

Once across the causeway and in the clubhouse though, as they settled into places around the room to listen to Twisted's proclamation of what they'd be doing for the next few days, Wildman did find it interesting Ruger wasn't the only member missing.

So was Po'Boy.

***

Justine

Pinching the bridge of her nose with thumb and forefinger, Justine pressed hard, hoping the wave of intentional pain would offset the growing ache behind her eyes. She released the hold and straightened in her chair, blinking at the reams of paperwork spread out in front of her. Commandeering a conference room with ample space to review the data had been a good call. The room was also windowless, which meant she'd been more focused than if she'd stayed in her own office.

Frowning, she flipped a paperclipped sheaf of paper to one edge of the table, shuffling through the pages underneath until she found the information she was looking for.

Over the past year, her office had been inundated with reports of trafficked women and children. Each case proved more disturbing than the last, and each incident was harder to track and document with prosecution in mind. She could disturb the route or the shipment, but finding those responsible had become nearly impossible.

"At some point I'm going to have to become okay with saving the people, I guess." Justine blew out a stream of air as she raised her gaze to the man seated across the table from her. "But the department doesn't care about that. They care about successful case prosecutions.

There's little chance they'll keep funneling money for the investigations if we can't produce the big payoff at the end of things."

Greg scowled and raked a hand through his hair, then patted it back into place. "My side of things is the same, you know? You're not the only one facing a decision here."

"Did you see this bit of intel?" She nudged a sheet of paper in Greg's direction, and he leaned forwards, fingers deftly plucking the corner to drag it closer. "I think that's a solid lead on the next shipment." She scoffed. "Listen to me. A shipment, as if the cargo were no more worrisome than a container of hijacked electronics or luxury purses. That's a lead on the next truckful of humans the cartel wants to sell into slavery. These are people, Greg. How can someone do something so heinous to another human being?" Justine pressed her lips into a tight line as she shook her head, swallowing hard against the nausea swelling alongside the disgust she felt. *Twelve out of twenty women dead at the last scene.* Walking into that container had scarred her deeper than she wanted anyone to see. "I'm always just floored the things the supposedly evolved species on this planet are willing to do for money."

"I'd say you're passionate about your role in stopping these assholes. It can be easy to get lost in the logistics, but you always bring it back to the people. Back to the individuals, and having that reminder is good for anyone working trafficking." Greg's hand landed on hers, and she pulled away, back ramrod straight. "Sorry," he muttered, picking up the paper again. "I see where you're pulling the idea from that this is a tell for a route." The sheet fluttered back to the tabletop. "But I don't see where the info is about the route's *actual* route."

She flipped the paperclipped sheaf back in front of her, thumbing through half a dozen sheets before she found the one containing the information she'd remembered. Turning it around, she handed it to Greg, top sheets tucked out of the way. Justine watched his face as he read the info, not surprised when his brow furrowed instead of raising in an "ah-ha" moment. This would be a slow slog to lead him into the info as she saw it, but one good thing about Greg was he didn't discount any theory until it had been beaten into submission.

She talked, referring to the information drawn from various sources the department had to offer. In-country chatter on known phones were tied to recordings acquired from the cartel members' home states in Mexico. That intel had then been paired with shipping manifests for containers unloaded in local ports—and as she'd slowly built the case for the route she'd identified, Justine had grown even more convinced this was a solid lead.

She watched Greg shake his head again, rejecting her argument about the facts that appeared plain as day. Justine sighed in frustration, smoothing a palm down the front of her jacket. *We're equals. Anderson doesn't get to nay-say me on this.* With that reminder she opened another folder, bringing out another stack of papers.

It didn't matter, though; all the rehashing of the evidence had cemented a plan in her head.

Now she just needed to figure out how to go about it.

***

Wildman

"Y'all ready for this?" Wildman scanned the group of men arrayed in front of the clubhouse. Members from half a dozen chapters had arrived as requested, and they'd all listened to Twisted's narrative on what came next. It was nearly go time, when they would split into three groups and pull out of the lot and onto the highways. Three hours would have them arriving at the destination picked for his group, over closer to Biloxi, where the cartel's containers had been stowed in the back of an abandoned warehouse. "I asked if y'all were ready for this?" His roared repetition of the question got responses at least, and he grinned at the prospects shouting the loudest. "Y'all aren't even fuckin' goin', man."

Shaking his head, he clapped one of them on the back. "Keep the house safe for us, yeah?"

"Yes, sir." Earnest and solemn, the prospect nodded vigorously as he agreed.

Rumbling of pipes from up the road made Wildman spin away, his hand automatically going to his back, where he kept his piece. He didn't relax until the riders were close enough to make out faces under helmets, and once he'd recognized the two leaders, he crowed loudly. "Fuck yeah, the gang's all here. CoBos are in the house." Whirling, he looked for Twisted and found a broad smile on his president's face. "Pleased you called 'em in."

"I am too." Twisted tipped his head a tad and grinned, eyes cutting to look at Wildman. "Wouldn't be a party unless we could throw a little Wrench into it."

"Par-*tay*." Wildman crowed again, then shoved his fists against his hips and waited.

Tonight, the Incoherent MC would take on an advance guard of the Mexican cartel that had been trying to horn in on their IMC territory, something locked down and undisputed for decades. This had been planned as a preemptive strike alongside their allies in the Caddo Hobos MC, and one that had every hope of being entirely successful. Tonight, the cartel would relearn the lesson that the IMC and CoBos didn't give a shit what the motherfuckers wanted and were entirely willing to pay in red if needed.

His old mentor Po'Boy didn't disappoint, appearing as if by magic in front of Wildman and pulling him into a hard embrace, fist pounding against his back. "Brother, good to see your fuckin' face."

Tension seeped out of Wildman's muscles, replaced with a strange sense of relief at Po'Boy's presence. It still killed that the man had patched out of the IMC a few months ago, and Wildman remained uncomfortable seeing the different colors riding on the man's back. Po'Boy had been the one constant for Wildman within the Incoherent club from the first moments of the hostile takeover of CEMC, to being the man's bitch of a prospect, and finally to a developing friendship filled with trust and a solid belief Po'Boy would always have his back. His leaving had opened doors for Wildman to move up within the organization, so shit wasn't all bad. "Fuck me, why do I miss you, motherfucker?" Wildman pulled back and scowled at the laughter bubbling out of the man's mouth. "See, I miss you, but then I'm around you again, and all of a sudden I remember why I can't stand you, and I'm fuckin' glad you're gone."

Po'Boy's mouth pulled sideways as he fought a grin. "I love you too, Wild."

"Quack fuckin' quack." Twisted's grin was a little wider, his shoulders a little more relaxed, and Wildman realized he wasn't the only one glad to see Po'Boy's face. "Glad you could join us, brother."

"Ride or die, my friend." Po'Boy grabbed around Twisted's shoulders, one fist already pounding the man's back as he pulled him close. "Always ride or die." He arched back and surveyed the men scattered in small groups. "We rollin' soon or standin' around with sticks up our collective asses?"

"Figured you and Wrench would want to know the score and plan, man." Twisted stepped away, one hand smoothing down his beard. "Gather 'round, kiddos. Got a tale to tell." Once every man was within earshot of his position, Twisted lowered his chin and raised his voice to cast across the group. "Cartel's shipping into our territory, as well as every goddamned port along the coast. We got word yesterday various smaller boats were being deployed, and have friendly eyes on two such boats docked in Eden Isle, just outside of Slidell. More are in Gulfport as well as Biloxi. They're shipping out in trucks that look legit, branded shit they bought at auction, complete with pizza place logos or cleaning service information. Fuckin' legit lookin', but filled to the brim with shit that's killin' our people.

"You all know I'm a man who looks the other way, with every expectation others will do the same. You wanna get fucked up and live in your own goddamned head, that's your fuckin' prerogative. Long as you don't kill someone else in the meantime, I'm down, man. Sellin' shit, again, long as you don't kill someone else in the process, knock yourself out." He shook his head. "They're bringin' in this shit knowing full well it's killing about seventy-five percent of their users. Now, that ain't good business for them, but when it touches our people, it's bad business all around. We've lost two, a brother from the Biloxi chapter and the oldest kid of a Baton Rouge brother. Club won't stand for this, and we're gonna deliver a helluva message today. Stay off our patch of ground. And we're claimin' every fuckin' acre of real estate between here and fuckin' Ocala if we have to. Every chapter has a role today. Some partnering with other clubs to get shit done. That's us, just in case you're wonderin'."

Laughter rose, defusing the tension as Twisted no doubt intended. Wildman was always amazed at the man's eloquence and in awe of the passion with which he spoke. Anyone listening would be crystal fucking clear where he stood and why he was taking these actions. Why Twisted had called the club to arms, knowing it would start a war.

Twisted slicked his hair back with both hands, strands sticking to his temples in the Louisiana heat. "We got ridealongs for all groups. We provisioned breakdown vans for each group too. I personally have warned the lawmen in every area to lay low for the day, because they do *not* want to get in my motherfuckin' way. We are gonna take back what's ours, clean up the coast, and give the fuckin' cartel a goddamned heart attack at the losses they are gonna hafta swallow, because there's no comin' back from this. I'm drawing a damned line in the motherfuckin' sand." He put truth to the words, dragging a booted toe side to side, and then stepped over it. "Here and now, shit changes, and we're doin' the work we need to do. Whatever it takes." Twisted pounded a clenched fist against his chest as he looked around the group. He took his time, and Wildman felt the weight of Twisted's gaze as it landed on him. "As our founders did before us, it's time to put on the colors and ride, brothers.

Don't matter what patch you wear today, you're under my protection, and I do not take your presence here lightly."

Wrench lifted a closed fist, followed by Po'Boy, Wildman, Ruger, and dozens of other men. As one, they lifted their faces and shouted their club's oath, the cacophony of noises rendering understanding of individual words impossible, but it didn't matter. Anyone watching would recognize these were warriors on the cusp of battle.

Wildman grinned, teeth bared as he shouted, "IMC is me, and I am IMC."

***

Justine

She crouched on the balls of her feet and ran a trembling hand down the arm of the woman in front of her. "Shhhh."

Bruised, with blood oozing from a split in the corner of her mouth, the woman stared up at her with an awed expression. "Thank you."

"Don't thank me. The son of a bitch still hit you." Ignoring the throbbing of the bruises on her own body, Justine leaned in and cupped the woman's cheek in her hand. "I promise you, we're going to get out of this."

Glancing around at the milling crowd of women and children jammed into the small space, Justine shook her head. *I just don't know how.*

Chapter Six
Wildman

Hands grappled for a hold on his arms, strong fingers digging in, blunt nails leaving furrows of red behind. Wildman dropped to a knee and countered, willing to risk a bite as he shoved his fingers into a gaping mouth and yanked hard on the jaw of the man in front of him. He pulled and twisted, dislocating the joints with a sickening snap and leaving the jaw grotesquely wobbling in the wake of the man's screams. A figure approached from the side, and Wildman burst from his low crouch and used the top of his head to blast that assailant's nose flat on one cheek, the instantly flowing blood black in the shadows.

Another one came at Wildman from the side, and he met them halfway. Tucking his shoulder low, he got underneath them and hefted the body high into the air before he wove his fingers into the clothing and yanked the man down across his lifted knee. The crunch of bone resonated through Wildman, and he caught the falling body to twist the man's head around until his neck popped and bulged obscenely. Dropping the still-twitching body to the shell-and-gravel driveway, Wildman fell back into his ready crouch. When there were no immediate threats, he took a moment to glance around, huffed breaths clouding in the chill air.

Po'Boy was in the middle of three men, but instead of fighting them off, Po'Boy was the one holding the men there. The wild grin splitting his face told Wildman Po'Boy was not only doing fine but was also likely enjoying himself.

Off to the side, Twisted straddled a man who was sprawled loosely on the ground, the president's fists pounding the face to an unrecognizable mass of flesh and bone. *Get him, man.*

All around him, Wildman counted four more individual skirmishes. A quick review of each showed they equaled four more wins for his brothers and friends.

A sound from behind him had him spinning around in a crouch, scanning the area close to him. They were in a trucking company's compound outside Biloxi, and until the first gunshots had ripped through the air not five minutes ago, the night had been riddled with bullfrog cries ahead of an approaching storm. Lightning played along the edges of the rolling clouds overhead, occasional bright flashes bringing everything into a stark focus.

It was one of those bursts of light that gave him his first glimpse of her.

The vent in the rear door of a nearby trailer had been forced wide and then wired that way so it would take a fuckton of intent to close it. *That ain't right.* The sounds of the fight faded to the background as thunder crashed, the accompanying flash highlighting a woman's face behind the mesh. The single eye he could see was wide and frightened—and staring straight at him.

The next lightning flash showed an empty hole.

He shook his head in disbelief, not trusting his own eyes, especially given the situation. He knew logically there was more than one reason for a person to be stowed away inside a truck trailer, whether parked on a lot or being dragged down the interstate. Innocent reasons, such as a haven from the storm. Malicious reasons, like bottling up warriors inside a current-day Trojan horse. However, given the owners of this company were the dirtbags currently breathing their last in the haze of dust floating through the air around him, Wildman was confident that whatever this woman was, the one thing she wasn't was a terrorist.

No matter how hard he stared, the vision of the woman's face didn't reappear. He trusted himself enough to believe, though, which meant it needed to be checked out.

Wildman ducked low and ran to the side of the trailer, dragging his piece from where it dug into his waist. Closer to the vent, an odor of unwashed bodies hit him, sweat and shit, and so much goddamned fear. The air reeked of terror, something he was far too familiar with. *Nope, not a foreign terrorist or one of the mules the cartel uses. Whoever she is, she's here involuntarily.* The faintest murmur of conversation from inside cut off in midphrase, echoes quickly silenced. *And she's not alone.* At the back of the trailer, he scanned the lot again, now seeing only friendly members still on their feet. All the bad guys were down and looking to stay that way. *Win for us, hell yeah.* There were clusters of folks here and there, but he couldn't spare any time to wonder what they were looking at, either opponents or good guys. *If whoever is inside poses a threat, we've got to know now.* It would be better to fight any remaining battles while still hyped up on adrenaline and the rush of winning than to be blindsided after they'd let their guard down.

Now's as good a time as any.

Lifting a hand overhead, Wildman waggled his pistol side to side as he gave off a soft whistle similar to a dove, gratified when Po'Boy's head immediately lifted and turned his way. With a single powerful blow, the man finished off the enemy he'd been holding upright with a fist around his throat. Then Po'Boy gave his own whistle and came in Wildman's direction, bringing three additional men with him.

Wildman met him at the doors, hand already on the latch. Under his breath, he shared what he knew. "At least one woman, but I heard other voices. From the stench comin' out of their hidey-hole, they're most likely unwilling guests of our friends."

Po'Boy stepped back, bringing out his gun while the rest of the men moved so they formed a deadly arc of iron and bone. *My brothers.* Same patch or not, he held the same emotions for every man here. *IMC stands with CoBos, and my brothers stand with me.* With a brusque nod, Wildman turned back to the trailer, shoving his gun into his belt at the back of his jeans.

The shoulder-high latches moved quietly under his hands, and he pulled in a hard breath, holding the air deep within his lungs as he lifted and pulled in the same movement, throwing both doors wide. Silence greeted him, thick shadows nearly fifty feet away at the front of the trailer holding their secrets. The lot's single functioning security light illuminated clothing and blankets scattered across the floor. A large rat sat on its haunches and stared at him with black eyes before scampering towards a drain hole along the side of the trailer.

Stepping back a half stride, Wildman surged forwards and jumped, feet climbing the safety bar to land on the edge of the door as he pushed upright. The sense of exposure was strong, and Wildman was entirely aware he'd made himself an easy target. The memory of that woman's face drove him forwards, though, his own safety less important than it should have been.

Lightning flashed through the open sky behind him and eliminated the shadows for an instant. There was a cluster of milling bodies where only darkness had been. The feminine faces turned towards him, showing a mix of emotions running the gamut from angry to terrified.

As he strode forwards, thunder and lightning picked up the pace, blasting them with a series of strobing flashes and bone-rattling booms. He watched, mesmerized, as one body broke away from the cluster of what could only be captives. Women, most appearing worn and exhausted, wore ill-fitting clothing that was tattered and stained, with rips and dirty hems.

A woman walked towards him, hips swaying side to side with deliberate movements. As she neared him, her arms lifted from her sides, so they were outstretched, as if she intended to herd him from the trailer. *Not happenin', darlin'.* Every twist of muscle seemed planned, choreographed into a dance of deflection, seduction, and her attempted use of her beauty to protect the other women threatened to take his legs out from under him as he imagined what she might have been subjected to.

Hers was the face he'd seen through the vent, the Siren call that had pulled him in here. Unlike the disheveled captives standing behind her, this woman had tamed her hair into a long braid that hung down her back. She was dirty and bruised, and flashes of lightning exposed dark circles on her neck mapping out the latest abuse she must have suffered.

Chin lifted defiantly, she glared at him, and another burst of light exposed her piercing grey eyes. Under the dirt, behind the blood pooled in marks under her skin, she held a beauty like nothing he'd ever seen. The symmetry of her features was poetry; her mouth, even twisted in anger, was a perfect mix of arches and curves. Her body was lush, breasts straining at the tight men's undershirt she wore, hips flaring from a waist he could easily span with both hands.

Jesus, what the fuck is she doing here? Why?

"You speak English?" The women were all Caucasian, but that didn't mean American. Wildman stepped closer, proud of how she held her ground as he looked past her. The clacking of teeth brought his attention back to the brunette, where the bared-teeth grimace backed up the threat she'd given. He leaned closer, focused on her eyes, the way her muscles moved. Sure, she could be crazy, and then he'd wear a scar for the rest of his life, but the intelligence in her gaze told him this was a deliberate ploy to keep him away from the other occupants of the trailer. "What the fuck, woman? Knock it off. I'm not the enemy here." She stared at him, lips pressed into a tight and silent line, those damn eyes considering and evaluating him, and he noted the instant she decided not to press her attack. In a low voice, aiming for reassuring, he asked, "Do you speak English? Any of you?"

Where they'd come together was in the center of the space, well away from the sides and the group of people at the nose of the trailer. The woman blinked slowly, muscles visibly tensing, and Wildman stared in confusion as she wordlessly folded to her knees. A supplicant's position—all grace and poise as she lowered herself to the floor. Here, in this filthy prison, this charismatic woman pulled off a pose change with an allure he'd seldom seen in clubs with padded floors. *What the actual fuck?*

Her lips parted, pink tongue darting into view for an instant before she said, "Yes, we all speak English."

And, God, what he'd give to have that tongue wrapped around the head of his cock. Her low and melodic voice carried a slight accent that wasn't local, but the roundness of the sounds reassured him English was her native language, and he nodded. At least the clubs wouldn't have to try and figure out how to repatriate foreigners. Cartel's reach being as far and wide as it was, and with the number of scattered connections the bad guys boasted, these women could have been from anywhere, brought here as slaves or sex workers.

With her still on her knees, Wildman had another flash of what would never be, seeing the broad head of his cock slipping past her lips, resting heavily on her tongue with her expression avid and hungry.

Fuck off and focus, dickhead.

As if she read his mind, her pretty lips pursed faintly, and she reached for him. He gritted his teeth, because damn if his cock wasn't waking up to say hello, not giving a shit if what she offered was coerced or not. If she wanted to suck him off with an audience in the middle of a growing thunderstorm, his dick would be entirely on board with the program. *Fuck, man, that ain't like me.* He might not mind hitting club pussy at a party or scening at the club intended for such activities, but that was an intentional public display. For moments of true intimacy, he'd always gone private, getting lost inside the act for however long his partner would let him.

"*Wild.*" The single word from Po'Boy yanked him out of the fantasy and into the world, splashed red by their enemies' blood.

Wildman quickly gave up the space he'd closed to her position, taking a long step backwards, moving away as quickly as he could from her clever fingers. *That ain't who I am, lady.* She stared up at him, and the anger in her gaze raised a chill up his spine.

Softly, she said, "I'm offering. You don't have to take from them. Mercy, please. They've been through enough." She swallowed hard, the muscles in her neck moving, and he focused on the bruises there. Fingertips had made those oval marks, which meant someone had choked her hard. He looked closer and marked the healing splits in her lips, the dark smears of old blood on her temple. "I won't fight," she promised quietly. Then, blinking fast, she struggled for a minute and finally got out, "Unless that's what you want."

"Jesus." Wildman shook his head, one hand held low to keep the distance between them when she looked like she'd start crawling. "No, no. That's not why I'm here. You speak English, that's good, because my Russian is the suck. *Da* and *nyet* about the extent. English is much better." He gestured behind him without turning around. "I guess we're rescuing you." It didn't matter what she thought she needed to give him; as far as he was concerned, she was an innocent in their war against the cartel. *Innocents should always be protected.* He had an instant flashback of his wife dead in their bed and clenched his teeth to drive back the dark memories. "You don't have to do nothin', darlin'. Come on, get up."

"You're not part of them?" He had no doubt the "them" she referred to were the cartel. Her gaze flicked down to his nameplate, then back to his face. "Not part of the bad guys?"

Well, now, that's a little more vague. He wondered how much she might know about MCs and the company they ran with. *Time to set her mind at ease.* Glancing around the trailer, he huffed out a frustrated breath. *Not much point in dealin' with this bullshit. Not when we've still got cleanup outside to deal with.* The group behind her shifted, and a much younger face peered out from between two adults. *There's always enough time to help the kids. If they have one memory of this time, let it be me.* Shoving his shoulders back, he shook his head in a delayed reaction to her question. "Not even a bit of it. They're assholes, and from the looks of things, I think you'd agree with me they serve their best purpose as worm food." A cough behind him had him backtracking. "So, yeah. We've cleared them out. You're all free, I guess. You got places to go?"

"We all have families, and names." She stared at him hard enough he felt the disbelief in her gaze. The expression on her face shifted from distrusting to something shading further towards wonderment. "You're just…letting us go?"

"Yeah." He stepped closer and reached down slowly, gratified when she didn't flinch away. Curling his fingers in invitation, he paused, then offered her a tiny smile, there and gone, the most he could give in this situation. Lighter, pushing a sense of teasing into his words, he cautioned her, "Don't bite me."

Wildman helped her to her feet and then steered her a step towards the side of the trailer when it shifted under their feet. The mass of women behind her stirred restlessly, and he glanced around to see both Po'Boy and Twisted standing in the opening. Lightning flashed, outlining their dark shapes in brilliant light, any stains of blood and dirt obscured by the contrast, and he looked back to see the women were all staring at the new men.

Except the one who still had hold of his hand, standing in front of him and now so close he could feel the heat from her body. That woman, the one he'd lifted from her knees, had eyes only for him.

***

Justine

With the storm threatening, the man—Wildman by the nameplate on his vest—recommended they stay in the shelter of the trailer for a few minutes as the group of bikers arranged transport. To where, Justine had not the faintest clue. The men had been very careful to keep any tactical conversations well out of earshot of her and the other women.

Wildman. What a conundrum of a man, who so far didn't appear to live up to his road name in any way, shape, or form.

When the sounds had come from around the trailer doors, and Justine realized the uncertain sanctuary of the trailer was about to be breached, she hadn't known what to expect. Without being able to watch the final moments of the battle outside, she'd had no way of knowing which group had been the eventual victor. Anyone entering the trailer would have been suspect—either remnants of cartel come to celebrate their win, or the unknown victors, who could be capable of anything, including killing witnesses to their triumph.

She knew it happened. Had personal knowledge in too many ways, from her childhood growing up with her father's club in California, the Outriders, to her brother's club, the Rebel Wayfarers, to her federal assignment sorting out the piece of work that was the Diamante. She knew regional clubs from coast to coast and definitely had heard of Incoherent. What had surprised her was seeing back patches of not just Wildman's club but also the Caddo Hobos, and she'd need to try and get a second look, but was fairly certain she'd caught sight of a Bama Bastards patch too. *What kind of shit is going down that involves so many clubs working in conjunction?* Justine blew out a breath, wincing when the muscles of her back protested.

My team's going to kill me.

That was not entirely hyperbole, either.

She'd have a lot to answer for when she returned home, back to work, back to reality. She'd argue the intel gained during her foray into the underbelly was worth every moment spent in filth, every bruise on her body. Every painful moment had garnered a wealth of information the team would have gotten no other way. *It had to be. In order for us to move on them legally, we had to have proof.* Justine glanced around at the women clustered at her back, youngest in the group held close to family or strangers; it didn't matter. *After something like this, none of us are strangers anymore.* She'd never truly understood the comrades at arms mentality before, but it certainly felt as if they'd all been to war together.

Movement outside the trailer presaged the arrival of a trio of vans. White, nondescript, no logos to mark them as anything other than personal vehicles. The side doors opened to show empty cargo floors. *They didn't take the time to put the seats back inside.* That either meant they weren't going far or didn't have any fear of the police catching sight of passengers in vehicles not correctly equipped. *Or, like Mason would do, they've explained things to the cops and have nothing to fear there.* Justine shook her head. She needed to not romanticize this group of club members into the kind of riding-the-legal-line mission her brother frequently followed. She wasn't an idiot. She knew the Rebels weren't lily-white by any means, but by and large, the laws they broke were victimless.

Wildman looked up at her, and their gazes locked for the briefest of moments. Then his eyes moved, trailing a look down her body, pausing at every visible bruise, lingering longest at the ones she'd felt on her throat, tiny pinpoints of pain marking each fingertip the bastard who'd choked her had dug into her flesh. Justine watched as Wildman's hand twitched, fingers stretching and contracting, and the heat in his gaze was unmistakable.

No fucking way.

Chapter Seven
Wildman

"What the fuck do you think we're supposed to do with eleven abducted women?" Po'Boy's clearly apparent anger was aimed directly at Wildman, as if by being the one discovering the trailer filled with captives, he was most culpable. "Huh? What do you think we're gonna do with that much bullshit? Neither IMC nor CoBos got time for that shit. We can't keep 'em, man. That's...there's no reason not to just take them to some fuckin' mall somewhere and dump their asses out. The less they know about us, the better, but here you are sayin' we need to take them back to the IMC house? Y'all's clubhouse? Fuck, brother, did you hit your head? Momma drop you when you were a baby? Not the favorite child, huh?"

"You see how many men there were when we got here?" Wildman jumped into the opening as Po'Boy took a breath. Once the man was on a roll, he was hard to redirect, and a body had to take opportunities where they were given. Po'Boy stiffened and glared at him. Wildman sighed and turned to Twisted, hoping for a more level-headed approach. "Did you? I did. Nearly two dozen." Sweeping an arm behind him, he indicated the bodies stacked to one side like cordwood. "We're missing six or so, which means we've got some cleanup yet to do. It's bad enough we didn't fully contain the shit, but if we compound it by turning the women loose, we'll be fighting against LEO to find those runners, and we all know what kind of fuckery would be involved if local lawmen get in the way."

"Why do you say that?" Twisted's voice was deceptively calm, but a single glance at him and Wildman could see the anger raging right underneath the lie. "What's LEO got to do with shit we're handlin'?"

"We take the women to the mall like Po'Boy wants, and what are they gonna do then? First thing, what are they gonna do? Call home, that's what. They call home, you think their loved ones aren't gonna wanna know where they been? Between us and the CoBos, we got a decent amount of control on everything right now, but if we turn the women loose, we will have a media shitstorm on our hands." He put his thumbs together, making an overlapping frame with his fingers. Using a falsetto, he imitated the talking heads on TV when he said dramatically, "This just in, nearly a dozen women appeared out of thin air at the local shopping mall, each with a terrible story of abduction and abuse. Video at eleven." He dropped his hands, and Po'Boy snorted. "Go ahead, laugh. But you take a hot minute to think about it, and you'll see I'm right. We need to take 'em to the clubhouse and tell them we're helping them out. Get them some clean clothes, offer up showers and baths, get some food into 'em. They'll cop a good, peaceful night of sleep while we finish dealin' with the trash that shouldn't have gotten away. And then we cut 'em loose like you want." He shrugged. "Put your mind to it, and you'll see I'm right."

Twisted turned away, fists propped on his hips as he glared at the trailer. Wildman had kept the ragtag prisoners inside the container, singing pretty lies about making sure everything was safe for them. The brunette's accusing frown had been the last thing he'd allowed himself to see, and her disappointed expression had torn at him. He'd still made it clear what was expected, though, keeping her and the other women in their secluded cell.

"*Fuck.*" The shout echoed off the trees encircling the parking lot, and Wildman bared his teeth because the anger warring with resignation in the word meant Twisted agreed with him.

Four hours later, the third vanload of women had been unloaded at the clubhouse in Hammond. Last out of the vehicle was the brunette, and she'd given him a lowered-brow scowl as she walked past, headed inside. Still in her role of protector, even now.

"Why can't I call my husband?" That was one of the other women, and the brunette shushed her absently, gaze still pinned to Wildman. *Something about that woman.* Confident in situations where that soul strength should be in short supply, she drew him to her, a pull he was determined to resist. *She's just an impediment to everything we need to be doing right now.* Maybe, if he could keep reminding himself her very presence was a threat, he'd find it a little easier. He snorted at his own flawed logic.

The delivery of the "we're rescuing you, but on our terms" speech had been left to Wildman, and he thought he'd done a decent job, explaining to the women it should only be a matter of hours before they'd be allowed to contact their loved ones. He'd cited the storm and lateness of the hour as the main reasons, making it difficult to transport them to the local authorities. Not one of the women had called him out on the lie or had pointed out they were, in essence, being abducted again, and he had the brunette to thank for that. Her willingness to go along with the plan had smoothed the way for the other former captives, since she held a position of trust among them. She'd helped, filling in the holes in his story with tiny supporting statements, but Wildman knew the brunette hadn't been fooled. Not one iota. He'd read the knowledge plain on her face, so her active cooperation had been a surprise. A welcome one, but just another layer of questions on top of his other ones where she was concerned.

"Our pros—*man* by the bar has room assignments for everyone. We don't have enough rooms for separate quarters, but there are three full private bathrooms with tubs and a communal shower room we've set aside for you ladies. Give you a chance to put yourselves back together while we get things rolling to take you back to your families." He followed them inside, nodding his thanks to the member who stepped in front of the door at his back, blocking the way out. The standing orders were to not hurt the women but still detain them at all costs.

His part of the transfer complete, Wildman turned to walk to the office where Twisted, Po'Boy, and other men were waiting for him, hopefully while they simultaneously worked contacts and information to find whatever hidey-hole the escape-artist assholes had taken cover in. A rough touch on his arm sent a lightning bolt through him and caused him to wheel around in an adrenaline-fueled instinctive response. When he stopped moving, the woman's wrist was in his grasp, and his other hand was at her throat. For a split second, his brain delightedly noted how neatly his thumb and fingers fit over the bruises, covering each with the tip of a digit as if the marks had been made as targets for his grip. Heart pounding, he dropped his hold and took a step back, getting out of reach so neither of them could touch the other.

It took a moment, but he got his breathing back under control, eyes on the brunette all the time. Voice steady and low, he growled, "The fuck you want?"

Tone matching his, she leaned in and said, "What you're doing is dangerous. For you, and everyone around you." She made a show of looking at his vest, then brought her eyes up to meet his. "Wildman." The rolling sound of his name in her mouth had him half hard in an instant, and in his mind, she was on her knees again, chin lifted and willing mouth open while she waited for him to feed his thick cock between her lips. *Goddammit.* She continued, her voice pitched low, sultry, and full of bad ideas. "It's a game you didn't intend to play."

A game. That word stripped the vision from him, leaving him wondering what had gotten into him in the first place. She wasn't a toy to scene with, surely wasn't a club whore, and wouldn't ever be in the position he'd found her again if he could help it. *If I can help it? I'm not in her life.*

She interrupted his thoughts with a solid tap against his breastbone with one stiffened finger. "You and your club are out of its depth."

"Who the fuck *are* you?" The question burst from him before he could think, and he shook his head, negating the need for her to answer. "Never mind. It doesn't matter. I'm not the one you need to speak to. He's over at the end of the bar and can help you find where you go next. *He* can help you. Not me."

Smiling with a fake shyness, she tipped her chin to her throat, gaze flicking up at his lips once before settling somewhere on his middle. "I'm no one."

The false answer to his blurted question was so disingenuous it pulled a chuckle from him. "You're far from no one, darlin', but what you aren't is foolin' me." He pointed at the prospect holding up a piece of paper. "He's got you, and we'll have you home soon. Just follow the path we've laid out for alla y'all, and it'll be over before you know it." With a stiffened thumb shoved over his shoulder towards the office, he finished with "I got things to do, and ain't one of 'em you."

Giving him a final long glance filled with a heat he didn't expect, she turned and walked away. Her firm, round ass sashayed in a slow shimmy he knew without a doubt was deliberate. Wildman didn't know what she thought she understood, but she didn't know him or any of the things he was capable of. *Woman's got no idea what kind of trouble she's tempting her way.* Not that he'd bring it, but a woman coming into a place like this with that kind of attitude would normally be looking for just one thing, and ordinarily, he'd be the first in line to take her up on the offer. Controlled passion—even with pain, if it earned pleasure—got him off, as long as everyone was consenting.

Focus, asshole. There's still a lot of work to do.

Work wasn't something he was a stranger to. Wildman's previous clubs had been waist-deep in a lot of shitty things, making risky plays in deep waters that had gotten a lot of good men hurt. He liked to think he'd learned along the way, though, and being part of an organization now that didn't just feel solid but was the definition of solid had become his reward. The trust he had in his brothers in IMC had been hard-won, through blood, steel, and iron, proving themselves again and again able to hold their own against all comers. His job, regardless of official station, was to make sure they *always* had the right tools at the right time to ensure complete success.

He took a deep breath, blew it back out slow and steady, eyes pinned to the brunette as she accepted her room assignment. She tossed him a long sideways glance on her way up the stairs, feet traveling each step surely, even as her gaze mapped every inch of Wildman's body. *My job hasn't a thing to do with her*. With that internal reminder, he made his way to the office, where hopefully good news waited.

***

Justine

"Stop it." Her hissed warning to herself was drowned out by the steaming water cascading over her naked body. "Jesus Christ, Justine, get a fucking grip." Her ribs complained with a hard push of pain as she lifted her arms, hands filled with shampoo to work through her saturated hair. She methodically cleaned herself, paying close attention to each sore spot, separating matted locks of hair to better clean any underlying wounds, counting the bruises mottling her body.

When she'd offered herself up in an effort to protect the other women from the guards, Justine had known what she was inviting and had thought she'd been ready for it all.

She hadn't been.

Offering to fight the bored men might not have been the smartest thing she could have done, but it was the only way she'd seen in the moment to accomplish both of her goals. Keep them from hurting and raping the other women, and protect herself from rape as well. They'd known she'd stop fighting the moment either of those happened, and a woman who could hold her own against a man had been enough of a novelty she'd kept their attention.

Just long enough for Wildman to ride to the rescue.

Snorting, she lifted her face into the spray of water, letting the heat seep into her, driving back the terrified cold that had encompassed her for too long.

This side trip will be interesting to be debriefed about.

It was hard enough for the men in the department to understand the limited background she'd provided them. Her association with the Outriders and Rebels was held under need-to-know status, but how could she explain her relief and ease with being rescued by one of the clubs the government considered deadly criminals without exposing the belief she had that they held family sacrosanct?

The existence of Wildman would need to be completely stripped from the equation. His name wouldn't be passing her lips in mixed company—"mixed" meaning her and anyone in law enforcement.

Gonna carry this one to my grave.

The attraction was undeniable. And it clearly went both ways. The man hadn't even tried to hide the lust he'd felt. And, even as he'd held himself in strict control, the way he'd stared at her throat meant only one thing.

Dom.

She knew it in her bones. Just as being submissive in the bedroom was baked into her psyche, being dominant held a primary place in his life.

She'd bet his face was known at all reputable clubs within a hundred-mile radius of this house. If she inquired through her developed network of people in the lifestyle, she'd place an even more certain bet she'd have his name within an hour, adding the title of Master to the one he wore on his vest—Enforcer.

"Stop it." Stretching out a hand to turn off the water, she was shocked to find she no longer trembled. Justine let her shoulders sag against the tile wall as she forced her lungs to suck in one deep breath, then another, surprised again when there was little tension to release. *Something about him makes me feel secure.* Not safe, that wouldn't be happening anytime soon, not through any fault of his or the other men downstairs. They'd been only solicitous and kind, firm in their resolution no one was to leave or contact family, but each denial had been made in a gentle way, taking into account the shredded emotions of the women doing the asking. In her gut, she knew how she felt wasn't about the clubhouse and wasn't tied to the men wearing a variety of club vests.

It's got to be him.

Roughly toweling off her limbs and torso, she ignored the pangs from each bruise and cut, uncaring of her own comfort. Urgency filled her, and Justine was driven to find him. *Had* to see him again. *He'll make things okay.* It didn't matter he'd turned down her fumbling sexual advances in the trailer or that he'd stepped away from her touch downstairs. The shock of electricity that had flashed between them at every touch, the way his hand around her throat had been steadying, not frightening, those were all things she couldn't ignore.

If I only have this one chance with him, am I brave enough to take it?

She stared into the eyes of her reflection, seeing a dark shadow of fear embedded there. No matter she felt protected, the repeated beatings had taken their toll. The captors had knocked her down again and again, until rising to her feet had been an act of sheer willpower. Each breath had fueled her determination to not see the youngest of the women raped or beaten. Every victory, no matter how minor, had reminded her the blows were a price she'd taken on and willingly paid. Now, with that behind her, looking at the bruised and battered woman in the mirror, she didn't think anyone would begrudge her the chance at pushing back the vicious memories, even if for only a few minutes.

Lifting her hand to push the fall of hair away from her face, Justine noted with rising anger how her fingers trembled again.

If she found the right way to ask, she knew Wildman could help her push past the pain and into the steady space she needed so badly. Validation was what she sought, nothing more. Surely he wouldn't turn her down a third time.

If not now, then when?

Chapter Eight
Wildman

"Go get some rest, brother." Po'Boy gripped Wildman's shoulder, giving him a rough shake back and forth. "You're dead on your feet, and ain't gonna be no good to us if your reflexes are slow tomorrow. Don't be slow, man, be fast."

"Truth," he responded, yawning wide, jaw cracking with the strain. "I'm gonna hit the hay here if my bed wasn't given away in the mix of things. You headed home?"

Po'Boy grinned, the expression turning into a sly and pleased smirk. "Fuck yeah, I'm goin' home. With what I got waitin' for me? Ain't sleepin' away from them if I don't have to." Wildman rocked his head back, staring at the ceiling, waiting. He knew what was coming next. For months now, it had been something Po'Boy managed to work into every conversation he could. "Coulda been gay for me, Wildman. Joined us all up in our puppy pile. Puppy pile with me and mine." Po'Boy's lovers were a woman named Crissy and the new president of the CoBos, Wrench.

The dig came from an observation Wildman had made in the heat of the moment after witnessing the two men share a reconnecting kiss, something Wildman had enthusiastically declared the hottest kiss he'd ever seen. It was far less amusing now, but he liked how it gave him and Po'Boy another thread of connection binding them together.

"Fuck you. I ain't never gonna live that one down, am I?" He rocked forwards and lightly shoved at Po'Boy's chest. "Get your happy ass home, then."

"No, you will not. Hell, brother, it's my leverage over you. I found I got a hold on your heart, and I know you're just waiting for me to act on that secret desire you got deep down inside." Po'Boy leaned closer, lips pursing comically as he made tiny smacking sounds. "I'm right here, brother. Right in front of you. Just gotta reach out and take what you want."

"I got nothing for you, deep inside or not. You're an asshole, and I hate you." Grinning at Po'Boy's put-on expression of disappointment at the rejection, Wildman walked away, middle fingers on both hands lifted over his shoulders. He glanced back to see Po'Boy still standing in place. "Go on, get to bed. As you said, we're both wiped. Get home to your crew, old man. We'll hit it tomorrow and find the bastards. Then it'll all be over." Po'Boy lifted a hand as he turned away, and Wildman pushed himself to trot up the stairs to his room, pausing before he eased the door open quietly, pleased when he found the bed empty. "Hell yeah."

He cleaned up quickly and crawled between the sheets, heels of his hands pressed against his eyes. "Fuck."

Confidential contacts with the promise of a big payday were looking for the missing men, but so far had turned up nothing. Without a viable target, Wildman and the other officers couldn't pull the trigger on a final raid, which meant come tomorrow morning, all the women would have to be convinced they needed to stay in hiding another day. *I'll make it about safety for their families.* He blew out a heavy breath, scrubbing at his cheeks with both palms, fingernails scraping through his rough scruff. *That'll work.*

Grabbing his phone, Wildman set an alarm to allow for four hours of sleep, then turned to his side and let his eyes sink closed. Exhausted, he took a couple of deep, calming breaths, and the world started slipping away. His last thought was he hoped he dreamed.

She knelt in front of him, chin lifted to expose her throat, palms cradling her bare breasts for his inspection. Knees spread apart to grant full access, she'd turned her body into a gift meant only for him. Naked and aroused, Wildman walked around behind her and sighed in pleasure at the expanse of unmarked skin on display. "So beautiful."

Trailing one fingertip in a tender side-to-side contact across her shoulders, he watched the rising goose bumps chase his touch, muscles sliding across her bones as they flexed in tiny, involuntary movements. "You want this?" He stopped in front of her again, hips squared to her shoulders, hard dick bouncing only inches from her mouth. "Me?"

Wildman woke when a hand slipped around his hip, nails dragging across the skin of his thigh, fingertips plucking at his sac. Quick as a snake, he gripped the wrist and twisted to his back, somehow already knowing who he'd see. The brunette pushed up on an elbow, head cradled in her hand. There was no smile on her face when she greeted him softly. "Hey, Wildman."

He studied her in the low light, finding only confidence and determination in her eyes. Not a bit of shame or fear, and that struck him like lightning—because in his gut, he knew she was here in his bed of her own wishes. Not because she wanted to wrest some secret from him, or because she thought him her new captor and wanted to earn her way into his good graces on her back, but because she'd found a hunger in her gut matching whatever she'd seen in him.

The sense of ownership from the dream had carried over, and he found himself reaching out to grip the hank of her braided hair. She let her body shift at the silent demand, movements flowing to tip her head back and give him a view of her throat, the strong, pale column bearing some other man's marks. A need to possess her rolled through him, and he asked the question from his dream in a voice gone to gravel and darkness. "You want this?"

Her mouth opened, but no words escaped, just a low, keening whine as she breathed faster. The pulse in her throat beat hard, pounding at her skin in an effort to escape. A burning desire to see her under him like this, wordless, with her sumptuous ass in the air, accepting whatever he gave her, stretched his patience to the limit.

He set his teeth, lips lifting in a snarl. "You came to me, girl. Came to my bed. Now—" He used his grip on her hair to bring her close. "—you tell me you want this. Give me your words, because in this bed, with me right now, I gotta know this is something you choose."

She blinked back tears he'd caused with his rough handling of her hair, staring into his face as her pink tongue slipped out, leaving a swipe of moisture behind. The movement wasn't an effort to seduce but a delaying tactic, because, from the lines at the corners of her eyes and mouth, it seemed she suddenly wasn't certain she'd picked the right play. Even so, she nodded slowly, head moving only slightly, the tug of the braid not enough to tear free of his grip.

Not giving an inch on the demand, he curled his hand around the back of her neck and snatched her head down until her lips hovered just over his. "You had to say the words." Speaking slowly and distinctly, he laid it all out for her. "I needed clear consent for what I want to do to you." He darted his head up until he could bite her bottom lip hard, not enough pressure to bleed, but firmly enough so she'd feel the sting for hours. With a final hard twist of his teeth on her flesh, he shoved her away and fell to his back on the mattress. "Not good enough."

Breasts heaving, she lay beside him. "Yes, this is my choice."

Too late.

"Shoulda said that about half a minute ago. Go on." Staring at the ceiling, he made a casual stirring motion with one hand. "Get outta here." She sucked in a wet breath, and he groaned at his brain's instant idea of her making a similar noise around his cock, mouth full of him as he roughly fucked her throat. "Dammit, girl."

He flung the covers off, the slight chill creeping against his skin not mattering to his dick, rock hard with wet trailing down the head. Hand wrapped around his cock, he glared sideways at the wall as he gave himself a stroke, slow and tight, fingers following well-memorized movements to end with a tight cuff at the base, using pain to beat back desire. She remained silent, and her continued lack of engagement pissed him off more. "If you don't leave, then how am I supposed to take it? Huh? I asked and you didn't answer, and now this is what you've left me."

The mattress shifted, and her hand curled around his hip to join his on the next downstroke as he groaned again.

"Take it as me being lost in the moment. By the time I found my voice, you'd closed the door." Her tone was low, naturally sultry, an edge of apology in her words. The change in tension underneath him revealed her movements as she crept closer to his side, each shift slow, as if uncertain of her welcome. "Gotta give me a minute to catch up, big guy." Her fingers tightened around him, and he let his hand fall away, giving her free rein of his cock. "Good Lord, you're just big everywhere, aren't you?"

Wildman rolled his head to look at her with a smirk. He liked she might be willing to tease and play, loved how she'd taken the initiative to turn things around after a near-disastrous false start, so he decided to reward her. "And you're talking entirely too much." He lay back on the bed and gripped her braid more gently than before, steering her head down and across his body. She kept her balance easily, gracefully, lips already open. "Suck," he ordered, hips lifting with the word. "Suck me off."

No argument from her before she gobbled him down, the wet and hot cavern of her mouth around him, cinching tight around his shaft as her head started the timeworn bobbing dance between his legs. He groaned quietly, feeling his balls already starting to tingle. She quickly fell into a perfect rhythm. Firm strokes from her fingers, tight suction from her mouth, and the teasing play of tongue all over him combined to be devastatingly effective, his cock growing impossibly harder. Like a heartbeat, she took him with a steady pace, moans interrupted by gagging noises as he thrust up and fucked deeper and deeper, forcing himself into her throat for several suspended breaths at a time.

Her hips shifted, and she rolled to her knees, balancing herself over his crotch with elbows out wide. Experimentally he released her hair, giving control back to her, and was pleased when she fought her own gag reflex to take him beyond what he'd pushed for so far.

Fuck yeah, she's outstanding. Time to praise her and see how she responded. "Goddamned good, baby." The brunette moaned around his cock and redoubled her efforts. *Mmhmm, somebody liked that.*

Hands now free, he reached over and grabbed her apple ass, yanking her closer to where he lay. The hand between her legs found her wet to the touch, soaked through, and naked as the day she was born—no panties, not even a string of floss up her crack to get in the way of his play. *Came to me ready.* Wildman smiled, knowing if she could see the expression on his face, she would have scrambled away, escaping as fast as she could, because this expression wasn't about pleasure. It was without humor, filled with teeth and the promise of pain.

"You like a little rough play?" She made a muffled sound in response, arching her back as he flicked a fingertip between her labia, coming close to her clit. "I'm gonna play, and if you want to stay with me tonight, you're gonna take it, hear?" His mind tried to argue, reminding him of her recent experiences by bringing up the image of her offering herself in exchange for the safety of the women at her back. *I didn't take what she offered then, and she knew I could.* She wouldn't be in his bed if she weren't up for whatever he threw at her.

He lifted his shoulders from the bed and angled towards her. He wouldn't be eating pussy tonight, not after where he'd found her, and knowing how likely it was she'd been taken unwilling, but he could play. Mouth to her hip, he tested her limits, setting his teeth deep enough to leave a bruise. She instantly squealed but just as immediately pressed into the pain, not away. Wildman moved his mouth, shifted a half an inch to leave overlapping marks, and bit again, harder, and gained the same result. A fast stiffening of her body, a wild sound far back in her throat, and then her adjusting closer to him, offering even more of herself to his ministrations.

With his middle finger, he circled her entrance, then shoved inside to find a well of wet there. "Fuckin' drenched." Plunging in and out, he added a second finger and watched as the liquid trailed down the insides of her thighs. *Bitch is turned right the fuck on.* "Wanna fuck you now."

As if he'd touched a cattle prod to her, she pulled off him and whirled, ass to the bed, and head pointed away, making it easy for him to climb on top if that's what he wanted. He watched her hips shift and sway, breasts bouncing with every hard breath, nipples drawn into tight peaks. He sat up and reached for a condom, hissing as he palmed his wet cock before rolling it on. Dark hair in a cord beside her head, hands in tight fists up above her shoulders, her pale body was laid out before him, legs akimbo with knees bent, sex glistening wetly. This was a conditioned response, one he'd seen from many a pain slut in the clubs, and one that promised him hours of pleasure if he'd gotten it right.

He shifted to his knees, looming over her as he asked, "You get off on sex, rough sex, or do you need the pain?"

"I need the pain," she told him honestly, not moving an inch to get away. "Sex is good, but I need the pain."

"You okay with being marked up a little?" He pressed his fingertips to the teeth marks already in place on her hip. Her neck arched as he dug in deeper. She quivered under his touch, and he smirked. "I don't want no cops comin' in and bustin' down my door in a couple of days over bruises if you're gonna freak out."

Her hips lifted, and the lips of her pussy twitched. Wildman knew she'd just clenched hard at the thought of him bruising her more. When she didn't answer, he pushed, asking again, "Well? You good with it?"

"I won't freak out. Just under my clothes, okay?" He hummed in agreement, because as negotiations went, her ask was completely reasonable. They'd gone from zero to a hundred miles an hour in a few short minutes, but this familiar back-and-forth was calming. She told him she felt the same way with her next words. "Not my first rodeo."

"No, I didn't expect it was." He was poised on the mattress. "Lift your legs, hands behind your knees." She complied, and he smiled at her, chuckling when her pupils dilated wider, blackness edging out the ring of grey. Without another word, without asking about any in-the-moment change of consent or any kind of fucked-up shit like that, he took his dick in hand and lined up with her entrance.

No turning back now.

The first tearing plunge inside her already had his balls pulling tight to his body, and he bent his head, teeth latching to one tit, biting down. She was wet through and through, and that helped him slide deep, but he didn't give her any time to adjust or stretch, forcing himself on her. *Goddamn, she's tight as fuck.* Hopefully she hadn't been violated by the cartel guards.

Her legs bounced up and down distractingly, and he reached a hand back and slapped her ass hard. "Wrap 'em around me." *Let's see how she does with a little permission versus direction.* "You're allowed to fuck me back." She shifted underneath him as her heels hooked behind his ass and her pussy lifted, hips tilting up. The next stroke was easier, his cock sliding deeper, the next round of push-and-pull even more slippery. "Goddamn, woman, fucking excellent. Do that again." He bit down once more, overlapping his teeth with the bruise he could already see forming, wanting to leave her another pair of linked rings to take with her as evidence of his possession. Pulling back, he watched her face as he slapped her ass, the sharp crack of sound not overriding her moan of pleasure.

Between fucking and spanking her, he'd worked up a sweat by the time she tightened down around him, offering a breathy request. "I need to come." He set his teeth in her earlobe, pushing a hand far underneath her, lifting her for another jackrabbited slapping of flesh on flesh. In a rising tone, she begged, "Please."

It was the plea that did it, and Wildman growled his permission through clenched teeth. "Come for me."

She'd stayed wet through everything he'd done to her, rivulets of her fluids running down the crack of her ass. He rolled his finger in the wetness, using it to coat his digit before he took her ass deep, hooking his finger around the ring of muscle and pulling hard. "God," she cried out, head tipping back, and he couldn't stop himself. Up on one elbow, he fit the fingers of his free hand over those bruises on her neck and gripped tightly, her pulse thudding heavily against his thumb as he constricted his hold. Her eyes rolled up in her head, and he gave her a sip of air before clamping down again. She stiffened as she came, mouth open in a soundless cry, and he plowed faster, hips beating at hers as he fucked her apart underneath him.

As if struck by the same lightning that had flashed through the sky at their meeting, he followed her over, finger still deep in her ass as he stayed propped up on his elbow and stared down at her. She had overlapping ornaments of bruises on each breast, deep enough to bring blood to the surface in places, her shoulders bore his marks, and now his bruises completely covered the ones some asshole had left on her. His cock pulsed, and he ground himself against her, coming hard, filling the condom in a flood of heat and satisfaction.

Fucking mine.

***

Justine

As she curled in his sheets, so many muscles in Justine's body were wrung out, alternately cramping and shaking. He'd held her close for a few breaths after he'd finished coming, then climbed off and arranged her like this before stalking away. She'd had enough uninspired bouts of aftercare to know what would be coming next. Once he finished cleaning up, he'd be back to ask some basic questions, then shoo her off to her borrowed room for the rest of the night. *I had high hopes for him.* She swallowed down her disappointment, keeping her gaze fixed on the shadowy details on the far side of the room as she waited for her dismissal.

A warm hand on her shoulder was a surprise; so was the gentle tug to turn her on her back. Wildman held a warm, wet cloth and used it to wipe the sweat from her face and neck, curling around to get the nape where heat had gathered underneath the heavy braid of hair. He methodically cleaned her body, shoulders to hips, then tenderly parted her legs. The cloth had cooled, but it didn't matter. The level of care carried its own sense of warmth as he wiped away all evidence of her pleasure, unashamedly delving into her crack as a last movement.

"Turn back on your side, baby." His hands gently adjusted her position again, finishing with a slow stroke of his palm down the length of her spine. "I'll be right back."

The weight of the air in the room changed, and light speared in through the doorway. She watched him walk into the hallway, jeans pulled to his hips, button left undone. He turned to the left and disappeared from view.

He'd be back, and the subtext was he expected to find her here in his bed when he returned. Her role was easy and simple, and knowing his expectations allowed her mind to stay quiet as she waited.

Justine let her lids slip closed, the pleasant buzzing from the orgasm still swirling through her body, nerves tingling from nipples to clit as she ran each moment of their encounter back through her mind. She'd thought he'd be good, but damn, Wildman had been *good*. She breathed in for a count of three, releasing the air through pursed lips before pulling in another deep breath.

For an impromptu scene, I got everything I'd hoped for and then some. She shook her head, trying to clear the thoughts threatening to creep back in. *Less focus, more quiet, please.* The bruises on her hips and breasts, along her ribs, all pulsed in time with her heartbeat. Delicate threads of pain twinged with each movement, and her body refused to be still, seeking that affirmation again and again.

Damn good.

She woke when he returned to the room, a glass of juice and a bowl of orange slices in his hands. He set them on the nightstand, crawled into bed, and then proceeded to haul her up against his torso until she nestled in the crook of his arm. The edge of the glass pressed against her lips, and Justine instinctively took a drink, giving him a quiet sigh of satisfaction when it was cold and tart, exactly what she'd wanted without knowing it.

"Here, baby. Eat this." A slice of orange appeared in front of her face, and she bit into the flesh, sucking the escaping juice from his fingers until he groaned and shifted his hips. "Bad baby. This is your time, honey. No teasing."

Justine curled tighter against him, burying her head against his shoulder, the tender chastisement enough to make her stop pushing for a reaction. *Oh yeah, he's good.*

"More juice." When she didn't lift her head at his verbal urging, the hand curled around her hip tightened, fingers pressing against one of the bruises in a stinging hold. "Drink the juice." Her body reacted to the growled order, chin rising as her mouth opened for another drink. "Good girl."

Oh, man, am I in trouble.

Chapter Nine

Wildman

A pounding on the door startled him from sleep only minutes before his alarm would have gone off, and Wildman called out a gruff acknowledgment. That kind of abrupt and demanding wake-up call likely meant they had news about the missing cartel members and was good, because the sooner he could wipe those assholes off the earth, the happier he'd be.

The brunette was a heavy weight sprawled across his chest, and he stared at her, only vaguely shocked that after everything that had happened, she was sleeping so peacefully. She'd fallen so easily into the submissive role last night, clearly needing the peace an intentional and consensual release of power gave her. He could tell it had comforted her to pull on that persona. Bonus points to him for pushing her just enough to ride the edge, without shoving her into free fall. *Never ignored base protocol before, though. Shame on me.* They hadn't discussed boundaries or safe words, and he suffered a sting of annoyance at himself for the breach of faith. *All turned out well in the end.* His cock gave a twitch. He ignored it. *Gave her what she needed.*

The blanket gaped as he shifted, trying to see into her face, and he used one finger to slowly shove it down, pushing it to her waist. He stared, breathlessly fascinated by the marks on her skin. Layers of them, covering bruising left by her captors, as if he'd reclaimed every inch of her back from their touch. As he traced a line of teeth marks, his cock gave more than a twitch at the proof of their time together.

Mine.

Wildman froze at the thought pushing to the forefront of his mind, then slowly shook his head.

Oh yeah, she's mine.

He snorted a quiet laugh at the ridiculousness of the repeating and futile thought.

And I'm an idiot. That'll hafta fall into the if-only bracket.

Just as carefully as he'd moved the covers down, he tugged them back up to blanket her, holding in the heat.

He swung his legs off the mattress and stood, eyes still on the nameless woman stretched out in his bed.

The unknown sub who seemingly fit every desire he had discovered, nurtured, and cultivated. *Made for me.*

With narrowed eyes, he considered the idea of her as a plant somehow, set in his path intentionally.

Nope. No way. There's just no way.

It was simple chance that had him noticing the trailer initially, and random need dictating he'd been first inside. Then came the million-to-one odds of them saying enough words to the other to recognize the resonance between their souls.

Nope, this is God's joke on me.

Wildman had been in a romantic relationship twice. His first hadn't stuck for long; eventually, she'd been turned off by what he needed. She'd said all the right things in the beginning, begged sweetly for his attention, and he'd been blinded to how she really felt, too excited at the idea of sharing the dark desires roiling through his imagination to truly question his luck. She'd grown up poor, raised her brothers and sisters almost singlehandedly, and had been looking for security via a relationship, thinking herself willing to do anything for it.

She'd been wrong.

The more he'd explored, the more she'd withdrawn until it was clear they weren't compatible. In the end, neither of them had gotten what they'd wanted.

The second had been taken from him, death and destruction something he was uncomfortably familiar with. Killed for another man's ambition, even though Shelly had been carrying his child. Then any chance at vengeance had been stripped from him by circumstance.

Since then, he'd cultivated a variety of submissives within the safe space of clubs devoted to those activities. Spent time learning their desires as he trained them in his preferences. While there'd been affection with each, the anchors on his soul wouldn't permit more than that. When they'd moved on in their own time, Wildman had understood, knowing himself stunted in the romance department. He surely hadn't believed they were meant to be his.

Still, each event counted in the tally that had put him on the path to come to Louisiana, and eventually here, with the IMC.

Found my brothers in the end.

He couldn't say it had been worth it, not given the cost. But if he'd had to pay in blood, at least the reward didn't suck.

This woman? Someone who'd been abducted and held in terrifying conditions, clearly paying with flesh for whatever sins her captors felt she'd been guilty of? And yet in his bed, she'd still met him thrust for thrust, begging for his mouth, his teeth, her voice rising and falling with cries of pleasure she hadn't tried to stifle.

Real, all of it. Nothing forced or faked in what we did last night.

Definitely not a plant. Not a spy set to trip him or the club up.

Serendipity and the universe having their fun with me.

She could be perfect for him. Was perfect for him. *Everything I could want rolled up in her gorgeous body and challenging attitude.* He grinned, remembering her poise yesterday dealing with the other women as she took the bits of information he and his brothers had given and wove it into something that helped them feel secure. *Smart, to boot.* Perfection.

Nope. Not mine.

After dressing quietly, he closed the door on the sleeping woman and made his way to the kitchen downstairs, surprised to find the room full, both IMC and CoBos well represented. Someone had made an urn of coffee, and he snagged a mug from the counter then flipped the lever to fill his cup before he looked for Twisted or Wrench. It would have taken their orders to call in this many brothers, and he wanted to know what kind of intel they had on the escaped cartel members they were tracking.

The office door behind the bar stood open, and Wildman threaded through the groups of men as he headed in that direction. Inside, he found Twisted and Po'Boy in what looked like a stare-off. *Well, shit, someone's gotta break the deadlock.*

"We goin' soon?" He kept his voice loud and strident as he pushed between them to get to the far wall. Leaning his shoulders against the flat surface, he turned back to find them still firmly engaged in whatever had them crossways. "What the fuck's up, brothers?"

Twisted sighed, not breaking the stare. "We find ourselves in dire disagreement on that exact topic."

"We go now." Po'Boy paused, his scowl deepening. "We roll heavy." He leaned forwards an inch, boots firmly planted shoulder-width. "We do that shit? Guarantee you we'll be back home in an hour, brother." Po'Boy clamped his lips tightly, ire in every line on his face.

"You know where they are?" The implications surprised Wildman. Chin tilting up, he considered the two men, heart beating faster at the thought of closing the door on this event. *Fuck yeah.* "Then why the hell are we still sittin' here? We wanted to make a clean sweep, didn't we? Weren't many, but we had some stragglers who slipped the noose last night. If we know where they're hiding, we roll. Now. Fucking *now*, man. Let's *go*. Go get 'em. Do this thing."

"Bitch in your bed, do you know who she is? Have that first idea who you slept next to?" Twisted transferred his stare to Wildman. Two careful breaths in and out, and he shook his head back and forth. Twisted's mouth pulled to one side as he demanded, "You sure about that shit, brother?"

"Yeah, I'm sure. I don't know her from Eve. Fuck, man, I don't even know her goddamned name." Wildman rolled his shoulders and reared back, bringing one fist in front of his crotch. Hips rolling in an unmistakable imitation, he curled his fingers and pretended to jack off vigorously. "She brought her own ass to my bed. Middle of the night, her crawling under my blanket wasn't something I asked for or expected. Still, you and every other brother know I wasn't about to turn the good shit down, brother. Wet and willing beats Rosie Palm every time."

"True that," Po'boy said through laughter. "But you might wanna ask the lady her name before you dip your wick again."

Low chuckles filled the air in the room. Wildman swung his head and let his gaze glance across each man, coming to rest back on Twisted.

Fucking hell. Knew it was too good to be true. She had to be a plant if her coming to him provoked his leadership to have this reaction.

"Clearly you know who the hell she is, and since that shit is obviously tied up with the business we need to finish and have done with, just get the info out there and tell me. Fuckin' tell me, man." The heat of blood rising in his neck and cheeks told him their efforts at provoking him were having a visible effect. Plant or not, if she wasn't an outright danger to the club, his gut was rolling with the selfish desire to keep what had happened between him and the brunette private. *I won't betray my club.* But if there was no overriding reason to share, he already knew he wouldn't, no matter how they rode him about it.

"That, my good man, is Justine LaPorte."

Wildman shrugged. *Justine.* Weighty and yet poetic, the name fit her well. *Jussie.* Yeah, he could imagine more moments of humor when the nickname would suit, too. *Wildwoman.* And there were even more times where a road name such as that would be a far better description of his woman. Cold as ice, blood pumped sluggishly through his veins at the thought. *Not my woman.*

"She happens to be tied to any number of interesting or *interested* parties." Twisted glared at him from the corner of his eye as he bent sideways and picked up a piece of paper from the table near him. "Uncle Sam bein' one of them."

Fuck.

This was worse than the worst nightmare come true.

Internally reeling, Wildman didn't hesitate to ask his questions, needing to know the facts. His truth would be IMC first and always, but the brunette? She was special. *Focus, idiot. Stay true to the club.* "She's a Fed?"

Twisted gave a slow nod.

Double fuck.

Wildman's gut cramped, chest tight enough it hurt to pull in a breath. "How do you know? Where'd this info come from, exactly? Who'd you squeeze to get the intel?"

"Well"—Wrench drawled, turning his chair to face Wildman—"we know because her brother recognized her picture last night when we floated it past a bunch of folks, plucking her out of the rest of the women. He reached out, personal like, to identify her and ask his own hard questions." He laughed, the sound hard and humorless. "Seems she's been missing for a few days, so he already had people lookin' for her. Just hadn't found her yet."

"Who's her brother?" Wildman pulled in a breath and blew it out noisily. "Fuck, man. Don't tell me. Way y'all trickle out information at a slow drip has done pushed me off into I-don't-care land. Don't matter anyhow. Let's get the discussion back to business. We got more important things to tend to right now."

"Well, seein' as she's in the middle of the business at hand, that woman is kinda the business, so to speak. And brother—" Twisted flicked his wrist and sailed the paper Wildman's direction "—you definitely do need to know this bit of intel. Look at it."

Wildman snagged the paper out of the air, the document crumpling in his grip. He scanned the room one more time, then angled his gaze down. The blood that had been cold in his veins froze solid, a heavy chill racing up his backbone, hard breaths rasping in and out of his nose. He scowled at the paper for a long time, the words detailing Justine's pedigree slowly but surely burning into his brain.

She might have seemed perfect, but she wasn't for him. Couldn't be, not like this. The association explained so much about her behavior, including the sacrifices she'd been willing to make to protect innocents. Every branch of her family was a powerhouse on their own. She would have marinated in understanding, witness to any number of examples she'd have internalized through the years. A girl growing up around strong men, learning from them the rightness of going to any lengths to keep safe those under their protection, not discounting how the evil ones would have served as a counter-lesson. Even her composure during the short vehicle ride made sense. The rest of the women might have been weeping and fearful, but she would have already known where they were headed, having personal knowledge about the safety looming at the end of the trip.

She ain't never gonna be mine.

He took in a steady breath, pushed it out slowly, and pulled in another. He chewed on the inside of his lip until he tasted copper, the pain centering him more. Once his heartbeat settled, pounding out a regular pace no doctor would find remarkable, he folded the paper once, dragging a thumbnail along the crease, marking it deeply. Another fold, followed by the same scoring process, and he yanked his wallet out, flipping the chain out of the way easily. Two seconds was all the time it took to secure the proof the universe was still a raggedy bitch, out to take everything from him, and he snapped the flap closed, cutting off sight of that innocuous, poisonous paper.

Lifting his chin, he glared at Twisted, shifting to pull Wrench into view to receive the same treatment. He felt Po'Boy at his back and trusted him to be there in support. Top lip flat against his teeth, Wildman dragged words out from deep in his chest, pushing them onto the air. "Don't matter. Let's go. You got wind of a place, got a possible direction, or got a solid line on anything, then let's go."

"Brother, we cannot keep a federal agent under lockdown at our goddamned clubhouse. That shit is inviting all kinds of trouble we do not need to wade through, and we all know it." Twisted lifted an arm, one rigid finger aimed directly at Wildman. He felt the gesture like a spike in his heart, because censure from his president pained him. Twisted's tone softened slightly, but he finished his thought with, "You did this, with your fucked-up plan."

"Naw, brother." Po'Boy thudded a fist against Wildman's shoulder as he walked around the table to reclaim his chair, then reclined far back, legs spread wide in front of him. Wildman held his peace, wanting to hear what Po'Boy's advice would be to the man who'd been his best friend since before high school. "It was a recommendation which held merit and was discussed at the highest level between two dominant clubs in the area. I may not have a great memory, but we all stood in that circle and said the same. Wasn't no circle jerk, and not a single man needed to build up a bank with Wildman that would cause them to agree without believing it was the right course." Po'Boy rolled his shoulders, holding his arms wide. "Brother, you know we all took it on, and it's club, man. Don't matter what patch I wear, the way of things is the same. It's always club, not any one member who decides the direction of anything. Don't lay this shit at his feet just because you're jacked up and on a rampage about what we're sheltering right now."

"Where are the cartel members?" Wildman interjected, trying to derail the brewing argument between the two men. *Time to get back on track.* "Give me a location and I'll go take care of it myself. Then there's nothing for the club to lay claim to."

"They're holed up in a place in Goodwoods, back over in Red Stick."

Wildman lowered his chin once, mentally running over what he knew. Goodwoods was a ramshackle neighborhood in Baton Rouge he'd become well acquainted with during his time in the Common Enemy MC. He noted the address as Po'Boy rattled it off.

"All right, I'll be back." He turned to walk out without any expectations but was pleased when he heard Twisted's groan behind him.

"Get your goddamned ass back in here. You aren't goin' off half-cocked and nomad. Fuck that shit." Wildman hesitated a moment to school his expression before looking over his shoulder, not wanting Twisted to see what it meant to him. "Oh, fuck you. Get back in here and shut the fucking door."

"Hard to run up on anyone quiet-like there. Damn few places to stage from, so anyone riding needs to have their assignments before we roll off the lot." Shoulders back as he closed the door, Wildman sent another glance towards Twisted to take his temperature. The scowl said he was still pissed, but his fists were perched on his hips, and Wildman breathed a little easier not to be on the receiving end of that accusatory finger any longer.

"I want a show of force. We roll from here in fives and tens, but when we get close, we'll close ranks, let our roar blister the paint from the fuckin' walls," Twisted said, beginning to lay out the strategy. Within another ten minutes, they had a plan, and Wildman sat astride his bike in the lot, waiting for his group's turn to head out the gate. A shrill whistle gained his attention, and he looked up to see Po'Boy waving him up to a different line of bikes, including his and Twisted's. As they moved through the gate three wide, he positioned himself to the back of the officers, protecting them with his actions. *With my life if need be.*

It was noon when they pulled into the parking lot chosen as the best staging point for the attack. A brilliant yellow sun hovered overhead, and he marveled at the dichotomy of bright daylight looking down on what was going to be a dark run. *None of them get away this time.* Within minutes, the rest of the men arrived, and they took off again in a close formation, bikes thundering up the street to the abandoned row of housing where they had good intel the escapees were currently squatting. The routed cartel members were supposed to be awaiting reinforcements, but after the drubbing the various alliance cells had received yesterday all along the coast from IMC, CoBos, Bama Bastards, and others, Wildman didn't expect their back-at-home officers would be as quick to send more soldiers into the fray.

People who'd been lazing around on porches along the way vacated, wisely disappearing inside their homes where it was far safer, because if this turned into a rolling shootout, slugs could and would go wild. The column had to go in fast and hard before any one of these helpful citizens became concerned enough to call in LEO. Reports of gunfire were not uncommon in the area, but a barrage of bullets and a herd of bikes would surely stand out. Twisted had opted to not alert the cops to this run, hoping to be in and out before their presence was much advertised.

Toe punching the shifter down into neutral, Wildman heeled the kickstand down and was off the bike fast, thumb hitting the kill switch a microsecond before his fingers uncurled from the clutch. Racing side by side with Po'Boy, he sprinted to the front door of their assigned building, a single-family two-story. Noting the mesh window was already splintered, he yanked up at a corner peeled back to allow for access. Shoving his arm through, he twisted the handle to open the door as Po'Boy slipped past him. Wildman ignored the threatened rake of the exposed mesh and ragged glass against his skin, withdrawing his arm without missing a stride.

Inside, he moved to the left, going around furniture clustered in the middle of the room and through the kitchen to meet Po'Boy coming from the other side. A loud crash from overhead had them both looking up, and without a word, he followed Po'Boy back to the stairs.

"On three," Po'Boy whispered loudly, and Wildman had to stifle his laughter. Long legs taking him up three stairs at a time, Po'Boy quietly made his way to the top. Hand around his mouth to redirect sound, he called out, "One."

Wildman hit the closed door with his shoulder, rolling with the impact and coming up with his gun in hand, already trained on the three men in the room. "Two," he said, pulling the trigger in rapid succession, noting the spray on the walls across the room as the first two bullets found their marks.

Po'Boy took down the last man, and in the silence that followed, said, "Three."

***

Wildman

"Not a single man?" Wildman scrubbed across his jaw with one hand, hiding the grin trying to shine through. "That's fuckin' outstanding, brothers."

Every IMC and CoBos member who had rolled into Goodwoods now sat their bikes on the grocery store lot that was their homeward bound staging spot. Not a one of them missing, and none sported blood of their own.

Wildman and Po'Boy weren't the only ones who'd found targets in their assignments, and he watched as Twisted and Wrench compared proof photos against the cartel intel they'd had about the men who'd run from the shipping yard the previous day. The fierce smile Twisted wore as he lifted his head told the tale, and his raised fist was all the victory sign Wildman needed.

"All of them, my brothers. Every fuckin' one, eliminated." Wrench flung an arm across Po'Boy's shoulders and pulled him close to plant a noisy kiss against the side of his face. "Goddamned well done."

Wildman stepped closer to Twisted, bumping his shoulder softly to gain his president's attention. "Brother."

"Yeah, man?" Twisted gave him a distracted glance, thumbs tapping across his screen. "Sup? I'm just updatin' Retro." Twisted's features sharpened, and a muttered, "Fucking hell" was all he said before lifting the phone to his ear. "What kind of situation?" Silence flooded the space around where they stood, as nearby men recognized the urgency of the tone. Wildman wished he could hear the other end of the call, waiting impatiently for Twisted to give any indication of whatever had Retro torqued over. "Fucking hell, man. That's some bullshit. In your motherfuckin' house? The kids okay? Jesus, you give the word, and I'll fuckin' roll to Birmingham, brother. Those are my kids now, too. You left them with me for the summer, means I got a goddamned claim."

The fact Twisted was speaking in terms of possible and not probable was the only thing that kept Wildman from rushing to his bike. He'd gotten to know Retro's kids well while they'd been staying with Twisted and Penny, and the idea of someone harming any of them set a flaming pit of anger loose in his gut.

"Goddammit, Twisted, you gotta give us something." Wrench's voice was thin with suppressed emotion, and when Wildman glanced over, he was reminded that out of all of them, Wrench had grown up knowing Retro best, his uncle friends with the man for decades. "Good or bad, tip your goddamned hand."

"It's all good." Twisted patted at the air with one hand, and Wrench leaned back a touch. "Retro handled the shit, but we'll need to cuss and discuss when we get back." Twisted tipped his head towards the group of men. "Wild, get 'em mounted, and we'll roll in a minute." Twisted quieted as Wildman lifted a hand in the air with a loud whistle, forefinger making a large circle to urge the men to their bikes. The man was listening intently to whatever was being said on the phone, then nodded in mute support of whatever Retro had told him. "Heard and understood. Talk soon, gonna run my ducks back home. Yeah, yeah. Quack fuckin' quack."

Wildman waited for the man to pocket the phone, waited for his gaze to lift, and once it locked with his, spoke his mind. "Don't mean to add to your pile of shit, and don't even know what it'll take, but if she'll have me, Justine LaPorte is mine." The idea had been bouncing around his head since they'd left Hammond, and he'd leaned in and out on the thought with every pass. One time yes, the next no, and sometimes for the same damn reason. Removing the "where she came from" aspect settled the notion firmly into the yes column, without budging an inch. "I know it ain't realistic, and fuck, man, she might laugh me out of the room for suggesting it, but if she'll have me, then I want that goddamned chance. She's mine, brother, and when I think or say it, the words resonate in a way I like. She fuckin' fits me. Against all odds, yeah, but I'd be a stupid man to turn my back on what might be fate's way of givin' me back just a little bit of goodness."

"Never knew you to be stupid." Twisted tugged on his fingerless gloves, flexing each digit to settle the garments into place, slotting his fingers together to push and pull the leather. "Saw your face this morning, man. Much as you tried playin' it off, I know that look."

"What look?"

A rare, broad grin split Twisted's face, lips parting his signature beard to give out a flash of white. "Owned. I see it in my goddamned mirror every fuckin' morning, but the first time I seen it was right before I made what could have been the biggest mistake in my life." Twisted's head swung back and forth heavily. "Pulled down Penny's sun visor and stared at myself for half a minute before I jumped down out of her truck and walked away. Every fuckin' step like sloggin' through molasses, and it never got any easier. Not until I hunted her down and took her back. Worst goddamned days of my life, tryin' to pretend I hadn't been rocked to my core. Tryin' to pretend I wasn't missin' a critical part of me." The smile faded. "That's the look you had this mornin', readin' that fuckin' paper. Like you were tryin' to reconcile what you knew in your gut with what your big head was tryin' to tell you." He leaned close, clapping a hand on Wildman's shoulder. "Trust me, brother. You're better off trying and failing than sittin' with the coulda, woulda, shoulda. That shit'll eat you a-live. We'll sort out the rest. It might not have sounded entirely like it this mornin', but I always got your back, and where I go, so does IMC. Incoherent for life, man."

"IMC is me, and I am IMC." Wildman rested a palm on Twisted's forearm, gripping lightly in thanks. "We should get this crew rollin' then, yeah? You got news from Retro needs more ears than mine." Backing away, he lifted his hand a second time, pulling all fingers into a rigid fist as he shouted, "Asses in saddles, bikes ready to roll. Stop yer bitchin', bitches." He strode to his bike and slung his leg over, pulling the bike upright to balance between his thighs. Just before he flicked the switch to start the engine, he called out, "Twisted." The man looked up from a similar position on his bike, chin lifted in silent question. "Never doubted you, brother." An expression of relief flickered across Twisted's features, and he nodded once. Bikes all around them roared to life, and Wildman followed suit, the rumble and shake underneath his ass as familiar as breathing.

This is right where I'm meant to be.

He understood the meaning of that phrase deep in his soul. Everything that had happened up to now had been in preparation for what would come, and the shitty moves the universe had made with his life in the past all had purpose. Wildman needed to have an unwavering trust most of all.

In this moment, what he wanted to believe was the woman created just for him was waiting in Hammond.

Chapter Ten
Justine

She had an instant of alert wakefulness as she jerked when a hard hand covered her face in a brutal grip. But a breath later, her brain was already groggy before there'd been a chance to fight or even catalog the bitter scent filling her mouth and nose. An instant and a single breath, and then she was gone.

Chapter Eleven

Wildman

The smile he'd worn the whole way rolling back from Baton Rouge didn't survive Wildman angling his bike into a parking space on the lot surrounding the clubhouse.

A quick glance at the men milling near the front door had his instincts screaming, and he looked over to see an alert, attentive expression also on Twisted's face. Even from yards away, the vibe was clear that something had happened in their house, and Wildman knew instinctively that whatever they were walking into, the scene wasn't going to be pretty.

The stench of smoke and burning plastic met them at the door, and Wildman wafted a hand in front of his face as he pushed inside. Coughing and cursing prospects were in the process of setting up box fans in the windows to push the tainted air out.

The women they'd rescued from the trailer were clustered to one side of the main room, farthest from the kitchen. The positioning avoided where the smoke seemed to be the worst, and most of them just looked tired, not frightened. *So whatever it was didn't involve them.* Wildman quickly scanned the group of women once, then slower a second time when he didn't spot Justine right away. *Shit. Fucking shit.* The smoke and stench, the tension in the air, it all had to involve her. He knew Justine wouldn't voluntarily be anywhere in the building except standing shoulder to shoulder with the women she'd claimed as hers to protect.

Wildman's heart thudded a rough set of beats as he grabbed a passing prospect's arm and pointed at the women with his other hand, growling out his question. "Where is she?"

The man shook his head and pulled away. But the expression on his face said he knew who Wildman was talking about, knew who he looked for. "She ain't there, man. This room holds every nonmember in the building right now, and we've counted more than once already. Apparently, we're down one body. But we don't know where she went."

Wildman let his arm drop back to his side, feet stuck in place while his brain worked overtime, turning over ideas furiously. The easy answer would be somehow Justine LaPorte had managed to avoid detection as she set a minor fire to mask and enable an escape, but he didn't believe she'd leave the other women behind. Not with how protective she'd seemed of them all along the way. *Not a chance in hell.* The women were her duty. And raised the way he knew she'd probably been, Justine wouldn't shirk that just to run off.

Nothing he could think of added up to such a scenario. Her brother could have swooped in, but the RWMC coming into the IMC Motherhouse with force or subterfuge would cause an inter-club incident of enormous magnitude, and nothing he'd heard about the man told Wildman he'd make such an egregious mistake. Could have been the Feds taking back one of their own, but the info from Justine's brother said they weren't even looking for her yet. *No, it's something to do with the goddamned, fuckin' drug runner business.* That felt right, somehow. Cartel wouldn't hesitate to smash anyone in their way, which was why the clubs hated them with hot fury.

One of the women was staring at him, eyes wide, bloodless fingers pressed firmly to her trembling lips. *She knows something.* Recognition struck him, and he barked, "Bring her to the office." The prospect had hovered close, knowing better than to leave without having been verbally released by Wildman, and set off immediately, long strides angling the man towards the women.

The one with the tell gasped, cheeks blanching as she realized she'd become the target of their attention. *Fear.* Oh, yeah, his instincts were gonna be proven right. This woman had some knowledge of what had happened while the rest of the club was out taking care of bloody business. Even if she didn't think it critical info, any tidbit could tell him where Justine might be.

He tilted his head towards Po'Boy, who responded with a nod. Twisted watched them from where he stood near a half-melted trash can brought out from the kitchen. He used a fire poker to sift through the detritus and shook his head. "Just trash. It was meant to make a mess and a stink. It's a distraction, brother."

Like I thought.

The woman had regained some courage and didn't wait for an escort, preceding the two men into the office. She quickly turned and stared at them, one hand curled tightly in the collar of her shirt. She tucked her chin behind her knuckles and opened her mouth, hesitated, and then asked, "You aren't like those other men, are you?"

"You mean the ones who kept you locked in a trailer?" Wildman didn't pause, jumping in before Po'Boy could respond, needing to get beyond the useless reassurance and on to the main reason he wanted to talk to her. "No, we're not a lick like them. Different as night and day." He waited, keeping his gaze pinned on her face as his fear morphed into anger. "Tell me what you fuckin' saw."

"The man who took her, he said you were bad." She held her peace only a moment longer before telling him everything he needed to know. Her unschooled imitation of the man's accent—*the man*—screamed anything *but* cartel. *What the hell?* "She was over his shoulder like a sack of feed, and he looked at me and said he was saving her." She swallowed, her body hitching in the middle so hard Wildman thought she might break in half. "You're Po'Boy, right?" She had it wrong, but close enough, so he nodded. "The second man said to tell Po'Boy she'd be cooking up where the sun doesn't shine, under the long blade of the clergyman." *Two men.* She paused and then said, "That's all. That's what he said. That's all of it." Her tone turned plaintive. "Can I go home now? I want to go home."

"Was she alive?" Wildman stalled Po'Boy's reach for the door and stood as stoically as he could, knees locked as he waited for a blow. *Two fuckin' men with chodes enough to bust into our clubhouse and take the only woman we'd roust a rescue for. Two informed men, and ain't that a shitty thought.* He pushed her on the piece he wanted—needed to know. "Did they take her breathin'?"

"I don't know. She didn't...she didn't move." The woman shuddered as if she'd been hit by the blow he'd taken instead.

I don't know.

His eyes drifted closed, a movie of Justine underneath him last night playing on the backs of his eyelids. Beautiful, courageous, submissive, strong, sexy. *She don't know if Jussie was breathin'.*

"Can I go home?" The woman's voice scraped along his nerves, the trembling and fearful tone like nails on a chalkboard, because Justine had risked everything to protect her, and she couldn't even be bothered to know if her champion was alive or not. *Not her fault.* He tried to believe his own thoughts.

"Soon, honey," Po'Boy softly soothed her as he opened the door and quickly ushered her out.

Wildman heard him giving orders about the women, and the creaking of the wooden stairs said he'd sent them back upstairs. None of them would be leaving in the near future, not until the IMC and CoBos members sorted out what had happened. A federal agent had been held in what amounted to forced confinement—in other words, kidnapping—and then had been removed from the IMC clubhouse either unconscious or dead.

Wildman's brain shied away from that four-letter word as he tried to hold tight to the woman's protestations that she just didn't know. *Need to move forward as if her survival is a surety.* Justine LaPorte hadn't vacated the clubhouse under her own power, and that fact was about all he knew with certainty. *Not the Feds, either. Nor her family.* But also not cartel. Whoever they were, they somehow had known which woman to take as the best possible bargaining chip. *She survived so much already.* Potential murderers and traffickers had Justine in their control a second time. *I'll set her free again.* All he'd been left with were three clues, deliberately obscure to keep him from finding her in time to prevent whatever had been planned.

"They didn't count on one thing." Po'Boy spoke from behind him as Twisted strode into view. Wildman turned to stare at both men, puzzled at the smug expression on Po'Boy's face. Stretching his neck with a low crow, Po'Boy told them, "I gots me a long-ass memory, which means those boys done fucked up."

***

Wildman

Standing in the gravel and dirt in front of the clubhouse, Wildman fought back his impatience as men gathered at what seemed a snail's pace. Knowing he was being unrealistic with his internal demands for speed didn't make it easier, watching the loose-limbed greetings between the IMC and CoBos men. They didn't have anything riding on this call-out. Nothing except the reputation of their clubs, and Wildman knew they'd kick it into gear as soon as the situation called for such.

Wasn't their fault Jussie was his and had been taken, location and health unknown for sure.

The three clues given by the kidnapper who'd stolen into their clubhouse to take Justine might hold everything they needed to find her, but tangled politics had already taken up too much time. Twisted had included the CoBos and Wrench via official channels, which then passed along the message to a half a dozen support clubs, while to Wildman, even a moment's delay was too much.

He lifted his head, closed gaze aimed upwards as the sun overhead painted white circles of light underneath his eyelids. Deliberately slowing his breathing, he held the position until he could feel tense muscles starting to relax.

That was derailed in an instant when the rolling thunder of bike exhaust bounced off the trees. A sound Wildman and every other member were well used to, but every man who'd been called in was here now, which meant these visitors were unexpected, and as far as Wildman cared, un-fucking-needed. *Motherfuckers.* All he wanted to do was find Justine and be certain she was safe. He'd let her go if that's what she wanted, hold her close if he found she was so inclined, but first, she had to be breathing and near enough to touch. Which meant whatever kind of bullshit protocol would have to be wrangled now between whoever was coming down the road and the IMC was time spent *not* doing what was needed. *Sons of bitches.*

"Twisted." He followed up his shout with a two-tone whistle, similar to the dove's cry he'd used at the shipping yard. *Hell, was that just a couple of nights ago? One night?* Across the lot, Twisted's head lifted, then angled towards the road with a nod. Wildman lifted a fist, pumped it twice, then pointed to where Twisted was stalking along the edge of the gravel so he could see farther up the narrow road. "Watch his back." A dozen brothers took off at a trot to close the distance between them and Twisted. "Ware the house." Wildman swept an arm in a circle, and Ruger nodded in response, twisting to tap the shoulders of ten or more brothers near him, heading around the edge of the clubhouse at a dead run, ready to protect against anything coming from the rear. "Ward our guests." This bellow wasn't accompanied by any gestures, just Wildman crowding closer to Wrench and Po'Boy, already encircled by their own men. Wildman positioned himself along the front edge of the cluster of bodies, ready to change tasks as needed.

He couldn't have said who he'd expected to see, but Retro wasn't high on the list, given Twisted had talked to him a dozen hours ago at about the same time some unexplained shit had apparently been going down in the man's own home. But there he was, riding point, rolling between two men Wildman knew by reputation.

Mason, international president of the Rebel Wayfarers MC, and Sparks, president of the Jailbreakers MC from Adken, Florida. The same hometown listed on the info about Justine.

Fuck me.

Then the column rolled past where Twisted stood and up to the front of the clubhouse, as if they had a goddamned right to be there. Behind him, Wildman overheard Wrench muttering to Po'Boy, who simply groaned.

Disrespect, right here on our ground.

Wildman didn't try to stop the men who flooded past him, a black river of potential pain, aimed directly at the man who was his woman's blood brother.

***

By the time the higher-ups had sorted out it was a friendly—if unannounced—visit and not an attempted takeover, there were a full dozen men on their bellies on the lot and handfuls more exchanging threatening words chest to chest.

No matter the bar of metal pinned to every stranger's chest, an old-school tell of a blameless pass-through, for every IMC member, the idea of a rival club coming to the Motherhouse as if they owned it was begging an explanation.

Only when he'd seen iron pulled had Wildman waded in, cursing and yelling with Twisted at his side, yanking their members back one at a time, leaving the cadre of foreigners in the middle of a ring of bikes. Retro was well known and trusted, of course, but the other two were shockers to more than just Wildman. It was chaos, voices lifted in shouts and threats while in the background Po'Boy and Wrench offered steady voices, kept control of their own men even as they helped calm the furor surrounding them.

Things finally ground to a halt, and Wildman dropped his hold on the last struggling brother, stepping back quickly as he retreated to the fringes. That buffer of distance was his sole barrier to keep him from killing anyone, because waiting even another goddamned second to roll their rescue felt like betrayal in the depths of his fear for Justine.

Long after Wildman had stopped giving a shit about what was unnecessary protocol, Twisted had finally walked to where Wildman stood, shoulders propped up on the outside wall, checking the time on his phone over and over again.

Twisted leaned a shoulder against the wall and blew out a lungful of air. "She ain't ours, but she was taken from our house. Makes us responsible." Wildman glared at Twisted when he paused, making a "hurry up" roll with his fingers that earned him a dark scowl. "CoBos are the only ones riding who don't have a dog in this hunt, but they're deep partners all the way around the circle, brother, and I can't find it in myself to deny them. Fuck, I asked 'em here before we knew it'd turn into a cluster. We got a history with them, and this honors that somewhat." Lips pressed tightly together, Wildman held his peace. "Rebels, Jailbreakers, and Bastards will be rollin' with us, goin' on my call too. For various reasons, I suspect you already understand, each of those men over there has a stake in the outcome today. You will be respectful." Wildman turned his glare back on Twisted, pulling it away from the group that had stymied him for far too long. "You will be, or I'll fuckin' own you."

"You already own me, Prez. Didn't have to be said. As Retro's fond of sayin', 'I'll abide.' I won't like it, but I'll fuckin' abide." Pulling himself to his full height, he stared into Twisted's eyes. "Just as long as we roll. Now the cock measurin' is done and over with, you think we could possibly get this goddamned show on the motherfuckin' road? Because I been standing around too damn long, and with every minute ticking past on the clock, I run the risk they'll move her. Or worse, give up on us showin' and just shift to erase their liability." He shook his head. "It's what I'd do if I was a shiteater like they are."

"*We* run the risk." Twisted thumped his chest and then Wildman's, the blow from the back of his knuckles stinging with the promise of a bruise. "Every single one of us runs the risk. Not just you, brother. That's a 'we' in there, not an 'I.'"

"Not the same, man. Not even close to the same, and you know it. She's *mine*. Not yours." Wildman shook his head to force his thoughts straight. "At least she could be. She's not, not yet, but dammit, Twisted, she could be, and standin' here even talking to you like this is fuckin' with me bad, man. I gotta go."

"Then we ride."

He took Twisted at his word and strode to his bike, leg over and thumb to the start button before Twisted had taken a single step. He rolled to where Mason, Retro, and Sparks sat their bikes and eased to a stop. "He's asked me for respect. I promised I'd abide by his wishes, and I will." Thumping his chest with a closed fist, he held Mason's gaze, the man's brows lifting in a painful shocked expression. "Jussie's mine, and you gotta know that's truth. I'm ridin' to bring back my woman."

Mason's headshake wasn't a surprise, but Wildman still hated to see it. "Man, you and her are a thing separate from why I'm lookin' for her. I won't get between her and whatever kinda shit she wants to drag home with her, but in this one, you'll play by my rules."

"And what makes you think I'd do that, you son of a bitch?" The shit statement had burned because Wildman knew Jussie was MC royalty, daughter of one, sister of another, but he wasn't worthy of that kind of dismissal. "If she's still there and we round things up the way we want, any decision won't be yours, and fuck, man, it won't be mine, either. It'll be hers all the way, but I'm gonna push my suit."

"She's got to get back to her bosses, or it runs the risk of callin' down more heat than any of us want to deal with." Mason held up a pacifying palm, and Wildman felt an unreasonable ire to see only honest concern in his expression, not any kind of bullshit reasons hiding there. "We clear the shit, I'm with you on that, and you can even make your verbal play, but she needs to be picked up by her own people. We can't bring her back here, can't take her to Birmingham—fuck, man, I can't even take her to my nearest clubhouse."

Shit. Every word Mason uttered made absolute sense to Wildman, and he hated the man a little for it. Breathing hard, as if he'd gone a ten-round fight, he glared down at his fuel tank. *She's a damned Fed. Don't even know if she's into me. Fuck, haven't seen the woman awake since just hours after we rescued her goddamned ass, so I can't know. Not for sure.* Lifting his chin, he stared at Mason and swallowed hard, giving a quick, brusque nod.

"I just want my fuckin' sister safe and sound, and I'm with you. All this shit took way too long to straighten out." Mason placed a palm against his chest, as close to an oath as Wildman had ever seen. "I already told Twisted, but you've my apologies for ridin' in like that. I didn't see him out by the road, or I'd have stopped the column."

"He ain't lyin', Wild." Retro leaned forwards, wrists propped on the peaks of his high handlebars. "None of us expected to find him anywhere but in front of his house, which was why we were aimin' at respectful placement. All kinds of bullshit y'all were ready to roll. We shoulda been ten minutes earlier, and none of this woulda gone down."

"Po'Boy thinks he knows where they've got her, based on the message left specifically for him." Wildman shook his head, frustrated. "Like I told Twisted"—he thumbed over his shoulder as the man rolled his bike up beside Wildman's—"they coulda moved her already. We need to roll."

"What's the plan?" Mason flicked his gaze towards Twisted, but then his eyes settled on Wildman, and just that nod to his claim on Justine helped mollify him somewhat. "We just pullin' a John Wayne?"

"Guns blazing, fuck yeah." Wildman nodded once, then looked for Po'Boy. "Bossman?" His call got a chin lift and a raised brow that told him Po'Boy was listening. "Brother, you pointin' the way?" Po'Boy flipped one thumb up, so with a wave to Mason and Retro, Wildman released the clutch and rolled the throttle, aiming his bike at the backend of Po'Boy's as the man whipped sideways on the gravel at the end of the drive. Wildman executed nearly the same maneuver, hearing the shouts and calls behind him growing fainter as he twisted the throttle more, shifting up through the gears quickly and catching up to Po'Boy's wild speed. *At least someone understands urgency around here.* He didn't push up next to him, just slotted into place behind him, letting a left-hand column roll up beside them, Twisted in the lead, Mason filling in next to Wildman.

Quack, fuckin' quack.

Chapter Twelve
Justine

Her body revolted, and Justine became aware as she retched hard, her stomach roiling inside her. She rolled to her side, head pounding so hard that getting away from the pain was all she could think about. Vomiting certainly didn't help, but lying still seemed to, so she scootched away from the small, vile-smelling puddle and relaxed as best she could. Other than her heart pounding, it was country-silent all around her. Cicadas and bullfrogs off in the distance spoke to a rural setting, while the lack of highway noise held a tiny blade of fear to her nerves.

Where am I?

Embracing silence and holding in place as she paid close attention to everything around her was a basic form of control she could exercise, so she did. Justine shoved her fear down and down, packing it away in a box in her mind until it was a distant emotion, already muffled by whatever had been used to incapacitate her. The nausea was slowly fading away, and she was awfully glad for small favors.

The more intently she listened, the more sounds were identifiable. From close by came the soft plink of a steadily dripping faucet, and in the far distance, there was a deep hum of some gas-powered yard implement, maybe a generator. The shuffling of boot leather across a rough plank floor marked the approach of someone.

Definitely not with Wildman and the IMC.

The road in front of the clubhouse hadn't carried heavy traffic, but there'd been a highway not too far away as the crow flies, and while in their house, she'd found the sound of trucks and cars had been nearly constant.

Where? God, where am I? Who has me?

The footsteps came closer, and Justine viciously tried to deny the spike in her fear, taking advantage of the cotton-headed feeling still muddling her thoughts. It took careful concentration to make sure her face would look relaxed, slack even, and every breath she took was controlled, steady, and slow. The footsteps halted near her head, close enough she could hear the squeak of the boards underfoot, and she had to fight a sudden terror threatening to break the rhythm of her breathing. *Don't touch me, oh God, don't touch me. Please, God, don't let them touch me.* Fortunately, playing possum seemed to have worked, because the footsteps retreated, faster than they'd approached.

Silence filled the space until the humming in her ears battled against the cicadas' rise-and-fall roar, then a man's voice muttered, "No, she's still out. You seen anything yet?" A pause where she could only make out the buzz of someone speaking on the other end of the call. "Let me know soon as, man. I gotta gear up for this shit. Can't just rock it without preparation, if you know what I mean." Silence, then a distinct metal and glass rattle as something was dropped on a hard surface.

Eyes closed, Justine pushed herself to remember the events that had brought her here. Fortunately, she remembered everything from the night with Wildman, or the soreness between her legs would give her a terrified pause. The last thing she held memory of was a hand over her mouth, jarring her from a sound sleep alone in Wildman's bed for only an instant. Then, lights out, and nothing at all behind the gray veil until waking to vomit. *Knocked me out fast.* Had there been a cloth in the hand, rough against her cheeks and chin? *Maybe.* The current headache and barely remembered bitter scent told her they'd used some kind of agent to immobilize her. *Chloroform?* Probably. The compound was easy enough to make via a home recipe, and that harsh and dangerous formula was alive and well in the dark corners of the Internet. *Wouldn't even have to worry about a paper trail that way.*

The conversation she'd just overheard gave her an idea of what had happened. She'd been working as an unauthorized undercover agent, posing as a victim of a Mexican drug cartel's flesh-trafficking scheme to gain intel on the source and routes of distribution. Then she and the other women had been inadvertently rescued by a local motorcycle club. Their patches had identified them as both Incoherent and the Caddo Hobos MCs, each a one-percent group who were deemed helpful by local federal authorities. They might not always stay on the legal side of the line, but for the communities where their clubhouses were, the illegal activities conducted weren't enough to override the beneficial effect they had of keeping other, more violent crime at bay. She'd studied all the known criminal elements in the area for years—and IMC, the club Wildman was part of, was one that had caught her attention.

So, first she'd been rescued by a member of the dominant MC in the area, in a clear strike against the encroachment of the cartel, and then taken in turn by someone else. *With an unknown agenda. Jesus, what a fuck-up.* This man was not part of the cartel. There'd been no trace of a foreign accent in his voice, and the cadence of the words on the other end hadn't carried it either. The man who was her current captor had likely been the one to hold the chloroform rag over her mouth, and his counterpart, whoever he was, was currently positioned far enough away that they expected him to see something before it could be known from this location. On the plus side, this guy was a clear amateur. Not only wasn't he standing watch over her, but by placing himself in the other room like that, he'd cut himself off from the line of sight. The dumbass also hadn't secured her at all, her wrists and ankles not restrained. *Not that I'm complaining.*

She just needed to get her pounding head under control and deal with him, then make her way back to the IMC clubhouse to verify the other women were okay.

Justine fluttered her lids as she slowly opened her eyes, blinking to adjust to the shooting daggers of pain blasting through her head. As things came into focus, she made out a duffel bag on the floor near a window. Barely visible inside were a plastic bottle lying on its side and a dirty rag. *No way. Would he really be that careless?* Her immediate response was an eye roll, but that attempt at derogatory humor had her wincing and biting back a groan as the effort earned her a headful of pain followed by a recurrence of nausea. *Okay, not moving anytime soon.*

She'd only have one chance at overpowering the man. Justine kept testing the limits of what her body would allow through the next twenty minutes, rolling her shoulders and neck, stretching out her hands and fingers, flexing and pointing her feet. The man had come back to check on her twice more, each time with the phone in hand as he reported in, leaving her lying next to her own vomit as he walked away. She'd taken the opportunity to size him up from the back, finding out he was larger than he'd sounded, tall but not broad.

I can do this.

Then the wooden floor under her cheek began to vibrate, rattling through her skull and setting up another wave of pain. Lifting her head to escape the vibration, she slowly pushed up to a crouch near the wall and crept over to look through the doorway into the other room. Facing a window, her captor was staring outwards with a hank of greasy hair falling across his face.

Focused on whatever was happening outside—she could only imagine and hope what that could be—he didn't turn when she scooped up the bottle. Holding it away from her body, she opened it and splashed the pungent-smelling liquid on the rag, forcing back a gag as she made her way to stand behind him. Outside the window, a dozen bikes had pulled up in an uneven row, faces covered with bandanas of varying colors.

Even with the bottom half of Wildman's face hidden behind the fabric, Justine easily picked him out of the lineup. *I'd know him anywhere.* His hand lifted to point at the window where she stood behind the man, and she stared at the pistol aimed directly at her. *Jesus, no.* With no time to hesitate, she lunged upwards and clapped her hand over the man's mouth and nose, wrapping her other arm around his neck to gain leverage. She had to work hard to hold the rag in place as, with muffled shouts, he tore at her fingers, his movements driven by an urgent strength. That ebbed, though, faster than she'd expected, his dexterity waning, and he wavered on his feet.

Outside, Wildman's gun was now aimed up at the dark sky, and she locked gazes with him. Her pulse raced, pounding faster in response to the expression of pride she read in his eyes, and she swallowed hard to keep back the tears.

He'd come for her, with nothing more than one night between them. *He came for me.* The body in front of her tilted, and she wrestled with his weight, deflecting him away from the window and letting him fall with a crash to the floor. Justine went down next to him on one knee and held the rag in place for another few seconds for good measure.

The door burst open, and Wildman was the first in, coming directly to where she crouched while other men flanked him, spreading out through the house, shouts coming back every few seconds promising safety as they found only empty rooms.

Wildman stooped until his eyes were level with hers, a question in them that somehow gained an answer in her silence, the lines in his face easing. Then his hands were on her arms, thumbs brushing gentle strokes over her skin as he stood, lifting her with him. An instant later, his arms were around her, and she leaned into him, letting the fear wash over her finally, fingers clutching his shirt, face buried against his chest between the front flaps of his vest as he smoothed her hair, holding her close.

"There's another man somewhere close. He spoke to him on the phone." Wildman had to know, just in case this wasn't done.

"Yeah, we clocked the asshole as we rolled in. Caught him before he sounded a warning. It's all good. He's tied up tight for transport, just like this asshole will be in half a minute." Justine pulled in the first easy breath she'd had since waking. His arms tightened around her. "You wearin' my shirt, woman?" His voice rumbled under her ear, the pounding of his heart outing the ease in his voice as a lie. "Damn, we ain't even a thing yet, and you're already stealin' my favorite tees?"

She sniffed and rocked her forehead against him, trying to keep the quaver from her voice when she retorted, "Seemed the thing to do at the time." When he'd left as part of a huge pack, the roaring of the bikes had woken the whole clubhouse. After staring out the window until she couldn't see any of the bikes anymore, she'd taken a minute to tug on her panties and his discarded shirt before lying back down. That had seemed a precipitous decision she was glad of now, since they were all the clothing she wore.

He took a slow, deep, even breath. "Mason says hello."

Goose bumps raced up her arms. That name in Wildman's mouth said he had to know exactly who she was. Grief welled tears in her eyes, but Justine brushed them away. *Maybe he knew who I was and came after me anyway.*

"He's not a bad dude." Wildman's voice gained a tiny thread of humor as he continued speaking. "Not a good one, either, but he ain't bad."

Davis Mason. Her long-lost brother, recently reunited, was the founder of a notorious one-percent club based out of the northern half of the States. A competitive counterpart to the Incoherent patch Wildman wore so proudly. Wildman learning about the relationship between her and Mason meant no matter how it had felt like coming home to be underneath him last night, them together wouldn't be something he'd ever consider continuing. *That blood connection paired with my job?* Justine allowed herself a single, final sniff, followed by a deep breath in, trying to imprint on her memory all that was Wildman, then shook her head and prepared to pull away. His arms tightened around her, and she froze.

His voice was quiet, pitched for her ears only, when he said, "See, here's the thing. I don't give a fuck who your kin is, or whatever you've done. Your job, that's gonna be a sticker, but if you want this, we can figure out a way to get over that too. You just gotta want this with me."

Bikes rumbled outside, engines revving high and loud, the multitude of exhaust pipes setting up echoes through the house. He turned her to look through the window, and she was stunned to find even more bikes, seeing back patches from a number of clubs.

Making mental notes, she made out IMC, to be expected since this was their war against the cartel. CoBos were next, and that could have been predicted, too, given the way the two clubs had become intertwined over the past years and their involvement along the way. Bama Bastards held part of the line, and when the rider carefully studying the house flipped his trademark long hair, she knew it had to be Retro, their president. Next was Sparks, the president of the Jailbreakers, out of her hometown in Florida. More goose bumps made her shiver when she recognized the final patch, one she hadn't expected to see in Louisiana. Strong arms tightened around her, and Justine allowed herself to lean back against the wall of his chest. Maybe especially with Wildman's words, she was shocked to her core that the man seated on that bike, one who shared her grey eyes and dark hair, wasn't in here tearing her a new asshole. That was Davy Mason, the brother who made her life far more complicated because he was bossy and straddled the line of legal more than she liked, but she was glad to see him nonetheless. Five clubs had thrown away the rule books and jointly ridden to her rescue, called together by the man standing at her back.

She twisted her neck to look up at Wildman and waited, because something in her said he wasn't finished, not by a long shot. He turned her again, and she braced her forearms against his chest, hands flat over the top of his shoulders. The bandana he'd worn to ride was still tied around his neck, but she could see the way he forced himself to swallow, feeling that same trepidation in her gut.

"I'm going to have to leave you here, baby. Have to. Do not fuckin' want to do this, but your brother had a powerful argument. There's a lot that could change, and not in a good way, if I take you back with me today." The look on Wildman's face said he wasn't happy about it, but she understood. "There's going to be a phone left outside. It's clean. Use it to make your calls. Do it immediately. Don't wait on us to get far, Jussie. Just do it. Take care of you. Make your calls and get your people here. Then, later, if you—" His voice cracked, and he stopped, taking in a deep breath as she pressed closer to him. "If you want to find me, I suspect you can."

She held her tongue, not speaking the words she wanted, because there was nothing else she could do. No pretty promises, no assurances. Just his offer, neither accepted nor rejected, and she knew leaving him in limbo was shitty, but just as he had to leave her here, she couldn't offer him anything more. *Not now.* He pushed her away, hands on her arms until she was steady on her feet, his gaze never leaving hers. *Not yet.* Then he gave her another thing, the gift of her name in his mouth. "Be well, Justine."

***

Wildman

"Don't know if I can, man." Wildman didn't lift his head, keeping his gaze fixed on shoving his sweaty fingers into the gloves he wore for riding. He was adjusting the same seam for the third time when the fingers on his shoulder clamped hard, pain forcing his head up with a snarled oath. "Mother*fucker*."

"Call me what you want, man, but you know we've got to roll." The look Retro gave him was a mix of sympathy and frustration, something Wildman entirely understood. "She can't call for help until we're past the tree line, and we can't get past the tree line until you're KSU and rollin'." His fingers dug into that bundle of nerves behind Wildman's collarbone again, hard and harsh, painful enough to get his point across and then some. "I can't get home to my family until you're KSU and rollin', and we hit the clubhouse to fully debrief. Come on, man. I get it's hard. I do, more than you know right now. I get how tough it is and that you want to walk back in there and make it okay for her. I see it in your face, brother, and I feel you deep." Retro's fingers relaxed marginally, easing off on the pain. "But you can't. Not and keep everything you want. Keeping her safe is letting her control this as she needs. Keeping your club safe is believing she'll be okay and rolling your ass up that damned road. The only gift you can give her is your confidence she can do this. That she can handle herself, come what may. We can't even leave men in the woods to ward her, because the Feds'll roll in heavy with drones before they risk a man, and those bastards'll spot our men a mile away. Wild, brother, you saw her take down that son of a bitch. You know she's got what it takes."

"She shouldn't have to." Wildman gripped his handlebars, tightening and loosening his fingers, anxious and feeling as if that tangible connection was the only thing keeping him on the bike. "You know I should be here."

"You explain it to her?" Retro's hand fell away, and Wildman stared up at the man. He'd always respected Retro, believed in the innate sense of honesty and rightness that bled from the man. He gave Retro a short, brusque nod, which Retro returned. "Good, brother. You paid lip service to your belief in her. Now you gotta show her. Come on, let's roll." He knocked knuckles against Wildman's helmet, then turned and straddled his own bike, looking over his shoulder at Wildman. "Drinks on me tonight. I have a feelin' you're gonna need someone to tell you when enough is enough." Retro started his bike, then looked pointedly at Wildman's, still leaning on the kickstand.

Slowly Wildman righted the bike, pushing at the metal rod with his heel until the kickstand flipped up into the lock position alongside the bike frame. He glanced at the window, catching a quick glimpse of Justine as she lifted a hand, then faded from view.

Makin' it as easy on me as she can.

He settled his bandana into place and pushed the ignition button, then gave Retro a thumbs-up, walking his bike into position behind the man. Less recklessly than they'd ridden into the clearing, which had been all slip-sliding sideways on pine needles and sand, the column straightened and rolled up the two-track dirt drive, dodging potholes instead of launching across them. At the highway, he didn't hesitate and picked up a gear as soon as the rear wheel hit the asphalt, then another as he tucked in closely behind Retro, working his way up through the rest of the gears until they were all rolling at highway speed.

Chapter Thirteen
Justine

Justine watched as all but one of the bikes disappeared, leaving her alone in the tiny shack in the middle of the Louisiana country wilderness. She wasn't concerned, not for her own safety, but as she sank to the floor, back propped against a wall, she glanced around the room at everything she could and would not be able to explain.

The shakes hit then, a drop in adrenaline she should have expected but hadn't. With a curious detachment, she watched her hands tremble at the end of her wrists, propped on each knee.

A scuff of boot leather to the side was followed by a huffed out laugh, the following clearing of a masculine throat familiar and comforting. Mason slid down the wall next to her, bumping her shoulder with his once he was seated.

She'd seen him wave his men onwards, watched as they argued with him, but then her attention had been captured by Retro's lecture to Wildman, their conversation entirely lost to her, but Wildman's reactions had telegraphed his unwillingness to leave, his final capitulation, and a last glimpse of his face before he hid from the world. No way could she have focused on anything except his unerring strength, back straight as he manhandled his bike up the sand-and-shell drive.

Still, it didn't shock her that Mason would want a word.

Private-like.

It's what their father would have done in his place. And no matter they'd each hated him, for similar and yet very different reasons, they were both products of their raising, strange as it all seemed.

"You okay, Justine?"

Mason's voice was pitched low but with ample volume for her to hear him seated so closely. It held a vibrating timbre of regret or longing; she wasn't sure which. She leaned her head against his shoulder and held that position. "Yeah, I'm good. No permanent damage."

"Goddammit, Justine."

There we are. That's more like what I expected. The weight of his anger rolled over her, and she took it, letting it settle in the room, hoping he'd see how ridiculous it was to be upset over something she'd done to herself.

"I'm fine, Davy." She rocked her head back to catch a glimpse of the side of his face. Tanned, sun and smile lines carved into the corners of his eyes and mouth, with his grizzled beard and hair, he was still handsome. "How's that pretty wife of yours?"

"Willa's fine, and you ain't gonna change the subject on me that easily." He huffed out another laugh.

"Yeah, I didn't expect I could dislodge your bulldog grip on the topic." She blinked slowly, then straightened just as slowly, settling her shoulder blades in an uncomfortable press against the hard wall behind her. *A little pain should help me through this.* Maybe he hadn't actually talked to anyone back in Adken. *White lies.* "I saw a chance and took it. Simple as that. Those who needed to know were aware of where I was, and if I were missing too long, they'd follow the trail to find me." She didn't shrug, didn't move, barely breathed as she tried not to give him anything to hang a hook into to pull her story apart. *It's true.* Schooling a grimace, she flexed her bones backwards, digging into the wall a little more. *Near enough for horseshoes, anyway.*

"They didn't even fuckin' know you were gone." Mason's tone dropped an octave as he continued. "Greg Anderson expressed significant surprise you weren't vacationing with family, as your last email to him indicated." He cleared his throat, and she could feel the weight of those grey eyes she knew were focused on her. "With my appearance at your home and office, he allowed as perhaps you hadn't been quite truthful. Seein' as that family you were with was supposed to be me."

Well, shit. "Are you kidding me right now? You went to my colleague to check up on me? You went to a coworker? What were you thinking, Davy?"

"No, Justine, what were *you* thinking? Forget it. You know what? Never mind that question. More to the point of what I need to know, what are you going to tell your people when you make that call Wildman told you to make?" Mason adjusted his position, easing one long leg out in front of him.

With his elbow propped on a bent knee, head angled so he could see her face, he looked so much like their father she nearly said so, stopping herself just before the words crossed her lips. Mason seemed intent on blending their families—once he'd found out about her, that was. But he did it without truly acknowledging the connection they held.

Especially once he'd eliminated the biggest threat that had ever existed to the two of them, shooting their father in a coffee shop directly across the road from her federal offices. And how he'd gotten out of that situation without anyone or any cameras catching sight of him was a wonder.

The official tale had Justice Morgan, their father, killing another son. Paternal filicide taking their half-brother John Morgan, Shooter, even as Shooter had lived up to his name earned in blood, committing patricide.

The truth settled somewhere in between the two different camps who'd been in the coffee shop. Patricide had been committed, as had fratricide, with Mason walking out the door head held high, his loyal brother Bones at his side.

"Justine?" This softly voiced question was so unlike Mason's more typically direct interrogation, she blinked and realized she'd been lost in her mind, considering the convoluted history they shared.

"You know much about Wildman?" She licked her lips, then cursed herself for allowing that tiny tell, angling her gaze away from Mason and out the window, watching the tops of the pine trees sway in the breeze.

"Good guy." He snorted and bumped her shoulder, then a second time until she twisted her neck to look at him. Mason's crooked smile was soft and affectionate. "I mean that, Justine. He's a real steady brother. Steady Eddie. Man has had shit luck in his life, and from what I heard, he seems settled into his evolving place with the IMC. He wasn't always from Louisiana, though, was originally a Florida boy if you can believe that, but farther to the south than your current stompin' grounds. He's got a story to tell, that's for sure. Question is, will you be ready to listen to it?" The pause wasn't long, just enough for her to offer a nod, and Mason's lips twisted into a smirk. "Do I know much about him? Yeah, once I heard whose bed you'd hit up, I had me a chat with Retro. Somehow, someway," he drawled the words out long, sounding amused, "he had the *very* info I needed, right at his fingertips, seeming to pull it from the air. Makes me wonder who else's been askin' about the man."

Justine's skin prickled into gooseflesh, every hair on her arms standing alert. Attention, in Mason's world as well as her own, was never a good thing. "You think he's on someone's radar? In a bad way?" Her fingers ached, and she looked down to see her hand had transferred to his arm, nails digging into his bicep in a way that had to be painful, yet Mason never flinched. Glancing up, she caught Mason's features as they shifted from surprise to concern, then settled into the blankness she knew he gave the rest of the world. "I mean, that's stupid. If Retro didn't even have to take a minute to dig, it means he's already been handed a shovel and hit paydirt. What matters is who it was." She retracted her hand, clasping her fingers together as she pulled her legs into a crisscross, head angled down as she considered the tiny bits of truth she knew. "Retro wouldn't tell you who else had been asking, would he?"

"Not without it costin' me more than the info is worth, no."

"Right. Right." Tip of her thumb pressing in turn along each large knuckle of her other hand, she mentally counted down her remaining questions, trying to settle on the one that would give her the most bang for the buck. Mason's hint at Wildman's past ranked high, way high, even as it felt wrong to hear anything about the man that wasn't from his own lips. Justine chewed the inside of her cheek, the sting and copper taste telling her she'd wound herself up past the edge of sanity. His Florida history sans-personal story would be good to know, yet she somehow suspected a lot of the info would be open to her normal channels of investigation. *Unless I don't want to bring the fact I'm looking into him to anyone's attention.* Huffing out an explosive sigh, she lifted her head and stared at Mason, features schooled into the same blank mask he wore. "What would it cost to find out if the interrogatory were malicious or benign? Not looking for the source's name, just the meaning behind the inquiry?"

"Now that would cost a sight less." Brows quirked together, Mason curled the corner of his lips in something that wasn't a smile but still strengthened her like a brand of approval. "Knew you'd come up with the right question. I'll call your home in two—" He pretended to study the ceiling, as if heavenly insights might be coming his way, and Justine laughed softly. "Maybe three days. Your people aren't gonna be pleased with you, darlin', regardless of the tale you spin."

And there it was. The real reason he'd stayed. This was his ask to her, to share what the repercussions might be for what Wildman had requested. *Might as well put him out of his misery.*

"One call will have an extraction team here within maximum couple of hours." She admitted to her ignorance of the exact location. "Baton Rouge if we're west of the Mississippi, Jackson if we're east of it. Tossup between NOLO and Mobile, depending on the southerly range."

"Red Stick, then," he said, using the born-and-bred Louisianians' nickname for the state's capital. "You got any personal contacts there? Need me to try to pass any information along official channels back to your folks faster than might otherwise happen?"

"Oh, it'll happen fast enough. Debrief won't be anywhere except Adken, unless it's in Jacksonville or Tampa. My story starts and ends with the human trafficking aspect. It would help if I knew what happened to the women left at the clubhouse." She tried to think of other important details. "And where the shipping yard was, exactly. Cartel's minions had us bagged when they took us there, and the IMC extracted us in cargo vans. I have a sense, but no real idea of the location."

Mason pulled out his phone and tapped an icon, using facial recognition to access the application. She angled her body to the side, trying to get a better look, but he huffed out yet another laugh and turned it away so all she got was the back of the phone. "Oh, fuck no, woman. I gotta keep some of the mysteries hidden."

A tinny voice said, "Boss, the loc puts you where you ain't supposed to be anymore. The fuck"—Mason's hands moved, and the volume soared, a clearly irate male voice filling the air around them—"do you think you're doing?"

"Got you on speaker, brother." Silence, broken only by a sudden and rapid tapping of keyboard keys. "Yeah, yeah, I know you could do all kinds of terrible things to me if you wanted to. Turn on the camera if you want to know who's here. I'll do a sweep for ya, show ya we're alone." He did as promised, still managing to keep the screen of the phone hidden. The phone paused longest aimed her direction, and another flurry of keystrokes sounded over the speaker. "You can fuckin' talk, man. It's all good."

"Boss. You're supposed to be pullin' up at the goddamned BR IMC house right fuckin' now." Mason's brows lifted, and Justine nodded, able to make the distance estimation based on timeframe. Made it clear why he'd thought Baton Rouge was the likely launch for rescue. "What the fuck are you still doin' there, and from the looks of things, alone except for your sister? Hell, just her and not a goddamned brother in sight? Really, Mason? This is how you decide to play this?"

Lips spread wide in a grin, Mason waited a beat but no more questions came through from whoever was on the other end of the video call. Gaze flicking between the screen and Justine's face, he chuckled loudly. "Damn, Myron, that's a load of cussin' for you. Mouse gonna need to take you over his knee, you keep that shit up."

Myron, otherwise known as Ronald Lyons, partner of Andrus Kasmouski, aka Mouse. Myron is blood brother to Bones' woman. Justine was pleased with herself at being able to quickly place both names. Once she'd known the relationship between herself and Mason, the casual, professional interest she'd had in the Rebel Wayfarers MC as one of the largest and most stable motorcycle gangs in northern America, expanding out into other countries including Germany, Netherlands, Spain, Brazil, and Australia, had shifted. Once it became personal, she had wanted to know everything, every single scrap of info she could dig up on Davis Mason, stunned by the direction his MC life had taken him but not surprised at all he'd been smart enough to surround himself with true brothers, not sycophants hanging around for the benefit the association could bring to them.

Myron was one of the most intelligent men he had, one she'd not met yet but who excelled in his role, based on rumors alone. A technical wizard who skipped standard schooling, learning as he went from everyone he met, and making up a shit ton of things along the way. All of it genius. Justine would bet good money the app Mason was using had been written entirely by Myron and was likely at least as secure as the most protected federal versions.

"Boss." Myron's tone took on a tenor she associated with forced patience, dragging the *ess* sound out long. "You gonna explain?"

"Mebbe." Mason's wink in Justine's direction was clearly witnessed by the man on the video, because she heard his labored sigh, loud and clear. "Just messin' with ya, My. I'm here for another ten, fifteen max, which means you can let the brothers know just when to expect me. And," his mouth pulled to the side, humor thick in his voice, "I'll even leave the loc tracker on for ya, so you can babysit my little green dot all the way back."

"Don't make me launch a swarm, Mason. You know I will."

"That I do, I surely do. Wouldn't want you to use up any of your banked drone hours just on little ole me." Mason smiled, and under that expression, she saw the bones of their shared ancestry, another instant where she was off-center in an unpleasant way.

Her final memory of their father was a picture of him lying in sprawled repose, across the uneven top of a shatter-legged table, head lolling to the side, the bullet that killed him having left no evidence of agony on his face. Mason had claimed the bodies quickly, release forms no doubt sped on their way with the slide of loaded palm against a greedy one. They'd both been cremated before she'd even known they were dead. With her being an active federal agent, the last thing she'd needed then was her family history on record, and any necessary restrictions were still the case. The gooseflesh was back with a vengeance, rippling up her arms and legs in harsh waves, leaving her shivering in their wake.

Mason's gaze sharpened, and he dropped the jocular act, if act it had been, instead adopting an on-guard posture, shifting to his feet in one smooth movement, his eyes angling through each window and door in turn, before falling back on her face. "What was that? Just now, what was that, Justine?"

She hated him a little as she struggled to her feet, ignoring the helping hand he extended. "Nothing. I'm just tired." Dusting off her palms, she pointed to the phone still in his grip. "Was this the request?"

"Yeah." Tongue tracing along the edges of his teeth, Mason stared at her then blinked, and when his eyes reopened, he was focused on the app. "Myron, need you to initiate a query with the Bastards. I'd go direct to Retro with this, but he's prolly in transit. I want the info ASAP, and I suspect one of his officers would have access to the info I need. You with me?"

"Ya, boss. What's the ask?" Myron's voice had been stripped of all emotion or humor, flat, affectless, and his words to the point.

"Who besides me has been askin' around about Wildman? That's it. Sum total. Got it?" Justine startled at the question, so much more than what they'd rehearsed moments before. Keystrokes sounded, Mason's electronic wizard behind the curtain working his Kansas whirlwind magic. "Me leavin' here depends on the rapidity with which you can locate the info, brother. Make it fast. Justine needs to make her calls and can't with me in proximity."

"Ya, boss." Less direct, Myron sounded distracted. "Retro just dismounted in the yard at IMC Motherhouse. You want him straight on this call, I can make it happen."

"Get him. It's better to get the mainline source anyway." Mason flicked a glance in Justine's direction, a considering expression on his face. "I'm going to stand where all interested parties can have a voice in the call, brother. Hide anything you don't want the lady to see."

"Jesus, Mason." Something rattled across a wooden surface, and then there was an anonymous scraping that could be anything. "Let me just check one thing. Shit, I left the…" Justine ducked her head, trying to hide her smile, before Mason's hand settled on her shoulder with a tiny shake. "Okay, I think we're good. You're a goddamned asshole, boss."

"Yeah, I know." Mason's fingers dug in a little as he adjusted their standing postures closer. "Myron, meet my sister Justine. She's the pretty one in the picture."

"Evening, ma'am." Wiry frame, dark hair in a cute tousle, Myron grinned at her through the video, and if she hadn't heard his rushing around to hide whatever it was he thought might be in jeopardy by her very viewing, she wouldn't have believed he'd been doing anything other than sitting in front of a computer. "Pleased to meet you."

"I've heard good things about you, Myron." Justine inclined her head slightly, gaze never leaving the screen as she mapped every inch of what she could see. The playground scene out the back window told her it wasn't the clubhouse, which meant Mason had reached out to him at home. "Thanks for taking Mason's call. I'm sorry he interrupted family time."

"As if I had a choice." He bent to put an elbow on the desk, propping his chin in his palm. "We're waiting on confirmation Retro's gotten private; then I can patch him in." She watched his eyes move side to side and knew he was cataloging the likenesses she and Mason shared. "She's definitely the pretty one."

"I know." Mason's arm tightened around her shoulders, and she let herself sag into his embrace a little. "Tough as nails. You hear she took down the guy here all by herself?"

"I heard something along those lines." Justine wasn't surprised the rumor mill already had hold of the story, but the idea of it getting as far as Fort Wayne, Indiana, was startling. "Finger always on the pulse, ma'am."

"Justine, please. You're not my subordinate, and I don't even allow them to call me ma'am." She gave him a smile she hoped edged into gracious. "Justine will do me fine."

Myron opened his mouth, then clamped it shut as he leaned forwards, hands disappearing somewhere underneath the camera as the clicking of his keyboard sounded again. "Okay, he's ready now. Give me half a minute—" His bottom lip rolled between his teeth, and he bit down. "—and he's here."

Retro's camera view slid in from the side, like a fancy special effect. He was in front of a blamelessly white wall, nothing in sight other than him. He stared at the screen in front of him and pursed his lips before smiling broadly, showing off his white, straight teeth. "Mason, brother. Thought we were lackin' a wad of hot wind at our backs. You hangin' out for a reason, man?" His gaze settled a little to the right, where Justine supposed her image was projected. "Justine LaPorte, well met, lady. Glad to see you're in such good company still."

She let the tiny dig about her job pass without comment. "Retro, good to see you."

"Brother, got an ask. You up for it? In a place where you can take it and respond as you need?" That would be Mason's only demand—that no one profit from what would cost him either money or favors.

"Mudd's behind the camera, as you might expect. We're alone and in a room I did not know the IMC had in their Motherhouse. Love it when I learn me somethin' new every single day." Retro made a show of looking around whatever room they were in.

She could only assume it was a tech-blocking isolation room, where the elite of the club could have truly private conversations without the worry of listeners-in, whether they were local club competition or the legal branches of the local, state, or national governments.

"Makes me homesick in a kind of way." He pretended to wipe a tear. "Gotta get rollin' soon, hie my own ass home. You already know why." The jovial lines of his features morphed, turning into a hardened version of the same face, but this a formidable man, not approachable as he normally appeared. "I don't mind layin' out a little here, because we may be able to do a tit-for-tat, depending on the ask." His eyes danced to the side again, so she knew he was looking at her. "Russian mafia in my goddamned backyard, playin' hopscotch with my goddamned kids. They're about to go to war with the Mexicans, and we're in the fuckin' middle, you get me?" Justine tried her best to hold onto her version of the family Morgan-face, a pitch-perfect deflection of any information leakage. She failed, and knew it when his chin came up, lips clamped tight as he cut his words off abruptly. "I see this is not news to you."

"It is not." She swallowed and coughed, ribs hurting not only from the beatings she'd endured but with however her body had been flung around while she was unconscious. She was also suddenly aware that although her legs were out of view, she would appear vulnerable, nearly naked from the waist down. The image in the video showed a disheveled woman, hair a rat's nest on her head, streaks of dirt across her cheek and chin. *Jesus.* Straightening, she lifted her chin as she elaborated, "I may have information you would want."

"Tell me what you need then, woman." His voice had dropped to a growl, and she knew it was because what was a growing issue along the coast had rocketed to the top of his displeasure list by involving his family. Retro was known by all to be a straight shooter, keeping his end of any bargain while still able to command men who would kill for him, and thus able to back up a demand of bargain-keeping from those he did business with. For him to be so visibly upset meant something, and the tension of Mason's arm across her upper back said his friend's discomfort was hard to see.

"I want—"

"We want to know who other than me has been askin' about Wildman." Mason's finger darted down to her side, where he gave her a hard pinch, telling her without words that him overriding her direct ask wasn't something he'd budge about.

"I find myself interested in what the lady would have asked on her own." Retro flicked his hair over one shoulder, intuitive gaze intent on the screen. "I was told it was an RWMC ask, which I'll entertain all day long. This though, is cloudy, given who signs her paychecks."

"You were just fuckin' willin' to barter with her about intel." Mason's barked response was loud, his body nearly vibrating with tension at her side.

"Rethinkin' that." Retro shrugged fluidly, a toned-back grin crossing and dropping from his lips. "My prerogative."

"Goddamn it, Retro. That's not how this is supposed to go."

"Supposed to go and actually goes. Those can be each end of the satisfaction spectrum, my friend." Mason cleared his throat noisily at Retro's words. "Brother," Retro amended, with a tiny, royal nod. "I'd like to hear the ask directly from Justine LaPorte, if I may. Mason, you don't have a marker large enough to offer for this. Not right now, man. Give me a minute to sort this out, and I suspect you'll be happy as a lamb in clover."

"I understand there has been more than one request for information on Wildman. One was Mason, when he heard I'd picked someone—Wildman—as a partner." Justine leaned closer. "Who else was asking about him?"

"Now, that wasn't so hard, was it?" Retro leaned back, face angled up as he addressed the ceiling of the room where he stood. "Let me think a minute."

"Goddammit, Retro."

"Oh, hush, you. Man's gotta find his humor where he can." Retro dropped his chin and stared into the camera. "This I know to be true. Three requests for information came my way. Two have been responded to, one to you, Mason, and one to Twisted, for reasons of his own that if you put your mind to what's happened in the IMC lately, you'll fully understand. The third was a tangled request, relayed just before we jumped on this video call. Silent Deaths offered a hell of a marker for info on Wildman and the woman in his bed." He leveled a finger at the camera, thumb cocked back like a gun's hammer. *What the hell?* "That woman would be you, pretty lady. So now the question is what do I do with that final request? Smoke and his boys are friendly with IMC, from what I understand. Why would they be interested in a man who may become a key officer, stepping up from the role he fills now? More to the point, what the hell would it matter to them who he's fuckin'?" He dipped a nod at the camera, uncocking his thumb as he lowered his hand. "No offense intended."

"None taken." Justine dropped her gaze as she ran over the information he'd provided. Silent Deaths were known to have solid ties down to Mexico, well beyond the Machos MC. *Their request could be in response to my recent trade-interrupting activities. Or it could be about Wildman.* Either way, it wasn't something she could afford to ignore. Justine realized she was staring at the floor again, seemingly for the hundredth time today. At least they were in the front room, and she didn't have to see her own vomit again. "I'm not on that task force any longer. Took myself off via request months ago. I'm purely trafficking, not on anything RICO-tinged. Anything to do with any outlaw clubs is strictly need-to-know in the bureau, and I'm no longer on that list. I have no idea why they'd be interested in me. Weren't they a club Tucker sought refuge with after he killed that little Texas girl?" In a split-second decision, she decided to downplay her knowledge of the SDMC. *All the better to get info with, my dear.*

"Essa? I didn't hear he'd reached out to Silent Deaths, but shit happened back on Watcher's patch of dirt before we brought the Southern Soldiers into the fold." Myron's interjection was sudden, and Justine half expected Mason to slap him down, but all her brother did was grunt in response. "I mean, we had Duck out there, but it all belonged to the Soldiers."

"They had old ties to the Machos, right?" Justine wracked her brain for any additional information she felt safe sharing. "Diamante was key back when. I don't know about now." That tinged on private pain, but she ignored the sting.

"Diamante is impotent." Mason shrugged, then pulled her close again. "Machos are a different crew now. They're allies."

"I would have called Silent Deaths allies too, boss. But they're askin' after your sister." Myron shook his head. "Don't seem too ally-ish to me."

"If I could interject." Retro swept a hand across the bottom of his face. "Cartel is what will help us piece this together. SDMC's ask will be sidelined, graciously, as we always do things. I'm heading home. I don't think they knew it was you, lady, but I wouldn't lower my guard for any reason. Way things looked to me today is you and Wild have set stones rolling. It'll be up to us to steer them downhill, so they avoid the things we want to keep and burst apart the things we want to destroy. We just need to know what and who falls into each of those categories."

"I agree, cartel is key to every one of these things. From Wildman's issues in Florida to the renewed VWMC presence in Louisiana. They'd certainly have contacts in SDMC, and the ask could be a pass-along, not direct from Smoke at all." Mason shot a glance at Justine as he finished speaking, and she lifted a brow to let him know she'd caught the reference. *We'll be revisiting that sometime soon, promise, brother mine.*

"I'll check into the veracity of that first thing when I get home. Call to clarify or some shit." Retro grinned. "I'll think of somethin'."

"You always do, brother." Mason's wide smile was visible in the video, and Justine felt the rush of affection he held for these two men. "My, no drones needed, brother. I'll roll in less than five."

"Promised to leave the loc on, boss. Justine, you heard him, right?"

"I did," she agreed, and Myron's grin lit up the screen. "Thank you, both of you." She twisted to look up at Mason. "All of you."

It was twenty minutes later, not less than five, when Justine was watching the taillight on Mason's motorcycle fade to dimness within the pine forest surrounding the shack, which she now knew had been a one-time meth-cooking spot.

Lovely. She tried not to think about all the corrosive and dangerous compounds and residues associated with the process, even as she balanced on one bare foot on the rough boards.

She'd counted to sixty twenty times and was launching into another round when there was movement at the edge of the forest. Something darker than the darkness behind it, a slinking silhouette low to the ground. *Fuck it.*

The number was at the end of her fingertips, branded into the front of her brain with training methods she wouldn't wish on someone she disliked, but they'd been effective. The number she'd learned nearly eight years ago and never before used still came easily to her.

Justine scarcely had time to suck in a breath before the call connected, middle of the first ring, no verbal answer.

Undeterred, she gave the phrase as practiced, not stumbling over the most idiotic aspects of it. "Rascal passes on their well wishes, but the press release is wrong."

"Rascal" was her, the call name assigned by her superior, who then—and probably more especially now—believed her a pain in his ass. "Well wishes" paired with "passes on" meant she was unharmed and alone, not held under duress. If she'd made the call at gunpoint, she would have said "designated a pinch hitter," something equally obtuse-sounding that was certain to make a kidnapper believe it was a token for a message. It would have been up to her to ensure they believed it would get them what they wanted. "Press release" stood in for pickup needed, and the use of a word such as "wrong" added the urgency of ASAP.

The line clicked, and she waited, gaze sweeping the edges of the clearing, searching for more of whatever had made the shadow moments ago. Another click, and she was treated to a voice steady as steel. "We've got you, Justine. Boots on the ground in less than fifteen. Can you...are you able to assist your rescue?"

"I am" was all she returned as she swallowed hard, not wanting Greg Anderson to hear a break in her voice if she tried to elaborate.

"Good." Then he gave her one of the biggest compliments he'd ever paid. A simple, "Talk soon," then the line disconnected.

Thumbing the volume buttons kept the phone awake and alight enough to see the room around her dimly, enough to keep her nerves at bay. She'd reached twelve iterations of sixty when she spotted the helo coming in low and fast, spotlights sweeping the trees ahead of the chopper until they landed on the shack, the bird banking in a quick circle before the pilot determined there was not enough room to land. They hovered low, scarcely twenty feet off the ground, the backwash from the rotors sending wavelets of sand across the clearing. Three dark bodies separated from the helicopter, dropping quickly to the ground as she thumbed the flashlight on the phone, turning the light on her own face as a willing target.

"SAC LaPorte?" Justine nodded at the faceless figure, the dark mask covering everything not shielded by the IR goggles the man wore. "I'm Michaels, the team's out of NAS JRB New Orleans, and we're here to take you home." He lifted his hand, and she placed the phone in it. The mask covering his mouth moved, and she could swear he was grinning as he pocketed the phone and held his hand out again. *Stupid.* She placed her hand in his, and he stooped as he tugged her towards him, swooping her legs up with one arm while the other circled her back. "Normally I'd do a fireman's haul, but—due respect, you're awake and, well, kind of exposed." She could hear squeaks from near his throat and kept her own mouth closed, assuming he had a coms device. "Ma'am, we'll have you back to Baton Rouge in just a few minutes. There's a blanket in the chopper with your name on it, right next to a bottle of water. You doing okay, ma'am?" Justine nodded again, jostled as he jogged back to the helicopter. "Mano, get me a cradle, yeah? Roger. Ma'am, you doing okay? You with me?"

"Yes, I'm good." Justine had to force the lie out between clenched teeth. Her adrenaline was spiking, no longer receding, and her jaw wanted to chatter, but giving into the physical impulse would reveal how fragile she felt.

"You will be, SAC LaPorte. We got a jacket on you when we got the call. Mucho respect, ma'am." He curled his body around her, protecting Justine from the worst of the downdrafts until he stood directly underneath the belly of the craft. Justine looked up in time to see another figure appear out of the darkness. He held up his arm and made a complicated series of gestures, to which Michaels responded, "Roger." A third figure came into focus against the darkness just over Michaels' shoulder, reaching up to guide a basket into place in front of Justine. Michaels deposited her into the cramped space, then climbed on with her, feet balancing on the side rails. "Hold on, SAC LaPorte. Short trip."

Inside the helo, she kept to the side seat they'd placed her in, the promised blanket and bottle of water appearing only an instant after she sat. The other two men launched themselves in through the side door of the helicopter, and she had to wonder if this was less than their training exercises demanded. The noise fell to tolerable levels when the door was closed and latched into place. Michaels had a quick exchange with the pilots, leaning into their space on one elbow. He pushed his mask up, leaving it bunched in a roll on his forehead, where it revealed strong features, burned dark by the Louisiana sun. Head tipped to the side as he listened, he nodded, then gave the pilots a thumbs-up, rolling to his feet. Hands wrapped in the rope mesh overhead, he swayed with the movement of the aircraft, his gaze fixed on Justine.

One of the other men crouched at her side, holding out another bottle of water. She hadn't realized she'd finished the first already, and took the second from him with a shaky, "Thank you."

"Our pleasure, ma'am." His words carried a foreign cadence, and she steeled herself from shrinking away; he sounded so much like the upper echelon of the crew that had held her and the other women.

"Brownstone." Lips trembling, she gave the warning call and watched as Michaels stiffened, growing still. "I have an urgent message. Brownstone."

"I'll hear the message, ma'am." Michaels took the seat across from her, leaning close, elbows on his knees.

She gave him the location of the shipping yard and information about the container where more than a dozen women had been held. These were not her women, the clutch of chicks she'd protected, but another cargo load that had come in after the initial raid and rescue, Myron finding out about them only after everyone had been dispatched to save Justine. The women who had been with her had each been deposited within feet of their homes, nothing more than a request to keep quiet about the club, no threats and no urgent demands, just a low warning that it wouldn't do Justine any favors to say anything about IMC. Sparse hope, but unless the women found each other and had a conference, it was unlikely anyone other than an idly curious family member would ever question the veracity of their miraculous escape.

The women the military would rescue would talk a vague story about a woman resembling Justine, and her clothing had been dropped into the mix of the offal at the bottom of the container. She'd listened to Mason and Myron concocting the story within a few sentences after Retro had dropped from their call, caught half the conversation as Mason chatted with Twisted, and Justine had found herself listening to the background, hoping she'd catch Wildman's voice somehow, somewhere.

Justine capped the bottle of water and dropped it to her lap, elbows to her knees as she bent forwards, fingers thrusting through her hair, coming up against each painful point of bruising. Heels of her hands against the bony sockets of her eyes, she rocked back and forth, willing the flight to be over.

No matter what came next, it couldn't be worse than having to watch Wildman ride away, taking a part of her with him.

***

Justine

Outside the trailer was war. There were loud shouts and gunshots, followed by cries of pain, grunts driven from lungs by powerful blows. Inside the trailer was chaos, and Justine did her best to keep the women calm, telling them what she'd seen through the vent. "We don't know who it is," she hissed, using the dim light that seeped in around the ill-sealing rear doors to catch every gaze she could. "Until we know, we stay quiet."

She'd been the final acquisition for the shipment. That's how the men had talked about the humans they held penned inside a metal box, which did nothing to retain heat after the sun went down. Chattel, possessions where ownership could be transferred as easily as a transactional phone call. Goods provided to men with an appetite for pain and fighting, and given how well and long she'd brawled with his men, the leader had boasted how much Justine would bring for his pockets.

At least in the two days she'd been imprisoned, she'd been able to keep the men from raping the captives. What happened before had been spoken of in whispers and tears, and the women had all looked at her with awe when she negotiated and bartered for a halt to the physical abuse. It had cost her, of course—that's the way these things went—but a few blows were a small price for the relief she'd seen on their faces.

Things quietened outside as Justine listened intently, shushing the women again when one would have called out. A sound at the doors had her cocking her head, trying to infer what was happening through scant clues. The door swung open, and an instant later, a man appeared as if by magic, not there and then there, and he was huge, blocking out the light with his body. Hands bloody, he had a tear along one arm of his shirt, as if a blade had come too close for comfort.

He took a step inside, and Justine marshaled every ounce of courage. Without a word to the women behind her, she stepped forwards and held out her arms, creating a barrier with her body. Fingers clutched at her shirt from behind, and she shook them off, taking another step and another. The man's gaze danced around the trailer, and she watched him catalog every detail before he locked on her.

Trembling now, because he was so much larger up close, she hoped if she could distract him enough, the women could escape. I've got to make myself vulnerable. Justine's arms shook with the strain, but she settled to her knees in front of him.

He lifted her to her feet and kissed her, lips soft and warm against hers.

No, that's not right.

"Jesus, Justine, you make me insane."

No, how could he know my name?

His fingers touched her gently, reverently.

No…

Justine jerked sideways, startled when her shoulder thudded against a wall. Heart racing, she blinked, moonlit aspects of her bedroom coming into focus. Hand flat against her chest, she settled back down in the bed, feet kicking off the constricting covers.

Even her dreams romanticized every moment they'd had together.

Once released by her superiors on her own recognizance, she had made her first stop a cut-rate tech shop where she'd bought several disposable phones. After the multiple days of debriefing, she'd forced herself to finish the trip home, had taken a long-overdue hot shower, and then gorged on Thai takeout before finally allowing herself a phone call.

Given who she was and what had gone down, only an approach through his president would do. If she'd tried to go direct to Wildman, he'd have taken her call, but it would have cost him. Even if he might have readily paid it, she hated the idea of him paying for her failure to follow protocol.

Her intent had been to connect directly with Twisted. She'd tried, truly, circling and beating herself against the protective wall surrounding anything to do with the national president of the IMC. Dropped calls, missed connections, and outright dismissal had met her every effort, until she'd passed the last door without it opening for her.

Next had come a call she hadn't wanted to make, but to get to Wildman the right way—Justine found herself willing to do nearly anything.

"Davy." She greeted her brother with a smile on her face, hoping he'd hear it in her tone.

"Justine, how are you?" The slightly aloof caution in his voice gave her pause.

"I'm good. How's Willa and the kids?" His sigh followed by silence was unnerving. "And you, of course, how are you doing since I saw you last?"

"Why'd you call? You never call just to check in, so if you're wondering how I know somethin's amiss, that's your fuckin' clue right there." She let the guilty silence hang between them. "My answer to the question you aren't asking is no. You don't really want this, Justine. IMC is no half-ass club, and you've stayed the course so far in keeping a distance from anything in the life. Not sure you want to break that streak for a man."

"Except you." She closed her eyes. *"I wouldn't change anything about getting to know you and your family, and you're deep in the life."*

"Getting to know, while keeping at arm's length." The deep scoff he made burned, because what he said was true. *"Justine, you don't owe Wildman anything. You don't owe IMC anything. Those debts only exist in your mind."*

"Owing him isn't why I want a chance to talk to him. Davy, that's all I'm asking for—a chance to meet with him and have a conversation." Justine's breath caught in her throat, and she had to push to get the words out. *"I just want a chance."*

That silence fell between them again, heavy and long, and filled with something that tasted like regret. He's done all the heavy lifting for what we've built so far, *she realized, and anger at herself burned red in her cheeks. She was glad he couldn't see her right now, because he'd ask and ask, never letting go of whatever it was making her behave this way.*

"I'll make a call." Short, brusque, his words chopped through the thick quiet. *"This number good?"*

"Yeah. Yes, I mean. It's a disposable phone I picked up for cash yesterday." The sound he made before disconnecting sounded suspiciously like surprise, and she grinned at the idea she'd been able to shock him a little.

The phone on the nightstand rang, and she glanced at the screen as she swiped to answer. Louisiana area code. *Hopefully this bodes well for me.*

"Hello?"

"Woman, what the fuck you thinkin'? You angled for a call, and I blocked your shit. I do not need some Fed thinkin' they can just chat me up willy-nilly. You gotta work for this shit. Yet here we are, talkin' at some godawful time in the morning because I was the recipient of a message and phone call from Retro. You just tap into the man's network and buzz him until he couldn't deal anymore, or what?"

Justine took a second to unpack Twisted's words, dialing in on the crux of the problem. "He at least took my call to hear my ask. Didn't try to decide what Wildman wanted without even a conversation."

"Oh, bitch, you think you can heavy-hand me into regretting blockin' your ass? Ain't gonna work. I've shredded better bitches than you, because you're in a fuckin' phase and lookin' to walk on the wild side for maybe the first time in your life, and my man don't got time for something that's gonna fuck up his head." Laughter rang through the line, hard and angry. "He ain't never gonna know about this convo, just so you understand where I'm comin' from."

The call disconnected, and she stared down at the silent device in her hand. *Shit.*

If his president didn't want her in Wildman's life, Justine knew she had zero chance at anything, much less seeing where this consuming desire could take them.

Then the phone vibrated, and she looked to see a video call was incoming.

With a heavy breath, she accepted, shocked to see two men on the call. Twisted and Retro.

This could be good. Licking her lips, she nodded at the camera. *Or not, but I won't know if I don't ask.* "I thought you were done talking to me, Twisted?"

Twisted made a rude sound far back in his throat. "Retro, you're an asshole." He adjusted so he faced the camera directly. "Now that we've an impartial audience, woman, tell me what the fuck you think you want to talk to Wild about?"

His question wasn't unkind. No, the inquiry was entirely reasonable and one she'd prepared for. But right now, with a cold phone held tightly in both hands, tiny screen able to give her his irritation and little else, Justine couldn't feed Twisted the answer she'd rehearsed. It was true, by the plainest definition of the word, but telling this man she wanted to thank Wildman was like saying she wanted the barest of sips when everything inside her wanted to upend the hose and bathe in the water.

She made a split-second decision, going with what felt right.

"I need him to know what he got from me was real. Wasn't the job, wasn't relief, wasn't misplaced gratitude for a rescue. I'd like to tell him he matters. A chance to connect without shit raining down from the sky around us. I need to make him understand that he matters to me."

Silence on the line for the longest time matched the seemingly frozen video, and she waited, breaths coming shallow as her lungs seized up from the terror that held her in its grip. Never had she wanted anything this badly.

In a direct change from his previous tone, responding in a voice gone soft and soothing, Twisted showed that he understood what she felt was at risk. "You got the time to put it on the line like that, I'll make it happen." He lifted his chin, gaze boring directly into the camera. "Shit's always swirling nearby, and your job makes it even chancier for him to reach across such a divide. You gonna have his back when Uncle Sam calls you to task? You ready for this, gal?"

"You know who I am?" He made a sound she took for a yes, and she laughed without amusement, knowing the sound was far from pleasant. "Then trust me when I say I was born ready."

"Then you've got six days to prepare. Be at the Hammond clubhouse, seven o'clock on the dot. You're late, you get a locked fuckin' door, no matter how hard you pound against that bitch. Be there, or—" Twisted shrugged. "Not. Don't matter to me."

"I'll be there."

"If we could be done now?" Retro's drawl broke the tension, and Justine flashed a smile she didn't feel. "Shut-eye is my friend right now, so I'll be obliged if neither of you called me again until sometime after noon, give or take a fast minute."

"Fuck you." Twisted thrust a hand towards the camera, the back of his middle finger filling his screen. Then it went black, and Retro's window shifted to take up the space.

"You got what you wanted, Justine." Top of his head tipping to the side, Retro let her see the concern in his expression. "Hope it shakes out how you want it in the end." Without a goodbye, Retro disconnected, and she was left staring at the blank screen of her phone.

"Me too, Retro." She shook her head, placing the phone back on the nightstand as she eased back underneath the covers. "Me too."

***

Justine

Seated in her car, she stared at the building in front of her. The wide windows gave her a glimpse into the world the home's residents occupied, made to look like any living room in an effort to help keep them engaged and calm.

Her mother was particularly attached to a low armchair near the window, and Justine could make out a figure seated there now. With a hard push of air outwards, she opened the car door and stepped out, stretching her back until ligaments popped in a satisfying way.

Most of the bruises had faded in the time since she'd been with Wildman. All of the ones he'd inflicted were gone, and she'd mourned each of his marks as they disappeared. The only major bruising was along one flank, remnants from a fall during a coerced fight with one of the cartel guards.

Is it too much to hope he'll want to do that again?

It was time to focus, and she pushed the thoughts away, walking towards the building. Justine held the fob attached to her keys next to a reader beside the door, pulling on the handle when the locking mechanism clicked.

The home had great security for the residents, and Justine had long come to a sense of thankfulness that her father had cared for his women enough to create this oasis for them. She was under no illusions it had been selfless, because she wasn't an idiot. But he could have easily killed them instead, and sinking so much money into creating a facility like this redeemed his motives in her mind.

Turning to the window, she smiled when her mother's gaze was already locked on her, awareness in the pleased expression on her face. It didn't happen often, so Justine took it as a blessing when it did.

"Mom, how are you?" Bending close, Justine brushed a kiss across her mom's cheek, smiling when she received one in return. "Lookin' good, lady."

"I'm feeling good today, sweetheart."

Pulling back, Justine stared into Lori LaPorte's face, taking in the beauty and grace her mother had always embodied. *One thing Daddy always liked was pretty women.* "That's awesome. Do you have time for a chat?"

"Oh, honey, I don't know." Her mom pulled a face, then laughed. "I've got a hot date with a Parcheesi board later, but I could squeeze you in now."

That set the tone for much of the afternoon, their easy banter frequently interrupted by laughter as the minutes ticked past.

"Now that you're comfortable." Her mom circled Justine's waist with an arm and pulled her sideways. Justine leaned her head against her mom's shoulder and breathed in her scent. The same perfume as always—a light vanilla and citrus. The smell of safety and love. "Tell me what's goin' on, baby girl."

Justine contemplated lying for half a second, until her mother's fingers and thumb found her side in a hard pinch. "Oww, stop it. I'll tell you. I'll tell you."

"I'm here, baby girl." The arm around her waist tightened briefly, then relaxed.

"I met someone." Her mother hummed far back in her throat but didn't speak. "Oh, Momma, he's perfect for me. Kind and giving, protective, and so much of what's him matches what's me, you know?"

"So what's the problem? Because sure as I'm sitting here, there's a problem, or you wouldn't have hesitation in your voice."

"He's in the life."

"So?" Her mother's instant response surprised Justine, and she pulled away to look into her face. "Don't pull that with me, baby girl. What does it matter if he's in the life?"

"You always told me you didn't want that for me." Justine shook her head. "Hell, I'm not sure I want that for me."

"Mouth, pretty girl." Her mom's gaze tracked across Justine's face, brows pulling slightly together. "What does it matter?" she asked again, with a deepening of her frown. "In the life, not in the life, it doesn't. All that matters is if he's a good man. Is he?"

"He is." Firming her quivering lips, she tried to give her words as much oomph as possible, needing her mom to understand. "So good, Momma. Good to me."

"Then why aren't you with him?" Her mom leaned sideways in the chair, putting more distance between them. "Why are you here chatting up an old woman when you could be building something with him?"

"He's in Louisiana." Blinking tears away, she laid her hand on top of her mother's, pleased when her mom's wrist rotated, strong fingers clasping to hers. "And I'm here."

"That's easily remedied, baby girl. If you want this with him, then you'll have to bend. Lord knows I bent with your father, time and again." Fingers gave her hand a strong squeeze. "And I don't regret a single minute. I love him."

Justine wavered but decided to ignore the fact her mother spoke in present tense. "I know you do, Momma. He's easy to love."

"No, baby girl, he is not." Her mom's laughter was surprising, and Justine leaned closer. "Doubt there's ever been a man harder to love. With everything that happened, it would be easier for me to hate him." Her mom's gaze swept the room, landing on the face of her best friend: Crystal Dawn Dixon, Mason's mother. "But he brought me so much beauty. Would go out of his way to find it for me and place it in my hands. Like you, my baby girl. Out of everything, there's nothing I'd change."

"I love you, Momma." Justine smiled when her mother's other hand cupped her jaw, holding her gaze.

"And I love you too, baby girl." Her mom patted her cheek, hard enough to sting. With a grin, she soothed the flesh with a brush of her fingertips. "Now get your head out of your ass and go find and claim your man."

Chapter Fourteen
Wildman

A herd of kids ran past him headed towards the kitchen, and Wildman gave a hip twist to avoid running smack-dab into at least two of the little cretins. Multicolored lights were strung off every available surface, and a Halloween-themed decorated tree stood in the farthest corner, donated presents already piled high underneath. Even if out of season, the effect was blindingly festive, something he would normally enjoy.

Today was the club's annual friends and family fundraiser blowout, and the excitement of being allowed inside the clubhouse still hadn't worn off the smallest IMC family members. "Fuckin' kids." He chuckled, not upset in the least to have the clubhouse full of the next generation of IMC. Sure, theirs was a club that had grown by absorbing members—including him—from organizations they'd taken over, but the core of their club was second and, in some cases, third generation, with patches handed down through families.

I didn't do so bad for myself. After being dealt a shitty hand so many years ago, he'd managed to find a good home, finally. He untucked a beer from under his arm and offered it to Twisted, handing a second to Po'Boy and finally popping the top on his own. They looked at each other and laughed softly, musical tones low, Po'Boy smirking a little. Wildman shook his head with a grin and gave his expected addition to their conversation, as they knew he would, this tradition having been in play for a while now. "Quack, quack."

"Heard me a tale," Po'Boy said, after he'd taken a long drink and leaned back in his chair. His gaze was trained on an IMC member by the bar, watching the man blow a stream of sweet smoke towards the ceiling.

"Do tell. What story is that?" Wildman asked as he reclaimed his seat, shooing Wrench's feet off it. The new CoBos president was an honored guest, seeing as he was not only a favored friend of Twisted's old lady, Penny, but was also in a poly relationship with Po'Boy. *So many fuckin' changes*. Not all bad. He scowled at the man when he threatened to put his feet in Wildman's lap, holding the expression even when Wrench broke up laughing. *Not all good, either*. "Fucker."

"Man, you were right. He's in a *piss*-poor mood." Wrench shook his finger at Wildman. "You need to get you a better attitude goin', man. It's a par-tay. Prezzies for the kiddies come Christmas."

"Yup," he drawled, tipping up the can for a drink. If they knew just how bad his attitude was, they'd have chased him out of the house before now. He forced a smile as the herd of kids ran past again.

It had been a long set of days since he'd ridden away from a run-down shack on the edge of a bayou outside of Sun. Well beyond the IMC normal haunts, the old meth cook house was hidden in CoBos territory, and it was only due to Po'Boy's history with informants in the region they'd known of it at all.

They'd ridden out arrow true to where Po'Boy had said she'd be, unexpected hostage to an old IMC war with a drug dealer and manufacturer, pure bad luck she'd been the one taken. Ten men had peeled off the column to deal with the lookout, the rest of them riding straight to the cook shack. Seeing the man in the window had curdled his stomach, but when Justine appeared like a ghost behind that fucker, his blood had run like ice. By the time the man went down—and it was only later he'd learned how she'd done it, proud as fuck of her taking her own out on the asshole—Wildman had been crouched beside her, finally believing in luck. The relief at holding her and knowing she was safe had been bolstered by the understanding that she was strong and wily, and far too smart for her own good.

Too good for the likes of me.

Then had come the moment he had known was coming at the end of the ride. They'd talked about it, talked it to death, and the outcome was set in stone before they rolled off the IMC lot.

Get there, deal with whatever threats there were, ensure her well-being, provide her a method of rescue, and leave.

The herd was back, kids chattering loudly and clattering up and down the stairs. It was so noisy in the room he could see Po'Boy's lips move but couldn't make out the words. Wildman leaned close and shouted, "What?"

"Turn around."

***

Justine

For the second time in her life, Justine stood in the middle of the IMC clubhouse main room. This time it was with cold, clammy hands clasped at her waist, nervously waiting for Wildman to turn and look at her.

Her debriefing had taken so much longer than it should have, but she'd understood. The last her staff had known, she'd been investigating the disappearance of two women in the panhandle of Florida in conjunction with reports of increased activity by a Mexican drug family. Only after Mason had alerted Anderson had she become one of the missing—car left parked in her own garage, identification and service weapon still in the bedside safe at her home in Adken. When she'd called for rescue, hundreds of miles away from home, not only had she been beaten badly, she'd borne Wildman's marks on her body, too.

"Ma'am, we need to catalog your injuries." The little duty nurse gulped at Justine's glare, the clipboard in her hands trembling enough to set the single sheet of paper fluttering, outline of a female body moving as if alive. "It's SOP, ma'am."

Justine nodded, cleared her throat, and stepped to the center of the sheet spread across the floor. "I wasn't raped. I'll identify the bruises caused by the kidnappers." The nurse made a sound, crouched near Justine's feet, looking up at her body. "Just point to something." She did, indicating an overlapping set of teeth marks high on the inside of Justine's thigh. "Consensual. Next." The girl shifted to the side and indicated a deep bruise along her hip, dark purple and red, sore, and still hot, days after being inflicted. "Bad guys."

Through the hours of questions—filled with curious sideways glances, all their whispered behind-the-hand conversations hovering over the charts and folders spread out on desks, information she wasn't allowed to see, not until she'd been cleared in Anderson's mind—all she could think about was Wildman. She knew the surface information, such as his government name, but that wasn't who he was. That man had been fed to the flame of anger and betrayal years ago, and Wildman was who had risen like a phoenix from the ashes.

She also hadn't been able to escape him, even in her dreams, and Justine shivered at the memories, glancing around the room again. It wouldn't do to get caught up in her own mind here, not now, surrounded by so many strangers.

I'm still convinced it was better to do it this way.

Except this moment, this spectacle, wasn't what she'd expected.

Justine's eyes cut side to side, and she worked hard to suppress a snort of amusement.

About the furthest thing from private she could imagine was this clubhouse during a massive fundraising party. And with Twisted's reputation for being a canny plotter, she suspected everything about the move was purposeful. He'd played first cool and eventually supportive on their video call, while completely playing her in the process.

Wildman's shoulders heaved with each heavy breath, visible tension running through his muscles. He shook his head once, then leaned forwards towards the man with the wild blond hair, and the vibration of whatever he'd said rumbled through the air.

Then Wildman turned, and she was lost.

His hot gaze ran down and then up her body, finally landing and staying on her face, and she offered him a trembling smile as she covered the small distance between them.

Any bravado that had bolstered her through those intervening days had fled the moment she drove onto the lot with her car and saw the hundred or more motorcycles parked in orderly rows. Fear had taken its place as she had been ushered inside, hard stares turned her way, the murmurs of "Fed" and "Rebels" and the hated "Justice Morgan" following every step. Now, as she finally stood in front of Wildman, the controlled lack of expression on his face drove out fear and ushered in despair.

Her being here was not something he wanted. *I didn't listen*. She should have. But, even with three men she trusted and respected telling her the plan was a bad one, she'd persisted, and now she'd somehow wrecked any chance she could have had at what he'd offered.

God.

Blasted to pieces any chances to be with *him*. Again, for a moment or a lifetime.

Just… gone.

Justine lifted her chin and deliberately squared her shoulders as she stuck out her hand. Her father hadn't raised a quitter. *In for a penny.* "I wanted to introduce myself properly."

He ignored her gesture, his head gradually tipping to one side. That was the only encouragement she got. He proved himself a master at holding his silence and maintained the same calm composure, each deep breath slipping in and out slowly. He gave every indication he could do this all day long. *Okay then.* She let her hand fall to her side.

"I'm Justine LaPorte—"

He cut her off, words brusque as he clipped out, "I know who the fuck you are. You fuckin' know that too."

"I work for the—"

"Shut up." He shook his head as she stared at him, her legs beginning to tremble. *If he'd only let me speak.* "Jesus fucking Christ on a goddamned stick. Next thing you're going to tell me you're"—he made air quotes around his next words—"thankful we rescued you." His upper lip lifted in a snarl. "Grateful for the help, or some shit." He bent at the waist, shoving his face right up next to hers, and Justine fought the instinct to back away. "You wanted this, tonight, with all these goddamned folks watchin' everything? You wanted to do whatever this fucking thing is *here*? With my brothers and family standin' by to witness everythin'?"

She shook her head and closed her eyes. The darkness didn't help, and she was unmoored, helpless to direct anything the way she'd wanted it to go.

"Goddammit." He huffed out an irritated sigh, heat from his breath a gentle caress against her cheek. "What'd you want? Justine, what did you fuckin' want from me?"

Swallowing hard, she steadied her voice and, with her eyes still closed, whispered, "To talk to you." She paused, then added, "In private."

"Fucking shit. People always getting up in my goddamned shit all the motherfucking goddamned time." His hand closed over hers with a viselike grip, and her eyes flew open as he whirled, yanking her along. He stomped through the crowd, broad shoulders moving like a wall ahead of her, the weight of his glare parting the people like a hot knife through butter. He stopped short, and she ran into his back as he allowed a gaggle of kids to run past, then jerked at her hand again, pulling her along in his wake. Up the stairs, which rattled loudly with every angry stomp, and then she was once again inside his room.

Wildman used his grip on her hand to whirl her around, then dropped it as if her skin burned him. "Strip," he ordered, backing up a step. His hands lifted his shirt off, sending the discarded piece of clothing sailing across the room in a flutter of fabric. "Goddamned strip."

"I...uh..." She didn't get more than those sounds out of her mouth before he was crowding into her space, shoulders blocking out the room. *I don't understand.*

His head dipped, and muscles in his jaw jumped and quivered with the force of his words. "I said *strip.*"

"I'm not wearing a wire." She offered the only thing that made sense, a possibility that hadn't even occurred to her until this instant, how he might see her visit as an attempt to damage the people and organization he was part of, those he called family. "Promise." She lifted her shirt and turned all the way around. "It's just me."

His hand was on her throat, and he gripped tight then lifted, bringing her to her toes as he slammed her back against the wall. "That's what you think of me?"

Confused, she shook her head, lungs working overtime to pull in air against the constriction around her neck. "No," she gasped, and he eased his hold a little. "I don't under—"

His mouth was on hers with an angry, dreadful possession like nothing she'd ever experienced. Teeth slicing at her lips, he fucked into her with his tongue, every stroke brutal and hard. Through the long minutes of the kiss, she let him dominate, giving way to his control until he took her wherever he wanted, drawing her along one path, then changing course and the angle of his head to cut off that course and find a different route. He ground against her and gasped into her mouth, his long, guttural groans forcing themselves down her throat, and she swallowed it all, taking and taking and taking until he eased back, softening his assault, calming her hammering heart. He tenderly broke the kiss and leaned on her, forehead pressed against hers.

Slowly, Justine came back to herself enough to realize her arms were wound around his neck, holding tight, fingers through his hair in a desperate grip. He surrounded her. His hot body braced on rigid arms to keep from crushing her. She was framed in on either side by a wall of flesh, his biceps, chest, and face all she could see. She lowered her leg from where it had hooked itself around his hip, and pulled in a breath. The harsh inhale broke into pieces, and she tried again, finding scarcely more success.

"Better?" He asked the question like it made sense, his heavy breathing balanced by the deep growl in his voice, gravel traveling across velvet, rattling through her head.

"Yes?" *Better than what?* The words in her head were what she wanted to say, but her mouth wasn't working yet. "Maybe?"

***

Wildman

She sounded and looked so softly confused he couldn't stop the chuckle from rolling out of him. *Kissed her stupid.* "Now, baby. Need you to strip so I can fuck you like I want." He took her mouth again, tasting her, slowly tongue-fucking her mouth, stroking and twisting in a sensual battle with hers as he amped her back up, satisfied by how quickly she lost herself. "We keep this up, I'll fuck you against the wall."

The way that caught at her breath, it wasn't an unwelcome idea, and he filed the information away for later use.

Because there will be a later.

He waited a beat, letting her catch up, until eventually she nodded, gaze lifting to his eyes.

She came to me.

He saw the weight of her giving this to him again slip sideways, her fears he'd reject her falling away, losing substance and growing lighter with every breath. "Okay," she said finally, eyes clear once more from the haze he'd brought her to with a kiss.

A single goddamned make-out session without even my hand in her pants.

"Did they rape you?" His words appeared to strike her like a blow, and he wished he could have found different ones, but he needed to know. She'd needed to purge, the first time, coming to him in an effort to tone down the howling in her own head. He hadn't thought it was to wipe another man's touch from her body, but maybe he'd misread the moment.

She shook her head slowly.

"Say it."

"No, they didn't rape me. I...bartered with them for something else, to protect the women."

He remembered the bruises, the way she'd dived deep with him, pulling roughness from him. She'd taken everything he'd offered. "A beating." She stared, gaze stuck on his face. "Why?"

Her expression didn't falter, watching him as she shook her head side to side, dark wings of her hair flying through the air.

Oh, honey.

Tongue pressed between his teeth, he stepped over to the door and locked it, making a show out of it so she'd know. Turning to face her, he stood still, breathing slowly, then told her, "You and me, we're going to come to an understanding."

Justine LaPorte might be the most dangerous woman he'd ever met. She didn't realize it yet, might be suspicious, yet still couldn't know for certain—but she held him in the palm of her hand, could break him with a single word and send him soaring with a smile. It didn't matter who she was, her name, or where she worked. No, what counted most was what she was—the other half of his soul. Something he never expected to find. He closed his eyes, pushing hard against the desire to be done with this, all this talking, all this chatter. To be done with it and inside her. *We both need this.*

"What you gave me was something I liked." She nodded, even though he hadn't asked a question, the statement seeming to settle something inside her. "Then before I could get back to talk to you, a man took you from a place I thought was safe." He swept his hands out to the sides, indicating the clubhouse, the people in it, and his room. *All of me.* "I dealt with it. This is my life, woman. I will always protect what's mine by force, because there are assholes who want to take it from me. This is who I am. It's all I am. The club made me, and then with my brothers, every single day I make the club. It's a give and take, always. You and me, we shouldn't work, but I think we do. We will. If you wanna give this a go, if that's why you came here tonight, then I'm all in on the idea. We'll push through whatever obstacles there are, and baby, given the fact me and your job are like polar opposites, there's gonna be a bunch of 'em. I got shit in my past, too, and we'll get to that eventually. But for the life of me, I can*not* get you out of my head. And I suspect you're the same, or you wouldn't be here."

She opened her mouth, but he cut her off with a firm shake of his head.

"Here's what's going on in this room tonight. It's you and me, and nobody else. I wanna fuck you, wanna see what'll make you come fast, drag it out of you slow. But I also wanna talk about what matters to you. I did some digging—"

She tipped her head to the side with a frown, and he laughed.

"Woman, we know a fuck of a lot of the same people, so I did some asking around. I think I know a lot of your secrets, but I wanna earn 'em. Wanna be someone you think's worth hearing them from your lips, and that'll take time. You live in Florida, and I'm here in Louisiana, but it ain't so far a drive and isn't a place I'm unfamiliar with." Wildman flashed her a smile, hoping like fuck it hid his trepidation. "Now, if you didn't come here for this, and I've misread every fucking thing, then you got a minute right now to go ahead and say your piece. Then you can turn around, take your sweet, *sweet* ass down the stairs and out the door, and you won't ever, not ever, see me again." She didn't move, and he pulled in a breath filled with the ease of relief because she wasn't scampering to escape, and her very stillness told him more than she knew. "You wanna get to know this old outlaw a little, I'm down for that, because there's something about you just fuckin' fits me. So what do you say, Justine LaPorte?" That felt too formal, and he smiled as he followed with something that rolled like satin off his tongue. "Jussie. You ready to take a walk on the wild side with me?"

Minutes rolled past as they stood on opposite sides of the room, and he waited. *Worth any time it takes for her to be on the same page as me.*

"I'm not the best submissive." The words burst from her, and he wondered at the desperation in her tone. "I like what we did in bed, need it, but I'm not always going to want to kneel at your feet. And it stays in bed. If that's not what you want, then we can—"

"Did I say I wanted more than what we have?" She shook her head in confusion, and he smirked at how cute she looked. "I'll tell you what I want, give you a lil' lesson. So, right about now—"

He thumbed his belt free, followed by the fastening of his jeans, sighing as the uncomfortable constriction around his rigid cock eased. Wildman marked how her breathing increased.

Aww, yeah.

She might not have come to the clubhouse for a fucking, but she'd take one with pleasure.

"What I want—"

He bent and tugged at one boot and sock, tossing them to the side.

"My dearest wish come true—"

He changed his stance to do the same to the other, his gaze never leaving her face.

"Would be for you—"

He shoved his pants down and stepped out of them, standing bare-assed before her, cock rigid.

"To fucking strip."

To his great pleasure, she complied.

When they came together, it was his arms around her, her hands in his hair, and he lifted her, turning back to the bed before resting her in the middle of it. The covers were neatly tucked and folded, this not being a place he could rest in with her gone, so he'd been sleeping at his own house. Right now, that simply meant there were crisp, clean sheets underneath the soft fuzzy blanket spread over the top. Pale silk of her skin against the midnight blue of the blanket made his heart pump faster, and it was already pounding like an overworked outboard motor in the middle of a sudden bayou storm.

Justine's chin lifted, and he obliged the unspoken request, trailing the edge of his teeth along the column of her neck, settling his mouth over the sweet spot where it joined her shoulder before he bit down. Gently at first, his hands roaming her sides and belly, cupping a breast before slipping along her hip, he bit until she moaned, lips against the side of his head, and he smiled around the mouthful of flesh, grinding his teeth in just a little harder.

"Wild." Her whisper was wispy, breaths sounding like broken shudders, and she quivered underneath him. He shifted, released his hold, and dragged the rough scruff along his jaw across the tops of her breasts, tongue following like a puppy, wagging its wet way behind, soothing the sting. "I didn't think."

"You don't have to think, Jussie." He lapped at her nipple, catching it between his teeth as it hardened, the rosy color darkening with her arousal. He nibbled gently, knowing the tease would be frustrating, but wanting to push her higher up the sliding edge of the wave. "That's the beauty of this. I've got you, baby." He cupped her breast in his hand, fingers molding and kneading the flesh before he fed it into his mouth on a hard suck. He slipped his other hand up the back of her neck, tangled his fingers in her hair, and twisted, yanking her head back as he bit down on her breast, mouth as full of her as he could make it.

He transferred his attention to her other breast, fingers tweaking and twisting the wet and swollen nipple left in his wake. "I've got you." Puffy and swollen, the nipple and areola were both red and pink and gorgeous—a testimony to what they both liked.

She arched off the bed, one hand landing on his arm, the other flying over her head, and he watched as she flattened her palm against the wall. "My baby likes a little titty torture." Sucking hard, he flicked the nub in his mouth against the edges of his teeth and twisted her other nipple again until she groaned, the vibration of her cry of passion filling the air around them. "Gonna be wet for me, aren't you, Jussie?"

"Yes, Wild. Always for you."

"Gonna come all over my cock, aren't you?"

"Yes, Wild."

"Be my wild woman, take my cock how I give it to you."

Her legs moved restlessly, and he draped a thick thigh over, pinning her in place as he kept up an intermittent pace with the nipple torture he'd begun. *Wish I'd thought to grab… fuck, anything.* His bag was at home, and in the room here at the club, all he had were fresh condoms and a tube of lube in the little table next to the bed. *Next time,* he thought, unsurprised at how confident he was there would be another time. And another.

"Wild." The word had an edge of pleading in it, like he'd lifted her just until she could see the finish line but didn't know how to get there on her own.

"I got you, Jussie." He let go of every hold and flipped her to her stomach, startling a tiny cry out of her. "Hush, baby." Covering her with his body, he used his knees to spread her legs, mouthing along the muscles of her shoulder, threatening with his teeth often enough to keep her attention there and not where his hands were. "Kiss me, Jussie." Her head turned, neck craning until her mouth met his, and he swallowed down her gasps and moans. Taking her bottom lip between his teeth, he razed it with a tight grip, letting it slip slowly free as she writhed harder from the pain. Working between their bodies, he rolled the condom down his length, then quietly popped the top on the lube, working enough of the gel onto his fingers to do what he wanted. Tube recapped, he tossed it to the side and rose to his knees, clean fingers once again wrapped in her raven tresses, making her arch her back.

"Knees, Jussie."

She rose to hands and knees, collapsing down to her forearms when he put weight against her upper back. A nudge with his cockhead against her entry found she was as sloppy wet as expected, and he didn't hesitate but dove straight inside, his steady push not giving her much time to get accustomed to the girth of his heavy cock. As her silken heat enveloped him, he had to tear his gaze away from the smooth lines of her body in front of him, the vulnerable knobs of her vertebrae aligned with the sweep of her ribs, instead staring up at the darkened ceiling. Once deep, he didn't give her a chance to breathe then, either, pulling out nearly entirely before slamming back inside, his balls drawn up so tight to his body they didn't have a chance to spank her clit, and he grunted when he bottomed out again, and again, fiercely ignoring the orgasm that kept trying to sweep him up as he kept up the punishing pace.

Deep again, he paused for a breath and ground hard against her, listening to the squelching sounds with a grin. Middle and ring fingers paired, he thrust into her ass without prep or warning, stretching her wide. She pushed backwards against his intrusion with a scream, and he bottomed out there, too, twisting and scissoring his fingers before hooking them at the edge of the rim and pulling with a steady force. Enough to have her hole gaping and fluttering but without danger of tearing. *Never hurt her.*

"Wild, God. Please. Oh. Wild."

The sounds Jussie made were unbelievable. From deep groans that came all the way up her throat to be swallowed back down, to these tiny keening noises he didn't think she could control. Every few strokes of his cock, tugs of his fingers, she'd pull in a breath on a gasp that broke in the middle, and he found himself living for and pushing harder to bring those sounds out of her again and again.

But she hadn't come yet, and as good as he was making it, she didn't seem close, not desperately so at least.

That'll change.

Wildman bared his teeth and thrust his thighs to each side, shoving at her knees until she was spread even wider for him. He released his grip on her hair, watching as her neck remained arched for a moment before she settled on the bed, cheek half on, half off the blanket, pillows fallen to the floor a while ago.

His fingers danced along her backbone, came down, and circled her hole as he watched it flex in anticipation around the improvised hook. Wildman grinned, thinking, *Not that, baby.* He slipped his palm around her hip, settling just above her pubic bone. Tracing random circles with his fingertips, he increased the speed of his thrusts, sweat covering his body and hers, her pale skin now rosy with arousal. Rocking his hips, he speared into her and made a claw of his waiting fingers, sliding down until he could feel the root of his cock grinding against her with each down thrust. Wet and slippery, he spread the lips of her pussy and clamped her clit in an unmovable grip. She wailed and bucked, an orgasm hitting without warning, and a rigid tension ripped through her as her body responded. Rippling waves of pressure surrounded his cock, her hole straining to swallow his fingers, and he pinched again, earning another wail of his name, the sound rising and rising until it mixed with his roar, seed impotently caught in the condom, but still deep inside her. *My woman.* He thrust again, his hips jittering back and forth before he rocked deep, releasing her clit as he slowly slumped over her back. *My Jussie.*

***

Justine

When Wildman left her body, it was slowly and with great care. His hand eased over her ass, one palm possessively cupping her swollen labia, gently soothing her. She knew it, felt it, but was so far inside the floaty space within her head his actions seemed separate. The mattress moved, springing up to the side, and a soft blanket drifted down to cover her sweat-filmed skin.

Then the mattress dipped again, and he cleaned her thoroughly. If she'd been less floaty, it might have been embarrassing, but because it was Wildman, probably not even then. Every part of her was his, and it was right that he care for what he owned. She flew for a few seconds before settling against crisp, clean sheets, still smelling of bleach and fresh air.

That's when it happened again, something she'd only felt once before.

He lay next to her, tugging her into the little spoon position, arranging her limbs as best pleased him, and she gave no resistance, liking the marionette strings binding her to him. Tucking her half underneath him, his weight against her back, heavy thigh covering both of her legs, he rested his cheek against the side of her head, so his mouth was close to hers.

"I know you aren't all here right now, but you'll remember enough of this so it'll matter." Justine tensed, but before she could move, his hand was gliding along her arm, down her side, curling around her belly until she was bound in place by his arms. "Shhhh. You don't gotta do nothin', darlin'. Just listen. Can you do that for me? Just listen?"

In the silence within the room, buffered from the sounds of the party below them and outside, Justine licking her lips sounded loud, and she bit down on them before giving him a response. "Mmhmm." Consciously relaxing her muscles, starting from her neck and shoulders, she tried to show him she could follow directions, even in this state.

His chuckle rumbled through her body, transferring from his body to hers, and rattling a soothing feeling into place in her chest. "Good girl, you're such a good girl." Justine wanted to preen, but he'd asked for stillness and quiet, so she breathed out a pleased sigh instead. "My girl's so good." His hand lifted and stroked hair from her face until his cheek was skin-to-skin with hers. "My baby." Justine smiled small, just a tiny recognition she knew he'd feel in the movement underneath his touch. "Just listen, baby. Just listen."

His body tightened around her, a bulwark against anything in the outside world, and she knew where this talk was going. Hoped she understood, anyway.

"You're mine. Came to me tonight, braved the gauntlet for me, hung in there even when you and me weren't on the same page, and that's earned you a spot at my side for as long as this old earth ball keeps turnin'." A soft kiss landed on her cheek, another on her temple, and as much as she wanted to turn her head to reach his mouth, she stayed true to his instructions, not demanding anything, just soaking it all up. If he wanted her to kiss him back, he'd tell her, and it wasn't her problem to figure it out. "Past days have been a special kinda hell, not knowin' if you would be back. I knew you were okay, were safe. Michaels is a member, so the minute they deplaned you at BRG, he was in contact." Wild took in a deep breath. "Said you were fuckin' brave, and I told him 'well, hell, yeah, she's my Jussie.' Man laughed at me, then congratulated me on findin' a woman wild as me." Another kiss against her cheek, then fingers lifted her chin, and his mouth was on hers, permission to engage, and she did, tangling her tongue with his as he thrust into her mouth, proud and possessive all in the same moment. "Mine" was growled down her throat as he turned her underneath him, sensitive breasts pressed against his hard chest as his mouth moved across her jaw, teeth to her earlobe in a stinging bite that had her neck arching and twisting, giving him better access. "Jesus, Jussie. Makes me fuckin' crazy. Every goddamned inch of you is temptation. Wanna mark you. Wanna own you. Wanna make love to you slow and sweet, but I wanna fuck you hard and fast in the same breath. Want everything you can give me. Can you give me this, baby?"

There was only one answer to that question.

"Yes."

Chapter Fifteen
Wildman

Staring up at the ceiling, this time from a different position, he slowly stroked a palm up and down Jussie's back. From her shoulders, all the way down to those dimples in her ass that were so bitable, and a gentle return sweep up to the vulnerable nape of her neck. She was nestled against his side, cheek to the hollow of his shoulder, with a delicate hand resting flat against his chest. *Fits me like a goddamned glove, no matter what we're doin'.* His smile was satisfied, his chest and head filled with hope and confidence that this time, this woman, this was where he was meant to be.

Boots up the stairs had him cocking an ear to the door, so the instant a single knuckle thumped quietly against the wood, he was already shifting her to the side, replacing his chest with a pillow and pulling the blanket up around her shoulders. Unbolting the door, he opened it a little, standing to protect Jussie from view. "Yeah?" he asked Pony, who had a happy smirk in place on his face. "Fuck you need?"

"Her keys. She's parked out near the road, so I wanna bring it in closer, make it easier to watch now most folks have headed out."

She hadn't held a purse, and he remembered her bared-torso twirl from when she'd imagined needing to prove she wasn't a plant. "Gimme a minute." He closed the door against Pony's chuckle, shaking his head at his brother's amusement. "Jussie, baby." He leaned close, pressing a kiss to her temple. "Where're your keys, honey?"

"Behind the visor. It's not locked." She didn't move, which meant she'd been more awake than he'd thought. "Tell him thanks from me."

The message passed through the slightly cracked door, he was about to close it when Pony paused. "Wild, you should know. Mason's downstairs."

"What the fuck, man? Are you shittin' me?" *She just fuckin' got here and he's already in our business?*

"Don't shoot the messenger, brother. He came to talk to Twisted, but he noted the car on the lot. It's hers, not a rental, and he tagged the Florida plates first thing. He hasn't asked about her, but you can see him lookin'. However, he *has* asked for you, somethin' like four times already." Pony shrugged. "Twisted just keeps sayin', 'Wild who?' like he's a dumbass, and you can see it's chappin' Mason's ass. Kinda funny in a way."

"Shit." Wildman made a quick calculation and knew there was no way anyone would be able to block Mason for long. "Tell Twisted quiet-like we'll be down in a bit, gonna take the back stairs, come in from the kitchens."

"Agreed it might be best if you didn't come down the center stairs like a parade, pushin' it in his face you're dickin' his sister." Pony's nod held as much sarcastic humor as a movement like that could. "Good call, brother. Good fuckin' call."

"Oh, fuck you." He reached out and gripped Pony's shoulder. "Thanks, man."

"I'd say anytime, but hopefully you'll take the loud action home next time, or at least wait until we don't have a houseful of kids askin' who's bein' murdered upstairs." He shook his head. "Brothers have had to deal with some shit from their ole ladies on this one, brother. Funny as fuck."

"Shit." He chuckled through the word, already anticipating the brushing elbows and "way to go" looks. "We had ourselves a little reunion." He gripped his bare dick and tugged. He was behind the door, but knew the movement was unmistakable. "Might need to reunite a tad more before we come downstairs."

"Your funeral, man." Pony's laughter was quiet as he turned and walked away, shaking his head. "Your goddamned funeral."

"Jussie?" He bolted the door and turned to see she hadn't moved, remained with her cheek on the pillow, hand resting on top of it. On second look, he saw her palm was no longer flattened but had been covered by her fingers, hand in a tight fist. "Sounds like you and me need a shower, then we'll dress and head downstairs."

Sitting on the edge of the mattress, he propped a leg up, resting his thigh along the curve of her ass. Eyes closed, she was breathing evenly, slowly, and if he hadn't already memorized every expression and movement of her so far, he might have believed she was sleeping. He used the back of his hand to pop the soft flesh of her lower cheek, just where it joined the top of her thigh, knowing the covers would blunt the pain. It got the reaction he'd looked for, her eyes opening and head turning just enough to bring her gaze to him. The expression on her face was so open and vulnerable, he immediately abandoned his position to crawl under the covers behind her, wrapping her up in his arms to erase any space between them.

"Baby," he crooned, dusting kisses across her shoulder and up the side of her neck. "My baby." His lips dragged along the edge of her jaw until he found her mouth, which he took possession of, molding their lips together in a hot kiss. Every touch was in sync, and they worked together as her fingers found his wrists, holding his hands in place around her. "My

Jussie." He rested his cheek against hers, closing his eyes when he saw she'd shut hers.

"I have a son."

Her words stilled his movements, and he stared at the inside of his lids for two breaths before responding.

"I nearly had a child once. Dead in my wife's belly, killed by my blood brother. Colder than cold, and still hurts, even if I dealt with everything I could at the time." He knew the story about Christopher Camp. Of course he did. It was one of the larger markers he'd given to Retro. But he wanted to hear her version, needed it from her like a gift, and if it required him peeling back the pain of his past a little to ease her way, he'd do that a thousand times over. "She and the child still inside her are buried in a little grove in southern Florida. Officially missing, unless her folks had her declared. That's been—" He had to do a quick calculation. "Way too many years ago now. Fuck, I hadn't counted up the years in a long-ass time, baby. *Shit*. The days just rack up, don't they?"

"Chris, his name is Christopher, is a little older than that. Married with two kids. He lives in Louisville with his family." She laughed, the sound wet and painful, his arm underneath her head damp with tears. He knew he couldn't console her, not yet. She needed to get this out of her somehow, and he was the catalyst and the cure, all at once. He just had to pick the time to soothe her. "I don't... I don't see him."

"Do you want to?" Wildman didn't know what it would entail, but if his Jussie wanted it, he'd upend heaven and hell to make it happen for her. She shook her head and shuddered, curling into a tighter ball, and he followed her with his body, keeping the zero space between them as best he could. "Want regular reports, then? Just to check in, know what's goin' on? You tell me, Jussie, and I'll make it happen, baby."

"It was club business that took him from me." Wildman stilled in place, not sure what her statement meant. "Your..." She took a tiny breath, then a larger one, pushing the words out on a huge exhale. "Your wife and child, was it club business?"

"Yeah. Was in a shit club because my half-brother was there, and I had it in my head he needed me at his back. Hurricane season came, and a storm swept through, takin' half the members' roofs with it. I helped get everybody back on their feet. Service to the club, you know? Powell Durrell, that was my brother, thought it was ambition on my part. So he called in a bullshit claim to the dominant club in the area, paid for a paper with my name on it. Shit happened"—*understatement, but she don't need to know I killed him*—"and he got hurt, died at the hospital. I went home, and the man he'd hired was sittin' at my kitchen table, eating the cold food Shelly had made for me. I dealt with him, then went looking for her. Dead in our bed, and the only blessing was she didn't look scared." He scoffed. "So yeah, club business you could say. I dropped that club like a hot potato, separated from them with prejudice and little care. Wandered for a bit, a long bit, but wound up in Louisiana. Took a couple of false starts, but I found my home, you know what I mean? Incoherent is me, and I am IMC. I know you get it, know you understand. No more shit clubs for me, baby. Found the club, and now I've found you, if you'll have me."

"Her name was Shelly?"

He mouthed at her ear until he could get her earlobe between his teeth, clamping down gently, not aiming to cause pain. "Yeah, Shelly. Out of the two of us, she was the ambitious one, always saw more in my future than I could see."

"What do you see in your future now?" She twisted in his arms, facing him, giving him a view of her pain-swollen eyes, red from weeping. He thought she'd never been more beautiful.

"You, Jussie." He kissed her hard and fast, had her gasping into his mouth within moments as he shifted over her, falling into the cradle she made with her legs like he'd been with her a thousand times. "You, and only you." He tested the waters with the palm of his hand, then a pair of fingers diving deep, finding her wet and ready.

Wildman held his breath when she rolled the condom on for him, her fingers dancing delicately along his shaft, paying close attention to the tip where she'd left an ambitious reservoir for his release. Then he was inside her again, slipping slowly between her intimate lips, clutched tightly in her arms.

They moved together like a dance, her hips rising as he thrust deep, taking as much of each other as they could. It was slow and sweet, and when she came with his name on her lips, he let the recognition that she was here, with him, carry him over the edge, falling so close behind her Justine was still spasming around him as he filled that pinched tip of the condom, his mind imagining what it would be like when he could take her bare, pushing the white semen back inside her with the tip of his dick, make her come with his mouth as he lapped her clean. That forced another few jerks from his dick, each movement inside her making her gasp until he covered her mouth with his again. He kissed her as his dick softened enough he had to pull back, ease out, holding the edge of the condom in place with finger and thumb.

"Okay." Her breathing had slowed considerably, but the word still sounded labored.

"Okay?" He questioned her as he disposed of the condom, turned on the hot water in the shower, and came back into the room, lifting her in his arms before he walked them back to the bathroom. "Just okay, baby? Damn, woman, I'm already losin' my touch? Fuck, hurt a man, would ya?"

Her easy giggle felt like a miracle, and he smiled as he pressed a kiss to the top of her head. Feet on the floor, she cocked a hip against the counter, uncaring of her nakedness as he stared at her. Steam billowed from the shower, and he reached in, adjusting the temperature to one that would be tolerable for them both.

"Okay, as in 'okay, I'm ready to go downstairs and face my brother down,' okay." Her palm landed in the center of his chest, and he covered it with his hand. "Not a criticism of your lovemaking prowess."

"Well, thank God for that." He pretended to wipe sweat from his brow. "I nearly couldn't tell if you even enjoyed it, woman."

After dressing, he led her down the back stairs hand in hand, about to take the turn that would lead them outside and around the rear of the clubhouse when she slowed. Her fingers clutched at him with desperate strength. "Jussie?" He turned and caught her in his arms, pulling her close. "What is it?"

"I think I do."

Wildman stroked down the fall of hair draped across her upper back, slowly traveling from her scalp to her shoulder blades, then again. He waited for her to elaborate, because he couldn't for the life of him think what she might be referring to. He'd dropped a load of info on her tonight, and at least her response to whatever had tripped her up was positive.

"You asked if I'd like to see Chris."

He hummed softly, his arms tightening around her to fend off whatever might be coming. "Mmhmm. And if you want it, I'll make it happen. Let me do my thang, and I'll sort out the best way."

"I don't want him to know about me." Her immediate terror was stark, fingers clawing at his chest as she tried to thrust her arms between them, fruitlessly attempting to push away. "He can't know about me."

"I got it, babe. You wanna lay eyes on him. Have a chance to make sure with your own five senses how he's happy and healthy, and has a good life. That your sacrifices were worth it, the pain you still feel, the way you've got a hollow spot inside you, because he's *good*. I got it, Jussie."

"Yeah." Her breaths came short and labored, bursts of panted air gusting across his chest and neck. "Yeah, please. That's what I'd like. Just to know."

"Then..." He gave her a squeeze, holding tight until she slipped her arms around his waist. "I'll make it happen."

They stood like that for a few breaths longer, then he pulled back and tipped her chin up with a bent knuckle. "You good to face the squad?" She rolled her eyes but pulled in a bracing breath before she nodded, so he knew she might be able to pull it off, but she was still more vulnerable than she'd like to be, given what was waiting on them. "Okay, then, let's do this damn thing. I'm right here, and I don't want you anywhere but next to me. You needa take a piss, take me with, yeah?"

"You want to go to the bathroom with me?" She stiffened then snuggled her cheek against his bicep, slipping around to stand next to him, fingers threading through his belt loops. With an even tone Justine told him, "That's either kinky or a Daddy need."

"Never had that before, but maybe it's a little of both, babe. I just want you safe and protected, and there's a fuckton of unknowns here tonight." He pulled her hand loose from his clothing and fit his fingers between hers. "You and me, we'll figure ourselves out, every single day. Don't matter if it's the same as the one before, or we need somethin' a little different that day. I'm tellin' you now that we can adjust on the fly. We get done with this tonight, and you're on the back of my bike, babe. We're gonna go to my house and be there until you have to leave. I'll let Twisted know I'm out of commission for—how long do you have?" They should have had this conversation earlier, and not on a public landing within the house, with his brothers and her blood brother nearly within hearing distance.

"I have two weeks, but I need to be back sooner to check on my momma. She's in a home in Adken and gets upset if I'm gone too long."

"We'll take a road trip, you can see her in a few days, and then we'll circle back to here in time for you to head home." She stiffened, muscles growing tense. "Baby, you don't have to try and intro me to her. This is me trying to give you what you need, while still takin' what I want."

"It's just the idea of her meeting you is…good." She laughed nervously, the sound jarring and sharp-edged. "Which is weird, because it might upset her, and normally I'd be a country mile on the other side of anything that might have that result. But meeting you, even if she didn't remember it the next day…" She laughed again, this more settled, low and easy. "That feels good. I'm being weird, I know. You don't have to—"

"Justine LaPorte, you're not being weird." Wildman turned to face her, cupping her cheeks in his palms and tilting her face up towards his. "And I won't sit here and listen to my beautiful woman putting herself down." Pressing their lips together in a dry, soft peck, he kept his eyes open, watching as her lids fluttered closed, lashes brushing against the apple of her cheek. "That's a hard limit for me, baby. I'm not blind to flaws, and God knows I got enough of my own, but I won't allow you to be unreasonably hard on yourself. There's enough assholes out there in this mean old world who'll be fuckin' happy as a clam to do it for you. So knock it the fuck off, hear me?"

She leaned forwards, forehead thumping against his chest, and he wrapped his arms around her again, waiting.

"Definitely a little bit of Daddy there."

"And you fuckin' love it."

"I thought I loved pain." This was low and ragged, the words exiting her body on a rough exhale.

"I think you do. Fuck, woman, I know you do. It turns you on like nobody's business. But you like to be controlled, too. No." He shook his head as she pulled back and looked up. "Not controlled, but you like to selectively give up control. Make it so you don't have to think, make a decision, or determine a path forward. You like giving that up to someone you trust. I'd bet big money on your previous playmates being more traditional Doms, mysterious scenes requiring you go with the flow, and then aftercare, which you probably liked just as much, or maybe even more than everything else, no matter how deep you'd gone. Am I right?"

"Yeah." She blinked, and the sparkle of unshed tears were like diamonds on her lashes. "Got it in one, Wild."

"We get to my house, we'll talk more about what we both want in that arena. Right now—" He reached down and adjusted his hard cock, so it lay more comfortably along his hip. "Right now, we gotta get to and through the meet-n-greet portion of the evening, and then we'll get the fuck outta Dodge, yeah?"

"Yeah." She fit herself against his front, her fingers grazing along the length of his dick, nails scraping across the denim fabric. "And then this is my play toy again."

He groaned into her hair, hips thrusting. With a sigh, he pulled back, gathered her hand up in his with a gentle squeeze, and turned her with a determined push. "Downstairs, now." They took the stairs side by side, went out into the humid Louisiana air, and he was glad for Twisted's insistence on citronella because there wasn't a single mosquito to mar Justine's skin with a welt. *That's my job,* he thought darkly, and stifled a chuckle.

We get to my house we'll have the discussion.

It wasn't like him to play without understanding his partner's hard, and more importantly, their soft limits, the ones he could push and tweak, looking for the interest that made a gray area of consent. He had a feeling that, like him, Justine would have her information on the tip of her tongue, readily available. And the tiniest twinge of jealousy he felt for the why—*can just go fuck itself.* She was with him now, no one else.

She came to me.

Not once, during the confusing time surrounding her rescue, but twice now, both of her own volition. This time, she'd been seeking more than a hot cock to help her rise above her experiences.

This time she wanted the whole shebang.

He opened the back door to the clubhouse, nodding at the prospect standing next to it, and followed Justine through. His hand slipped underneath the waistband of her jeans, fingertips resting just above the crease of her ass. The sound levels had decreased from before, and he no longer heard the running thuds of children's footsteps. A glance at the clock over the sink said he and Justine had been upstairs far longer than he'd thought, and he smirked. *Mason's gonna have a good idea what was takin' so long.* Now to see if the man could look past the personal relationship his sister had with an officer of a rival club and be sweet to her. *If he doesn't—* "Justine, this is your only warning. Your brother gives you shit above a level I think is warranted, which is less than ankle-high, if you get my meaning, then I'm gonna shut him down. I wasn't kidding when I said there were assholes out to tear a body down, any chance they get. If he's one of those, then I'll drop the hammer on him in a heartbeat."

She laughed, the delicate belling of her humor preceding them into the main room, so everyone within twenty feet of the door was watching as they walked through.

"He's not like that." She leaned against his side, and he adjusted his hold, draping his arm over her shoulder. Her fingers threaded through his belt loops again, and he reached back with his other hand to pat them, telling her silently he liked her claiming him like that. "Promise."

"Well, mine's a promise too." He wiped the smile from his face as he steered her through the clusters of men and women towards where he could see Twisted's back. His president had placed himself in the most vulnerable spot in the circle of men where he stood, as always, taking on the uncomfortable-feeling position to give his brothers pride in his trust in them, believing they'd protect him at all costs.

Someone must have said something, because Twisted glanced over his shoulder, then slowly spun in place as he put his palms together forcefully, leading the entire room in a round of enthusiastic, if also sarcastic, applause.

"Well done, brother. Was quite a fuckin' show, and we didn't even get to see a damn square of flesh. Well fuckin' done, man." Twisted reached out, and Wildman gave Justine a squeeze to tell her to stay right next to him, then met Twisted's palm with his own, letting himself be pulled in for a one-armed clinch. "Out-fucking-standing, brother."

"Fuck you." He pulled back and reclaimed Justine's shoulders, tracing along the edge of her sleeve with his thumb. He kept up the caress, grazing her skin in a back-and-forth movement meant to reassure. *Always on my mind, baby.* "And the horse you rode in on."

Pony grinned at him from across the circle, and Wildman realized he'd parked himself and Justine next to Twisted, taking up space with their backs to the room. *Measure of trust.* He scanned the other faces, noting the three not smiling, as he nodded in equal greeting to the rest of his brothers. Only then did he bring his gaze back to meet Mason's.

To give the man credit, he adhered to protocol and didn't so much as glance at Justine, who was close to Wildman's side as she could be. Wild pulled her in front of him, then arranged her at his other side, so he wouldn't have to move away from her again, and she snuggled in tight against him. Her tiny sigh of contentment had his lips curling up, and he knew Mason didn't miss the expression.

Twisted elbowed Wildman, chuckled, then began the introductions, both needed and unneeded. "Wild, you've met Mason." Wildman inclined his head, receiving a brusque chin lift in response. "Gunny's parked next to him, and on the other side is Hoss, both from Fort Wayne."

Wildman reached out, giving Gunny's hand a double-pump as he said, "Seen you around, here and there. Well met." Gunny was silent, his side-eye of Mason saying enough for two conversations. "Hoss, I know your brother well. Retro's a helluva man, and I've only heard good things about you. No surprise that. Welcome to our house, man."

"Good meetin' you, Wildman. I've heard things too."

Wildman squeezed Justine's shoulders when he heard her soft giggle, and he grinned broadly. "I just bet you have, Hoss." Turning back to Mason, he leaned in a little. "We should probably have a private conversation soon." His hesitation was momentary, but he wanted to make a statement with his words. "Brother." Mason nodded. "Anyone important to Jussie is gonna be high on my list of folks to get to know, because this is stickin'."

"Is it now?" Mason looked down at Justine, features wreathed in a smile that was soft and heartfelt. "You're lookin' good, Justine."

"I am good, Davy." She tipped her head so her temple rested against Wildman's bicep, and a coal of warmth bloomed in his chest at the possessive gesture, clearly designed to telegraph her feelings. "I didn't get a chance to thank you for everything." Glancing up at Wildman, she leaned forwards, and he released his grip on her shoulder, watching as she moved towards her brother to be enveloped in his arms. Mason cradled her to his chest as if she were the most precious thing in the room, and Wildman liked what that said about the man, about the relationship these two complicated people had carved out for themselves. "Not just riding all over while you were looking for me, but your words of wisdom."

"Older brothers are supposed to have a bit of that, sweetheart. I'm just glad it all turned out okay." The rumbled words were intended for an audience of one, but Wild was highly focused on this reunion, determined to ensure it went well for Justine's sake.

Looked like he had nothing to worry about. Mason's eyes had dropped closed, and he appeared to be drinking in the affection Justine had for him. Wildman remembered hearing through the grapevine a few years back how Mason had found unexpected family in a couple of places. Justine must have been one of those he'd grown up not knowing about. *More of his father's fuckery,* Wildman thought.

The instant Justine pulled away, Wildman's hands were on her hips, guiding her back in front of him. He folded his arms across her chest, head next to hers as he pressed a kiss to the soft skin just behind her ear. "You good, Jussie?" Hair tangled with his, she nodded, and he gave her lobe a tiny nip. "We'll only stay as long as you want. Gimme a sign and we'll head home." He didn't miss the way she melted into him when he said that word. Home was something that clearly held importance to her, and he locked the info away to dig into at some point in the future. "You know Hoss and Gunny?" She nodded again, cheeks creasing into a smile. "It's all good here, baby. This is a family night."

"Was a family night," Twisted butted in, humor thick in his voice. "Kids are all gone. Just us grown-ups here now."

"Yeah, we're acquainted." Justine leaned against his chest as Wildman straightened. "Hi, boys." She gave a little wave, arms restricted by his hold. "I'd hug you, but this man seems to be determined to tie me up tonight." Wildman's shoulders started shaking, and he chuckled in her ear. "So to speak."

"I'll tie you up, woman. Just give me the green and we'll have a playdate like you won't believe." Wildman pressed a kiss to the side of her head. "Behave, Jussie."

"Yes, Sir," she retorted back, sassy as all hell.

"Before y'all start another noisy session here on the main floor, may I have your attention?" Wildman glanced at Twisted, who was no longer smiling. "I'll give you tonight, but we'll have business to discuss tomorrow. So don't get a wild hair up your ass and go for a run. Need you here well before lunch, say ten or so. You can bring your woman, but she'll cool her heels in a chair out here. I'd honestly recommend leavin' her home." Twisted tipped his head at Justine, who returned the gesture. "No offense meant."

"Like you meant no offense having me show up here tonight, when I'd specifically asked for an opportunity to talk to Wildman in private?" Justine delivered the words quietly, carelessly even, no tensing of her muscles to say she understood she was poking a very dangerous bear. "No worries, Twisted. I'm kinda hard to offend."

"Worked out for ya, didn't it?" Twisted shrugged easily, his smirk never entirely fading. "Big bad Fed caught herself an outlaw. Sounds like the setup for a bad TV drama. How the fuck is this supposed to work in real life, huh?"

Justine's rib cage expanded under Wildman's hold, and he tipped his head to look at the side of her face, surprised to find a brilliant smile there. "That's something I have a few ideas about, none of which my bosses are going to like." She turned her face to his, and he captured her lips in a soft, slow kiss, ending with a tiny smack. "Conversation number two after we get home."

Resolute, certain, secure, and fearless—and he loved the look on her.

***

Justine

She'd had people at her back before. Formidable people. People she trusted, who believed in her, showing it in word and deed. She'd made promises, knowing she could carry through on them in her own right, having confidence in her abilities to negotiate, fight, or cooperate with whoever she needed to.

She'd never felt as powerful as she did with Wildman's arms wrapped around her. Protected by his public claim, visible on her throat in the form of purple bruises, and with his possession of her implied and apparent in his physical hold on her. Most important was the way his belief in her saturated every word sent her direction. She could do anything with him at her side.

She'd caught Hoss' gaze on her throat while he was introduced to Wildman, and from the tiny quirk of his lips, thought he might approve. Then, Davy's words during their embrace had very deliberately avoided any introduction of her relationship with Wildman, or even her presence in this clubhouse at his side. Her brother had chosen to focus on their hard-won sibling closeness, circling her safety with his promises of supporting her.

Facing down Twisted, however, might have been an ill-considered gauntlet. The silence surrounding them grew until her words to Wildman sounded louder than they should have, and she closed her eyes as she turned her head away from Twisted, cheek pressed to Wildman's chest.

"Actually," came a new voice to the circle, and she angled her gaze to see Wrench had approached from the side, "the little lady's take from the Fed side of things might be pivotal to have in the mornin'. If she'll share her wisdom." He patted the air as if anticipating an argument. "Not sayin' you've got to compromise anything you've oathed on. Just mentionin' we've got knowledge of shit you don't, and if you want a voice in shit, now's the time to step up and toe the fuckin' mark."

Wildman's sigh gusted out over her head, his breath stirring her hair as he sucked in another hard one. "One fuckin' day. Is that too much to goddamned ask around here? I'd planned on ditchin' for a couple of weeks, but forget that shit, you tellin' me you can't do without me for one goddamned day? I've got to be back in here in the mornin', and you know I've got shit I want to do at home, but it don't fuckin' matter?"

The shaking of his chest transferred through to her, and it was uniquely satisfying to know they were pressed so close, he couldn't laugh silently without her knowing.

"My Jussie wants to ride in with me in the mornin', wants to bring her unique perspective to what-the-fuck-ever you want to talk about, I'll take a seat beside her at that goddamned table, you can bet your fuckin' boots. First time for everythin', right, Twisted?" He huffed, no longer able to hide his laughter, and the shaking grew in intensity. "Oh, wait, that was your own Shiny Penny, back when you were all tied up." The men around the circle were smiling or chuckling—even Davy—and Justine understood whatever the story was, it wasn't complimentary to Twisted. "Rode the column, too, didn't she? Jussie'll be with me, her sweet, sweet ass and legs wrapped tight around me, there and back, and no matter what happens." He leaned forwards, the action taking her with him as he looked around the faces of the men nearby. "And not a motherfucker in this room better say one thing sideways to my ole lady. If we're not fuckin' clear, then let me know. I got five fingers that'll send a body to paradise if they wanna start shit." He straightened, and she echoed his posture, his hands tightening on her ribs. "Mine."

"Shit, man, you gonna piss on her next to make your fuckin' point?" The voice was recognizable, and she turned to see Pony stalking up on Wildman's other side. "Jesus, man, we fuckin' get it. She's yours. End of story." He shook his head, smiling and laughing. "Fuck."

"Oh, fuck you." Wildman released her, reaching out to clasp Pony's hand. He tugged, and Pony bumped against his shoulder, then they both released. "You hear what they're askin'?"

"I did. I caught wind of the shit earlier. Honestly surprised to still see your skanky ass here, Wild. Figured you'd have taken the lady home already." Pony dipped his chin at her. "Justine, glad to see you in one piece." He'd been very helpful with the rescued women during the original rescue, and she gave him a friendly nod in response. "Wrench, who's the guy movin' into your old apartment?"

"Tale for another night, brother." Wrench grinned as he shook his head. "Always got your nose in somebody else's business, man."

"It's how I find out the best stank." Pony pointed at Mason, then Gunny and Hoss. "Y'all dry yet? Got a prospect primed for my yodel, you need another drink."

All three men demurred, and Justine noted the high levels in their beer bottles. *Staying sober, but why?*

Pony continued with a quiet, "Just let me know," and she suspected the intent of the entire exercise had been to bring it to their attention how their behaviors had been noticed and noted by the hosting club.

Politics, everywhere I go.

Wildman bent, and with his mouth at her ear, breathed, "Baby, gotta keep your ass still, you don't want to put on a show here."

She twisted and glared up at him. "What?"

"You, dancin' to the music, Jussie. Rubbin' that aforementioned sweet, sweet ass right over my dick. I don't like ridin' with a hard-on, which means we'll have to go back upstairs if you don't stop it now. I wanna take you home and fuck you there, in my personal bed." One hand dropped, and the sting of a hard swat registered before she heard the impact of his hand against her ass. "So be fuckin' still, woman."

Her breath had caught in her throat, and she didn't fight the feeling sweeping over her as she angled her chin down, lowering her shoulders as she widened her stance. Service, ownership, rightness—it was all mixed up in her mind, but her heart was singing one word. *His.* Her arms might be trapped by his hold, so she couldn't assume the pose properly, but she cupped her fingers around his wrists with a squeeze. "Yes, Sir." Her murmured words couldn't have traveled far, but she knew Wildman had caught them when his cock stiffened more and he thrust against her ass.

"Minx." Cheek stroking against hers, he gave her affirmation she'd gotten it right. She'd gotten everything right. "That's my good girl, Jussie."

Boots stepped into view, and a hand curled around her chin, lifting her gaze to meet one as grey as her own. Mason studied her for the space of two breaths, then nodded. He still questioned, and she understood the need to put a line under it, given how she'd come to be here. "You want this, Justine?"

She looked deep into his eyes, trying to project the positive from all the confusing emotions swirling through her as she nodded slowly, a deliberate down and up and back to center, his hand never losing contact with her skin. "More than anything."

Mason stepped back between his two men and flicked his gaze up, over her shoulder, nailing Wildman with a hard look. "She's my blood."

"Yeah, yeah, yeah. Pain and suffering if anything happens to her. Chance of maiming up to and including death. We get it. It's a family thang." Twisted's voice was light but carried a thread of anger. "Woman is here of her own volition, man. She's choosing this, every moment she stands right fuckin' there. So you go ahead and do your yada, yada, yada, get it outta your system now, so my man can take his woman home." She didn't miss the extension of his ownership to her through Wildman, and knew Mason caught it when his features tightened. "Go ahead." In the periphery of her vision, Twisted's hand flapped in a circle. "Yada, yada, yada yourself to where you needa be."

"No, man." Wildman's voice had dropped to a low rumble, one that rattled through her whole body. "That's Jussie's blood standin' there, askin' if I'm gonna do the right thing by her. I get it. If I had a sister, I wouldn't want her with an outlaw like me." The grating chuckle should have shaken the rafters, it was so powerful. "But me bein' who I am, I like this woman the way she is. Ain't gonna try and change her. Why would I when I've already found we're compatible in so many fuckin' ways."

Another chuckle, this lighter, as she silently took in the meaning of his words. "Take that how you want it, but the reality is she's hooked me, and I'm the one left tryin' to reel her in. You can bet your ass I'll work hard to land her, catch her, and tie her tight to me. Part of that is respect to her family, and this is me givin' it."

His hand lifted to her jaw, trailed a touch down her throat and body until he latched onto her hand and threaded their fingers together. She gave him a squeeze, hiding how her hands trembled.

"She's your blood." His thumb thrust upwards until her bare ring finger stood above the rest. The inference lodged a lump in her throat. "I'll do whatever it takes to keep her. Happy to do anything from the least, to the most complicated. Her job's not a problem, because me and Jussie are gonna deal with both sides. I'd like for her family to not be a problem too. And I guess that's partly up to you, Mason." He disappeared from Justine's back, his arm draping over her shoulder, hands still joined. She leaned into him, giving him her weight as she tried to come to terms with everything he'd declared. "More'n halfway, you wanna meet me. This ain't no game to me. Ain't a scene, done and over in hours. This is—she's something I've been lookin' my whole fuckin' life to find." The idea that he valued her enough to worry about how Davy would take them being together shouldn't have been surprising. Everything about this exchange fueled her joy, validating the strong feelings swooping through her chest. The core of this man was filled to the brim with good faith and loyalty. *And love.* Those attributes, along with so much else, were what had brought her here tonight. Wildman fairly vibrated next to her, the intensity of his voice carrying a ring of truth through it. "Patience by the bucketful. Won't win her overnight. Spend the rest of my life makin' my pitch, seein' if she'll have me."

His arm squeezed her shoulders, and she rested against him, memorizing his every word.

"Fuck, brother, how in the hell are the rest of us supposed to give you any shit after you come through with a goddamned declaration like that."

Gunny's sigh burst from him, and he swung his head side to side, looking down. "Boss, need to see about gettin' goddamned Wildman on the payroll as a speechwriter. That's some powerful shit."

And with that, the heavy atmosphere was broken, grins around the circle of men, and as Justine glanced up at Wildman, she saw the broadest smile of them all.

Chapter Sixteen
Wildman

"You got a bag or something in your car you need for tonight?" Wildman didn't wait for Justine's response as he paused in their path to the door and bumped shoulders with Busk, a member he was friends with. "Hey, man, you still keep a spare lid here? I need one for my lady. Mine'd fuckin' swallow her."

"Wild, yeah, man. Hang on, I'll grab it." He looked around Wildman, and the instant his gaze fell on Justine, all humor fled his face. "You can keep it when you're done. I won't want it back."

Busk turned to walk away, and Wildman tongued the inside of his cheek, taking a moment to decide how to handle the subtle disrespect he'd just been handed.

Justine tugged on his hand, and he angled his gaze at her, his "Yeah, baby?" not giving away his rising anger towards Busk. Justine was shaking her head, a tiny movement he would have missed if he weren't looking directly at her. "What?"

"I'm not going to tell you how to manage your brothers"—the easy way the word rolled off her tongue reminded him this wasn't her first rodeo around a club and the men who filled the ranks under the patch—"because that will *never* be my place." She took a breath, and the unsteady nature of it revealed how uncertain she was in his acceptance of whatever she was about to deliver. "But parties mean booze, and booze means emotions are closer to the surface. I've got a mighty thick skin, Wild. Little dig here or there won't bleed me, won't even welt me. So you do whatever you need to do for you, but don't assume I need defending."

Her eyes never wavered, didn't drop or slide away. She held his gaze like a champ, and he was reminded the woman she was for him in bed would never be the one she was on the floor of a clubhouse, unless she gave that to him. Chin high and shoulders back, she was strength and poise, holding confidence he knew wove through her core. That made her submission to him even sweeter, because it was a part of her nature she wouldn't show just anyone.

"Fuck me, you're so gorgeous, Jussie." He gave her hand a tug. "Come on, he'll find us on the lot. Lemme introduce you to my other girl." From the way she rolled her eyes, he suspected she already knew what he was talking about, and sure enough, she didn't question him as they walked through the door and outside to stand next to his bike. "This is the only other girl in my life. Tempest, call her Tempe for short."

"Tempest, the wind." Justine's fingers squeezed his. "She's very pretty."

Hands to her waist, he lifted her onto the queen seat behind where his ass would ride. "You're prettier," he whispered against her lips, brushing a kiss from one side of her mouth to the other. "No competition there."

The front door opened and closed, and footsteps headed their way. He looked up, expecting to see Busk, but instead found Pony, helmet in hand. He took it from him without a word and fit it to Justine's head, fiddling with the strap until he could snap it into place. "Thanks, man." There was a jingle of metal, and he looked up to see Pony dangling keys from his fingers. Wildman accepted them with a wince. "Oh, shit. Man, I'd already forgotten the car. Thanks."

"It's what brothers do. Make sure our friends don't fuck things up." Pony took a step back and then hesitated, reclaiming that space with a wry expression on his face. "I know you know this, but just don't get sideways with folks before you have a chance to talk with them. I saw Busk, heard him, and the man will be pissed at himself tomorrow. It's just—" He cut his gaze to Justine, then back to Wildman as he huffed out a sigh. "—not everyone got a chance to meet her yet. Between club affiliations and other things, you both are gonna have some swamp to wade through."

"I know." He gripped Pony's shoulder, then pulled him in for a hard embrace, the familiar thudding of a fist directly over the patch on his back settling his anger. "I get it, I do, but brothers need to believe I'd never do anything to risk the club."

"Memories run long. Gonna be an uphill road for a while." Pony pushed away and ran a hand over his hair, smoothing it back. "I've got your back, brother."

"Back atcha, brother. Much appreciated. Later, man." He clasped Pony's wrist and gave it a squeeze, then turned to Justine, Pony's "See ya" trailing off as he walked away. "What do you need from the car, baby?"

"There's a little bag on the front passenger seat. That has everything I need for tonight. Phone and all. I knew better than to bring it inside." She smiled at him, the edge of the helmet shadowing her eyes, so her expression was unreadable, but her tone was open and tender, backing up the sweetness of her smile. "Thanks, baby."

"Mmhmm." Wildman pursed his lips in a request she easily read, leaning forwards to press her mouth to his in a soft kiss. "Be back." He glanced around the lot, seeing an unfamiliar car parked near the end of the building. "Be right back."

"I'll be here."

Her declaration aside, he couldn't keep his eyes off her, glancing over his shoulder every few steps to see her smiling at him, hand lifted in a wave she renewed each time with a sweet waggle of her fingers. The lights of the car flashed when he clicked the fob Pony had given him, and it was the work of only a moment to gather her bag and make it back to the bike, locking the car as he walked away. Crowding into her space, he murmured in faux surprise, "You're still here," rewarding them both with a kiss that was hot, and wet, and deep.

Breathing like he'd run a mile, aware of how uncomfortable his hardening cock already was behind the folds of denim, he slowed down, smiling against her lips when she gave a little whine of disappointment. "Let's go home, baby."

Bag strapped on top of the back fender, he lifted his leg across the tank, settling into place in front of Justine. Her fingers fumbled with the dangling straps of his helmet as he started the bike, and he felt the click as she locked the quick-snap into place for him. Her hands came to rest at his waist, then threaded around his belly, and he didn't wait, took her position as readiness to roll, easing out the clutch until they weaved their way through the remaining bikes on the lot, to the end of the drive, and with more care than he'd ever left the clubhouse, out onto the highway.

She rode bitch like a champ, thighs tight to his hips, arms steady around his middle, head resting against his spine, and Wildman gave himself a breath to take in the knowledge that Justine, the woman he'd wanted since setting eyes on her, was with him. *She talked her way past Twisted to get into the clubhouse.* No matter how the evening had started—including her trepidation at being on display for people who might have reason to hate her—Justine had persevered, stayed the course. *Like a motherfuckin' lioness, saw what she wanted and went for it.* Then she'd given herself to him, completely, so naturally, exactly what he needed and wanted—he still couldn't believe his luck. *Fate, more likely*. They needed to do some serious talking when they got home, but he believed she, like him, was already deep into this thing between them.

His house sat outside of town, off a small oil-topped road, where there was a mile or more between neighbors. Lights in the landscaping cast a low but welcoming glow around the periphery, and as he rolled past the sensor at the end of the driveway, the door of the detached garage began lifting. He rode inside, looped around the end of his truck parked on the right, and pulled into the bike's parking space.

Justine wisely stayed put, and he climbed off the bike, turning to her. "Good girl." Hands at her waist, he lifted, bringing her off the bike before letting her feet take her weight. Taking off her helmet, he smoothed her hair, grinning as she unfastened his lid, straps dangling along his throat. "Welcome home, baby." She hummed against his lips when he kissed her, then pulled back, looking up at him with saucy mischief in her eyes.

"Tempest is well named."

That brought a grin to his face. "Liked that, didja?" She nodded. "Was good to have you with me, Jussie." He leaned into her for another kiss as he unstrapped the bag. "Let's get inside before the skeeters discover us. I got some kind of sonic shit, but I never trust it really."

"It's too late for the worst of the bloodsuckers."

She placed her hand in his outstretched one, and he wondered if he'd ever get used to even that small thing, hoping not. The sense of wonder was addictive. "There's always an outlier."

"Yeah." Her voice was soft, and he slowed, gaze on her face, taking in the mix of emotions passing over her features, glad when a mix of amusement and pleasure remained. "Gotta plan for the edge cases."

"That what I am, woman? Am I your edge case?" He slid his thumb across the lock at the back door, pushing on the knob when it clicked. It opened into the kitchen, motion-detecting lights flicking on under the cabinets. He paused because there was an electric movement to the air, setting the fine hairs at the back of his neck on end. Scanning the room, he asked, "What all did you plan for in your campaign to get into the clubhouse?"

Security lights are all amber. I'm imagining things. Nothing was out of place, and his suspicions were based on no more than a gut feeling. *Trusted my gut enough times, though.*

Unaware of his inner dialogue, Justine continued, "I wasn't planning on getting into the clubhouse, per se. I'd only plotted out what I wanted to say once I got to see you. Tonight," she said with a light laugh, clearly not holding any grudges against Twisted no matter what she might have said earlier, "didn't really go anywhere near what I'd planned."

"Do tell?" Shuffling her, so her back was to the wall next to the door, he pressed close, head angled so he could see her face as she spoke.

"Oh, once I got to you, it was off the charts beyond anything I'd hoped for. But before that?" She tried to bury her chuckle, but it bubbled out. "So not what I'd expected. Before *or* after, honestly." Rolling her eyes, she amended her earlier statement. "I hadn't braced for being on display in front of the whole club. Nor had I prepared to remind my brother I'm a big girl." She shrugged lightly, lifting a hand to drag her fingertips along his jaw, a graceful touch that buzzed through him. "Everything in between was a far and away better outcome than I'd hoped for."

"Were you prepared to negotiate?" He leaned in and brushed a kiss along her cheek, flicking at the lobe of her ear with his tongue. He was rewarded by a soft hum and a movement to arch her neck. Only a small portion of his attention was on the rest of the house, listening, that gut feeling not entirely leaving. "We recognized each other long ago, maybe that first moment."

"Lightning flashing and fighting all around, and there you were, larger than life. Hard to believe it's barely such a short time." She hummed again and turned her face to press a kiss at the hinge of his jaw. He let out a low groan at the initiative, liking how she wanted to touch him. "Big and powerful, it was like you sucked all the air out of that trailer."

"Strong. Smart. Loyal." He emphasized each word with a gentle kiss along her throat, ending with a bite he knew would sting. "Iron steel wrapped in a velvet fist." She arched into his touch, bodies pressed together. "Topping from the bottom from the beginning. No, Jussie." He cradled her jaw in his hand, turning her face back to his from where she'd tried to hide against his shoulder. "Nothing wrong in knowing what you want, especially if you don't trust anyone around you to know well enough to give it to you. That night, you needed the women with you to be safe and didn't know me from Jack. Willin' to do whatever it took to keep them whole and healthy. There's not a damn thing to be ashamed of there."

"I'm not forward. Not like that."

"Woman, you came to my room, you remember that? Bold as brass, crawled into my bed, me asleep."

"Yeah, but there was just something about you. I knew you'd take me out of my head, keep me safe. Plus, you didn't mind much."

"And did I keep you safe? Make you floaty where the world no longer mattered?"

"Yes." Her breath hitched, but she didn't fight his hold, exposing her emotions for his approval or censure. "Oh, yes."

"Justine." He drew her name out slowly, pleased when the corners of her lips tipped up. "My name's Lyle. Wanna hear you say it." Bending his neck, he dusted kisses across her mouth and back again, lapping at her bottom lip until she opened for him. After taking a long taste, he rocked back slightly and reminded her. "Lyle Woolsey. Say it."

"Lyle," she murmured against his mouth, the tip of her tongue touching his. "My wild Lyle."

He deepened the kiss, moving closer, pressing her tight against the surface behind, lips, tongue, teeth—wrecking his senses with the way she tasted, how she took everything he offered and begged for more. Tiny noises came from deep in her throat, not quite a whine but a definite plea he answered until they were both panting for breath.

Then, he deliberately slowed them down, keeping the heat but dampening his desperation, knowing she was echoing what he was feeding her. *My good girl, Jussie.* "Wanna take you on a tour." Cupping his hand around hers, he drew her fingers up his chest, flattening their palms together. "There's at least one more room I wanna see you in." Lifting her chin, he captured her mouth again, a slow exploration that had her trembling against him. "Come on, Jussie." Taking a step backwards, he looped their fingers together. "Come see."

The kitchen went past in a blur, as did the living room with the large freestanding fireplace, empty of even ashes this time of year. Walking fast, not giving her much chance to look around, he pulled her down the hallway towards his room.

Once inside, he leaned sideways and tapped his code into the security panel beside the door, arming the exterior system, which protected the windows and doors, and included video inside the garage. Then he crowded back into her space, so close her breasts pressed against his chest, her neck stretching and chin lifting to keep her gaze on his face.

"We've gone about things halfway backwards, baby." A tiny divot appeared between her eyebrows, the puzzled expression making him smile. "Our dynamic won't ever be like anyone else's, but there's a right and wrong way to go about this, and I've been skirting the issues. If we're going to play in addition to fucking, then we've got to have the right information about each other."

"I'm negative." The frown didn't ease with her soft statement. It might even have darkened, muscles in her face tensing. "If that's what you want to know."

"Nope, guess again." He shrugged, aiming at an easy movement, trying to hide how her instant expectations stung. Just like before, when she'd thought he'd believed her a plant with a wire. "Traffic light system works for me, if that's comfortable with you. I'm going to want a lot of control over you, but I understand your career is at odds with any kind of a round-the-clock lifestyle. You said you're only subby in bed, not out of it, but honey—and I hate to be the one to break it to you—you publicly submitted so sweetly back there in the clubhouse, I nearly couldn't catch my breath. I don't do roleplay, and dubcon is a hard limit for me. I'm not going to bleed you, but seeing your sweet ass going dark pink from my hands on you is fuckin' hot. I fuckin' love impact play, and I know I can make you fly." He pressed his lips to hers, working side to side until her lashes dipped, her mouth softening underneath his attentions, a tiny gasp opening her to him. Plundering the depths of her mouth with his tongue, he cradled her jaw with one hand, the other coming to rest on her waist, steadying her as he pulled away. "That's my starting negotiation, Jussie."

"I..." She leaned into him, and he gave her that tiny slice of privacy, wishing he could see the expression on her face but understanding how in the past six hours he'd stripped her bare enough that not having to school herself would be a relief. "Everything's different with you. All my rules are thrown out the window. I've always needed the pain to get to that place in my mind where I could just exist. Often it was without penetrative intercourse, just an application of predicament bondage, or a demanding pose needing constant attention and focus, something to push everything away. My most recent partner—" He tried to stop his muscles tensing, but when she cut-off midsentence, he knew he hadn't been fast enough. The idea of her giving herself willingly to a man—and he had no doubt it was a male partner, since the chances of her finding a Domme she would trust were even less—churned his stomach.

"Go on." Circling her throat with his hand, he tightened only enough to feel the slide of muscles and tendon, but it was possessive and what they both needed right now. "It's all right, Jussie. You're my good girl."

The softly keening sound that broke from her throat made his arm around her shoulders tighten, folding her against him closely when she cut herself off. *Fuck, I like that reaction. My good girl.*

"Always gonna be my good girl. Mmhmm. Jussie's my good girl." And if he put emphasis on the *my*, Wildman didn't think any man would blame him. "Go on, now, tell me what you need me to know."

"He"—*damn it, I didn't wanna be right*—"wanted to be intimate sexually, but we work together. Taking what I needed from him was bad enough."

"Stop it right there. There's nothing to be ashamed of in making sure you're happy and healthy. The fact you worked together shouldn't factor. Any Dom worth his water should be able to help you without it becoming a source of embarrassment." He rested his cheek on top of her head. "Let's take this somewhere more comfortable." Scooping her up and grinning at her tiny yip of surprise, he stalked to the bed and knee-crawled to the headboard, twisting around, so she rested in his lap as he sat and leaned back. "There. I'm more comfortable. How about I go first after all?"

"But you already—"

"Nope, I told you what I like, not what I've done. Big difference, Jussie." He took a breath. If she was going to leap into the deep end of past relationships, he wanted to get out in front of everything, give her a chance to say *sayonara* in a clear way, so he'd know what it'd take to get her back. "My first relationship was a matter of circumstance. She was the earliest one I explored anything I'd been thinking about, and she seemed into it, enough to fool me, anyway. I wasn't real smart back then, or I should have probably cottoned onto her true feelings sooner. In the end, we weren't what the other needed, and once her youngest siblings were out of the house, she left my sad ass." He licked his lips and swallowed. "The only thing I hated was how blind I'd been through the last couple of years. Here I thought I'd been exploring something we both wanted, only to find out she believed I was sick in the head." Justine sucked in a breath, and he stroked the backs of his fingers down her face. "Shhhh. Wasn't her kink, would never be her kink. I get it now. Don't mean it didn't hurt like fuck at the time, but I get it now."

"You said your first relationship."

The emphasis was tiny, but he caught it, nodding once, then dropping a kiss against the top of her head.

"Yup, my second lies buried in an unmarked grave. I've done talked about her a little with you, but I wanna be an open book, so ask me anything."

"You said it was club business, like my Chris being taken?" The uptilt of her tone indicated a question, but it was a statement of information he'd already given her, so Wildman just hummed in response. "And you left that club because of it?"

"I left the club because my brother was VP and talked his way into buying a paper on me while he tore up the club to get the president patch. All of which meant not only wasn't he family anymore but those who allowed both weren't my brothers under the patch either. I left the club after he died because of a fight. I didn't know I was fighting for my life. I thought it was a test to see if I was still loyal, but he was gonna kill me himself if he could. Tangled himself up and tripped, clipped a corner going down, gave himself a TBI that did for him." He took a breath. "I killed him. Didn't mean to, but I did."

"My brother killed my father. Then my other brother killed him." She pulled in a ragged breath. "Chris' dad turned traitor to his club, was involved in the death of Watcher on orders from his own father, then was killed by the man. I'm rethinking what I asked earlier. You know? Maybe it's better Christopher stay well away from anything to do with the life. With genetics like this—" She broke off with a choked sob, her fingers clamping tight on his wrist where he once again held her throat in his hand.

"Diamond, right?" She nodded. "Deacon's boy." Less of a question, but she still moved in a way that was agreement. "Stories tell the tale, baby. Everyone knows how Deacon fucked the Fiends sideways. He's the poster child of what a club president shouldn't be. Man's dead, too, because of his fuckery. I've heard stories about that takedown. You know Bones?" The "mmhmm" was nearly a lilt, and he was pleased by the fact she clearly liked Bones. "Climbed the man like a tree and took him down. Wish there were video because that'd be good as fuck to watch. Don't care what it says about me, but the stories are epic. He didn't go down easy, Jussie."

"What do you think about Chris?"

The vulnerable trembling of her tone tightened his throat, made it harder to get the words out, but he wouldn't leave her hanging like that, so he muscled through, speaking the truth as he knew it right now. "I can approach him anonymously, and we can leave it in his hands whether he wants to meet you, if you're okay with that. But baby, I'm happy to get monthly reports and pass them along, if that'll settle your soul about how your boy is doing. Hell, we'll get weekly or daily if you want. I think it's a good idea for you to wrap your head around him and his life, and if he's open to a meet-and-greet, then that's what we do, as long as it's what you want too." He tightened his grip on her throat when she swallowed hard, the thud of her speeding heart against his palm growing faster. "I can't imagine what it was like to not know for so long if he was even breathin', so you wantin' to keep your eye on him now you know he's livin' what looks like a good life, that's not a bad thing. That's a good mom wanting to make sure her boy's okay. You're a good girl, Jussie."

"I don't feel so good today." Pulling in a deep breath, she melted against him, going boneless, which told him he'd hit the mark with his response about her boy. "I don't know up from down, seems like."

Her shifting in his lap had his dick chubbing up, but he ignored it in favor of making this a suitable introduction for her to his home. *A place I hope like fuck she spends a lotta time.* "Let's grab showers, get a bite to eat, and then slip into bed." She shifted, and he groaned softly, the pressure on his cock enough to make it pay more attention to how close she was to him. "To sleep, Jussie. We both need it before we go back for the war meeting in the morning."

"And if I don't want to sleep just yet?" She pushed against his chest with one palm, and he relaxed his hold enough to let her move away a few inches, her chin coming up so he could look down into her face. "And showers, as in plural? Haven't you heard about the world water crisis? We need to cut that down to a single activity and double up in the tub." She flashed him a smile that wasn't confident, wasn't assured, but held a hint of hope he wanted to cultivate. "Unless you have a strange shower fetish you haven't shared?"

"I'd love to share my shower with you, baby girl. Pamper you, get you all soaped up and slippery, see where things go. Then I'll feed my baby, and we can get some shut-eye." He thrust his hips up against her weight, ensuring she felt the hard rod of his cock as it ground against her ass. "And seems to me you know up from down just fine."

Her laughter pulled him in, and he bent to catch it with his mouth, fitting his lips over hers, taking her tiny gasp of pleased surprise and eating it down, storing for later the happiness he felt just from that. Then he slipped sideways, curled his arms to lift her, and climbed from the bed.

"Another surprise for you. I *may* have a bit of a shower kink, as in I like it large, with plenty of hot water and water pressure." He shoved the bathroom door wide with his shoulder, fitting them through the opening so she could see the room. The smile on her face reflected off the several mirrored surfaces, and he liked how the bright expression lit up the space. "And"—he turned to face the walk-in shower, sliding door pushed partly open—"it comes with accessories." Reaching inside, he tapped the control for his normal setting, the instant on of the water making her jerk in surprise, moving back against his chest as he let her feet settle on the floor. Steam rolled out of the shower already, and he again thanked his brothers for the tankless water heater idea. "See that?" He pointed to the handheld wand. "That's going to be your new best friend."

Her laughter rang out, and he spun her, again capturing it with his mouth, kissing her hard and fast, tongue thrusting into her mouth in imitation of what he'd be doing in a fast minute, soon as he got her wet. *No condom in here. Can't forget to pull out.* He'd seen a couple of tiny scars on her stomach, old incisions from some kind of surgery, but it could have been anything. She wasn't too old to conceive, not by a long shot, no matter how old her boy was. She'd been a child when she'd birthed him, and until they had *that* conversation, he'd take care of her even if she didn't know he was.

Backing her into the shower, he angled himself, so his back caught the bulk of the spray to test the temperature. "Too hot, Jussie?"

Breaths coming fast and heavy, she gusted air across his lips when she answered. "Just right."

With the door closed, he twisted them sideways and reached for the wand, flicking the control to a light, pulsing spray with a practiced movement. He took her mouth again, one hand holding her nape tight, angling her head like he wanted; then he placed the tip of the wand at her clit, eating down her squeal of surprise, then doing the same with the low, rattling moan that escaped her throat. Working the pulsing jets of water in tiny, unpredictable circles, he had her crying out against his mouth time and again until she went rigid in his arms. Wand back in its holder, he replaced it with his hand over her mons, fingers finding that glorious slipperiness the raining water couldn't wash away.

Two fingers tucked inside her, he swiped the tip of his thumb over the hooded part of her clit, feeling the softness returning as she turned boneless against him.

"My good girl."

***

Justine

She rocked side to side, movement of the surface underneath her subtle but enough to rouse her to the edge of being awake. Without opening her eyes, without him saying a word, she knew it was Wildman slipping into bed beside her. He smelled clean with a citrusy edge, the same scent of the body gel he'd used to clean her after whiting out her mind in the shower with an unexpected orgasm.

The memory swelled, and Justine's breath caught in her throat.

It had been nothing but pleasure.

There'd been no pain.

No pain, and still he'd wiped her brain of all conscious thought, so much so he'd had to support her as he cleaned her up, keeping her hair dry as he could. Then he'd wrapped her in a towel and laid her on his bed, chasing stray water droplets before chucking the towel towards the bathroom and tucked her under the covers with a gentle kiss against her forehead. Hand braced around her throat, he'd stayed bent over her, face close enough his mouth was only a breath away, and he'd watched her go to sleep.

She had no sense of time passing, so it could have been five minutes or five hours, but from how tired she still felt, Justine thought she'd lean more towards a shorter period.

Wildman curled himself around her, his arm slipping under her head before he wrapped his other hand around her hip, erasing the distance between their bodies.

"You awake?" The rumbling of his voice transferred through her back and into her belly, where it set up a shop of butterflies from the fluttering.

"Barely." Her words came out hoarser than she expected, and she lightly cleared her throat. "You good?"

His arms tightened, and his lips brushed the back of her neck in a soft kiss, light as those butterfly wings. "Got my Jussie right here. I'm right as rain." The tip of his nose trailed across her nape. Then his mouth was on her ear, nibbling and sucking gently. "Need some juice or a snack before we sleep? We kinda skipped the meal I'd intended to feed you."

"Nah, I'm good." Her fingers curled around the edge of his bicep naturally, and she nestled her cheek against his warm skin. "This is nice."

"Mmhmm," he agreed. "More than nice, Jussie. This is what I want."

"Well, good. That's one goal knocked off." She yawned, and his hand on her hip slipped down to cover her belly, making her feel surrounded by him, something she was coming to love. "Sleep."

She must have taken her own advice, because the next thing she knew was the mattress shifting underneath her again, Wildman's hip on the other side from where he'd been lying. She blinked up and watched as he rested two mugs on the table beside the bed. A discreet sniff confirmed he'd brought her coffee. She flicked a glance around without seeing a clock and concentrated on the edge of the curtain covering the window, seeing light filtering in around the bottom.

"Morning?" She caught herself before shoving off the covers, realizing she was naked underneath the sheet. Instead, she tucked them underneath her arms as she pushed to a seated position and held out one hand. "Hand me the magic potion and no one gets hurt." His chuckle was unpolished, rough as gravel, and sounded tired. Lines of tension gathered around his eyes and mouth, and she frowned. "Everything okay?"

He lifted a mug and surrendered it to her grip before grabbing the other one. "Yeah, Jussie, just long nights catching up with me. Slept better with you than I have in a long time." Sipping noisily from the mug, he cut his eyes to her. "You sleep okay?"

"Did I snore? I snored, didn't I." The coffee was hot and rich, filled with flavor and blessed caffeine. "I'm sorry."

"Jesus, Jussie. No, woman." He chuckled again. "You didn't make a peep at all. Just curled up against me and took your rest. Made me happy to see."

"Oh, well, then that's a relief." She shook her head, huffing air up to fluff her bangs. "What time is it, Lyle?" She knew she was taking a chance using his name, but the way he'd demanded it last night gave her confidence it would be what he wanted.

His smile was blinding, his entire focus on her as he leaned in close to brush his lips across hers. "We've got about an hour before we need to head out. I've got breakfast warming in the oven, so finish your coffee—" He twisted away, setting the mug down before reaching down to the foot of the bed. "Slip on my shirt, and come to the kitchen when you're ready."

"You want me to wear your shirt?" She thought she understood the gesture but wanted to verify his motives.

"Fuck yeah, woman. You in my shirt? Gonna be hot as hell. Rile me up right before a war meeting, and I'll do my best work. Then when we're all done there, we'll come back here and make our way through a couple sets of sheets before we hit the road." He smiled broadly, not as brilliantly as before, but close. "Now, give your old man a kiss." She reached for the shirt as he leaned close, fingers wrapping around the fabric, so she had a handful of material and a hot mug of coffee in her hands when he pulled the covers down around her waist, his hands immediately going to her skin. One broad palm skated along her ribs, his work-roughened thumb scraping across the side of her breast in a titillating caress. His other hand cupped and lifted a breast, fingers and thumb tweaking the nipple until she felt the burning sting of pain from the pinch. Breaths coming out choppy, she stared at him as he watched her face. "My Jussie."

Closing the distance between them, she offered her lips as he'd demanded, and he instantly took control of the kiss, using tongue and teeth as his mouth worked against hers.

"Kitchen, honey." He pulled back, tweaked the stinging nipple a final time, picked up his mug, and sauntered through the door.

Justine watched him stride out of sight, those damn jeans clinging to his ass and thighs like they'd been made for him. His broad shoulders stretched the fabric of his T-shirt thin to give a great show of the muscles moving underneath.

"Man's a menace," she muttered, gulping at the cooling coffee. She set it on the table and spread the shirt out over her lap, casually bringing the covers back up to cover herself because the sight of her one nipple red and puffy was distracting. It wouldn't have been as bad if he'd given both the girls the same treatment, but he'd apparently picked a favorite. She snorted a quiet laugh.

Support your local Incoherent was on the back with iron-on vinyl, and the same material displayed *SYLI* on the front.

Something he'd just said struck her, and her brain reeled back to last night as she stood next to him in the clubhouse, shoulder to shoulder. *My old man.* Justine pulled in a shaky breath because this wasn't something she'd ever wanted. In fact, this was something she'd actively avoided, moving away from her father's club as a teen, staying at arm's length from Davy's club. Hell, even her job had been selected as the most opposite thing. Sure, she'd told herself—and still mostly believed it—that she'd gone into law enforcement studies because she'd wanted to help women like herself, those who had their loved ones stolen, those whose lives were made impossible by criminals—*like my dad*—but joining the agency? That had been the biggest stick she could push into her father's eye. A virtual scream of "I'm not like you, not at all."

"And here I am." She looked at the doorway, wafting scents of eggs and bacon beginning to make their way in through the air. "I'm an old lady."

Wild—Lyle isn't like Daddy. Not at his core. She had no illusions that if there'd been money to be made running flesh back in the day, her father's club would have been all over that. *Davy's not like Daddy, either.* She'd understood as soon as she'd realized who Davis Mason was, her half-sibling, but one who had also angled his path well away from the line their father had trod.

There were no hard and fast rules about this relationship with Lyle. He'd claimed her in front of the men who mattered in his life, but hadn't she done the same thing? *We'll do this get-to-know-you tour on his bike, and then I'll have decisions to explain.*

But she didn't have to turn her mind to those changes yet.

She flipped the covers back, picked up the shirt, and shimmied into it. *He wants to see me wearing his shirt.* When she stood, the hem swung midthigh, so she smiled as she picked up the nearly empty mug and very deliberately stepped past her panties on the floor.

The only thing she had to do in the next hour was tease and please her old man.

And that sounds pretty damn fine to me.

Chapter Seventeen
Wildman

Backing his pipes to the building with the ease of long practice, he stabilized the bike and held up a hand, smiling when Justine's palm confidently met his. She stepped off the pegs, swinging her leg over, so she stood next to his left side, and he grinned again. First, it put her opposite the hot pipes, so no chance of getting burned, but he was also right-handed, and it put her well away from the piece holstered along his thigh.

"Fuckin' champ, woman." Kickstand down, he stood up and off the bike, taking the helmet she'd already removed and hanging the chin clip on a metal hook welded to the bike's frame. Dangling his from the handlebars, he slipped in behind her and captured her hands, replacing them in her hair with his own as he fluffed her bangs and stroked stray strands behind her ears. "Love havin' you wrapped around me."

"You're not half bad yourself, Wild." She twisted around in his arms, and he waited to tighten his hold on her when she'd turned to face him. His hand on her ass brought their lower bodies flush. "No slouch."

"Lovin' the approval, Jussie." Eyes open, he leaned in to kiss her, grinning against her mouth. "You ready to head in?"

She pulled back and glanced around the lot, seeming to take in the elevated number of bikes in the lot. "Is this the whole club? All chapters?"

"Nah, we'll just have Mother here. Maybe BR. Not everyone, though." He pointed to a bike with distinctive handlebars parked two rows out. "Retro's bike. His crew is here." He scanned and gestured towards a clump clearly parked together, a prospect set to watch over the machines. "That'll be the Rebels delegation, and I'm not going to venture a guess how many chapters they've pulled from, but it's probably safe to say most of their southern contingent." Another line of bikes was pulling into the lot, and he lifted a hand in a welcoming gesture to the lead rider, earning a head-nod in response. "That's a Georgia club right there. They may or may not be in the negotiations but will definitely be around for assignments afterwards. Support shit, that's what they do. Capone there took over from Big Nico when he was deposed, runs the South Coast Devils with an iron fist. I like the man, like how he is with his members more."

"So Twisted is willing to lean on leadership of other clubs?" She shook her head slowly, gaze following the movement of the bikes and riders as they found a space large enough for the whole group to park. "Isn't that something he would normally avoid?"

"Being capable of doing something yourself but understanding if you band with others who have the same abilities then the result will be stronger—that don't make someone weak. Just means they're confident enough to see the endgame and be willing to apply whatever tools are needed to get there fast and sure." She hummed and turned to face the road, leaning her head against his chest as another group turned into the drive. "That's Wrench and the CoBos. They're probably the last to arrive. That'll be an intentional move on his part, guarantee. Kept Po'Boy out of the clubhouse for the earlier introductions, which makes his defection less of a topic of conversation."

"Politics never change, do they?" Placing her palms flat on his chest, she angled her head up, and he looked down into her face. "In the government, in the agency, asking or accepting offered help without a fight is seen as an inability to manage resources or solve issues. Everyone is always pissing in the corners of their territory to keep other agents out of the way. Cross-department endeavors often need a mediator to even start to talk about whatever it is needs doing. I saw one case stalled in committee for a year, and then it was just dropped, because no clear hierarchy was ever established."

"That's why your guys were so pissed, because you stepped over that process and took things into your own hands." The club had ears in the DEA, and it had been brought to his attention this morning via series of calls and texts how much shit Justine had earned for her part in the recovery of the women. Despite the positive outcome, there were rumblings of an official reprimand coming her way, which was shit. "And not one of those fuckers have your back. That's the biggest difference in doing things their way or our way. I go out on my own and source a solution that works, I know Twisted will be right there beside me when I need him. No coulda, woulda, shoulda around, just him and his 'fuck yeah, get it' as we deal with the shit."

"That sounds sorta freeing." She laughed, but the strain in her voice was echoed in the tension lines around her mouth. "I can't imagine not needing to requisition things in triplicate."

"And I can't imagine you being happy with that process for long." He gave her a squeeze, then turned them, heading towards the door. "Hence your rogue status in the DEA." They reached the door the same time as Capone, and Wildman held out his hand, grinning as the man removed his riding gloves before gripping his thumb, hands wrapping around in a warrior's greeting. "Capone, good to see you, man. This is my old lady, Justine."

"Ms. LaPorte." No surprise, Capone knew exactly who she was. He lifted a finger to his brow in an abbreviated salute, not trying to touch her. *Saved himself some pain there.* "I'd say it's a pleasure, but you know how things are." Capone must have noted Wildman's instant offense, because he scoffed and shook his head. "Not trying to insult your old lady, man. It's the day, brother. I fuckin' hate this shit, and we did it not even a decade ago. Those cartel boys don't gots long enough memories, seems like, and I'm tired of learnin' 'em. Note I didn't say it was good to see you, either."

The feel of Justine's fingers slipping into Wildman's back pocket was good, a silent vote of confidence. He tried to reel back in his anger, listening to Capone's tone as well as his words.

Capone continued, "That ugly mug gonna haunt my nightmares for the next few weeks, no doubt." Capone's face wreathed in a grin, corners of his mouth lifting his beard. "So unfuck yourself, man. It's all good."

"No, man. I get it." He lowered his shoulders and rolled his neck, grunting when it caught and popped loudly, telegraphing to anyone within earshot the level of his tension. "I'm with ya, brother." Tipping his head towards the door, he reached out and opened it. "After you. Let's get this show on the road."

Capone gave him another grin as he walked past, his shout echoing into the building, "Fuckin' South Coast Devils are in the house, motherfuckers. Where the hell's Twisted?" Wildman chuckled, tightening his arm around Justine as he held the door for the SCDMC members following their crazy president.

A hand fell on his shoulder from behind, and he turned his head to see Po'Boy standing there. Justine ducked under his arm as he spun and wrapped his arms around the man's shoulders, pounding against the patch in the center of his back. "Good to see you, brother."

"Wild." Po'Boy's muffled voice in his ear sounded strained, and Wildman gave another brutal squeeze, forcing a groan out of the man, who then matched force for force, gripping Wildman hard enough he lifted him off the ground an inch, and Wild gave out a groan of his own. "You're a fuckin' asshole, Quacker."

They released at the same time, both men stumbling back a few inches with broad grins on their faces. Wildman shook his head and sighed, reaching his arm out, and was pleased as fuck when Justine immediately reclaimed her spot at his side, her fingers tucking in along his waist this time, curling underneath the fabric to stroke his bare skin.

"Justine, you know I nearly kissed this man once? Was just going to be an experiment. Just to see how it was to be on the other end of all that intensity." He shook his head, feigning sadness as he glanced down to see a crooked, questioning smile aimed his way. "I'd seen him kissin' Wrench, and it sparked a curiosity in me." He leaned close, hand up for privacy he negated by raising his voice instead of lowering it. "Bastard took offense, if you can believe that. 'Keep ya tongue to yaself,' he told me. So instead, the next time I went to the club down in Orleans, I found myself a...well, that's neither here nor there, but let's just say I'm glad I found you, baby girl."

Laughter rose from the men who had clustered around their little group, Wrench standing at Po'Boy's back one of the loudest.

"And that's how it's fuckin' done, boys." Po'Boy shook his head, then tipped his chin towards Justine. "You're a stronger person than I am, woman. Takin' this old troublemaker on like you're doin'? Hope you got the patience of a saint, because a saint he ain't."

Justine's headshake and sigh came with a smile as she said, "Already got that memo. Think there's still time to get out?"

"Hey." Wildman glared at Po'Boy, then gave Justine a shake. "Hell no, you ain't gettin' away from me."

"Good thing I wasn't going to try then, isn't it?" Her fingertips dug into the soft skin under his ribs, and he flinched, which only pressed them more tightly together.

"Let's get inside," Wrench offered, pounding Wildman's shoulder as he stepped past them. "Found your match, I see. You're in for a helluva ride, brother."

"Don't I know it." Wildman ignored the rest of the CoBos as they filed past, dipping to brush his lips against Justine's. "Can't get enough of your taste. Can't get enough of you." He kissed her again, flicking his tongue against her lower lip, delving deeper when she opened for him, as uncaring of their audience as he was. "Want you right fuckin' now and can't have you. Told you that shit'll rile me up, and we'll get through this meeting faster. Good job, baby."

He caught her laugh in his mouth, only moving back to let her speak when her shoulders had stopped shaking.

"Just doin' my part for the cause." Head against his chest, she stayed close as he led her into the clubhouse, which was bursting at the seams with so many members and guests present.

It struck him immediately that Justine was the only female face he saw. No party dolls, no old ladies, not a single woman present—except Justine.

"Quick primer, since you've been out of the life for a long time. I'm going to do my best to keep you right here with me, Jussie. If you're barred from any closed-door meetings, then you look for any IMC with a Mother rocker. Don't speak to them. Just let them see you and then get close, so it's clear you're looking for protection. I guarantee you they know why you're here, and they'll keep you safe if I'm not in the room with you. Don't speak to a soul unless you're under my arm and I give you the nod. Even direct questions, hear me?" He gave her a shake and stared down at her, watching as her lips pressed thin. She clearly wrestled with the directive before nodding her acceptance. "Not fuckin' around here, Jussie. This is unprecedented, this many clubs in one fuckin' room, and I expect shit to start at some point. Someone's gonna bump someone, and it'll be a shitshow for a minute before our guys wade in. Just don't want you caught up in any shit. I don't think anyone'll be targeting you. If they do, then they're too stupid to keep breathin', and I'll introduce them to the concept myself. But don't put yourself in a position where you can be compromised."

"I won't embarrass you." Low and clipped, her words carried a thread of anger that had him shaking his head.

"You mistake me, lady. I have no doubt you can handle yourself. Fuck, saw you do that with my own eyes just days ago. You got the goods, baby, but in this situation, it is counterproductive to use them. One on one, or even two on one, you got your shit handled. No doubts." He pressed her against a wall, curling around her the best he could, creating a space for just them. "I'm not worried about that. I'm worried about shit breakin' out behind you that's got nothin' at all to do with you, but you get swept underfoot because folks are tryin' to keep it toned down and no weapons drawn. I expect you noted we weren't checkin' at the door, which means every one of these motherfuckers has at least one piece on 'em. Last thing we need is for someone to need a doc today, so we'll be squashing shit fast. It's in those moments between 'not happening' and full-blown where you could get hurt. I don't want that."

"What if I pull a chair behind the bar and sit?" Brows furrowed, she angled her head to look around him. "I'd be below casual line-of-sight, and I can stay out of the way of the prospects. I'm guessing they won't be serving much more than cans of beer today, if that. Would that work? This way I'm not a distraction if one of your officers needs to wade in and stop whatever altercation is brewing."

"Beautiful and brilliant. I'm the luckiest motherfucker around." He kissed her hard, turned, and walked into the room. His hand on her hip pulled her with him. At the bar, he pointed to an upturned bucket near one end, shoving it behind the bar with the toe of his boot. "There's your throne. You won't be on it long, if at all, promise." A low whistle caught the attention of Ruger nearby. He waited for the man to be within hearing distance before he again pointed at the bucket. "If I have to be in a closed door, Jussie'll be here. You'll watch out for her for me?"

"You know it, brother," came the easy answer, Ruger's fist bumping against his shoulder. "I got you."

"Problem solved," he told Justine, then pulled her in front of him and folded his arms across her chest. "Ruger, this is my old lady, Justine. Jussie, I've known Ruger for a long fuckin' time. Trust him with my life, and now yours. Trouble by the bar, you look for and run to him. We won't be in the same conversations, so should be an easy swap." Her nod had soft hair drifting across the side of his neck, and he smiled, smoothing a hand over the curve of her head and tucking those strands back behind her ear. Looking at Ruger, who appeared to be watching the interaction with interest, Wildman asked, "Twisted?"

"Cross the room, near Mason and his boys. Guessing they're the biggest dom asked in, other than us, so they're getting a somewhat VIP treatment."

"Or my man Twisted wants to keep a close eye on this crew himself." Wildman shrugged. "Either way, two birds, one stone for me right now. Come on, baby." He dropped a kiss on the top of her head. "Let's go see the fam."

"Oh, Lord," she muttered, then giggled and pressed tighter to him. "You gave me a couple of marks."

"I know." Chin high, he led her across the room. "Boss." He leaned towards Twisted, looking neither left nor right, arm firmly around Justine as Twisted greeted him with a slap on the back. "Timeframe for gettin' this shindig started?"

"Well now, my good friend Mason and I were just discussin' that very topic." Twisted turned to look at Mason, forcing Wildman to do the same.

Mason's eyes were focused on the IMC-support shirt Justine wore. Then his gaze flicked up to her face and back to the shirt before moving more slowly to the junction of her shoulders and her neck, where Wildman had left two very distinct overlapping marks. One of his teeth, and then a dark bruise from a hard, sucking kiss. Mason's jaw moved side to side, and Wildman watched as one hand folded into a fist.

"You couldn't give it one fucking day?" Mason turned his glare on Wildman and took a half step forwards, chin up.

"You should know, old man, there ain't a single fucking thing about this between me and Justine that's got shit-all to do with you. Everything I do is for her, and if you'd think with your strategic hat on for just one goddamned minute, you'd see clearly." Wildman leaned in, chest nearly brushing Mason's. "She's wearin' my shirt because I fuckin' *need* my brothers to see the depth of this commitment. She's not a plant, and you and I know that to our bones, but the scrutiny and skepticism will live on in deep, thick bands of still water if I don't get out ahead of it and make a goddamned statement. It's one thing to know, and it's another to take something that feels like a risk on just fuckin' faith. So I picked the shirt with care, my man." He shook his head, inching another fraction into Mason's space, the big man's chest rising and falling with each hard breath, their gazes locked on each other.

"She's mine. *Mine.* I know you get that, at least, havin' a good old lady of your own. One to keep. Keep her for you, and keep her safe." He pulled in a breath, watching the muscles in Mason's jaw jump, hearing the circle of silence around them grow as attention was brought to bear on this potential altercation. *Gotta make my point and then back the fuck up.* Justine was tense under his arm and hand, drawn tight, poised for action. *Shit, woman. Last thing I need right now is a boner to deal with too.* He glanced down at her to see her head on a swivel, watching his back and all around them. "Easy, Jussie." His mutter was quiet, but she caught it and looked up at him with a quick, decisive nod. Arrowing his attention back on Mason, he considered his next words.

"There ain't a single other woman here, which puts a spotlight on her. By reputation you're supposed to be a cagey shit. I bet you can imagine all of what that can do. Some man in here gets to thinking she's not spoken for, and there might be a possibility of grooming themselves for some of your consideration? I'd have to kill them, and I'm against spillin' red today, because these are friends and allies in this room, and we're going to need every fuckin' one of them to do what's needed. Me puttin' my marks on her, having her under my arm, draping myself all over her—I'm keeping her. You feel me? Keepin' her for me, keepin' her safe, hell, keepin' her whole so your family doesn't have to deal with any fallout. Your blood family." Time to drill the message home how she'd shifted allegiances. She'd still have loyalty to her brother, but the RWMC? *Fuck them.*

"Your club family, those patch brothers you've talked about setting to watch her? They got nothin' to do with her no more. She's IMC now, Mason, and you're going to have to understand this situation. This relationship, this fucking woman I have at my side, don't got shit-all to do with the RWMC anymore. Loyalty, brother, and I know you understand that concept. She's mine, I'm hers. You know our saying, too. I am IMC, and IMC is me. Well, now, she is IMC, and IMC is her, which means she's covered. You feel me?"

He took a deliberate step backwards, taking Justine with him. Boots behind him shuffled to give him space, and he retreated another few inches. Head high, he held Mason's gaze until the man gave him a tight nod, the barest dip of his chin to his throat, but not a single muscle eased from the tension forced all over the man's frame. *This ain't over, got it.*

Wildman waited. Still and silent, he waited.

And Mason surprised him.

Slowly, so slowly he missed any first indications, only picking up on the way the man's cheek creased as if holding back a smile. Grey eyes the mirror of Justine's blinked, and Mason sucked in a deep breath, then let it out in a slow sigh. "My sister picked well." Mason's hand flashed out, and Wildman avoided flinching by only the barest measures, his palm lifting quickly to slap against Mason's, hard and stinging. There was no grinding grip, no attempt to cow him, just a firm up and down shake, followed by a change in grip so Mason's fingers wrapped around his wrist. He accommodated and went with the flow when Mason pulled him forwards, dipping until their shoulders met briefly. "You'll do, Wildman."

The fuck just happened?

Twenty minutes later, he and Justine stood against a broad pane of glass at Twisted's back, their positioning entirely intentional, as they were exactly where Twisted had told him to place themselves. Wildman watched as the presidents and VPs of the various clubs filtered into the room, half shooting daggers at Twisted, half looking questioningly at Wildman and Justine. Mason had to break protocol, bringing in four men with him, so that Wrench made his way back to the door and whistled, gesturing. Wildman was unsurprised when Po'Boy poked his head into the room, grinning as he took in the makeup of the crowd.

Since Po'Boy had patched over into the CoBos, he'd been trapped in an uncomfortable gray zone. No longer an officer in the Incoherent MC and not even a voting member of the CoBos, yet he was still someone the standing presidents of both clubs leaned on heavily. Him being in here only made sense to Wildman, though, and he gave the man a nod as he parked up next to where Wild stood. He split the difference between Twisted and Wrench, somehow managing to be behind both. *Message received.*

Movement on the other side of Justine had Wildman's head whipping sideways to watch as Retro and Mason had an impressive standoff, their staring glares caught immobile. Finally Retro dipped his chin and took a step back, letting Mason move past him and into the spot in front of Justine. Retro and Mudd lined up after Mason and Gunny, though, splitting the RWMC men with practiced ease.

All of this accomplished in near silence, broken only with muffled coughs and a couple of whispers between the groups lined up on the other side of the table.

Without any kind of signal Wildman could suss out, three prospects swept into the room, six different buckets held in their hands. Each bucket labeled with an MC's initials was deposited on top of the table near the identified groups.

"Phones in the pot, please, folks." That was Busk, standing next to the door. "You can understand our desire to keep our conversations private-like."

"You bring in a phone, baby?" Justine answered his murmured question with a headshake. "All right." He pulled his phone from the inside pocket of his vest, hand hesitating over the gun tucked in alongside it. "Just the electronics, right?"

Twisted laughed out loud, and Busk hung his head, swinging it back and forth. "Yeah, Wild. Keep your iron, brother. It's all good, man." That broke the silence in the room, and there was a steady rattle and thump of devices being deposited into the containers. The prospects gathered the buckets when the men had all returned to their former positions, stacking them and withdrawing from the room. The doors swung closed and latched, and only then did Twisted pull his chair back from the table, dropping heavily into it.

The men nearest the table around the room followed suit, toppling into place like rows of obedient dominos, until there was a ring of black leather framing the tabletop and a secondary ring of observers standing at their backs. Wildman took stock of the faces and names, the intent expressions each man wore, and a shiver drilled its way down his spine. *This is historic shit.* Justine's fingers clamped around his hand, tight then released, then tight again, and he used his peripheral vision to track where she was focused.

The man behind Sparks was glaring at her. Likely a member of the Jailbreakers, but what would his beef be with Justine? Wildman knew the club had been tasked with being her babysitter often enough by the RWMC, the dom they owed allegiance to, so he'd expect she'd know most of them reasonably well. *Guess we'll see.* He met Justine's grip with his own, giving her hand a tiny shake, and she tipped her head to brush against his arm, acknowledging his response.

Twisted had started talking minutes ago, the lead-in for the reason behind this meeting, but hadn't gotten to the bone of the issue yet, so Wildman kept observing. Gaze flicking from face to face, he kept returning to the Jailbreaker VP, trying to remember the man's name. The plate on the front of his vest only held his position, and Wildman found he didn't like not knowing.

Silence fell, and he glanced down at Twisted to see his national president taking a long look around the room. *Showtime.*

"Cartel dropped a list. List that's got all kinds of names on it. They're makin' it real clear they wanna do a sweep of the coast, push back the power we got until they can take over and run their business any damn way they want. Part of that list is threats. Generalized threats, followed by information." He leaned his chair back on two legs. "Right now, every club in this room is noted on that list."

Busk had a stack of paper in front of him, and he flicked half of it on the far end of the table, half nearer this end, then passed a handful of the sheets backwards without looking. Wildman took the sheaf, kept a piece, and shoved it at Po'Boy. Glancing at the words in the screenshotted image, he skimmed, keeping his mouth shut. When Justine pulled at his arm, he passed the paper to her, focusing again on the other men in the room.

"How'd you get this?" Mason's gruff question broke the tension. "That looks like a private server setup."

"It is. I got a guy who knows a guy. We light-fingered our way into the server background and have been watching, waiting. Hoping they'd fuck up." Twisted thumped a hard finger against the table, then pointed at the paper in Mason's hand. "They fucked up. We were in a position to catch it, and here we are."

"My man can help with that."

"Oh, I'm countin' on it, Mason. Countin' on Myron bein' able to dig deeper, faster, and farther than our fumbling attempts. He's the real deal, and as successful as it feels to have this shit in front of us right now, I know he'll do a better job." Twisted looked past Mason to Retro. "Lookin' for the Bastards to lock ranks with this shit, man. You see those names under your club? I know you're not even out of the last sack of shit that dropped on your doorstep, but this is gainin' critical mass with every fuckin' minute."

"I have a member missing." Retro tossed the knowledge out there like it was nothing, like he didn't protect every one of his men with his life, like whoever it was didn't matter, but Wildman saw the way the man's hand shook as he flattened his palm on the table. "That sack of shit you mentioned done landed on my doorstep? Sometime between then, when we spoke on the phone about it as it was barely over goin' down, and when me and mine were ridin' to Ms. LaPorte's little rendezvous, an officer failed to check in. We had dialed out a touchstone, got nearly a hundred percent response, which ain't enough. Zeroed in and tagged him with dozens of calls and texts and still got nada." Retro took in a deep breath. "One thing after another comin' our way. Got someone to his house couple of days later, nobody home. But there was food on the table, dresser drawers in his little girl's room hangin' open, and blood on the floor." He lifted his chin, angling his gaze around the room. "His name is on this fuckin' list, Twisted." Voice rough, breaking in half, he choked out, "Brothers, I need your help."

Chaos descended on the office. Men standing and sitting, men pacing and posturing, shouting with hands up by their heads. Wildman kept his attention on Twisted, and sure enough, it was only a moment before his president, his friend, held out one hand, finger pointing at the only official gavel the IMC had ever had. Wildman pressed against Justine's belly, settling her against the glass firmly, then stepped away and around a half a dozen men. He reached for and retrieved the bat, splintered and worn, wound round with a bicycle chain which held more residual red than was safe for the club—what with the advancements of DNA and whatnot—and turned to slap the handle into Twisted's still-outstretched hand, holding it steady as Twisted's fingers gripped, relaxed and shifted, then gripped again. Wildman popped his fingers wide just in time to avoid being shredded by the chain as Twisted swung it overhand, so it whistled through the air, thudding in a crash against one end of the tabletop, the end nearest the Jailbreakers, Wildman noted, and had a moment of pleasure when it looked like the man behind Sparks was going to literally shit himself.

But he'd left Justine alone long enough at that point, a half a dozen breaths between now and when he'd last touched her, so he reclaimed his position in the line against the window and scooped her close with his arm around her. Somehow he wasn't surprised she hadn't cowered, hadn't looked frightened at all, was standing there and evaluating every man in the room, her gaze marking where they stood and who they looked to, and he thought she was the most magnificent woman he'd ever had his hands on.

The roar had settled instantly when the report of the baseball bat hitting the wooden table had crashed through the room. A profound silence followed as Twisted whirled the bat through his fingers with ease, displaying how frequently he'd handled the weapon. He finished with the flourishing movements and rested it crossways in front of where he sat, folded his hands and forearms over the wood and metal, and deliberately scanned the room.

"When's the last time anyone saw your man, Retro?" Twisted flicked a finger towards the end of the table. "Swap seats with Capone there, take the lead, man. Or stand or some shit. Let's get to the bottom of this."

"Pretty sure you can hear me from here, brother." Retro's drawled response held no notes of humor, just tension and plain need. "Last time we laid eyes on Einstein was at my house. Ran Chulpayev off, had ourselves a little cookout, and the men headed home. That was the day of the big raids."

"Ten days ago." Twisted thudded his finger against the paper as he had before. "This wasn't posted until yesterday. You sure it's cartel?"

"Nope. I can tell you it's not the Bratva, but that's about the extent of my certainty. I don't know who the fuck might have scooped him up."

Mason cleared his throat and scooted his chair backwards, creating a tiny triangle of space between himself, Twisted, and Retro. He propped his ankle on his knee, looking like he could be in any backyard conversation. "Been my experience that if the obvious isn't the culprit, then it's the next obvious thing you need to look at. You cut anyone lately, bad blood or lose anyone to a patch out for good reasons?"

"Not a one. Bastards don't patch lightly, we prospect diligently, and I've never had to cut a man for doin' shit. Few who have surrendered their patches over the years have been a location thing, because I'm not interested in nomads. Jobs move, and family matters, so shit happens sometimes." Retro shook his head, then shoved a hand through his hair, flinging it over his shoulder. "Einstein's a good man. Good member. Good officer. Eatin' me up that I can't put a finger on where or when. Coulda been that same night or anything between then and days later when we put out the touchstone."

"Where'd he come from?" Wildman leaned over, locking gazes with Retro. "He didn't grow up in Bama, did he? Man's got an accent, am I right? I remember from earlier in the summer, when we rode over. Remember meeting him."

"Yeah, he's from Philly. Old lady's family got sickly, so he got out of the MC he was in there and came to Alabama so she could be with them. Did his homework on the Bastards, and we recruited him, because we did our homework too." Retro shook his head. "He'd been in a shit club, ties to the Italian boys, if you get my drift."

"Club got a name?" Wrench leaned forwards on Twisted's other side, eyes bright as he stared at Retro. "If they're shit, you think they'd be lookin' for him for some reason?"

"Monster Devils." Mudd spoke up from over Retro's shoulder. "And Einstein delivered a message a few weeks ago that was surprising. Was about the same time you"—he pointed at Po'Boy—"and Twisted rocked up askin' about that shitstorm in Florida."

Wildman stiffened and turned his head slowly to look at Po'Boy. The man met his gaze, a pained and brutal honesty staring back at him. Po'Boy had dug into his background. Without a word to Wildman, without a single question aimed his way, he'd dug around that bloody past.

"Aww, fuck." Mudd's soft curse was background noise to the loud buzzing in Wildman's ears.

"Retro, someone pay you for information on me lately?" Without looking away from Po'Boy, Wildman asked the question he wasn't sure he wanted an answer to. He got the answer right away, not from Retro, but from the sick look on Po'Boy's face.

"Son—"

He'd never know what Retro was about to say, cut him off with a slice of his hand through the air. "Never mind. Neither here nor there right now. The problem is in Philly, and is the Monster Devils." He couldn't pull his gaze away from his friend, possibly his best friend, his mentor, a man he'd trusted with his life—who'd gone behind his back for some unknown reason. "They're in a war, been in one for a long time. But it's ratcheted up in the past six months. Ain't no rhyme or reason to their strikes. They're just flailing around and trying to keep some semblance of control." With a giant breath that stretched his ribs to their limit, he tore his eyes away, locking them on Retro. "He got a message after he patched into the Bastards. Chances are that's the direction you need to look, brother."

"Who'd reached out, do you know?" Mason had an elbow over the back of his chair, still looking as relaxed and easy as ever. "Could be telling."

"Current president, who is a shitbag cumstain I wouldn't let within a hundred miles of my club."

Retro's statement had the conversation volume increasing in the room, not quite to previous levels, but enough so Twisted lifted the bat again, waggling it through the air.

Wildman got it, why they were all questioning. A club president didn't reach out to another club via an old member and ask for anything.

"What'd he want?" Sparks' first question was key, and Wildman raised his opinion of him by a notch.

"Was lookin' for a soft place to land. Didn't like the fact they'd gotten into a shoot-on-sight war, probably felt vulnerable, since he was bleeding members and had just lost two more officers to drive-bys." Retro stood slowly, each movement looking heavy, weighed down. "I think you've hit the right of it, boys. Now I at least got a direction to start checkin'." He sighed. "Mudd, let's—"

"Brother, you do not need to do this alone." Twisted pushed to his feet, too, angling his body towards Retro. "IMC stands with the Bastards, thick and thin. You ain't gettin' rid of me. So sit your ass back down until we have a goddamned plan. We'll deal with this and get your man and his family back, and then we'll circle back around to the next threat, the motherfuckin' cartel. Or the Bratva. Or the Feds. This group right here?" He punched a finger at each president seated at the table. "We're the law when it comes to our territory, and we need to start acting like we give a shit about our clubs, our lives. We go things alone, and we're easy to pick apart. Pick off, like a sitting fuckin' duck." He whirled and shook his head at Po'Boy, who slowly closed the mouth he'd just opened. "Between the cartel, the mob, pop-up clubs who don't have a fuckin' clue about the life, the other outlaws in North America always pushing at our borders, and the goddamned fucking government, if we don't stand together, then we'll all fall eventually. I've been puttin' my money where my mouth is, lately, and I gotta say, life is better with allies. It's a lot fuckin' better." He patted the air, and Wildman grinned as Retro settled back in his chair. Grinned again when Mason's hand reached out and clasped the man's shoulder. "I'm not finished, dammit. I say we do what we should have done a year ago, and we work together to not just fix this current line of shit we got trending to our doors, but whatever else needs doing. You can do it alone, Retro, but brother, you don't have to."

There was a rap on the doors leading into the clubhouse main room, and Wildman traded a look with Twisted, who nodded. Wildman pointed at the man closest to the door, the South Coast Devils VP, and gestured for him to open it.

Pony's head popped around the door, his gaze zeroing in on Twisted, broad smile stretching his lips.

"It's time, boss."

This time when the uproar happened, it started with Twisted's joyful shout, followed by him standing so quickly he toppled his chair over backwards. The baseball bat swung wide, straight into Wildman's deflecting hands, and Twisted shoved between men on his way around the table to the door. When he got there, he put a hand on each of Pony's shoulders, dipped his head to stare into his eyes, and asked, "You sure?"

"Yeah, she called and said her water broke, so she's in it to win it this time, brother."

Twisted's shoulders rose and fell once, then again, and when he finally whirled to face the room, it was with a blinding grin. "Y'all motherfuckers gotta figure your own shit out right now. My Shiny Penny's been tired of being pregnant for a while now, had a couple of false starts, and there ain't nowhere I need to be but next to her." He pointed at Wildman. "Acting chapter president, effective immediately. So decreed." Wildman stiffened, but Twisted wasn't done. "Justine LaPorte, do you hereby swear that you have no ill intentions to the Incoherent MC or to any club so represented at this table today?" Wildman glanced down to see her nod. "Nope, pretty lady, you need to voice this loud and proud so everyone can hear. Do you swear?"

"Yes, Twisted. I swear no club embodied in this room will come to harm by my action or inaction. You're all safe with me." Her chin trembled, and Wildman curled his arm tighter around her while Mason reached out and brushed the back of her hand with his fingers. "I swear."

"Use whatever assets or resources are needed from the IMC to find and retrieve your man, Retro. My word is oath for the club, brother. But right now," he took a step backwards, Pony moving out of his way, "I got other places to be."

He whirled and ran, sprinting through the clubhouse. The door hadn't closed behind him when Twisted's pipes roared as he took off, gravel spitting against the outside wall.

Wrench cleared his throat, and Wildman looked down as Po'Boy lifted the chair Twisted had used, the same one his grandfather Jimbo had sat in as he founded and then ruled over the club long ago, and placed the seat back in its place at the table. Then Wrench kicked at the legs, angling the chair towards Wildman.

"I believe that's your seat, Wild." Po'Boy's hand on his shoulder should have burned but didn't. It felt supportive and proud, if a touch could carry such emotion. "We can talk later, and I'll explain everything, but right now, your nat prez placed a burden on your shoulders you need to pick up and carry." He was pushed, pulled, and weighted down with a hand to settle his ass in the old leather, worn and molded by only two sets of asses through the years. "We need to get ahead of this, brother. There's a two-pronged approach that might work, but only if everyone agrees." Po'Boy's head was close to his, the whispered words for Wildman alone. "First off, recognize the change here and now. Plant the understanding of what he did when he called on your lady. Make sure they all get the idea. Then you'll know she's safe."

A quick look over his shoulder found Justine standing directly behind him, as he had stood behind Twisted. This was her show of faith and loyalty, in a way that every man in the room would understand. Chin up, she was again taking the measure of every man, and he could almost see the list she was ticking off in her head.

When he went to fold his hands on the table, he realized he still held the baseball bat. He studied it briefly, then rested it across the center of the table. "When we're done in here, we'll ride to the hospital and celebrate with our brother. It would be the IMC's honor to have every man present when our prince is brought to air." He took in a breath that came easier than any had since Twisted left the room, left the house, rolling away from this shitshow. "I'd like official recognition of the oaths sworn in this room prior to Twisted's exit. If we're going to work together and leverage everything we need to get shit done, then we can't afford any infighting, or fuck, even any suspicion. Justine answered Twisted's question, and I throw my trust behind her in that response. Anyone around the table have anything else to say about that?" He waited a beat, glancing left to right and back again, seeing only headshakes from every president. "And your seconds, can you oath they'll stick to the same plan?" He arrowed a look at Sparks, who nodded, then looked at the man at his back just in time to see the man's mouth twist in disgust. "You sure about that, Sparks?" He didn't beat any harder at the man, simply made the statement and moved on, calling out one other president, because he hadn't seen Capone's second before and didn't know Rocket personally, just through the grapevine. Capone's easy smile put him at ease, but when he turned back to Sparks, it was to find him embroiled in a heated, if quiet, conversation with his VP. "Sparks, can your man give his word?"

"Seems not, brother." Sparks stood, hands on his hips as he towered over the other man. "Needa vacate, brother. Head out, now. We can talk about this later, but you can't be in here no more."

"Bitch had my brother arrested, and we're supposed to just believe it's all puppies and happiness now? Fuck that noise, man." The man backed up, shoulders to the wall. "Never thought you'd pussy out, man."

"Not pussying out to say it like it is. We need her now. And Doth, your brother's a fucking asshole." Sparks sighed, the air hissing out of his pursed lips. "You gonna make me do this here?"

"Do what? Pussy out in front of the big dogs? Thought you wanted to impress 'em with your leadership, or some shit."

"Well, I'm sure doin' a stand-up job right now, aren't I? My own man won't even follow a simple direction to unass to the other room." Sparks sighed again. "You are gonna make me do this here. Shit, man." Quick as a snake, his hand flashed out, and it was only then Wildman saw the blade. His shout died in his throat as instead of stuffing the metal into the man's chest, Sparks sliced at his vest, coming away with a hunk of leather and the officer patch. "Return your other patches in Adken. Tomorrow. That's all you got."

"You can't do that."

"Oh no, here we go." Sparks leaned close, nose to nose with the other man. "My fuckin' club. My fuckin' rules. You got no goddamned place there anymore. Now fuck off and get out of here." Sparks turned and settled back into his chair, staring down at the patch for a breath before shoving it into a pocket. "He gone yet?"

Wildman shook his head.

"Fuck, he's gonna make me do this other thing, ain't he?"

"Likely, brother." Wildman shrugged. "Or I could help it along."

"I'd appreciate a hand, man. Appreciate it a hell of a lot."

Wildman whistled, and the three prospects from earlier flung the doors open, staring openmouthed at him sitting in Twisted's seat. "Yeah, yeah. There's been a few things goin' on. We'll have a meeting in a bit, but for now, can you get this mouthy piece of shit out of our clubhouse? Man needs to head back to Florida, and if a couple of you would trail him out of our territory, that'd be sweet." To their credit, none of the prospects questioned him, the seat, the bat, the way the other men still sat at the table—all the proof they needed that for now at least, Wildman's word was law. They swarmed the sputtering and cursing ex-VP of the Jailbreakers, taking him to the ground, then rose up with a man on each arm and the third holding the kicking legs. They toted him out of the room like a bag of garbage, and the doors closed behind them, Pony's grinning face mouthing "I'm your VP now, bitch," the last thing Wildman saw as the gap closed.

"Where were we?" Pinching his lips together, he looked around the room, latching his gaze on Retro. "Findin' your man. Let's hunker down, see what we can come up with. Mason." He angled his head to look in Mason's face. "If I get your phone in here, can you get your tech guy on the line? If the Monster Devils are imploding to the point the president is vacating, there's gonna be all kinds of meaty info around. He'll know where to look first, and best."

"I can do better than that." Mason pointed at the doors. "He's out in the main room. I had a feeling I'd want him close for this meeting."

"Out-fucking-standing," Retro said, slapping a hand on the table. "Now we've a direction and a tool, we just need a break."

"We'll find that break, brother." Wildman nodded at the South Coast Devils VP again, who grinned good-naturedly at being reduced to the doorman and reached out to open it. "Myron, with the RWMC, the pleasure of your presence is requested. ASAP."

The skinny biker slipped through the door, looked straight at Mason, and asked, "What can I bring in with me?"

"Whatever you need." Wildman's voice cut through the air before Mason could open his mouth, and he experienced a tiny flicker of pleasure when Justine's hand landed on his shoulder in a silent ask for acknowledgment. "Yeah, baby?"

"If you can get me Wi-Fi and a tablet, one that won't lead back to anyone here, I can do my own digging. I've got my own ways into the nuts and bolts of various investigative data."

Wildman nodded without hesitation. "Myron, do you have a clean tablet for the lady?"

Myron reached out a hand, and someone out of sight dropped a backpack strap into it. "I've got that and a lot more. Pretty boys have the best toys, don't you know that?"

Wildman waited for the door to close and Myron to make his way next to Mason. Someone shoved a chair in their direction, and Mason and Retro moved down to give Myron room. Wildman reached back for Justine, linking their fingers together as he guided her to sit on his leg. She adjusted herself, then accepted the device from Myron. With a smile, she bent her head over the surface and started tapping, only stopping to ask Myron, then Retro, a couple of questions.

Myron was much the same. He had a laptop he'd reinstalled a battery in, a tablet, a phone, and another device Wildman couldn't identify but appeared to be a satellite connection. As the two worked their technical magic, Wildman, Wrench, Po'Boy, Mason, Hoss, Retro, Mudd, Capone, and Sparks pooled their knowledge of the Monster Devils and the malignancy of the leadership there on the East Coast.

More than two hours passed before Justine stiffened, putting her nose within a few inches of the tablet and squinting. "Hey, Myron, I think I found something." She shoved the device down the table, and Myron picked it up, studying the information on the screen.

"Yes, you did." He tapped the device, then laid it on the table, opening another window on the laptop. A rendering of the tablet showed, and he deftly toggled something, so the document snapped into focus on his screen. "Check this out."

A picture slowly resolved. Grainy and shot from an awkward angle, it was security footage of a gas station. A van pulling a short trailer slowly rolled into view, two motorcycles lashed tightly in place on the trailer. If the angle had been any different, they wouldn't have seen inside the van.

A man, trussed and tied, lay with his arms stretched over his head towards where they were anchored to the struts of the driver seat. On the floor of the vehicle next to him were fabric bundles: one small, one large. The man was moving, struggling, though weakly. The other two blanket-covered lumps were still. Very still.

"Your man Einstein, he has a wife and kid, right?" Mason's question was quiet, nearly gentle.

Retro's voice broke, rough and filled with gravel. "He does. Little girl. That's him. Where are we, man? Can you find him?"

"Oh, yeah." Myron's tone held anger and sadness, grief. "I've had a fuckton of experience at this part of the job." He shifted and glanced at Mason, who held his gaze. "Well versed in the mechanics."

"Just find him, My. Fuckin' find him so we can get him and his family back."

"This was taken twelve hours ago, just off I-75, outside Ocala. They're headed south, for whatever reason." Myron's fingers flew over the keys, and a series of camera angles popped into view on the computer. "This'll take me a hot minute, but I should be able to track them downstate. Where would they be going?"

Wildman had kept his eyes on the initial video, the vehicle rolling just out of view, then backing up closer to the gas pumps. There was nothing for a moment, only the bugs flying in and out of the shot proof that it hadn't ended, was still playing. Then boots came into view, followed by the rest of a man, the driver, he supposed. He kept his attention there, watching the man with growing disbelief.

"Myron, can you pause this? Enlarge it? Make it better?" He tapped the screen, and the video disappeared, Wildman pulling his hand back like he'd touched something hot. "I think I know that guy."

"The driver?" Mason's question was tight and low, filled with anger. "How the fuck would you know him?"

"Get me a good look at him, and I'll tell you if I fuckin' know him or not, okay?" Justine squeezed her legs around where she sat propped on his thigh, a quiet reminder he wasn't alone. *Never be alone again if I have anything to say about it.* "Just get me a good look, yeah?"

"On it. I just need to download the video so I can enhance it." Whistling tunelessly through his teeth, Myron tapped, tabbed, scrolled, clicked, and typed on the laptop, working through a variety of screens.

"Oh, is that the Niesha software? Such amazing stuff." Justine's quiet question split the silence, and she jerked in place, looking back at Wildman with a mouthed, "Sorry."

"What's the Niesha software do?" Mason's question wasn't quiet, and he made no apologies at the potential interruption.

"It's an enhancement algorithm that's illegal in the US right now, because it comes from China via Cuba," Myron said as he clicked again, then expanded the results of his efforts. "Best I can do."

The image had gone from being a shades-of-gray thermal rendering to a full-color shot, all the graininess removed, and even the perspective was different, more straight-on than before.

"Holy fuck," Wildman muttered, waggling his fingers towards the laptop. Myron grinned and shook his head, then slid the image sideways off the screen, where it appeared on the tablet. He picked it up and handed that to Wildman.

"It picks up on reflected imagery in the photo, building out the most viable representation of the subject. It's also a facial recognition tool in China. They use it to control who comes in and out of various neighborhoods, where there's an ethnic component." Myron shook his head. "Doesn't matter except for the results. Do you know this dude?"

"Yeah, I do."

Staring at the tablet, Wildman again felt the rolling burn of anger blazing through his blood. The death of Powell, of Shelly, the night it all went down, this man had been there for it all. Every bit of it. The only time he hadn't been was those two fucking days when the cops were around and Wildman had hoped for support.

"Curtis Bassil."

Chapter Eighteen

Justine

The name niggled at her brain, and she pulled back from the table, leaning against Wildman's chest as she followed the tiniest thread of memory down whatever track it seemed locked on. *Curtis Bassil.* It meant something; she was certain of it.

Eyes closed, she relaxed into the warm cradle created by Wildman's arms and body, feeling safe and secure, kept from harm. In this way, she sank deep, letting her mind worry at the information behind the name that was on the slim side of recognizable. Bassil wasn't a common surname, not one she'd encountered often. *But I have heard it.* She let her head rock to the side, forehead pressed against Wildman's throat, the steady beat of his heart underneath her cheek.

No one had ever made her feel like this. Protected. Cherished. Loved. Lyle Woolsey was unique in that way, and she tried to tame back her instinct to soak it up, holding onto it for the time in the future when it would be ripped away. *He's not going anywhere.* He already knew everything about her that might cause a man to go running for the hills, and he was still here.

Male voices buzzed around her, growing in strength and volume before decreasing again, that cycle unending as they discussed how and where to find this Bassil.

Time bent, and she was eighteen again, one arm holding a bundled-up Chris in a safe cocoon pressed against the edge of the cheap kitchen table.

The tiny apartment had been renovated two decades earlier, when the former four-room place set in the projects, the poorest-of-the-poor housing, had been refactored into the current two-room configuration. A booklet was spread in front of her, and Justine held a short, tooth-marked pencil in one hand, fingers clutched around it awkwardly. Studying for her GED, she read and reread the section on constitutional law, making notes on the back of leaflets that had come through the mail slot in the front door.

Jimmy walked into the apartment, another man at his heels, their angry voices overlapping as they shouted over each other. Jimmy's words rang loudest as he tried for control over whatever situation he'd brought into their home. Chris writhed in her grip, and she carefully loosened her hold, hoping deeper sleep would again overtake him. No such luck, because the man with Jimmy roared loud enough to rattle the glasses in the cabinets.

"I don't give a fat fuck who your father-in-law is, you son of a bitch. You owe the chapter here, and you're gonna fuckin' pay your goddamned dues to the club."

Chris wailed, the sound thin and terrified as Justine brought him to her shoulder, her hand moving in a soothing pattern across his swaddled back. He hiccupped, air catching in his throat; then he let loose with another cry, this one stronger and louder.

A face appeared in the doorway, dark skin flushed red, sweat beading along his temples. The smile he flashed her was ugly, sinister, and as filled with danger as anything she'd ever seen.

"Boy sounds hungry, bitch. Whip a tit out and shut him the fuck up, yeah?" Tall and broad, this stranger sauntered into the room where Justine held her crying son, Jimmy's face showing just over his shoulder. Surrounded by hard men all her life, Justine had learned quickly which ones were to be avoided at all costs. This man, whoever he was, pinged at those same instincts, so she turned sideways, offering him her back as she brought Chris to a protected position low across her chest, rounding her shoulders to keep him from view. Of course it just angered the infant more, and his frightened cries deepened, growing more robust, showing off the strength of his lungs.

"Lemme see him."

The man shoved her backwards and plucked Chris from her arms, her fingers catching only air as she tried to scrabble for a hold on her son.

"Give me my son."

"Give me a fuckin' minute, bitch. Wanna look at the prince."

Her blood slowed, clogging so much her heart had to beat heavily to push it through her veins. Prince. A word only someone who knew her bloodline would use.

Jimmy spoke over Chris' screams, one hand out to the man. "Bassil, give my old lady my kid back, asshole. You're scarin' him."

Bassil lifted his head from where he'd been staring down into Chris' red face, shooting a killing glare at Jimmy. "You owe the fuckin' chapter. Gonna pay your debts? Ready to ride it off, man? We need you for tonight, and you fuckin' owe us."

She realized Jimmy had on a vest, something he hadn't worn since California, and her heart sank. Then he turned to the sink, and she saw the same emblem she'd known her whole life. The same mark she'd tried so hard to put in her past. The rocker might indicate a different region, the town of Cynthiana, only a few miles away—but the patch was evil incarnate, something that had cast a destructive shadow on everything it touched.

"There was a Bassil in the Cynthiana chapter of the Outriders. Long time ago. He came to the apartment with Jimmy once. We're talking decades ago, but I think he'd be the right age now for the guy in the footage. I don't remember much about him other than he was terrible." Arms tightened around her, and a hand gripped her thigh, turning her in Wild's lap, so she leaned closer, draped across his legs. "I don't know if that's any help, but I remember the one time I met him. He was as scary as my daddy ever hoped to be."

"Sounds like the same guy." The words rumbled through Wildman's chest and into her, and she snuggled closer, the terror of those long-ago memories not out of her system yet. "Asshole who studied asshole to be a bigger asshole."

"What was he in the Keys club, Wild?"

Wildman's thighs turned to steel beneath her ass, and the muscles of his chest trembled as he pulled in a slow, deep breath. "Suck-up, mostly. Fuckup, often. He was my half-brother's ride or die from middle school." She angled her eyes up to see Wildman's expression. It was carved out of stone, not a twitch or movement other than his lips, forming the words. "Some kind of shit you should know about, yeah? Was Powell's ride or die, until he wasn't. Backed him until he didn't. Shoulda seen the look on Powell's face when that happened. Shock, surprise, pain, disbelief. Ran the gamut. Day I found out my own brother took a paper out on me, paid a dom to assign a bullet to my name, that's the same day Bassil stepped away, leavin' Powell to fight his own battles." His head swung side to side, gaze fixed on the blank wall across the room. "Found out later Bassil had ousted the old president at the end of a blade, put the patch on Powell, then forced him to take me on." Slowly, as if Wildman couldn't help the movement, his neck twisted until he stared at Po'Boy, whose own features had bled dry of blood, pale and white, muscles and tendons taut under the skin. "But you already knew a bunch of that, didn't you, *brother*."

Things clicked into place suddenly for Justine. Mudd's comment earlier, Wildman's reaction to it interrupted by Twisted's pending fatherhood. The instant shift into a seek-and-destroy mission to find Einstein. But this amount of anger was rooted in a feeling of betrayal and something that could tear her man to pieces if she didn't get out ahead of it.

Arching her back, she reached up to wrap a hand around the back of his neck and shifted, so her mouth was close to his ear as his hand tightened on her hip. "Blow it out, big man. Let all your anger go. If it were malicious, you know Twisted wouldn't have sanctioned it. If it *was* intended to be malicious, then they'd have pulled you in here on your knees and taken your patch." He became impossibly still, the only movement the slow in and out of breath. "Likely it was to confirm what they already knew, which is you are a good and trustworthy man, a brother through-and-through, and worthy of the weight of power. Something Twisted handed your way tonight. Acting chapter president isn't a small jump, Lyle. That's not something done in haste either. This is a shift he's been thinking about for a while, so you blow all your anger and rage out. Let your butthurt emotions go, then take this as credit to who you are as a man. As their brother."

Settling back into his lap, she waited, unsure if her interruption would be brushed aside. Then his hand landed on her thigh, big fingers giving her a squeeze, thumb riding up between her legs. "Fuck, woman, you set out to talk strategy you need to warn a man. Gets me hot and bothered to know my old lady's got a fuckin' brain in her head." Mason's snort at her back said he'd overheard. Po'Boy's expression at her front was controlled, warily skeptical, and she understood it. The venom that had been in Wildman's words was gone in an instant, derailed by what she prayed had been good advice.

Then Po'Boy stepped up a rung on the ladder of her thoughts of him, attacking the elephant in the room directly, not waiting until later when it could be more private and not backing off. "Twisted knew. Knew I was leavin'. Knew he'd have to shift shit around yet a-fuckin'-gain, because I was not going to be the one to tear down IMC. It coulda, and you and I both know it, brother. Club is club, blood is blood, and brothers are brothers—but when things get tangled, sometimes there ain't no easy solution. I can't wave a magic wand and fix anything, but I will tell you the desire to know more about you was my fault, if not instigated by me. Because Twisted needed—*needs* brothers he can trust. And he'd thought he could trust me, yet here I am wearin' another patch proudly. Man may never say it, but the idea I *could* leave still wears at him. We're findin' our way, friends for life, and fuck me, but I'm still his ride or die, and him and me both know it. But club is club, and I ain't his anymore. So he set out to make sure he had others around him, just like you. And you're his, Wildman. No fuckin' joke there, brother. You're IMC to the core, because you've been around the bend and back again, and you fuckin' know this is your spot on the old earth ball. I've always been here, but my spot is a little farther down that bend than it used to be. Close, but not inside, not anymore."

He bent slightly, resting his hands on Wrench's shoulders, fingers digging deep, thumbs tucked underneath the black leather vest the CoBos president wore. "This right here is my inside circle now. And thank fuck I didn't have to pass no kind of background check, or I wouldn't have made it in. You, though, you've only ever been looking for brothers worth your loyalty, and you've got it with the IMC. So you gonna be pissed, be pissed at me. It was my moves what caused him to reach out and touch someone to find out a little bit about the man he intended to hand Mother to." Po'Boy shrugged as Wrench tipped his head back, staring up at Po'Boy's face with features pulled tight with regret. *So much pain here in this little room.* "Which, in case you fuckin' missed the goddamned memo, is you, motherfucker. So quack fuckin' quack, brother. You're the big man in the room right now, and fuck me, but I'm proud as any big momma quacker to see it."

Wildman's head dropped forwards, so his cheek rested against Justine's. She heard and felt slow, even gusting of his breaths over the shell of her ear, then heat from a dry, soft press of lips against the side of her head. "Fuck me, woman. You are something else, Jussie." He lifted his head, and she met his gaze, steady and hot, drilling into her as they stared without blinking. "Fuckin' mine, you hear me? You don't get to give this to me and then try and ever fuckin' take it back. Been lookin' for you all my goddamned life, and I'm—fuck, woman, you're mine."

"I am," she confirmed, not wanting any misunderstandings between them. "Here, at home, anywhere, Lyle."

"Lyle?" Wildman scrunched up his face at the shrill question from behind him. "Fuckin' Lyle? That's your goddamned name? Jesus, and you were my prospect. Fuck, man, shoulda told me that one a while ago. Gonna take a bit for the sting to go away. You shoulda been named Rocky, or fuck, I don't know, some kind of strong-ass name. Fuckin' Lyle? Jeeze."

Wildman straightened and twisted, turning to look at Po'Boy. Beyond that man was Wrench, who was wrestling with Po'Boy, one hand half over his mouth as they both laughed. "Shut up, asshole." Wildman leaned in closer, then hissed, "Ralphie." He snorted. "Ralph Lewis."

"What the fuck about it, *Lyle*?" Po'Boy straightened, hands on his hips. "And there ain't a damn thing wrong with Ralph as a first name."

"Sure, not if you don't mind being confused with a drunken spew session, man. I get it." Wildman leaned back in his chair, one elbow going up to the back, his other arm slung securely around Justine's waist. "I totally get it. Not everyone can have an awesome moniker, brother. I feel ya."

"Lyle what? What's the rest of it, you bastard?"

"Lyle Woolsey, right here in front of you. Read my lips and weep, Ralphie."

"As amusing as this is, I may have found something we should pay closer attention to." Myron's soft words snapped everyone's focus back to him, Wildman jostling Justine, so she straddled his leg again instead of sitting on his lap. "There's an old Diamante clubhouse by Timber Hill, on the Gulf Coast. I think that's where they're going. Sat imagery shows movement in and around the compound, which had been sealed by federal warrant about two years ago. Shouldn't be anything there now, at least nothing larger than the furry kind of rats. But I see four vans that look a lot like the one Bassil has, which makes me think he's got help."

"Why would Bassil have picked Einstein? He wouldn't have had any trade with the Outriders. That club stayed strictly off the East Coast boys' radar, best of my knowledge." Wildman looked at Retro, then Mason, then down into Justine's face. "Something doesn't make sense."

"Agreed, man. Who would this asshole be tied to that'd want to rile the Bastards? Retro, you got anything else in your big ole bag o' tricks, man?" Wrench shook his head. "We all agree it don't taste organized, right?" Grumblings around the table said his statement was true. "Which means it's club. Didn't you deal with the asshole who cost you a member not long ago? That Florida rally?"

She angled her head to see Retro considering the tabletop, eyes moving in aimless patterns as he paused. His memories were signaled first by the firming of his lips, dropping them into a bloodless flat line slashing across his face. Then a muscle ticked in his cheek, his top lip curling upwards into a snarl. "Yeah, man." Elbows to the table, he rubbed his face between his palms, curling one hand over the back of his head, fingers tangled in the long hair draped down his back. "Mason's play, but my gain. Yeah, that shit was found and dealt with not eight months ago, right, Mudd?" Soundless movement behind Retro was Mudd's nod. "You thinkin' this has something to do with that and less to do with Einstein's shit-for-brains former club president reaching out? You against serendipity?"

"I know the saying about zebras and horses, but this goes back, brother." Wildman leaned forwards, and Justine went with the change in position, keeping her hands along the scarred tabletop, places smoothed like silk from the passage of other hands, other palms. "Bassil is tied to it all, and from what I know about the man personally, he's not above starting a war that would benefit only himself. Talk and talk, rile folks up, then stand back and watch it burn. Fuckin' psychopath."

"What if Bassil is looking to raise another patch for his own back? The club you left in tatters never recovered, man. They died a quick death when you refused the president patch." Justine saw Wildman's pupils react to Retro's words, larger in a flash, then dialed down after a long blink. "There's a lot you don't yet know, brother. Nothing bad, but I've been watching over you for a long time, man. I've got your back in anything, you hear me? Even before I realized who you were, I had your back." At Wildman's terse nod, Retro cleared his throat. "What we know of this Curtis Bassil could fit in a thimble, but Myron sent out a message to my network on my behalf, back while y'all were still huffin' and puffin' around shit, and we've already got some info in the hopper. Your little Keys club wasn't the first one he'd been in. Outriders was. Right there in Cynthiana as Justine recalled. We've got his every move tagged and categorized. After Kentucky, he wavered his way east to throw his lot in with the Monster Devils, then finally broke with them to move away from the harsher climate. He'd gotten into the heat, politically speaking. That's when he settled back into home territory. I bet you either weren't aware of his time away from your neighborhood, or he played it off as something else. Every time he wound up a failure, though, which has to sting. Only way for a man who can't be voted into an office to get his hands on a particular patch is to raise his own, you feel me?"

"Oh, yeah, brother. I feel ya," Wildman muttered. His hand curled around the top of Justine's thigh, his grip relaxing and renewing until she threaded her fingers between his. Then he lifted their joined grip to pull against her belly, sliding her more securely against his body. "Miles to that clubhouse, Myron?"

"About twelve hours, give or take a fuel stop." Myron had another screen open on the laptop, an overhead view of metal buildings grouped behind a fence. "I got live eyes on them. I can hold this for fifteen hours before swapping birds. I've also got some alerts built into my system, so I'll watch for the tags on the van as they get closer to arrival."

"And Bassil is, what, like six hours out, max?"

"Something like that."

"Fuck." He raked his thick thumbnail across the rough edges of the wood where the baseball bat had scarred deeply, the tick-tick-tick sound barely audible in the silence around the room. "They coulda killed him at any point up to now. Man likely won't be dead when we get there."

"Lots worse things than dyin', when family's right there in it with ya." Mason's low response had every man around the room sucking in air, making Justine believe they'd all lived at least some part of a nightmare of their own. She knew Davy's regrets where it came to his wife, Willa, and genuinely understood them. He'd been hours late to keep her from being savaged by his and Justine's blood kin, a wound that lived on in their family to this day. No matter Willa might claim it had healed over, Justine knew Davy still wrestled with it at times.

Wildman nodded. "Yeah, I get that. And IMC has brothers we can roll from the Big Bend Country. They'll split the time it'll take us, but it's not like being there and putting hands on him myself."

"I got a friend who has a friend." Mason held up a finger and pointed to the door. "If I could have my phone?"

"Get him the goddamned phone." Silence in the room, and Wildman groaned. "Oh, Lord, give me strength in these moments of strife." Wildman gestured to the South Coast Devils officer again, and the man shook his head as he stood off a stool, which had appeared at some point, and opened the door.

She heard a muffled, "Man wants a phone in here. RWMC bucket, prospect."

An empty-handed prospect appeared and, at Wildman's dark scowl, quickly retreated, returning with a stack of buckets under his arm. He strained, pulling until he was out of breath. "RWMC is here, in the middle." It took four men, finally, to separate the buckets of phones.

"Just pass 'em all fuckin' out. Jesus. Comedy of errors right here." Wildman's frame shook under her, and it took a quick glance at his face to realize he was laughing silently. "Fuck if I know what to do, Twisted."

His muttered comment didn't go unheard, because Po'Boy leaned close, licked a broad stripe up Wildman's cheek, and stage-whispered, "Yeah, you fuckin' do, brother."

Wildman's backhand of Po'Boy was casual, without sting or heat, and left the man standing tall behind Wrench and grinning ear to ear. "Mason, gonna give us a clue what you're pullin' together?"

"Yeah, got a guy who owes me for life, and I collect every fuckin' chance I get." Mason lifted the phone to his ear, the tinny and distant ringing ending with a buzz. "Daniel, good to talk to you, man. Hey, I need a jet. You know anyone who might have one?" He paused, and there was more buzzing in the background. "Oh, no shit? Sold it? Well, fuck." More pausing, and Mason grinned, flipping a wink Justine's way as he listened. "So like a timeshare. Anywhere in North America? Well, how about New Orleans? Yeah, NOLA to Miami." He sighed and rolled his eyes. "NOLA. New Orleans, Louisiana. No, not like yolo. Fomo? What the fuck is fomo? Know what? I don't care. What I do care about is you havin' this timeshare-like arrangement. How long does it take to spin up?" Pulling the phone away, he said, "Hold on, I'll put you on speaker. Myron's here. He can do whatever needs doin'. Thank you"—he laid the phone on the table—"my friend. I owe you one again."

Deep and smooth as dark chocolate, a man's voice rolled through the phone's speaker. "No talk of owing between friends, Mason. You know how I feel about that shit. Myron, what do you need from me? I've got an agency number and a membership number, and I think you'll need both of those. I can text you if that'll work?"

"Text Mason. His phone's right here, and I can get what I need." Myron stared at the phone until it vibrated, then he flicked up and down on the screen, isolating the information in view before turning back to the computer. "Okay, found the agency. Now for bookings." He tapped for a minute. "We can have one leaving in just over an hour. Means we gotta haul ass to get to the airport like now." He looked at Wildman. "No time for a hospital stop."

Wildman's hand patted Justine's ass, and she stood, stepping to the side as he rose behind her. "Gonna call Twisted. Get and give some updates, so he's in the know." He bent, put his mouth to her ear as he steered her behind the chair. "You can stand here or sit out behind the bar, but you do not place your ass in any seat at this table, you understand?" She nodded, and he pulled back, staring into her eyes. Whatever he saw there reassured him, and the somber aspect of his expression eased. "Fuckin' made for me. My wild woman. You get it, because you just fuckin' know."

Justine placed a hand on his shoulder and rose on her toes, pressing her lips to his. "Go, call your brother. Make sure all is well in Twisted Land." She smacked her lips against his again. "I'll be here, and I know protocol. I won't fuck up, Wild. Swear."

"I believe you, baby girl." As he loomed over her like this, his hair hung down on either side of his face, framing his features for her eyes alone. The expression he had just for her was patient, and the look in his dark, bright gaze was love.

Chapter Nineteen
Wildman

Phone to his ear, Wildman leaned his forearm against the doorframe leading to the smaller office off the kitchen. Normally used by old ladies organizing charity runs and other clubhouse duties, it seemed the only place in the whole clubhouse that wasn't currently neck-deep in people. He listened to the ringing, already preparing himself for the voicemail he'd need to leave when the call connected.

The high, thin wail of a newborn babe greeted him, followed by Penny's grumbled, "If you'd just give him back to his momma, I could help out, Bell."

Wildman allowed himself a smile, and the instant it broke the scowl he'd had on his face, a hand clapped his shoulder, and he looked up to find himself fucking surrounded by men. Wrench was right there, eyes bright, question in his lifted brows that he wasn't willing to put to words.

Twisted still hadn't spoken, the only sounds through the phone right now a stumbling tune followed by tiny snuffles. "Lemme put you on speaker, brother. I got an audience." Wildman put action to the words, balancing the phone on one palm as he said, "We got you, brother. All's good, yeah?"

Thick, maybe thicker than Wildman had ever heard his voice, except for the day Penny had laid her hand in his while saying her vows, Twisted responded, "Yeah, it's fuckin' good, brother. Our boy is strong, so fuckin' strong. Penny's a champ, too. This boy wasn't waitin' on his daddy, oh, no you were not, were you, little one? You had your own timeline, and my wishes didn't matter a speck. Got here just in time, brother. Just in time."

"Tell Wrench I need gumbo." Penny's complaint came through loud and clear, and the men around Wildman laughed. "Twisted, tell him. Hear me? They don't have any good food here."

"Tell her we get the message, brother." Wrench was pounding his fist against Po'Boy's shoulder, none too gently if the tiny flinches and winces from Po'Boy were real. "Loud and clear. Glad to hear they're both hale and hearty."

"Double that, Twisted. Congrats from the whole of the RWMC, and especially from me. Not an event you want to miss, and I'm glad you didn't." Mason's hand came to rest on Wildman's back, and he tensed up before he realized it wasn't anywhere close to his patch but lying a respectful distance away. "Be there with them, soak this up, man. These are precious times."

There was a brusque noise, and Wildman looked up in time to see Hoss step backwards, the expression on his face broken and tired as he turned to walk away without a word. Retro flashed his palm at the men around Wildman and retreated with him, angling his blood brother towards the back door and out into the lot beyond.

Po'Boy reached out and steadied Wildman's hand where he held the phone. "Twisted, brother, we've got a handle on everything here. You worry about your woman and your babe, and we'll catch you up when we get back, yeah?" Po'Boy's lips pulled sideways in a grin. "Your man's doin' a damn fine job with the shit you slung at him, so good job on that."

"What's the boy's name?" Wrench leaned closer, turning his head to look up at Wildman. "Wild, man. You couldn't have fuckin' video called? Shit. Twisted," he called out louder. "Hey, man, Twisted, we need some pics, yeah?"

"The fuck you boys goin'?" Cold, dark, and hard, Twisted's words came through the phone slowly. "Here, pretty momma, take our boy a minute." Wildman looked at Po'Boy, shocked to see he was still grinning, as was Wrench. There was a slight commotion in the background, murmuring between the couple followed by another tiny cry quickly soothed. "Okay, that's sorted. Tell me what the fuck's been goin' on. Baby," his tone changed, softening, "I'm just goin' out in the hall for a minute. I'm right here, you call me I'm with you. Back in two shakes, Penny."

"Tell Yousa we love her," Po'Boy yelled, and the chuffed laugh from Twisted was audible.

"Asshats say they all love you and wish you and our boy every blessing." There was a pause, then Twisted said, "Hold on, pretty momma. Wrench was askin' for a pic. Lemme get one of just you and our boy for that motherfucker." Wildman's phone buzzed in his hand with an incoming message, but he saw the other four men standing around had their phones out immediately, so it must have been a group text.

Wildman leaned to look over Po'Boy's shoulder at a picture of Penny's smiling face, red hair caught in a braid along one shoulder, a miniature bundle of blue cradled to her chest. Curls of dark hair peeked around the knit cap covering the boy's head, and Penny's pinky had been captured in a tight grip by tiny fingers. "There, that should soothe the masses for a minute at least. Back soon, baby."

The sound of a kiss implied an intimate moment between the new parents, complete with the close-by coo of the baby, and Wildman had to swallow hard. *Wish Justine was here for this.* This was the kind of thing that tied clubs together tighter than blood ever could. Shared life changes, shared challenges, full support from friends and family—this was what he'd wanted in a club. Exactly this.

"Now, I'm away from my old lady, who is bound and determined to go home today yet, fuck my life, and I want to know what the fuck is going on. Where are you headed, brothers? Tell me. Share a little, so I got a good feelin' about what's goin' down."

"Found Retro's man." Wildman was glad Mason didn't insult Twisted by asking if he was safe to talk, knowing Twisted wouldn't have asked for the update if it wasn't a secure line and location. "They're in Florida. Might have his family with them, and if they do, it don't look good, man. Name's Curtis Bassil, who is a fucked-up bounce-around through a few clubs, all of which we know the goddamned names of, but most telling is MDMC out east, where Retro's man came from originally. That, with the ties to the south Florida club Bassil was in with Wildman and his brother, tells us he's headed to familiar territory, but with some kind of leverage. Don't know yet what he thinks Einstein will earn him in that arena, but none of us are willing to let it play out. They've got a couple hours yet before they get to the old Diamante compound we think they're headed for, and I've got a line on a plane that'll get us there nearly the same time. Myron's working his magic with transport on the other end, and then we're headed to the airport, where we'll park on the fuckin' tarmac if needful." Mason swung his gaze around the small group, taking each man's face. "That about cover it?" Nods all around had him looking back down at the phone. "Telling you now, I second Po'Boy's words about your man here. Steady and smart, and yet, I still don't fuckin' like him."

"Your sister—"

"Oh yeah. I get *why* I don't like him. Do not feel you need to spell it fuckin' out, man. I get it." Mason aimed a half-grin at Wildman, the smirk fading as he continued speaking. "And I'll get to where I like him, I'm sure. I'm just not there yet." Fingers tightened on Wildman's shoulder, and he realized Mason still was propped against him, keeping him close. "You got any questions for us, brother? Otherwise, we gotta get in the wind here chop-chop, get our asses movin'."

"Nope. No questions from me." A heavy sigh said there might not be questions but there was some regret. "Give 'em hell, boys. Retro don't deserve to lose another man, and fuck me, but Einstein's a good one. And his family?" A low growl floated through the air. "Fuckin' deal with them, Wild. You hear me, brother? You're my voice and hands on this, and you've the full backing of the IMC. You are IMC, and we are you, and we've got your goddamned back."

"I hear you, Prez." Wildman angled his head down to stare at the Enforcer plate still in place on his vest. "I got this."

"We all got this." Po'Boy leaned close. "Twisted, get back in there and build memories with your woman. You fought hard and long for her. Now show her you're gonna spend your fuckin' life with her. Build that with her, brother, then keep buildin' it day by day. Proud as fuck of you, man. Straight up, Jimbo would be fuckin' proud too. That old man would be on his knees praising God you'd not only found a good woman, but you had a family to grow. So suck in all the goodness Penny's got in there for you, and we'll see you on the other side."

"George Tyler Lewis Bell. Boy's got a hell of a life ahead of him, livin' up to you motherfuckers. I wanted to throw Jimbo in there, and Penny got testy, so I gave it up as a bad idea for this one." The low chuckle revealed the depths of Twisted's pleasure, as did his voice when he continued. "Next one, all bets are off. She gets happy with that gas they gave her. If I'd known and waited, I think I could have negotiated pretty much anything I wanted. Anyway, that's the boy's name. George Tyler Lewis Bell."

Myron appeared next to Mason, the backpack zipped and strapped, slung by one strap over his shoulder. "We gotta go if we're gonna make the filed plan."

Wildman glanced around the circle one last time, tapped the phone to put it back on the normal speaker, and lifted it to his ear. "Prez, brother." He turned away from them, stepping farther into the little office and kicking the door closed behind him. "Bassil, there ain't no comin' back from this, brother. I just want to make sure there's no misunderstandings."

"What the fuck do you think I'd do if I was standin' next to you, him on the floor and my boot on his spine?" Twisted's words weren't impatient. No matter the makeup of phrasing, his tone held a note of patience. "You think I'd let a family-killer walk away, give him a potential target with my patch on it?"

"No, but—"

"Wild, brother. You've been the arm of my vengeance before, never questioned it."

"Yeah, because I'm the Enforcer. It's my fuckin' job."

"Yeah, it is, brother. And now you've got a harder one. I won't be takin' back the chapter. Mother's yours from here out. We'll confirm with an officer vote, but this is your gig now. You think the president don't make hard calls? Fuck, man, we don't have certain offices for every chapter, because I like to keep some power closer to hand. Enforcer is one, and so is shot caller, who typically is me. In this, you need me to be, I'm callin' it. But what I'm tryin' to get you to fuckin' understand is I trust you. I fuckin' *trust* you, much as I ever did Po'Boy. I know you got the grit, and I know you got the bone under the muscle to stand whatever the fuck comes to the club's doorstep. So I'm callin' it, and what I'm callin' is you got this, brother. You got this, man." Twisted's voice receded, and Wildman's phone vibrated. He pulled it away from his head to see a different group text. "Want to sew it on your fuckin' vest before you get on the plane, you need to get a move on it, brother. Busk'll have your plate, hear me? Unass yourself if it matters to you. But to me? That plate don't matter for today. What we're doing right now will be woven into the lore and history of the club. The day the enforcer stepped up and took on a different burden, and then executed masterfully."

"Brother." Wildman swallowed hard. "I got this."

"Fuck yeah, you do, man. And now, I need to get back in there and put my arms around the most beautiful woman I've ever met and hold her while we get to know our boy a little more." Twisted's tone turned businesslike, his words quick and final. "Don't text me updates. Text me over-withs."

The line disconnected, and Wildman thumbed the text message open to see Twisted's words: **Get the motherfucker the right goddamned officer patch, fuckers**

He snorted a laugh and opened the door, headed back out into the main room. Walking up to Busk, who dangled a piece of fabric between his fingers, he shook his head as he took it and tucked it into the man's vest pocket. "Keep it safe for me. Don't got no sewing kit and less time, brother. Now, did we get a count of how many we can take? Any ideas if all clubs are interested, or are we just takin' our main allies?" And just that easily, he swung back into the final planning stages of what he hoped would be another bloodless coup.

Please, God.

Ten minutes later, he had Justine pinned against the wall, leaning on an arm propped next to her head. Staring down into her stormy grey eyes, he shook his head for the second time. "No, Jussie. This ain't something you get to ride along with."

"You need me. Myron's already said he could use my information. How it'll make things easier." She lifted her chin, glaring up at him. "The access comes with a caveat, which is me in the flesh on the op."

"It's not a fuckin' op."

"Doesn't matter what you call it, I've been on and running these kinds of missions for years, Wildman. All I need is a gun, and I'm good to go." Arching her back, she put her mouth to the hinge of his jaw, and heat from her mouth burned into him. "I can handle myself."

"Your job—"

"Will be moot in three days, and you should already know. I'm not staying in the agency." Her steady breaths bore the most precious of promises, and Wildman felt the most immense sense of relief at her words. "Won't be staying with the government. I'm with you. All in." Her hands latched onto the lapels of his vest, and she shook the fabric, fists thudding against his chest once, twice. *God, woman. She has to understand how important she is to me.* "I'm with you, and if you don't allow a trained asset to take part in this because of gender, then you having me in that room all day is another moot point. No one will take me seriously, no one will trust me, and Wildman, that has an extension of negativity pointing straight to you."

Shit. Shit, shit. She isn't wrong.

"I hate it when you make sense." That feeling of pride in her swelled, and he leaned back, resisting the urge to aim a broad smile at her.

"Get used to it." Mason's laughter came from behind him, but Wildman kept his position, staring down at Justine. Mason finished with, "She's like that."

"All I need is a Glock or Ruger—"

"I got a Ruger she can—" Mason's and Wildman's negative responses stepped on each other, their "No," and "Fuck no," eliciting a backpedaling, "No worries, brothers," from Ruger.

"I got a Glock." She smiled at Wildman's words, beaming even more at the unspoken subtext of acquiescence. "What I don't got is ammo for that caliber. Bummer for you." The expression of pleasure fled. *Gotcha.*

"Oh, I got ammo aplenty." Mason chuckled through his words. "My pleasure."

The smile that had dropped from her face at Wildman's statement returned with Mason's, and Wildman groaned, bending to bury his face against her neck. "It always gonna be like this, Jussie?"

"Probably." Her arms wound around his neck. "I'll make it up to you later."

"And that's my cue to head out. We got three groups already KSU and en route, be good if we can get the rest of us rolling now." Mason's voice moved away. "RWMC, get your asses in your saddles. If you do not have knowledge of the destination, then do not take fuckin' point. I ain't followin' anyone who can't find their own way."

Forehead pressed to Justine's flesh, Wildman breathed her in, filling his lungs with her scent, impressing it on every part of his mind. Cupping her cheek with his hand, he turned her face as he pulled back, gliding his lips across hers in a tender kiss he tried to fill with all the longing and hope he had inside him. "Let's ride, my wild woman." He caught at her hand as he moved away, pulling her behind him through the door and outside. At the bike, he handed her the helmet and watched her deft movements as she put it in place securely. "Magnificent." He threw a leg over the bike and started it, then held up a hand without looking back. Her palm slipped into his, her other hand going to his shoulder as she straddled the seat behind him, legs placed alongside his hips and thighs.

By the time they got to the airport, he'd somehow become accustomed to riding in the front of the multiple columns of bikes, all wearing different patches, and as he rolled to a stop on the tarmac next to the hanger Myron had provided as the correct location, Wildman was settled and strong, confident.

And ready.

Chapter Twenty
Wildman

The private jet offered many luxuries, but the one Wildman found himself taking advantage of was a full-length couch set at right angles to the fuselage. It was actually a sectional, bolted to the floor, but still a structure with a corner. He was propped in that corner, one leg spread long across the cushions, one boot planted firmly on the floor, Justine in his arms and draped over his lap. She'd dozed off not long after takeoff, after telling him how flying always put her to sleep, but she'd wake up on the other end. Her back was to the rest of the plane, and the unspoken trust set up a resonance within him. She'd followed his lead all day, showing everyone they were a unit. He snorted. *Almost all day.* If he'd had his way, she'd be at his house right now, taking a bubble bath or something. *That ain't the kind of woman I've fallen for,* he reminded himself, choking back another laugh.

On the other couch, Po'Boy and Wrench held nearly the same positions, with Po'Boy's chest being the pillow for Wrench's head. They'd whispered for a few minutes, then Wildman had watched as Wrench directed Po'Boy's lips downwards for a kiss that lasted, deepened, and eventually trailed off. The smile Po'Boy had worn as he lifted his head stayed there, even through his whisper-shouted, "What? You still fixatin' on that kiss, brother? I done told you, got me all the man I can handle right here." His hand smoothed down the back of Wrench's head, fingers tangling in the short hair at the nape. "We are fuckin' lucky men, aren't we?"

"Yeah, we are."

A few minutes later, the intercom crackled; then a low, professional voice announced, "Folks, weather's great in Miami, temps are warm and comfortable, and we've got a very light breeze from the water. We are third in line for a runway, so about twenty minutes out. Please follow the attendants' instructions to prepare for landing. I'll let you know our taxi time when we're on the ground."

Wildman gently shook Justine's shoulder, and she blinked up at him, going from asleep to wide awake and aware in a breath as he smiled down at her. "Need to buckle up, baby." She scooted off his lap and swung her legs off the couch, arching her back in a long stretch followed by a satisfied groan.

"Sending everyone their transport assignments before I lose the Wi-Fi. If you don't have it on your phone by the time we're ready to get off the plane, let me know. No bikes or vans for this run. Best I could do were high-dollar rentals, which means we've got dually trucks with crew cabs, and two Hummers. Swear to God, Florida is the worst for rentals." Myron's voice decreased in volume, but Wildman could still hear him complaining back in the rows of seats. "Four-door sedans everywhere, but can I rent a motorcycle? Not from an agency, nope."

"You ready, brother?" Wrench lifted his chin as he caught Wildman's gaze, holding it until he nodded. "Luck rides with us today."

"As she always does." Raising his voice as he called out their last set of orders, Wildman turned to look at the faces staring back at him from the seats arranged across the plane behind him. "Myron's your point for transport, but the run is mine. Mason, Wrench, Retro, Sparks, Capone, and I have a roster for the rollout. We're going to hit the compound from three directions. Myron will alert us if anything looks out of place. The timing is close to when we think Bassil will be arriving with Einstein, so if he tells me we're not far enough ahead of them, we'll hold and wait until they get settled. Last thing we need is for them to bust a gate and roar out of there." He held up a hand with a smile that felt toothy, sharklike. "But if they do, Myron's promised me he can follow them anywhere. I've rousted the Big Bend chapter, and Ragman is ready and willing to be the pincers to our hammer if needed. There's a lot of info points to this potential club launch as a trial run, and we all know what happens when unmonitored pop-up clubs start raising hell."

He glanced down at Justine, who had her gaze angled towards her legs but her head turned enough to indicate she was listening closely. "The worst time the Feds get involved is when we can't control our own. So think of this as a proactive treatment. We'll keep these boys from getting more baddies involved." Looking back up the plane, he met Mason's gaze with a nod. "We do not have permission from the resident dom to be in their territory, which is one reason I'm glad Myron wasn't able to roll iron for us. We're ridin' heavy, every fuckin' one of us, and the intent is to do this with prejudice. That's *my* call, and I'm telling you now there won't be any IMC blowback for stealin' a shot. I just want us all back on this plane in ten hours, crew rested and ready to haul our asses back to NOLA. If the dom gets wind, while we're here or after, all that shit's also on me, so do not fuck around. We're not here to tag vests, not here to rile clubs, no matter any bad blood or history you may have with them. That's not this run. You want to petition for assistance down the road, we'll talk. Right now, we want to disassemble this snake pit, get Einstein back, and assure the safety of his family and everyone on this fuckin' plane."

He gave it a beat, saw only a few heads nodding, and roared, "You fuckin' get me?"

Mason grinned as he nodded, as did Retro, and when Wildman turned to face the front, he found Po'Boy had sketched a salute at his brow, middle finger firmly extended as he returned the shout, "Aye, aye, Lyle."

"Fuck me."

Debarking happened in record time, the men lining up quietly and moving down the short set of stairs quickly, some of them showing off what looked to be naval skills of sliding the rails at speed. Multiple pings filled the air as they cleared the plane, and Wildman watched as each man checked his phone, then made his way to whatever vehicle had been designated as his ride. Eight pickups and two Hummers were lined up in front of the hangar, and he followed Myron with his gaze as the man walked to speak to a crew exiting the building. A few words, a handshake, and Myron aimed himself back to where Wildman stood with Justine, Mason, and Wrench, waiting.

"Maintenance and refueling will happen on schedule. We've got an hour or so to get to the clubhouse." Myron looked around the lot, and Wildman noted he glanced up too. *Cautious little shit.* "Everyone looks sorted. Are we ready?"

"Yeah, My. We're golden. You're riding with me, Justine, and Wildman. Hoss is drivin'. Po'Boy's just waiting for Wrench to climb his ass up in that Hummer he tore away from Mudd." Mason put action to his words, striding across the hot surface towards a large black pickup. "This is the rig with your hookups, right?"

"Yeah, that's the one." Myron slung his backpack around to carry on his chest, unzipping and digging into the main compartment. "Should have a couple of built-in monitors in the back of the seats for me to tap into. Makes my life easier."

"No doubt," Justine muttered as she visibly lengthened her stride to keep up with the men. When Wildman would have slowed for her, she shot him a glare and added a hopping skip that made up the distance tidily. "Surprised you don't have a command vehicle."

"Too much scrutiny. Construction bosses and contractors fly under the radar with some fun toys, which are the kind of vehicles I settled for, but a full-on comm-sat would be noted, marked, followed, and likely cause us a hell of a lot of trouble for little gain." Myron patted his backpack. "I honestly have everything I need right here, but the extra real estate for the computer screen makes some shit easier to do."

"Makes sense." She trotted for a couple of strides, then tucked her fingers around Wildman's belt. "If you have the tablet, I can work the entries we discussed from that, leaving you the screens."

"Sounds good." Myron ducked under Mason's arm, climbing into the back seat of the truck as Wildman and Justine rounded the bed. They angled into the seat next to Myron, Justine in the middle, and even before Mason had his door closed, Hoss had floored the accelerator, barking the tires against the tarmac.

Wildman glanced behind them, seeing Wrench and Po'Boy in the front seat of the following vehicle, the rest of the trucks and other Humvee filing out behind them. It was the work of minutes to navigate the surface roads around the airport, given they'd come in on the west side, opposite the normal passenger terminals, and then they were out on the highway, headed south.

Looking out the window, Wildman noted the many things that had changed about the area and the few places or locations that appeared to be the same. A thick fog settled over him, the sense of déjà vu making his skin itchy, had his fingers twitching for something—anything. He checked and settled his guns in their holsters three times before Justine's hand covered his, pressing his palm flat on the top of his thigh.

"Tell me what I can do?" She leaned close, chin to his shoulder as she looked at him. "I've got Myron hooked up, so you've got my full attention."

"These are my old stompin' grounds. See the next turnoff up there? I had two members lived on that road. I had organized a roofing party for their houses the week before all the shit with Powell went down." He shook his head. "Everything looks different, but it's not. It's all just the same. All the shit that was here before, still out there, waiting."

"No, it's not." She was on her knees in the seat, plastered along his side. "Nothing is the same, baby. You've got allies and friends here, right now." She hesitated, and he glanced away from the window in time to see a tender look cross her face. "And you've got me at your back. Always. Everything's different for you now. You found your place, found your way, and found your family."

"Family." The word felt like a gut punch. He opened his mouth and closed it without saying another word.

"The van is only fifteen minutes out. We do not have time to enter and stage before Bassil arrives." Myron leaned up between the two seats, motioning for Wildman to do the same. He sat forwards as Justine settled back, moving out of the way. "Wildman, do I have your approval to make the call to divert? We'll set up along three streets, spaced three and four blocks from the compound. I'll have eyes on him the instant he hits the fence, and if I've got things right, even inside. Still workin' that angle, but I'm close now. Another twenty will ensure we've eyes inside, too."

"Yeap, do it, brother." Wildman sighed and twisted his fingers tightly with Justine's. He looked into the front seat, and Mason's grey eyes, so like Justine's, met Wildman's as he nodded in agreement.

"You got it," Myron muttered, toppling backwards into the bench seat, laptop balanced on his knees. "Less than twenty. Down to a science."

There was no chatter in the text channels, no responses to the change in plans Myron fired off to the groups, and no conversation in the truck. Wildman found himself watching Myron's screens, seeing a bright green dot come into view moving south, traveling quickly as it exited the highways. *That's Bassil.* He'd never thought he'd see the man again. Remembered the feel of the bastard's blood on his fists the last time they'd had an encounter. *Something wasn't right that day either.* Hard to pin down, especially when the remembered anger was enough to white out the edges of Wildman's memory.

"He's on-site." The screen changed, now a top-down view of the compound, entirely unfamiliar territory for all of them, except where Myron's tools had pulled back the curtain. They knew most of the men in the compound were in the main building but were also running what looked like a chop shop from a smaller garage near the back fence. "Looks like we've got folks converging." Wildman watched intently as small gray blobs traversed a slightly different gray representing the parking lot. "Bassil's vacated. They're taking one person from the van." Myron's voice cracked, and he cleared his throat. "Confirm, they've only retrieved one person."

"Call it, Myron." Wildman's fingers danced across the holsters and handles of his guns, slipped the hilt of the blade strapped to his thigh up, then snicked it back into the sheath. "They'll have him inside in half a minute. We need in there."

"Back gate is already jimmied open." Myron split the screen, dual focus on the back fence near the garage and on the van. "Front gate's on a code, and I'll have it open before we get there. No one'll hear anything." Hoss put the truck into gear, and they started rolling as Myron split the screen again, this showing a long view of the inside of a metal building, all industrial struts and columns, dangling chains, and overhead lights. "I've got eyes inside. I'm counting more than twenty bodies in there. Repeat, twenty or more hostiles, one friendly."

Wildman thumbed at his phone, opening the text thread. He responded with just one phrase: **Roll quiet**

That would ensure no one drove in guns blazing but would get everyone moving. Justine pointed at the screen, and Wildman gave her leg a squeeze; he'd seen the same thing. "Mason, they're dragging him up the center. Looks like a stage or some shit. Got chairs set up." He shook his head. "Fuckin' church? What the hell?"

"Hold, brother," Mason muttered, leaning forwards as they drove through the open gate. "Fuckin' hold, man."

Wildman glanced in Hoss' mirrors and noted the six vehicles filing in behind them. The rest would be at the back of the property. Fingers curled around the handle, he waited for Hoss to drift to a slow, silent stop, then flung the door open, leaving it wide for Justine. Every instinct in him screamed to protect her, but he knew in his gut she really didn't need it. She could hold her own, and more—she needed to do this. Not for him, but for herself. Something he didn't yet understand, but he hoped he'd have a chance to soon.

Gravel crunched under their boots as the men in the other vehicles bailed out, running alongside and behind him. Their goal was the door at the end of the building, an opening that fed into the metal shell near where that damn stage had been constructed. From the inside video, he knew they'd be protected for about twenty feet by a metal hallway before a barn door opening would feed them into the main area. Hopefully right in position to take Bassil by surprise. If fate was with them today.

That fickle bitch was, for a change.

Gun in one hand, blade in the other, he burst around the end of the hallway and, along with a dozen men he trusted at his back, swarmed the stage. He kicked Bassil in the chest, pleasure blooming in him as the man starfished through the air, landing on his back with a racketing thud. Einstein fell to the side, rolling off the stage quietly, shoulders and elbows as swollen and deformed as his face was, but Wildman didn't have a moment to spare. He was on Bassil, skidding to a stop next to the man before flinging a knee in the center of a chest still trying to suck in air after the fall.

The moment Bassil recognized him, Wildman saw surprise replaced with hatred, thick lips pulling back from yellowed, ill-spaced teeth, the man's broken snarl still showing the effects of their last meeting. "You?" Bassil's wheeze lacked substance, and Wildman ground down against his bones, leaning more heavily where his knee was compressing the man's chest. "The fuck you doing here, boy?"

"Not your boy." Wildman shook his head. "Never was. The fuck you think *you're* doin', snapping up a member of an ally of the IMC? You always were stupid as fuck."

"Not as stupid as you and your brother was." Bassil grabbed for his hip, and Wildman's hand met his there, ripping the pistol away and flinging it into the dark at the back of the stage. "He was a tool, but he was my tool, bent and broken to my hand. You fucked that up for me, just like you're fucking this up too." Bassil bucked underneath him, and Wildman sprawled to the side. Both men rose to their feet. "I'm gonna kill you, boy."

"Let's see you try." Wildman took a risk, holstering his gun. He was vaguely aware of multiple altercations happening at his back but trusted Justine and his brothers to keep everything at bay. Blade in hand, he feinted at Bassil. "Bring it, old man."

***

Justine

Trailing the men into the building, Justine noted the small group splitting off towards the van as she found a place for herself in the line, well back from the front runners. This was their beef, not hers, and even if she hadn't let Wildman see her uncertainty, she'd wondered a dozen times why she'd been so insistent on making this trip with them.

Her reasoning was clear, and she believed the basis of what she'd said. So did Wildman and Davy; otherwise, they would never have agreed, no matter how she'd have argued. If they didn't understand how her reputation within the club—and thus Wildman's—hung on the men trusting and believing she would never act against their interests, then not only Wildman's presidency but probably even his membership would be default within weeks. Justine had no illusions how things would have been handled otherwise, and being locked in a room in the clubhouse while people she loved flew a thousand miles away wasn't something she could have tolerated.

Now, though? In the thick of it, there was no uncertainty. Her sole goal was to watch Wildman's back. Make sure none of these assholes who'd started shit with the clubs had a shot at him. *And make sure there's no chance of friendly fire either.* Not that he didn't trust the men with them. He'd not said a single thing against any of them. But he'd made it clear he didn't know many of them well, if at all, and was taking their leaders' word they were true and loyal.

Daddy didn't raise no fools.

Loyalty couldn't be bought, but betrayal could, and she'd earned herself enough enemies through the years. Her upcoming defection from federal ranks was already making the rounds through the outlaw world. It'd have to be, based on the number of calls and emails she'd ignored from various agencies she'd collaborated with through her career. Next would be her office, and while she knew Wildman still held out hope they'd make their grand tour of her life after this business in Florida was settled, she was more interested in not being scooped up and detailed as a risk. Which meant she'd need to go through channels to get a clear pass. But not right now. *Focus, Jussie.*

The line of men rounded a corner and disappeared, and as she ran three steps beyond, putting her back to the wall as the men behind her continued to flood the room, it took her half a breath to find and lock her gaze on Wildman.

Hands wide for balance, he was dancing in a crouched circle on top of the stage she'd seen on Myron's screens. The man from the van was opposite him in nearly the same position. The only difference was Wildman held his knife in a defensive pose against his forearm while Bassil appeared unarmed.

Appearances could be deceiving, she knew, so she moved around the backside of the stage, keeping her back to a wall, ensuring the dozen fights remained in front of her.

Mason and Hoss had a man on the ground and were taking turns kicking at the guy's back and legs. Intimidation rather than pain and injury, which meant they didn't feel threatened.

Retro was stooped beside someone lying next to the stage, Mudd protectively hovering nearby. That would be his man, Einstein.

Po'Boy and Wrench stood back-to-back, taking on three men at once. She angled forwards when Po'Boy appeared to stumble but then stood upright when she realized he'd nearly lost contact with one of the men and was pulling him back into the melee.

On the stage, Wildman and Bassil continued to circle each other. The men's mouths moved, but their taunts as they tried to gain the upper hand were lost in the noise and chaos around her. Then they made another half circle, and she saw the gun at Bassil's back, tucked low into his belt.

Bringing her gun up to firing stance, she steadied her double-handed grip and kept the sight on the center of Bassil's spine. If he went for the gun, she'd know it and deal with him before he could lay a finger on the weapon. A gunshot echoed through the building, the first such sound, and her gaze was drawn beyond the two men to find the shooter.

Then Wildman and Bassil collided and went down, elbows and knees flying as they fought for advantage. Another gunshot, this closer, and Wildman's body lifted up a couple of inches before falling back down on top of Bassil.

No!

Heart in her throat, she ran for the stage, leaping up the three feet like she'd risen on wings. Neither man moved, and the sound around the elevated platform fell away. At the edge of her vision, it looked like every fight had stopped in place, suspended as dust wafted through the air, brilliant sunbeams piercing the gloom as she fell to her knees next to Wildman. She laid a hand on his shoulder, and he shuddered, rolling away from her and the unmoving body, knife in his hand dripping. Justine launched herself at Wildman, hands searching across his body and clothing looking for a cut, a tear, a hole. For bloody flesh, a wound, or trauma.

The front of his shirt was wet with red, and she pushed the leather of his vest to the side as she ripped at fabric, tearing it apart in her hands. "Wild. Please, no. *Please.*"

His hands on her arms stopped her, finally. She'd found nothing, but it took his words to break the hold the terror had on her.

"Not mine, baby girl. Shhhh. It's not my blood. It's okay, honey." His arms circled her, and he stood, lifting her with him as he climbed to his feet. "It's not mine. I'm okay."

She cradled his face in her hands, staring up into those eyes she'd come to love, into that face she adored, and at the man she lived for. "Scared the shit out of me."

"It's okay." His head lifted, and he shot a glance over her shoulders. "We're on the tail end of this shit now, baby. Bassil's a goner, which is a good fuckin' thing, trust me when I say that."

She backed away a step and turned, looking down at the man lying on his back. Blood pooled from underneath him, concentrated along his waist, where his hands clutched at a long tear through his abdomen. Bulging intestines threatened to break free, held in place by connective tissue and his fingers.

"You." Bassil's eyes never moved from staring straight overhead. She didn't know if he knew what he was saying or if the blood loss had scrambled his brain. "Done it now." His grip on his side slipped, and he groaned, slapping one palm over the gash and pressing. "Shoulda died by now..." His words trailed off, becoming breathy and jagged. "Shoulda." His chest fell, and his hands dropped away, a tiny gush of blood cascading along his side.

"You okay, Jussie?" Wildman's question seemed odd, and she looked at him, surprised to see uncertainty on his face. "You're good?"

Smiling, she lifted her chin and stepped closer, realizing why he seemed hesitant. "I'm good, Lyle." Gesturing with the gun in her hand, she indicated the men spread out over the inside of the building. "Let's check on our folks."

"We'll come back to this later." He brushed a kiss across her cheek; then his palm connected with one globe of her ass in a stinging swat. "You're good."

Chapter Twenty-One
Wildman

There'd been a moment when he'd seen the gun in Bassil's hand where Wildman wasn't sure how things would end.

He shook his head. *Last thing I should be thinking.* Then the man had aimed the weapon at Justine, and there had been no hesitation. Wildman had struck hard, burying the blade deep in Bassil's belly before jerking it to the side, tearing through the aorta before he was done.

Bassil'd gone fast, too fast for Wildman's way of thinking. But on the other hand, he'd been glad it hadn't drawn out. Once Justine had latched her eyes on Bassil, she hadn't turned away, hadn't said anything, just watched the man die. Wildman had a moment of fear, wondering what she saw or thought, the man dead from his hand. Then she'd pulled herself together, moving close to give him what he'd needed.

Bassil and two others were the only casualties. Po'Boy would have a black eye, but his bruising was truly the only damage on their side.

Except for Einstein.

The man had been beaten unconscious, as well as dislocating a shoulder and elbow trying to get away during the long drive from where they'd taken him hostage. Mudd was still working on him, trying to keep the man calm while he prepped him for transport without getting an actual doctor or EMT involved. Mudd had men in both professions on video providing guidance in the form of one Bama Bastard and one IMC officer from the Big Bend chapter, and Justine had settled nearby, appointing herself Mudd's runner as needed.

Retro claimed to still be unsure at the motivation behind the madness, but Wildman had watched his face as Mason and Wrench dispatched men to question the ones they'd restrained. Retro had an idea; he just wasn't ready to share it yet. One of the first things they'd learned from those interrogations was Bassil hadn't acted alone. No, not at all. The Monster Devils were in this neck-deep, but it would take time to extract the information they needed and then for the puzzle to be pieced together.

The blanket-covered forms in the van were Einstein's wife and daughter.

Wildman had stared into those faces for a long fucking time.

Eyes closed, expressions peaceful—if not for the bruising and paleness in contrast, they could have looked asleep.

Like Shelly did.

Myron was already working on a story that would allow Einstein to bury his family without hiding. Could lay them to rest respectfully, with friends and loved ones around him.

Standing alongside the building's outside wall, Wildman widened his stance, folding his arms across his chest as he counted back the years and then shook his head. *Nothin' but bones by now.* The baby in Shelly's belly had been so small, so new—*likely nothin' left.* He shook his head again, more viciously, punishing himself for the anger and resentment welling through his chest, choking him. *Man shouldn't be envious of another man for gettin' to bury his family.* "It's a goddamned horror he'll have to do this. I'm glad he won't be alone with it."

A hand landed on his shoulder, and he jerked around to find Po'Boy within reach. The grip rocked him back and forth, feet firmly planted but swaying as if in a strong wind. "It is a goddamned horrible thing, brother." Po'Boy bent close, mouth near Wildman's ear. "I fucking hate this shit. Beyond everything, the fact anything we do can touch family like this? It scares the bejeezus out of me. Someone targeting me? Or Ty, due to club business? I get it. I don't like it, but it's what we choose every day. Crissy though? Or someday soon—please God—a babe of ours? That doesn't make any goddamned sense."

"Bassil said he was the one who talked my brother into taking out a contract on my head." Wildman scooted back to rest his shoulders against the wall, trying and failing to pull out of Po'Boy's grip. "Man stood there and basically admitted to being the reason my wife died, man. Who does that shit?"

"No compass in that one. His true north was one thing and one thing only. Power." Po'Boy crowded closer. "That'd be the reason you didn't stay and deal with him when it all shook out. Because you probably got how he was, having seen him around for a while. You're a smart boy. You were bound to figure shit out, you know?"

"Not fast enough. Didn't change a damn thing, did it? Me leavin'? Me pullin' up stakes and puttin' it in my rearview? Didn't change a damn thing, and now another man's family is dead. How is this happening again?" He fastened his gaze on the van, watching as someone moved it into the shade of an overhang. "I understand Myron's got a plan. Got somebody out buying supplies, so we can take them on the plane. I'm real glad Einstein'll have them close to home. It won't help with the pain, but just knowing they're where he can go visit has got to help somehow."

"I talked to Mason and Retro, then I called our man Twisted." Po'Boy's forehead hit the side of Wildman's temple. "You want to bring your ole lady home and plant her in the family plot out back of Mother, they'll have a place ready and waiting for her."

Wildman reared back, turning to look at Po'Boy, heart pounding in his chest. "What?"

"Retro said he knows where she is. Where they are. Said it's twenty minutes south. Myron already accounted for it somehow, like he knew, but whatever." Wildman watched as Po'Boy's throat moved, Adam's apple bobbing deep in his throat, like the words were hard to get out. "Be my honor to help you bring them home, brother. It'd be my honor."

"There's nothin' but bones left. It's been years, man. I don't know if I can—I don't know if I can see her like that, you know? All that was Shelly, reduced to a few scattered bones? I don't know." He closed his eyes. "But I'd be lyin' if I said I didn't want it. It's fuckin' killed me how things had to be left. Fuckin' tore me up for years, how disrespectful it was to her. How fuckin' cold it made me to know she'd been discarded, because the triggerman pullin' her number was inconvenient for the club. But I don't know if I can see that."

"Then you don't see that part." Po'Boy made the statement like it was easy. "You bring us to where she is, make sure we know where we're lookin', and then you stay where you can have your hands on Justine. We'll bring her home for you, brother. I ask, we'll have a dozen hands in the air, ready to help, and you fuckin' know it. Because you're our brother, and we've got your back. Patch don't matter in this, man. This is the life, and this is what we do."

"Justine. What would she think about it? It's one thing to hear it as a story, but to see the fallout? To know what she's potentially signing up for? That should be enough to have any woman running, sure thing."

"Bitch is not just any woman, though. And I think you know it, brother." Po'Boy grinned. "Hot as fuck to watch a woman who can handle herself, even distracted as I was in there just tryin' to match my strides to Wrench. Her sole focus in there was you. Just you, Wild. *Lyle.* Every threat to you, she had it locked down, eyes on, gun drawn. And you know that kind of devotion won't break because it's already factoring in the worst options and just bustin' through the backside of the territory to look for any more threats to her man. Hot as fuck, brother." Po'Boy leaned close. "She's only going to give a fuck about the impact it'll have on you. Nothin' else. She's not going to see it as a foretelling or augur about possible futures. She's going to see the settled look on your face once we get your family home, and she will not only be good with it, but she'll also be grateful your brothers take care of you, however we do it."

"Fuck, I want that, brother. Been tearin' me up for so long, I won't know what to do when the pain's gone."

"Let's get you to that place, then. Where you can see how it feels to not carry so much goddamned weight, man. Let us do this for you." Po'Boy shook Wildman's shoulder a final time before stepping back. "We want to. Hell, if I'm honest, some of us—me included—are desperate to feel any kind of a win out of this. You heard the stories these boys been telling?"

Wildman stared at him, then shook his head slowly. "Been out here since Mudd got Einstein's elbow back into place. Wanted to watch over his family for him. I know it's stupid—"

"Nope, not a bit of it is stupid. I get it, man. And that's righteous of you, brother." Retro stepped up behind Po'Boy and gave Wildman a nod. "Very much appreciated, and this is me telling you how as of right now, Lyle Woolsey has a marker from Jeremiah Rogers. You stepped up, brother, and I owe you."

"No, man. It's what we do, right?"

"Yeah, but I fucking owe you." Retro's lips pinched flat. "Cast your mind back years ago. You remember calling your dominant and askin' for help after Shelly was murdered? After you got home from holding death watch over your brother and came home to find your wife dead? After you killed the man who had the audacity to still be in your home, shittin', and sittin', and eatin' food she'd prepared with her two hands?"

Wildman didn't respond, frozen in place, fists clenched tightly enough to set up an ache in his joints.

"That dom flung a request wide, and I snagged it. There'd been lots of talk about a brewing shitstorm in southern Florida, and I deal in information, so it seemed a good way to get intel. Little cleanup, little investigative work, and I could pull my net back in closer to Alabama." Retro shook his head, one hand coming up to rake through his hair, flipping it over a shoulder. "I didn't know you. Never learned a name other than Ogre, but I'm the one who did a shit job of takin' care of you back then. I coulda done what Myron's doing for Einstein right now, made it so it could have been an official death. Was easier not to, and I didn't know you. Feel like shit right about now because of that weight you've been carrying, man. I don't know it, don't need you to speak it, because I've seen it in your face since I met you. That's on me. So I fuckin' owe you, okay? Suck it up and deal, because you've got a marker with me. A personal marker, in addition to the one the Bastards owe you for takin' up our cause today."

"I don't know what to say." The knowledge it was Retro who'd assisted floored him. He vaguely remembered it being an Alabama club, but back then, Retro's name wouldn't have meant anything to him, other than a way to get Shelly into the ground as gracefully as possible. "But I can tell you the help I got was the only thing kept me sane. My own club had refused me. After holdin' out the president patch to me one minute, then pullin' back on the brotherhood the next? I didn't know what to do, but after the shit with Powell dying, I knew I couldn't call the cops in. Blood staining the bastard's shirt from my old lady, and I'd shot him at the table, him fallin' over backwards into his own bone and brains. Shelly dead in the bed, sweet smile on her face even as she'd started to—" He shook his head. "Retro, you don't owe me, brother. I owe you. Kept me outta jail. Might not have been my choice of places to lay Shelly to rest, but at least she wasn't rolled off into a ditch somewhere. That was the advice offered by Bassil back in the day, make it look like a random killing that couldn't be traced back to the club. Thank you, man. Sincerely. Thank you."

"Wasn't enough, brother. Not fuckin' near enough. But I'm gonna do what I can now." Retro lifted a hand and turned. "Y'all need to come back in and witness. We've got more business to deal out, and while I fuckin' hate it, it's got to be done."

Wildman glanced at the van, seeing three men standing nearby, backs to the vehicle, focus outwards. "These are some fuckin' good men, Po'Boy."

"Yeah, we are." Po'Boy crooked his elbow around Wildman's neck, tugging him sideways towards the door. "Come on, let's see what kind of story we've got to hear."

Retro was in the process of jumping up on the stage, and Wildman was surprised to see Bassil's body was gone. Someone had scattered sand over the bloodstained wood, and it was clumping into lines and ridges, the circle impossibly large to have come from only one person. Wildman and Po'Boy stopped near Wrench along the back row of chairs, and Wildman scanned the men seated in front of them. Legs and wrists were restrained, tied to the chairs where they'd been positioned, and on two of the men, fabric bags of some kind had been pulled over their heads, making them anonymous, featureless in a way that bothered Wildman. *Not my gig.*

Retro stomped his foot twice, the booming sound of boot against metal rolling through the building. Head high, he looked out at the men gathered along the edges of the space, ignoring the ones who were the reason they were there. Most of the clubs had divided the space, so they stood next to those who were best known to them, IMC and CoBos the only ones who were interwoven without regard to patch.

"We've got news, brothers." Fingers danced along Wildman's waist, and he lifted his arm, snuggling it tightly around Justine as she slotted herself next to him. "And lady, because some of this impacts you."

Fingers balled into fists, Retro propped his hands on his hips, and the great gusting sigh that came from him was loud and tired. "Mostly, this is for us all."

Tipping his chin down, Retro seemed to study the wood at his feet, then lifted his head and shot a hot glance towards where Mason stood with his men. "This rockets back to Tucker and the bastard he was." Mason didn't react, but Retro went on as if he had. "Oh yeah, blast from the past, brother. Dead and gone for a while now, but reachin' out from beyond the grave right here and now. Seems he grew up in this neck of the woods. Long before Powell struck a deal, before Bassil twisted brotherly love into hate, they ran around with Tucker. You'll remember he hooked his star to fuckin' Lalo, may he rot in hell, and was the main threat behind my man dying two years ago. So he's dead and gone, but Bassil wasn't forgetting about it." Retro pointed at the two men who'd been masked and muffled. "And neither are they. I'm done making mistakes when it comes to this kind of shit, so I'll deal with them before we roll out of here. The rest of these assholes, well, you've heard it said the worst sinners are in the first pew at church, and that seems true here, as well as in the secular world." He pulled in a harsh breath. "There's four more here who I do not trust as far as I can fuckin' spit, but I lack the weight of true belief I'm right. They've been in bed with the Monster Devils and were followin' Bassil's lead, but it don't feel right, brothers. It don't feel right. This is what it would feel like if I were convicting a son because of a father's sins, and it don't feel right."

He shook his head and tossed his hair over one shoulder with a grimace. "Ain't entirely my call, because this is all our asses. I'd like nothing more than to do a 'scorched earth' move, just for Einstein. But this needs a vote or some shit." He gestured to the two with their faces hidden. "Those are mine, I'll remind you." He pointed at the back row of men secured to their chairs. "Most are apparently harmless pawns. They're scared pissless and won't be angling back into the life anytime soon, or probably ever. In over their heads, and out of their league, and just want to be able to run home to momma at the end of the day." He leaned forwards, gaze sweeping the four men in the front row. "These are my dilemma. Feels like a catch-22 no matter which way I head, my friends. Tell me what you need to hear in order to vote a thumbs-up—" His gaze swung across the men they'd brought with them. "—or down."

"I got questions, Retro." Wildman took a step forwards, Justine's fingers falling away. "Based on what you've shared over the past days, and what we know of those East Coast bastards. You want 'em out here, or want to take it private?"

Retro stared at him, then raked every man in the room with his hard gaze, took a deep breath, and seemed to settle his stance as if for a fight. "Ask 'em."

"Your newfound family?" That was as close as Wildman was willing to go to say Retro's old lady and her baggage, but he knew Retro marked his intent by the fire in his eyes. "They have a certain association with them that runs directly counter to the history of the MDMC." He walked up until he stood at the end of the row where the four men sat in limbo. "And those are the questions I think we need answered most of all." Staring down at the men, Wildman marked the visible tattoos each wore, unsurprised to find a mark etched into the flesh of each man's right hand. In the soft webbing where the thumb met the body, they bore a star surrounded by five dots, and tattooed between the first and second joints of that same thumb was a stooping bird of prey worked into a ring shape, the letters VVZ underneath.

He could nearly hear the pieces in his head snapping into place. Closing his eyes, he remembered the first overheard phone call that had caused him doubt in his heart for his brother, Powell. Dug deep to pull out the name Powell and Bassil had discussed at length after the call ended. Remembered again the newly etched ink on their hands.

Wildman opened his eyes and took a step towards the stage, turning and sitting on the edge. "Thief-in-law." Two of the men jerked in place. Their flinches were nearly unmentionable, except they'd reacted.

"Scarloucci." That earned him a hard glance from a third man. "Chulpayev." The fourth man spat on the floor. "I've got my vote." Wildman stood and lifted his hand, thumb pointed straight down. "Not worth the risk, brother."

Metal screeching against metal sounded, and he looked up to see Hoss and Sparks dragging two chairs up the center aisle. They deposited them at the end of the row, roughly turning them to face Retro. "Reckon we found two more, brother." Hoss pointed at the two new additions, who had the same hand tattoos, and said, "Negative reaction to our friend's words, same as those."

Wildman shifted, twisted, put his boots to the stage, and stood. Crowding close to Retro, he laid it out for him. "The tattoos on their right hands make them made men in the Italian mafia. That's not done lightly or without cost, and I wouldn't trust any of the men in this room who share the same marks. Their reaction to your old lady's blood father ain't good, man. Means Chulpayev is being discussed. Actively discussed. Either he's in the middle of makin' a move or about to have a move made on him. Either way, this is a fuck of a lot bigger than a squabble over territory with the Mexican cartel. We should look for the black hand tattoos on their chests, as well, just to make sure there's no fuckin' crossover in enemies, man. Cover all our bases since we've got a captive audience." He lifted a hand and settled it on Retro's shoulder, the tension in the man's muscles fairly radiating outwards. "Those six, though? Might be the worst of it, but they gotta go today. I will gladly stand tall and take care of it, brother. I know you understand me. I know you get it because IMC stands with the Bastards." He took a breath, thudded his fist against Retro's shoulder, and finished with "I have your back, brother. Always have your back."

There'd been another six men culled from the larger group, based on ink alone. Then two more had outed themselves as Scarloucci men.

There had been an unspoken agreement of presidents-only in the building when the men were executed. Wildman had thanked God

Justine didn't argue, glad when she'd followed the example set by the other members of their party, officers and patch members alike, with her moving outside amongst the larger group without even a look back. No lingering glances filled with guilt, no admonishments of any kind. She'd accepted the need and given him what she could. Not a blessing to take another life, but an acceptance of, and clear trust in, him.

Two shots from each gun, and the twelve bodies had jerked and sagged against the ropes binding them to the chairs.

Retro had taken longer with the final two men he'd marked for more, and Wildman had stood in the circle around where he worked on them, staring, restraining as needed, and witnessing.

He'd immediately decided Retro was not someone he wanted to be on the wrong side of. The man was brutal, thorough, and inventive. Seventeen bodies had been wedged into a utility van turned food truck they'd found on the lot, and then one of Mason's men had gotten busy rigging it with explosives—which Wildman had no idea where Myron had sourced from, but he was another man who had far more depth and darkness to him than expected. Chemicals were sprayed over every surface inside the main building as well as the food truck, supposed to do who knew what, but everyone trusted Myron at that point, so they did as he said.

Then they were rolling out of the lot. All told, only four from the Florida crew walked away from the building. Well...had been driven away, far up the coast, no phones or identification, and doped to the gills so Wildman, Mason, Retro, and the rest would have time to get back to the airport and vacate before any possibility of an alert was raised. Two vehicles angled north and east, going upstate to drop off the men who lived. Three vehicles would follow their original path straight back to the airport, carrying Einstein and his family. The rest of them headed south towards a remote area of woods Wildman prayed still stood. Myron had promised it was the same, said nothing had been done, no building in the area, no razing of the trees. Just a small copse of woods that held what once was his family.

Sitting sideways in the back seat, Wildman stretched his leg out along the bench and motioned Justine to unbuckle and slide closer. With Myron in a different vehicle, they had more room, and he wanted to stretch out as much as he could, but more, wanted his hands on her in whatever way she'd allow. She crawled across and settled herself between his legs, shoulder pressing against his side, head on his chest, and he sighed so loud Mason's head twitched sideways to glance back at them.

"There's not going to be much left of them." He pressed a kiss to her temple. "You okay with this, Jussie?"

"Yes." Her immediate answer was gratifying, as was the firm tone in which it had been spoken. "God, yes. You of all men deserve to be able to bring your family home."

"Shit, woman. You fuckin' slay me." He trailed his fingers down her arm, circling her wrist with his hand and bringing it to rest flat against his chest. "Feel that? That beats only for you, Jussie. I fuckin' love you. You understand that? I fucking love *you*."

"I know you do." She nestled closer, fingertips drawing tiny shapes against his chest. "And it's returned a thousandfold."

***

Myron settled into the seat next to Wildman, laptop already open and a frown on his face.

"Hey, My." Wildman glanced around, seeing Justine still engrossed in a conversation with her brother. They'd been in the air for about ten minutes, and he'd been going over the day in his mind, so Myron's distraction was welcome.

"Busk gave me access to the security for the club." Myron slid a glance at Wildman, fingers tapping along the top edge of the laptop screen. "At the time, I didn't know he'd tied some personal residences into the system. Makes sense, and I do the same for the RWMC, but there's a way to keep it separate. I plan on showing him when we get back."

"Okay." Wildman studied him, then addressed what obviously was the issue by telling him, "Busk set up the security at my place."

"Yeah." Mouth pulling sideways into a scowl, Myron shook his head. "I wasn't looking for anything in particular. Just snagged all the vids from the server and ran them through a processor I use. The AI behind it is pretty sweet in how it learns real quick what's normal and what's not, so property owners coming and going become background noise."

"And anything not normal stands out for review." He blew out a breath. "And you found something not normal at my place?" Myron nodded. He glanced behind them, seeing two rows of empty seats, as most of the men had gathered nearer the galley. "Show me."

"It's from this week. When Justine showed up at the clubhouse. You were at the party, then stayed a while, and then you went home late. With Justine." Myron's words came in choppy sentences as he tapped keys on the laptop. "Someone was in your house just before you got home."

Gooseflesh crawled up his arms, and he remembered the gut feeling of things being not quite right. "Who?"

"No idea yet. I didn't get enough for recognition or identification, so I can't pick him out of a group. But I've got scans running on traffic cameras around the same time, hoping I can find him as he came or went." Myron twisted the laptop to face Wildman. "Here. Watch this and tell me what you think."

A man stood in his kitchen. Dark coat, too heavy for the season in Louisiana. Dark hat pulled low over his eyes. He brought something out from a pocket, shook it, and then crouched near the base of a wall in full sight of the door, windows, and the camera. With economic movements, he wrote something on the paneling, focused in on his actions until Wildman noted what had to be the lights of his bike swing across the kitchen windows, announcing his and Justine's arrival. Still, the man lingered, crab walking along the wall to continue what he was doing. Moments before Wildman and Justine walked into the kitchen, the man left through the front door. The camera view changed, and he could clearly see the man deftly circumventing the alarm on his way out and then reenabling it from the outside.

"What's he writing?" Wildman frowned. "There's nothing there."

"No idea. That's all I have. There's nothing else on your exterior system and nothing in the logs that says he brute-forced his way inside, which means he's more sophisticated than a burglar."

"Plus, he didn't take anything."

"No," Myron agreed with a sigh. "He left something."

"What?"

Justine appeared at the end of the row, head tipped to one side. "Hey." She looked at the laptop screen, frozen on a shot of the man standing in Wildman's kitchen. "What's that?"

"Come here." Wildman stood and lifted her past Myron, settling her in his lap. "Watch this, tell me what you see." When Myron didn't immediately play the video, he flicked a finger at the screen. "Run it again, My."

The video snapped into play with the man in the kitchen, cycling through nearly the entire video before Justine sucked in a deep breath.

"You know him?"

"Coworker in the agency." She shook her head. "Sometime...playmate."

"What'd he use to write on the wall?"

"UV ink." She shook her head. "Probably. I mean, he left the pen in the cup near the wall." She wiggled to get free, and Wildman clamped his hands on her waist. "Wild, we need to see what message he left."

"I'd like to know more about this person who broke into my house, Jussie." Keeping his tone even and free from anger was hard, because, after the past two days, he'd had plans for them getting home tonight, and dealing with some fucking government asshole leaving secret messages wasn't on the agenda. "Tell me about this coworker."

"Greg Anderson. My counterpart on the anti-trafficking task force. He's a good agent but uses questionable tactics at times." Her backbone was arrow straight, shoulders back as she waited for him to question her further, but Wildman held his tongue, hoping her natural inclination to explain to him would take over. "He's the one who introduced me to the scene, and always respected I didn't want intercourse with him. He was over-the-top angry about the op, about me 'going rogue' as he put it. I don't get why he'd be there." She twisted and stared into Wildman's face, and he let his gaze search hers, seeing only concern and fear there. *Fear for me.* "We need to know what he left for us."

"I don't disagree. What's key about him leaving the pen?"

"It likely has the UV light needed to disclose the message. Cheap party tactics these days, but still an effective communication tool. As long as someone knows where to look for the message, it'll remain unremarked unless the right light shines across it."

"Myron, can you get someone to my house?"

"Already on it. Busk should be there momentarily."

"Then we wait."

A few silent minutes later, Wildman's phone buzzed with an incoming call, and he handed it to Myron. Within moments, the video had been transferred to the laptop, so they could see using the better graphics.

"Thanks, brother," he told Busk, and waited as the man took in the image from their end of the call. Myron next to him, Justine in his lap. "There'll be a marker in the cup next to where my coffeemaker sits. Brand-new. See if you can find it."

Busk wordlessly pointed at the mug filled with pens, pencils, and markers, and Wildman nodded. Sure enough, there was a bright blue one he didn't recognize sticking straight up out of the crowded mess. Busk grabbed a cloth, then picked up the pen, experimentally flicking a switch he found on the side.

Aiming the light at the baseboard of the wall where Anderson had crouched made scrawled words appear, incomplete letters flashing as Busk swept the area randomly. Hunkering down near the bottom of the wall, he started at the left and kept a steady movement of the light, revealing the message.

NOBODY LEAVES ME. NOT EVEN YOU, JUSTINE.

"What the actual fuck?"

Justine's question seemed to sum up everything well, so Wildman didn't bother responding.

Chapter Twenty-Two

Wildman

Something tickled his nose, and he halfheartedly slapped at whatever bug it was, surprised when Justine giggled. Blinking up at her, he caught her hand as she went to bring in the lock of hair again, growling as he rolled them, pinning her underneath him.

"The fuck you doing, woman?"

They were in his room at the clubhouse, deciding to crash there last night after way too much to drink and the lingering uncertainty about the security of his house. Justine could have driven them home in her car, now covered in a thick layer of dust after being parked on the clubhouse lot for so many days, but he'd wanted to fuck, and the closest bed won out.

God. He brushed hair away from her face, curling one long strand behind an ear as he bent close to take her lips in a long, slow kiss. *Fuckin' mine, and don't I know just how goddamned lucky I am.*

"Waking you?" She lifted her chin, and he obliged, dropping a series of kisses at the corner of her mouth, trailing along the edge of her jaw. "It's nearly noon already, and I wanted to make sure you had time to wake up and get ready."

Grief landed in his gut like a lead balloon, and he dropped his forehead to rest against the side of her neck. "Thanks, Jussie." He tightened his grip, stretching out over her as he registered her arms wrapping around his neck. "You take good care of me."

"Kinda in the job description." She sniffled, and he pulled back, staring down into her face. "I just want you happy, Lyle."

"With you. I'm happy with you. That's all it takes, baby." Pursing his lips, he gave her a quick peck. "Just." He kissed her again. "You."

"You ready for today?"

Wildman smiled as he buried his face against her neck. "That's my Jussie, tackle the hard shit head-on, in such a way there're no surprises." Nibbling along the tendons and corded muscle of her throat, he scrubbed his bristle-covered cheek against hers. "Yeah, baby. You beside me, my brothers behind me, I'm ready for anything." He sighed. "Will be good to get it done with."

They'd arrived back in Louisiana yesterday evening, and after being shocked as shit every bike was still present and accounted for next to the plane's hangar, Wildman had watched as three boxes were loaded into two trucks. Einstein had walked a slow procession to climb into the front passenger seat of the vehicle headed to Alabama, and Wildman and Justine had ridden Tempest back to the compound, following the truck with Shelly inside.

Einstein's family interment would be tomorrow, limited to close family and friends. Wildman knew even though the man had extended an invitation to every IMC member who'd been on the flight, none of them would take him up on it. Too close, too hard to see, and too much pain and uncertainty in watching a man bury his wife and child, freshly dead.

The Rebel contingent had split down the middle, Hoss taking a full dozen guys to back up his brother's club and officer, and Mason sticking around Louisiana, with a couple of new faces showing up. Sparks and his

Jailbreakers were angling their way back around the curve of the coast, headed home to Adken, and Wildman knew both Po'Boy and Wrench would likely make an appearance in the clubhouse today, if not for what came next.

"Kiss me, beautiful." He lifted over Justine and settled a forearm on either side of her, fingers steepled over the crown of her head where it rested against a pillow. "Kiss me, and then let's get a roll on shit."

"Yes, Sir." She smiled and rose to meet his mouth, tongue dancing across his bottom lip until he groaned and dove deeper, leaving her lips swollen and red at the end of the kiss.

"That's my good girl, Jussie." And fuck him, but the sigh she gave out at his words had him harder than the kiss had left him. "Baby girl, you're gonna be the death of me. You slay me, baby."

Rolling off her and off the bed, he bent and grabbed his jeans from the floor, then stepped into them commando, turning around as he adjusted his half-hard cock along his thigh. Tangled in the sheets, Justine stared at him with a hot hunger in her gaze. "I've got a surprise for you when we get home, baby." *That should pique her interest enough to get through the next bit.* He had no illusions it would be easy for her, no matter the words of support she'd given him about bringing Shelly back here.

He'd been right how time and the natural order of things had made their mark on the body. The only surprise had been the change in the scenery around the gravesite. The last time he'd made his way to south Florida and stopped to see her, the dirt was dead, a sunken-in oval, looking exactly like an abandoned grave did in the movies. Yesterday, however, the vegetation growth had taken over, lush and green in the Florida humidity, turning the whole scene into a surreal explosion of life.

Digging her up had been hard. The plastic sheeting was tattered, weakened with age, pierced through by beetle jaws and roots. Her clothing was gone, the few leathery patches of skin over her joints the only place remaining covered. Then there'd been a tiny pile of dust in her low pelvis to mark what had been the beginning of a new life. Mason and Hoss had been methodical about the excavation, Po'Boy and Wrench gathering the remains and placing them gently into a box Justine had prepared, lining it with a brand-new shower curtain and sheet. Shelly's necklace had tangled around her neckbones, and he'd stared at it for a long time, finally leaning over to snap the chain with a slight jerk, shoving the medallion deep into his pocket.

His brothers, his friends, these people he loved more than breath, hadn't let him lift a finger. They'd let him watch and take it in, let him see each bone as it was uncovered, gave him the gift of their care for him and his, and he'd taken it. Like a greedy bastard, he'd taken it and sucked it down, savoring the goodness of the support and loyalty he felt rolling off the men.

Justine's hand hadn't moved from the middle of his back, just under the angry eagle that was the IMC patch. She'd opened water bottles with her other hand, wedging them under an arm to break the seal, and passed them out, but that left hand had stayed in place. A promise he intended to make bank on soon, locking her to him even more than emotions allowed.

"What kind of surprise?" Justine's question pulled him out of his memories, and he grinned easily at her.

"Somethin' you'll like. Let me just say, we're gonna re-create a scene I want to play out, again and again, only this time, better." He bent close and kissed her again, hard, quick, closed-mouthed, then pulled back. "See you downstairs in a minute, baby. Get up and get movin'." He smiled and gave her a slice of truth pie she needed. "I'm gonna need you with me today."

"Then I'll be there beside you." She sat up, letting the covers fall to her waist, and he groaned at the sight of her bare breasts, nipples pebbling in the chilly air, globes swaying with her giggle.

"Fuckin' minx, woman." He opened the door, turned and tapped the doorframe, and grinned. "Mine."

Through the closed door, he heard her response, "You better believe you're mine."

Wildman grinned a little wider, then took the steps down two at a time.

Twisted stood in the kitchen, and Wildman wasn't sure why he was surprised to see him there, but he was.

Then the man turned and revealed what he held, and the adoring expression on his face was worth anything—everything.

"Come meet my little man." Twisted's slanted grin over the baby's head was filled with joy and pleasure; it took everything in Wildman to keep walking, keep closing the distance. Gaze aimed down, focused intently on the infant, Twisted adjusted positions, letting the baby recline in his arms. With his upper body rocking slightly, he looked so natural and at peace with this change in roles—all Wildman could do was grin, hoping he didn't come across as crazy. There was such a stark contrast of heavily scarred, tattooed hands cradling new life with such grace and tenderness, the darkness of the skin and history of the man set against the pale perfection of this infant child, that Wildman was a little sorry Hoss wasn't there to see it, because he suspected it would have made a perfect sketch. "GTL, meet your uncle Wildman. He's your daddy's newest chapter president and is gonna make daddy's life a lot easier. We like this one, boy. So take note."

"GTL?"

Twisted angled an amused glance at Wildman before settling his gaze back on his son. "Sure as fuck not callin' him Georgie. I lived that nightmare. Tyler's a hard nope from me, and while my Penny's not against settling on Lewis as a nickname, for now, I'm just goin' with initials."

"You can't call that boy GTL." Wildman tore his eyes away from the sleepily blinking baby to see the RWMC officer Gunny walking into the kitchen. "That's like a hundred shades of wrong, brother." Gunny grabbed a mug off the countertop, flipped it over, and placed it under the coffee urn, leaning his thumb on the lever to begin dispensing the dark liquid. "GTL. Gimme that lovin'. Man, you cannot call your kid that. Nicknames matter, and he'll be stuck with them for a long fuckin' time."

"Then what the fuck do you think I should call him? This him that's *my* boy, just so you're aware." Twisted tucked the baby's flailing fist back into the blankets with an absentminded movement, as if he'd done it a thousand times already. "I am not callin' him Georgie."

"I don't know, but you hung that on him, so you need to find a way to fix it, man." Gunny slipped another mug under the flow of coffee, angling the first to Wildman, who accepted it with surprise. "You shoulda known better, brother. In fact, if you had a nickel for every time you shoulda known better, maybe you'd have enough sense to not do this shit."

"Nickel." Twisted shook his head, moving his lips close to the baby's forehead and brushing a soft kiss there that made Wildman's chest clench with pain. "Nickel to my Shiny Penny. There we go."

"What?"

Wildman looked between Gunny's confused expression and Twisted's serene one and busted out laughing, quickly lowering the volume when Twisted fired a frown his way. "Gunny, I've heard a lotta shit about you. Shit I liked, some I didn't, but mostly good shit." Wildman reached out and clapped a hand against the man's shoulder, fingers biting down in a hard squeeze. "Mostly I heard things like 'if I had a nickel for every time that asshole rubbed me the wrong way, I'd have a sock full of nickels to hit him with,' so this actually makes perfect sense."

"What?" The dark scowl on Gunny's face deepened, and Wildman caught Twisted shooting him an amused glance.

"Don't matter. Matters you're here for me today, and I appreciate the fuck out of that." Wildman squeezed again, then backed away, lifting his mug. "Helluva thing, gettin' a road name when only days old. But I like it. Twisted, you like it?"

"Fuck yeah. Names matter, and this one'll stand the test of time. The moment in my life when I developed enough sense to know a good thing when I'm holdin' it in my arms." Twisted started swaying again, looking down. "My boy, my boy, my *boy*. You've got smart uncles, loyal ones who'll do anything for you. My boy." His gaze caught Wildman's, and his expression grew somber. "Fuckin' honored you wanted to bring your family home to Mother, man. Got the call yesterday and couldn't say yes fast enough. If nothing good comes out of this whole shitstorm, you've got this at least."

Pressing his lips together, Wildman hid behind his mug until he could trust his voice. Low, guttural, moved beyond measure, he finally told Twisted, "Thank you, brother." Clearing his throat, he made a show of looking around. "Where's Penny?"

"Some shit in the bathroom. She's tryin' to not let me know she's hurtin', but my boy ain't exactly a peanut, so I know there's pain. I'll let her run with it for a while, then rope her back in and force her to accept some help." He shrugged, that subtle weaving back and forth never faltering. "Doin' all I can with our boy, and somehow that's not helpful. Calls me a baby hog, if you can believe the audacity."

Wildman set his mug down and held out his arms. "Come to Uncle Wildman."

Twisted took two steps backwards, suspicious eyes on Wildman as he shook his head. "Nu-huh, we're good, just like we are. He's fine. Right where he is, Nickel is just fine."

Gunny laughed, drained his coffee, and turned the mug upside down in the sink. "Baby hog," he confirmed before walking out.

Wildman laughed at the expression on Twisted's face, then shook his head. "Baby hog, brother. But I don't blame you. Hold onto that tiny slip of sweetness and never let go. You and Penny, you've been through enough. Came out the other end, and here you are. You hold that boy long as you want. Ain't nobody gonna blame you even a little bit."

"How can something I never knew I wanted mean so much?" The frown on Twisted's face faded as he stared down into the again-sleeping baby's face. "In isolation, it seemed like an idea. A thing people do with someone they love. Then Penny got pregnant, and it was real, we were buildin' a family, and I chased how good it felt. Now? Watchin' her with our boy, seeing him suckle or sleep, hell, even his I'm-pissing yell makes me grin. Means everything."

"As it should." Wildman refilled his coffee mug. "Gonna go outside, see how things are set up."

"Better be as you requested, or these motherfuckers are gonna have to answer to me. Yes they will. These old assholes will answer to Daddy. You better believe it." Twisted's voice had taken on a singsong that made Wildman bust out in laughter, closing the door behind him on a continuing litany of imagined slights Nickel's daddy had taken on himself.

"Brother," Busk called, gesturing with a come-here movement. "Got something for you to look at, man."

Wildman made his way across the lot, approaching the open back gate leading out into the wild area nearer the back edge of the property. As he got closer, he saw a stand had been erected, with a small wooden box resting on the risers. "Check out what Ruger made, brother. I think it's fitting for her to be so recognized."

Not a coffin, the container was smaller and thinner, made to hold exactly the remains they'd retrieved. He could only assume they'd already transferred Shelly, and he was ashamed of how glad he was to have missed the process. He had no doubt they'd done it with respect, but he could go the rest of his life without seeing the bones again. Burned into the top of the box was her name, birth year, and death year. No mention of the babe, which was fine, he guessed, since it wasn't more than a promise at the time. *But…*

"Can we add something?" He slipped his fingertips along the curving letters, coming to a rest in the center of the box. "Ruger around?"

"Right here, brother." Ruger's hand landed on his arm with a squeeze, then fell away. "What'd you want to add?"

"I was Ogre then. Her PO read that." He spoke of her "property of" vest, the patch and pieces of leather the club had assigned to her. She'd worn it proudly, pleased to be his. "It'd be nice to see her belonging."

"How about Ogre's OL?" Ruger traced a line above where Shelly's name rode the surface of the wood. "I got room just here."

"Yeah, I'd like it. Nod to the past, because the man I was isn't who I am now. But still, it's about her belonging."

"You got it, brother."

He stood and watched Ruger work, acknowledging every man who came up to pay respects, nodding and shaking hands without speaking. Justine came outside and pulled up to stand nearby, but out of reach, which nearly pissed him off before he realized he needed to cut her a break. She was attending the funeral of his wife, and this was her being respectful. Wildman leaned sideways and lunged, clamping a hand around Justine's wrist. He gave it a healthy tug, sending her flying into his body. "It's been twenty years, baby. Stand with me." Then he wrapped his arm around her, settling and taking in a deep breath when she rested her weight against him, proving once again that she was perfect.

Eight men took shovels in hand, turning sod made of sand and clay, grass roots tearing free as they lifted the first bladefuls out of the small hole. The entire proceeding took less than an hour, from first thump of the blade into the earth until the last deliberate thud of the back of the shovel against the reset sod.

The next breath Wildman took in was somehow easier, lighter, and the next came easier yet, until he turned his head to look down at Justine, not surprised to see her staring up at him, shining tracks glistening along both cheeks.

"Let's go home," he suggested, pleased when she wordlessly turned with him to walk away.

***

Wildman

"Climb off, baby." Balancing the bike between his thighs, he held up a hand to steady her and drew her knuckles to his lips once she had both feet on the ground, brushing a kiss across the backs. "Been a couple of days, yeah?"

"Hard couple of days." She handed him the helmet he now thought of as hers, and he fastened it to the lock on the frame. "You okay, Lyle?" Her arms came around his waist with a squeeze; then she was wiggling underneath his arm, angling around so he could look down at her. Concern drew her brows together, and he cupped her jaw in his hand, lifting as he pulled her close for a kiss.

"I'm good, Jussie." They exited the garage, and he aimed their steps towards the back door of the house. "Just ready to have you to myself for a few days." He laughed, the sound harsh. "Fuck, I'd take a few hours of you and me at this point."

"Long as you need me." Her fingers dipped into his back pocket. "I won't lie, it'll be nice not to be on display to everyone for a change. It's going to take some getting used to, folks not trusting me."

"Those who don't already, will soon. Shouldn't have had to prove yourself to anyone, but you did, and that shit? That good shit what you did? That'll seep faster than anything else. Tales and stories, folks'll get caught up in it, and you'll have cred beyond our family." He opened the door and led her inside, glad when the lights came up automatically to show nothing out of place. Toeing off his boots, he lined them up next to the door, smiling when she did the same.

Myron had found the flaw that allowed Anderson to access the security. Something as small as a manufacturer's password was all the man had needed. Busk was currently upgrading systems as well as segregating them per recommendation by the RWMC tech wizard. Long and short of it, Busk and Myron had promised Wildman his place was more secure now than he'd likely ever need, which meant he was comfortable bringing Jussie home.

Anderson was a ghost. In the wind, and distrusted by his colleagues and bosses, based on the few conversations Justine had initiated, answering a variety of calls she'd been ignoring for two days.

Mason was blaming himself for the Anderson part of things. While it was true alerting the Feds that his sister had been missing might have been the first rock over the ledge, Anderson himself had shuffled through the shale on the way down, starting his own human-sized avalanche.

There would be more to come from Alabama. Wildman had met with Twisted and Busk, and gotten Ragman on the video, discussing the information that had come out of the Florida trip. Eastern European mob clashing with old-school Italian mob, and mixed with Mexican cartel? Wildman wasn't sure who'd been the first to suggest taking advantage of the new collaborative atmosphere, but it had been the work of minutes to get Mason and Wrench in the room, then Retro on the horn, only to find out Justine herself had been the authoress of that particular idea, back when she'd rescued herself.

"Come on." He tugged at her fingers, turning to walk backwards, his gaze fixed on her face. "I got something to show you."

Busk in full-on apology mode was a delight. It had only taken a single please, and the man had agreed to install what Wildman wanted. No arguing, either, which was a miracle. Now to see if it matched up with his hopes and her desires.

"What kind of surprise is it?" She grinned, crooking her fingers to lock with his. With her head tilted to the side, the dark wings of her hair framed her face beautifully, grey eyes bright and inquisitive.

"You're so pretty, Jussie." He checked behind himself, angled through the bedroom door, and stopped about a yard from the foot of the bed. "Beautiful when you're strong. Courageous. You're fuckin' fierce, woman, and that is a miracle to behold."

Her gaze scanned the room before landing back on him. "What's going on?"

"Gorgeous in your submission, too. My good girl, Jussie." He tugged at the hem of her shirt, and she lifted her arms as he dragged it over her head. He was there to smooth her hair back from her face, twisting it into a hank to hang over one shoulder. Arms around her, he flicked the clasp on her bra and let it drop to the floor. "Gonna make you fly."

Teeth to her quivering belly, he nipped and licked as he unfastened the button on her jeans, grinning when she stepped on the legs to get them off her body faster, taking her underwear with them.

Shrugging out of his vest, he tossed it onto the dresser, then followed with his shirt, leaving him just in jeans and her bare entirely.

"Knees, baby girl." A hand on each shoulder eased her to the floor, and he took a moment to position her arms as he wanted them. Fingers tight, palms flat towards him, she took on a mirror of her pose the first time he'd laid eyes on her.

"Saw you, and the first thing I thought was how fuckin' strong you were. How brave." He circled her, angling her chin down slightly. Hands on her waist, he lifted so she rose off her heels, balancing on her knees. Chafing the skin of her back with both palms, he stroked softly, then more firmly to bring blood to the surface, making her more sensitive. "And how much I wished I deserved someone like you."

Smiling, he caught her rising chin and tugged it back into place, tapping her nose with one finger. "Shhhh. I get what you want to say, but this is about my initial impressions of you. I've already heard yours of me. Larger than life, strong, handsome, fuckable." Her breath stuttered, and he chuckled. "Don't you dare laugh, Jussie. I'd like to think I'm very fuckable."

Stroking the long muscles across her shoulders, he took the weight of her arms, shaking them, then left her suspended again. Careful attention kept the metal pieces from clanging together as he lowered the bar from the ceiling, then fastened one cuff to each strong wrist. She tensed, and he waited for a protest, but Justine settled against the bonds, arms still at that perfect angle.

Like wings.

Standing behind her, Wildman stripped his jeans off, tossing them to the side as he opened the closet and withdrew a light flogger. As exhausted as they both were, it wouldn't take much to overdo things, so he planned on starting very small. They would have a lifetime to work up to more, and wasn't that a sweet thought.

"Traffic signal system." He circled to the front and lifted her chin, staring down into eyes already hooded and dark. "Red, yellow, green. Where are you right now, Jussie?"

"So green."

Rolling the flogger in a slow figure eight, he made sure she could see and hear the falls shirring as they brushed against their neighbors. "Still green, Jussie mine?"

"Still green." She didn't try to evade his touch or his gaze, and he saw her settling into the space that gave her peace. Where if he needed her to do something, he'd tell her, and she didn't have to make any decisions.

"Let's fly."

Fini

THANK YOU FOR READING
Tarnished Lies and Dead Ends!

ABOUT THE AUTHOR

Raised in the south, *Wall Street Journal* & *USA TODAY* bestselling author MariaLisa learned about the magic of books at an early age. Every summer, she would spend hours in the local library, devouring books of every genre. Self-described as a book-a-holic, she says "I've always loved to read, but then I discovered writing, and found I adored that, too. For reading...if nothing else is available, I've been known to read the back of the cereal box."

Want sneak peeks into what she's working on, or to chat with other readers about her books? Join the Facebook group! **bit.ly/deMora-FB-group**

deMora has a spam-free newsletter list she'd love to have you join, too: **bit.ly/mldemora-newsletter**

~~~~~

ADDITIONAL SERIES AND BOOKS

Please note that books in a series frequently feature characters from additional books within that series. If series books are read out of order, readers will twig to spoilers for the other books, so going back to read the skipped titles won't have the same angsty reveals.

Rebel Wayfarers MC series

A motorcycle club can be a frightening place, filled with hardened men and bad attitudes. Rebel Wayfarers is a club with their own measure of hard and dangerous, led by their national president, Davis Mason. This book series follows members as they move through their lives, filled with anguish and heartache, laughter and love. In the club, each of them find a home and family they thought long lost to them.
~~~~~

Mica, #1
A Sweet & Merry Christmas, #1.5
Slate, #2
Bear, #3
Jase, #4
Gunny, #5
Mason, #6
Hoss, #7
Harddrive Holidays, #7.5
Duck, #8
Biker Chick Campout, #8.5
Watcher, #9
A Kiss to Keep You, #9.25
Gun Totin' Annie, #9.5
Secret Santa, #9.75
Bones, #10
Gunny's Pups, #10.25
Not Even A Mouse, #10.75
Fury, #11
Christmas Doings, #11.25
Gypsy's Lady includes *Never Settle* (#10.5), #11.5
Cassie, #12
Road Runner's Ride, #12.5

Occupy Yourself band series

Stardom doesn't happen overnight. Hell, it doesn't even happen after a decade in the business, as the members of Occupy Yourself have found out. But, with the right talent and the right representation, they might still have a chance to make it big. As long as they can keep their lead singer sober, keep their drummer focused on the music, keep their guitarist out of trouble ... well, you get the idea. Come and join us, stand side stage for a close-up view of the backstage happenings in a rock-and-roll band. It's guaranteed to be a show you won't ever forget.

Born Into Trouble, #1
Grace In Motion, #2 (TBD)
What They Say, #3 (TBD)

Neither This, Nor That MC series

Legends are born from moments like these. Folktales spun around a single point in time so perfect, you can almost hear the click resonating through the universe as things align. Meet Twisted, Po'Boy, Retro, and Ragman, good old boys from southern states who have many things in common. First, is a bone-deep love of the biker lifestyle. Second, would be their love of the brotherhood, and knowing that you trust the man at your back. Finally, these men have the love of a good woman. None of these come without a price, and it is our pleasure to journey along with them as they discover the blessings that can be won, and lost along the way.

> *This Is the Route Of Twisted Pain*, #1
> *Treading the Traitor's Path: Out Bad*, #2
> *Shelter My Heart*, #3
> *Trapped by Fate on Reckless Roads*, #4
> *Tarnished Lies and Dead Ends*, #5
> *Tangled Threats on the Nomad Highway*, #6 (TBD)

Rebel Wayfarers crossover stories

Enjoy these stories that tie the different worlds of my MC universe together, bringing Rebel Wayfarers MC and the clubs of the Neither This Nor That series into glorious alignment.

> *Going Down Easy*
> *No Man's Land*
> *In Search of Solace*

Mayhan Bucklers MC series

The Mayhan Bucklers MC has been part of the rolling hills of Northeast Texas for decades. Now, new life is being breathed into this reborn club, a legacy resurrected by grandsons of the founder. The MBMC is set to surpass its original glory, fortified with an honorable purpose: Helping wounded warriors reintegrate back into society, gifting those who've given so much with a safe place to land.

Learning how to navigate life while war still echoes inside you isn't easy, but with solid brothers at your back, and the love of a good woman, anything is possible.

Most Rikki-Tik, #1
Mad Minute, #2
Pucker Factor, #3
Boocoo Dinky Dau, #4

Borderline Freaks MC series

When you can't count on anyone else to save you, there's only one real choice. Borderline Freaks MC is a series of books about the men of the club and their brotherhood—and of course the love they have for their women. Take a trip along with Monk, Blade, Wolf, and Neptune, and feel for yourself the connection these men have for each other.

Service and Sacrifice, #1
More Than Enough, #2
Lack of In-between, #3
See You in Valhalla, #4

Alace Sweets series

Dark romantic thrillers, these books are not light reads. Filled with edge-of-your-seat suspense, these intense stories command the reader's attention as they drive towards their explosive endings. Alace Sweets is a vigilante serial killer, with everything that implies and is sure to trip all your triggers. Be ready.

Alace Sweets, #1
Seeking Worthy Pursuits, #2
Embarrassment of Monsters, #3
All the Broken Rules, #4 (TBD)

With My Whole Heart series

Sweet as pie and twice as delicious, these romantic love stories are a guaranteed happily-ever-after read.

With My Whole Heart, #1
Bet On Us, #2

If You Could Change One Thing:
Tangled Fates Stories

When threads in the tapestry of life are cut short, inexorably changing the future for those you love, would you be willing to tempt fate to set things right?

There Are Limits, #1
Rules Are Rules, #2
The Gray Zone, #3

Other Books:

Hard Focus
Dirty Bitches MC: Season 3

~~~~~

deMora's Rebel Wayfarers MC and the Neither This Nor That MC series do cross over, along with the Occupy Yourself band books, so readers have a couple of choices. The series can be read independently beginning with RWMC, OYBS, and then NTNT without too many spoilers. There's also a crossover between deMora's RWMC world and Lila Rose's Hawks MC world. Or they can be read intertwined—in chronological order.
~~~~~

Here's the recommended reading order if you want to follow according to timing:

Mica, RWMC #1
A Sweet & Merry Christmas, RWMC #1.5
Slate, RWMC #2
Bear, RWMC #3
Born Into Trouble, OYBS #1
Jase, RWMC #4
Gunny, RWMC #5
Mason, RWMC #6
Hoss, RWMC #7
This Is the Route of Twisted Pain, NTNT #1
Harddrive Holidays, RWMC #7.5
Duck, RWMC #8
Biker Chick Campout, RWMC #8.5
Watcher, RWMC #9
Treading the Traitor's Path: Out Bad, NTNT #2
Living Without, Lila Rose's Hawks MC: Caroline Springs #4
Shelter My Heart, NTNT #3
A Kiss to Keep You, RWMC #9.25
Gun Totin' Annie, RWMC #9.5
Secret Santa, RWMC #9.75
Trapped by Fate on Reckless Roads, NTNT #4
Bones, RWMC #10
Gunny's Pups, RWMC #10.25
Not Even A Mouse, RWMC #10.75
Road Runner's Ride, RWMC #12.5
Never Settle, RWMC #10.5
Fury, RWMC #11
Christmas Doings, RWMC #11.25
Gypsy's Lady, RWMC #11.5
Tarnished Lies and Dead Ends, NTNT #5
Going Down Easy
No Man's Land
In Search of Solace
Cassie, RWMC #12

More information available at **mldemora.com**.